ROTTERS

Also by Daniel Kraus

The Monster Variations

ROTTERS

DANIEL KRAUS

DELACORTE PRESS

Visit us on the Web! www.randomhouse.com/teens
Educators and librarians, for a variety of teaching tools, visit us at www.randomhouse.com/teachers

Library of Congress Cataloging-in-Publication Data
Kraus, Daniel.
Rotters / by Daniel Kraus. — 1st ed.
p. cm.
Summary: Sixteen-year-old Joey's life takes a very strange turn when his mother's tragic death forces him to move from Chicago to rural Iowa with the father he has never known, and who is the town pariah, although no one imagines the macabre way in which his father earns a living.
ISBN 978-0-385-73857-6 (hc) — ISBN 978-0-385-90737-8 (glb) —
ISBN 978-0-375-89558-6 (ebook) [1. Fathers and sons—Fiction. 2. Moving, Household—Fiction. 3. Bullying—Fiction. 4. High schools—Fiction. 5. Schools—Fiction. 6. Recluses—Fiction. 7. Grave robbing—Fiction. 8. Iowa—Fiction.]
I. Title.
PZ7.K8672Rot 2011 [Fic]—dc22 2010005174

The text of this book is set in 13-point Perpetua.
Book design by Vikki Sheatsley
Printed in the United States of America
10 9 8 7 6 5 4 3 2 1
First Edition

for Amanda

My tale was not one to announce publicly; its astonishing horror would be looked upon as madness by the vulgar.

—MARY SHELLEY, *Frankenstein*

He who digs a pit will fall into it.

—PROVERBS 26:27

CONTENTS

Prologue
So Many Worthy Deaths 1

BOOK I
Fun and Games 9

BOOK II
Lamb and Slaughter 211

Epilogue
Next Lesson, Then 435

ROTTERS

So Many Worthy Deaths

This is the day my mother dies. I can taste it right off: salt on my lips, dried air, the AC having never been switched on because she died from heart failure while reclining in front of the television, sweating in her underwear, her last thought that she needed to turn on the air because poor Joey must be roasting in his bedroom. Pulmonary embolism: it is what killed everyone on her side of the family and now it has killed her, while I slept, and this salt is the bitter taste of her goodbye.

Turns out, her heart is not what got her. There are her usual morning noises. The apartment door unbolts and unlocks. I kneel on my bed to look out the window. The dawn is piss yellow but beautiful because it is another day and she is alive, and I am alive, and the city around us is screaming with life. Birds push one another along branches, their alien feet peeling bark. There is an empty birdhouse; I hear my mother's utilitarian humming and realize that she is somewhere beneath it, and that as the birds battle they will bother the string that straps birdhouse to branch, causing it to fall. Given the right trajectory it can kill her and will. I built that birdhouse. It is my fault. This is the day she dies.

I'm standing on the bed now. The birdhouse rights itself. My mother is still alive; I catch sight of her confident shadow darting around the corner of the apartment complex, her direction indicating the building's laundry room and the homeless murderer crouching behind the row of washers. Since childhood I've watched her claws flash at the barest hints of danger; she has nearly attacked strangers whose only crimes were giving me disapproving looks. Now she is the one in danger and yet I display none of her courage: I let her die. My failure is too much to bear. I bolt up the stairs and into the shower to hide the tears. I love her too much, I know this. I'm a teenage boy and it's embarrassing. Her constant, hovering, demanding presence should irritate and infuriate me, but it doesn't. She's stronger than I could ever hope to be. She's all I have, and even if that's her fault I love her anyway, especially today, the day that will turn out to be her last.

Then I hear her noises again; she's back inside and there is something unwelcome playing on the stereo—she has turned it on now that I am awake and suddenly I remember the vase. Oh, god. Her birthday was two days ago and I bought her stupid flowers at Jewel and, on impulse, a silver helium balloon with some crap about turning forty. The balloon's ribbon was tied around a vase. Our apartment, cluttered with enough nonperishables to outlast a nuclear winter, photos of the two of us in various Chicago locales, other evidence of a life spent isolated from the wider world, has forced my mother to put the vase on top of the stereo. In moments she will reach to skip the CD's second track—we hate the second track—and her knuckles will bump the vase and the balloon will pitch and rise. The vase will overturn and spill and there will be water in the stereo, through the wiring, down the wall, and into the power strip. She will reach in there to wipe it up and will die the way she warned me against incessantly when I was little. Electricity takes her.

Or not. She barges into the bathroom, burdened with freshly dried towels, singing along grimly to the loathed second track. Her voice is loud, and then there is the rattle of water to contend with, and I wait for a gap of silence during which I can implore her to turn back from certain doom, but she is already ranting that I get up too early, wasn't I up all night playing video games with Boris, and how do I survive on so few hours of sleep—all this despite the fact that she is the lifelong insomniac, the lifelong paranoid, not I. What do you want for breakfast, she asks. I don't care, I say through a mouthful of water—how about eggs. There is a leak in the tub and she will slip in the puddle and strike her head on the edge of the toilet—at least this death is quick—and the final thing I will tell her is not how much I owe her, not how much I need her. It is *eggs.*

She's tough, so tough: I find her alive and well in the kitchen, curls arranged sloppily, cheeks freckled, shoulders pink, wearing a tank top and cutoffs and red flip-flops, hunched bored in front of a frying pan. It's all for me, this tedious routine. She could've been a nuclear physicist, a powerhouse attorney, a mountaineer. Her intelligence and ingenuity are proven on a daily basis—she knows all the *Jeopardy!* answers, can disassemble and reconstruct a toaster oven in under five minutes, is steely in the face of injuries, crafty in the face of collection agencies—yet for me she accepts the indignities of raising an ungrateful sixteen-year-old, the stultifying grind of an insulting desk job. Despite these sacrifices, I won't eat. How can I? The room twitches with menace. Grease pops in the pan; it will burn holes in her ever-watchful eyes and she will flail, and I do not have to list the number of sharp objects waiting for her on the counter.

I choke down the eggs. I watch her as she cleans up. She

raises the edge of her cutoffs to brood over cellulite. Contorted in this way I can see the unnatural groove that passes through the curvatures of her left ear. It is a wound she suffered from my father. I don't know my father and she has offered neither information nor emotion. The injury is part of a puzzle I've been too self-absorbed to wonder about, the true origin of her sleepless nights. The pitiful little I know is this: to draw attention away from the disfigurement, she stretches her lobes with extravagant earrings; those she wears now are turquoise with mini-dangles that swirl and catch themselves in knots. So *this* is how she dies. Today's chores include mowing the grass along the building's front lawn (for a few bucks off our rent), changing the oil in the car, and cleaning dust from fans that over the summer have caked. It seems inconceivable that such trifling devices could take down my invincible guardian, but they will. Mower, car, fan: each has spinning components that will snatch dangling earrings, gears that will pinch the skin, then shudder against live meat before self-lubricating with blood. I have time to disable only one device, and the choice immobilizes me.

She's unrelenting. As usual. Already she's down the stairs seeking my dirty laundry. There is a rip in the carpet on the third stair, wide enough to snare a flip-flopped toe. When she somehow survives, she is out the door, laundry basket on her hip, shouting to me that I need to get off my butt and practice my trumpet. The door bangs shut. Outside there is nothing but trouble. Strung-out punks with knives and a need. Gang members not caring who gets caught in the cross fire. There are a million ways to bite it in the big city, even if you're as fearless as my mother. I lift my trumpet. The song I play will be her requiem.

I play poorly. My fingers stiffen in sympathy with the rigor mortis already setting her joints. I am one month away from beginning my junior year in high school, and this room of mine provides further proof that I am helpless without her as my vigilant protector. Tacked to my bulletin board are the past six years of straight As, a testament to her skillful badgering. Scattered around the room is evidence of too many weekends spent together playing board games. She should not have sheltered me so much. I try to get mad about it. It might make losing her a little bit easier.

The flops have been replaced with flats, the tank top with a blouse. I must leave the house. She says so. Summer is half over and my face, she says, looks like Wonder Bread. She is leaving, too—groceries don't buy themselves. She moves fast, mirrored sunglasses planted, purse shouldered. I stand there in bare feet. This unstoppable force is my mother and I will never see her again. I need to thank her and tell her the truth: I love her. Her perfunctory smile tells me she has other things on her mind. She is saying something about how I should shut the windows before it rains, and do I want Thai later, no, no—let's do Vietnamese. It is food I will never taste. The space between us plummets and we stand on edges of opposite cliffs. It feels like I have played the trumpet all night: my lips are numb, my fingers tremulous, my lungs bruised. She stomps out the door, and ten minutes later, at 10:15 a.m., the time of her actual death, when she jaywalks and is broken to pieces by a city bus, I turn where I stand in our living room and glare at the apartment that used to be our haven. So many more-worthy deaths available here, all things considered, than the one that chose her.

BOOK I

Fun and Games

1.

My father's name was Ken Harnett. I was told by my caseworker from the Department of Children and Family Services that she had tracked him down in a small town in Iowa not far from the Mississippi River, not even five hours away from Chicago. My caseworker, a young woman named Claire, was proud of the discovery. When she had told me after my mother's funeral that she was giving top priority to the search, it had sounded like one of those things she was required to say. I think I nodded and maybe even smiled. It never occurred to me that Claire would succeed. I don't think it occurred to her, either.

I tried to imagine what he looked like; I subtracted my mother's features from my own. The exercise was not only futile, it was boring. I didn't care. He was not real, at least not to me. Even the name felt fabricated. My last name was Crouch. I knew no Harnetts and had never met anyone named Ken. Such thoughts compelled me to fish out my passport and consider the moronic face staring back at me. I'd had the passport all my life, a childhood gift that made little sense; perhaps there had been a time when my mother had fantasized that we might leave the confines not only of the city but of the country as well. Over the years, I had taken it upon myself to renew the passport as a personal promise that I would not turn out like her, that one day I would see the world, any world. If I used it now, right now, maybe I could escape this faceless father.

Claire was assigned to my case the same day that my mother went under all eight wheels of the bus. Death was instantaneous, though the paperwork wasn't signed until about noon. Around dinnertime, the intercom buzzed and I asked who was there and it was a woman's voice that was not my mother's. Our speaker was crap, so I went downstairs to see who it was and it was a pretty Asian girl with a pixie cut and purple fingernails, possibly still in her twenties, and suddenly it didn't matter if she was homeless or a Jehovah's Witness or planned on pressing a knife to my throat. All I could think of was how stupid I looked with my Kool-Aid-stained tee and pleated shorts. Not that my attire mattered much: I was short and scrawny and not anyone people spent time looking at, and I knew I was kidding myself that this female, any female, saw me as anything but a blur of pimpled flesh and uncooperative brown hair. "Your mother has died," she said. She said it before introducing herself, and I couldn't help considering my reaction almost abstractly. There was an attractive young woman at my door; masculine protocol required that I not cry. It was tough, and got tougher as the night progressed, and I found myself wishing that Claire were less cute, much older, and had, for instance, a mustache.

Claire attended the wake and the funeral. I guess it was part of her job. My best friend, Boris Watson, met her for the first time there, and was as disheartened as I by her inappropriate good looks. The two of them shook hands, her grip business-like and warm, his limp and humiliated, and I realized that, with my mother gone, this mismatched pair was all I had left. It did not bode well that their handshake was short, their conversation strained and doomed.

The service took place at our usual church with our usual pastor—my mother had taken me there almost every Sunday of my life. I don't know who arranged the funeral details and chose the casket or where exactly the money came from to pay for the service and flowers. Claire surely knew; maybe Boris knew, too. I was steered around, sometimes literally by the shoulders, from a hospital morgue to Boris's living room to a dreary Italian restaurant and back to Boris's, and on and on until it was two days later and there was my mother in her casket. I first caught sight of her face from the corner of my eye and it was like noticing someone you didn't expect to see. Behind me, Boris and the rest of the Watsons kept their distance. The funeral home doors would remain closed for another twenty minutes; this time belonged solely to the family, and that meant me. Red carpet led me to her. She was fantastically still and her cheeks lay unnaturally flat. On those cheeks was far too much makeup—the only freckles I could see were in a patch below her throat.

A few seconds of this was enough. I craned my neck. That spider bobbing in that ceiling cobweb—there was more life there than in this expensive silver box, and I devoured its every detail, the delicate probe of the spider's leg, the responding sink and shine of its net. It was a talent of mine, or a problem, depending on whom you asked, to obsess about trivial details during stressful situations. In fourth grade a school therapist called it an avoidance technique. My mom, who didn't mind it so much, had dubbed it "specifying." Once, in a doctor's office, as the old man ran through the grim details of my impending tonsillectomy, my mom caught me specifying toward the floor. As we left, she didn't ask me about the procedure. Instead she asked me about the doctor's shoes, their color, the number of lace holes, and their general condition. I could not help smiling and responding—

—*greenish black*—
—*twelve*—
—*ratty as hell*—

The skill hadn't come from nowhere. My friendship with Boris aside, my mother and I had lived in solitude as hermetic as it was mysterious. Fiercely dependent upon her from an early age, I was seized by anxiety when she was even a few minutes late coming home from work. To distract myself I would concentrate—on the insectile innards of lightbulbs, the landscapes of dust on the blinds, the caricatures hiding within the ceiling spackle—and when she arrived, I could recite to her every last detail. She applauded and encouraged this practice, but for me it came far too easily. There were plenty of things in life I wanted to forget. By the time I was nine or ten, I considered specifying a curse.

At the request of the Watsons, and with Claire's recommendation to her department, I was placed with Boris's family until other arrangements could be made. Boris stood beside me during the endless handshaking of the wake and sat next to me at the funeral. When the graveside service was over and people were filing away, Boris was the one who told me that I needed to touch the casket. "Just put your hand on it," he said. I didn't see why it was important. "Now, dumbass," he hissed. "I did it when my grandma died. Trust me."

People were squeezing past us; it was my only chance. I leaned over and touched the casket with two fingers. The solidity of the hard surface was unexpectedly reassuring, and I pressed my entire palm flat against the beveled corner. I could feel through my hand the thunder of the exiting crowd. These vibrations were life, and for a moment my mother was part of it. I let it last for several seconds. It was the first time I had touched a casket and I presumed it would be the last. I was wrong, of course—I would touch hundreds, and soon.

Ken Harnett was out there, but it was still two weeks before Claire would find him. Two duffel bags and my beloved green backpack in tow, I moved into the Watsons' dusty ambiance of paperback books and vinyl records, all of which quivered with thatches of dog hair. My mother and I might have never crossed state lines, but going to the Watson condo was like traversing the world. Boris's parents, Janelle and Thaddeus, were an interracial couple—he was from Vermont, she from Kenya—and their place was decked out with bizarre and frightening artifacts they brought home from their travels only to have them dutifully demolished by one of Boris's hysterical little sisters. I moved through the familiar museum of masks and swords and sculpture, crashed onto an army mattress on Boris's floor, and found myself staring at a scattering of glow-in-the-dark stars that we had stuck on his ceiling in third grade. As the sky darkened, I marveled at the number of years that had passed since we had placed the constellation, how little we must have been, and how those stars—little scraps of sticky paper—had outlasted my mother. "The stars are still there," I finally said, unable to close my eyes and unwilling to start specifying—here, nested within the Watson home, it just seemed cowardly. "Huh?" Boris answered right away. He was awake, too. "What stars?"

"The stars," I insisted, and he responded, "Yeah, but where?" I thought I was going crazy. Then he said, "Oh, *those* stars. Wow, I guess I forgot about them. Huh. You sure are an observant bastard. I don't know, I guess that's just how my ceiling looks. You better get used to it." I wiped the sweat from my face and peeled away the dog hairs. He was right. I had better.

Boris wasn't just my best friend, he was my only friend, really. By the time you hit middle school, one good friend was all you needed. We were not popular, Boris and I, but we were hardly Mac Hill or Alfie Sutherland. It was a big school, seething with nearly two thousand jocks and dorks and burnouts of every conceivable ethnicity and IQ. Within such pandemonium, it was blissfully easy to be overlooked.

If the adults were to be believed, each one of us possessed some sort of special talent, though they were kidding themselves if they thought all talents were equal. My straight As, for instance, were hardly something I went around advertising. Fortunately, there was one other place Boris and I shined: we both played trumpet. Boris had been playing since he was little—trumpet lessons were but one of the dozens of cultural pursuits foisted upon him by Janelle and Thaddeus. My mom was uncomfortable with anything that kept me away from home, but I guilted her into buying me an instrument in sixth grade and naturally chose the same one as Boris. We were both pretty good. We could sight-read and even improvise over changes a bit. We played at school pep rallies, football and basketball games, and seasonal concerts, and between the two of us we had scored four or five solos. We spent a lot of quality time bitching about what an idiot's contraption the trumpet was, how it barely rated above a first grader's recorder, and how we both planned to melt the brass for money as soon as we hit college. In reality we loved it. The trumpet is, in fact, a pretty unimpressive thing, but it's different when you're playing as part of an eighty-piece concert orchestra or twenty-member jazz band. There is power there, and we both felt it after every performance, even as we rolled our eyes at the applause and made lewd gestures involving the bell ends of the trumpets.

Since the beginning of summer, I had practiced maybe two or three times total, and each of those had been a reaction to my mother's badgering. Now, bunking alongside Boris in weird imitation of the sleepovers of our youth, I couldn't get practice out of my head—practice had been my mother's final request. I sat up beneath the glowing green stars, the sheets clinging to my skin. I checked the digital clock. It was nearly two in the morning. I counted on my fingers. My mother had been dead for almost sixty hours. It was dark in Boris's bedroom, much darker than my room at home, and I patted the carpet until I found my backpack, then dug past clothes, the flimsy folds of my wallet, the crinkled pages of my passport, until my hands felt the hard plastic of my trumpet case. Keeping my eyes focused on the phony universe six feet above my head, I removed the trumpet and ran my hands over the warm metal, slid my palm over the valves, gave a little tug to the water key. I settled my fingers onto the buttons and nested my thumb into its crook.

"Shit, man," came a voice from Boris's bed. "If you wanted to play, all you had to do was ask."

"Oh, sorry."

"I'm sure you are." He paused. "It's a nice night."

"It's dark in here," I said. "I tried to be quiet, sorry."

Boris drew a long breath through his nose. "Sound always

carries best at night anyway. Think about how we sound at football games."

"Boris," I said. "It's late. Real late."

"Hell, if this was Birdland, we'd just be getting cooking right about now."

"Your parents would kill us."

"Janelle and Thaddeus? Tonight? Tonight we can get away with anything, and I say we take advantage of it." I heard rustling covers. He was out of bed. Next came the bang of his trumpet case hitting the desk, the crack of undone latches.

"What about your sisters? They will go bat-shit," I said. "Come on, forget it, let's go to sleep."

I heard the soft squeal of his mouthpiece being inserted and saw his outline in the dark, blotting out star systems in silent laughter. "You want to play or what?"

And so we played. The notes were tentative at first; "Blues by Five" never sounded so twiggy and fragile. Boris took the lead on "Salt Peanuts." At what passed for the conclusion, I started "Oleo" without even thinking about it, and there it was, what we had been searching for: a true sound. He met me a few lines in, dodging around, finding the gaps before I could guess where they might be, and now we were playing, really playing, and Boris shoved open his window with an elbow. The night came inside, the music went out. Only after twenty minutes did I realize we were loud; we both played louder. I kept waiting for the pounding from his sisters or angry neighbors, the phone calls alerting us to the police who were on their way. Nothing—it was as if the performance itself imparted its magnitude. Boris kicked open his bedroom door and we snaked through the kitchen and living room, and I thought of the second-line funeral marches in New Orleans, the sepulchral celebrations in the streets of Mexican villages.

Another window tossed open and we were on the fire escape, the sound taking on crisper properties in the night air, the notes electric at each apex. At some point I became aware of Janelle and Thaddeus standing behind us looking on silently, their hands gripping each other's pajamas. Behind them, yawning dogs and the progressively shorter lineup of Boris's bedclothed sisters, their perennially cross faces loosened with something like awe. Below us, faces on the street tilted our way. All this listening made me listen, too: our notes no longer made any sense. It didn't matter and no one seemed to care. In the end, everything is noise.

2.

Bloughton, Iowa, population: 4,000. Claire came into her office at the DCFS with this curse written on a piece of notebook paper printed with calico kittens. She collapsed into her chair and tapped the words with purple nails.

"Okay, relax. *Relax*. It's a nice place, Joey. Before you ask, no, I haven't been there, but I checked it out online, and, you know, seriously, I want you to give it a chance here before you freak."

"Who said I was going to freak?" I asked. I squeezed my hands into fists beneath the table, well into the process of freaking.

"Because I know I would," she said. "In fact, I did. My family moved when I was in sixth grade, and that's an even harder age to adjust to a new school, believe me."

I saw no reason to believe her.

"You told me you've never been outside Chicago. Which

I still find hard to swallow, by the way, but fine, it was a quirk of your mom's, whatever—you're not the only one uncomfortable with the countryside, a lot of people are, the countryside gives them the creeps. But can I stress that Bloughton is not just a couple shacks in a cornfield? Now, it's true, a town Bloughton's size," Claire said, shrugging, "their Web presence is minimal. A great way to get around that, though, is real estate listings, and I looked up maybe three or four homes, most of them with little slide shows. I don't suppose you're into woodwork? Of course you're not, but regardless. It's nice, Joey. Kind of idyllic, if you want to know the truth."

"So you've spoken to him," I said.

She paused for a moment, tapping her bottom teeth against her upper lip, then looked at the calico paper and made an ambiguous gesture with her head. "There have been communications," she said.

"What's that mean?"

"Look," she said, giving me her eyes, which she must have known were her best weapon. "He doesn't have a phone."

"You mean he doesn't have a land line."

"I mean the man does not own a telecommunications device."

I felt my pulse race. "Who doesn't have a phone?"

"You're freaking, Joey. Don't do that. You want a water?" She looked around her office. There was no water cooler, no bottles. I planted my fists on the table and made hands of them again, laying them flat. I inhaled and meditated upon calico cats.

"He at least knows about me, though, right? There's been some kind of communication. That's what you said, right?"

She reached over and laid a hand atop one of my own.

"It has all been explained to him," she assured me. "The old-fashioned way. With letters. We've received a response. It's all set."

I shook my head. "This just sounds like a bad idea."

Her hand slid away from mine. She bit her lip, as if she were holding back words suitable only for more mature clients. This had not been an easy case for her, I knew that. There had been thrilling surprises and unexpected setbacks, far more than she had bargained for when she took the job, which, from the looks of her, couldn't have been more than a few months ago.

"We are out of options, Joey," she said. "Unless you've remembered another blood relative."

"Blood," I said, thinking of Janelle and Thaddeus, Boris, and his three shrieking sisters. "Why is that so important?"

She shrugged. "It just is. In the eyes of the law, it is. In the eyes of a lot of people, actually."

I took back my hands and left parallel smears. We both regarded the moisture. She would have to wipe it up later, before the next sad sack took his seat at this table. Without looking at her, I got the impression of shoulders slumping. I heard her chair creak, a file cabinet squeak, and papers shuffle.

"Ken Harnett," she recited from the page. "He has been told that his son Joey Crouch will be arriving via Amtrak train on August twenty-fourth. On August twenty-fifth Joey will begin eleventh grade at Bloughton High School. By no later than August twentieth, Joey's textbooks will need to be picked up at the school and all arrangements made for the transfer of credits. Mr. Harnett has been advised to establish a relationship with a local physician for Joey, as well as a grief counselor if a need presents itself. Contact information for Joey's present general practitioner and dentist has been forwarded."

"Through the mail," I added gloomily.

"Mr. Harnett has been advised that Joey has not been diagnosed with any health conditions that require immediate attention. Mr. Harnett has been advised that Joey's health insurance under his mother's plan will extend to his eighteenth birthday. As is standard procedure, social services of Lomax County has been contacted to ensure that Mr. Harnett's dwelling meets acceptable standards. Mr. Harnett works as a garbageman."

"Wait. What?"

Claire flipped back a page. "Mr. Harnett works as a garbageman." She raised her eyebrows at me, waiting for a follow-up. I said nothing. Again she lowered her head and turned the page.

"As specified by Ms. Crouch's will, her liquid assets transfer to a savings account for Joey accessible to him on his eighteenth birthday. Her physical assets, aside from those claimed by Joey by August twentieth, will be put up for public auction, the resulting funds of which will be placed into the aforementioned account."

Claire paused on the last page. A purple nail tapped the last paragraph. I didn't like the look of it.

"It is the explicit wish of Ms. Crouch, as specified in her will, that Joey be placed into the sole custody of his biological father, Ken Harnett," she said, with a tone approaching regret. Claire stopped reading and looked at me. "Not that there are any other options," she said softly.

I looked past the piles of papers that I had become so accustomed to during our twice-weekly visits and peered out the window. In the distance, I could see the Hancock Center and Tribune Tower, almost perfectly aligned. We had never gone to the observation deck of the Hancock, my mother and I, though we must have talked about doing it a thousand times. It's easier to do those things as a tourist; you sweep into town with a bulleted to-do list and you get it done because the clock is working against you. It had worked against my mother and me, too; we just hadn't felt it.

There was packing to do.

"There are always options," I said.

3.

ON AUGUST 24 JANELLE and Thaddeus paid for a cab and with Boris accompanied me to Union Station. As Janelle practiced her Arabic with the driver, I stepped onto the curb like a newborn, into the shadows of giants, deaf with traffic, blinded by glass. Exhaust settled into my skin. Pedestrians brushed past too close and their shirtsleeves nipped me like mosquitoes. The scissors switch of businessmen's slacks, the chalkboard squeal of a police siren, some sort of subterranean moan: all sounded to me like blood rushing through my ears. *Blood, yes, it is important, Claire, and this is mine, all around me.*

Janelle and Thaddeus were the type of parents who hugged kids, any kids, whenever the opportunity arose. Their hugs hurt. When they'd had their fill, I turned to Boris and shrugged, and he gave me a hug, too, but just for posterity. What mattered was the handshake. His hand, frailer and bonier than even my own, clamped hard and shook with reckless assurance, and I experienced a surprising certainty that we would never see each other again. He would recede into the human morass of the train station, then the tangled skein of the city. Then it happened: they walked away and up an escalator. Alone for the first time since I had stood above my mother's open casket, I thought again of the spider that had watched her from the funeral home ceiling. I imagined it swinging down on gossamer and catching a lucky breeze. I saw it dancing over her folded hands, racing past her necklace, and defying gravity to scale her upturned chin before disappearing inside her, where it would live out its life. We were all disappearing: the spider, my mother, Boris, me. The wind whips, even down here in the cellar of the city, and we swing from our invisible strings. The strings break and we land, and where we land is called home.

4.

Each town dwindled. First, city suburbs with clean parks molded carefully from surrounding concrete. Then other towns, smaller, but with train stations painted a reassuring summer-camp yellow. Rust was next, abandoned tractors, followed by shirtless children who didn't look up at the train. Finally, spoil: ancient barns swallowing themselves, paved roads crumbled, a bald man on a seatless bike listening to the radio duct-taped to his handlebars. Never in my life had there been no tall buildings to impede the view; the silos made but weak notches in the infinite blue. I peeled my neck from the brown vinyl of my coach seat and let the quaking train rattle me down the narrow steps toward the exit as one might shake a glass to settle a tower of ice.

The train stopped at Bloughton for no more than five seconds. The attendant nearly pushed me out the door. On solid ground again, I swayed beneath the pressure of multiple shoulder straps and felt the square shape of my trumpet case knock against my knee. The station appeared deserted. On one side of the tracks was a small park, mostly barren of trees and rubbed to the dirt. The remains of a swing set sprouted against the late-day sun like the claws of a demolished building. A squirrel nosed at an overturned trash can, flinching each time the breeze snapped the inserted Hefty. On the other side of the tracks, an electrical cage and, beyond that, a light blue trailer home with a sunflower pinwheel spinning implausibly fast. Nothing else in this town, I was certain, moved with such speed.

With each gravel crunch beneath my shoes, I expected him. Ten paces away, nine, eight. He would step from the interior of the one-room train station, the roof's shadow slipping away like a robe lifted from above. Seven paces, six. He would not look like I expected; I expected that. Five paces, four. There would be shyness, possibly faked camaraderie. Three paces, two. Almost certainly a handshake, though I was willing to accept a hug.

My last step hit cement and then I was inside the station. Two empty wooden benches contemplated each other. There was a snack machine with a yellowed OUT OF ORDER sign applied over the coin slot with masking tape. I turned toward the drone of an electric fan and crossed the room to the ticket window. There was an old man inside and I knocked on the glass. He looked up from his book of word jumbles. He wore thick glasses and had a bandage on his forehead.

"You Joey?" he said.

My heart skipped. I felt myself nod.

"Got something for you," he said. He set down his book, his eyes lingering on the puzzle for several seconds more, and then retrieved a piece of paper and pushed it through the slot. It was pencil on rumpled notebook paper. It read:

Hewn Oak Rd.
Dead End
Off Jackson

That was it. No names—not mine, not his—and no map. I looked again at the old man. He was back at the jumble, his glasses sliding down his nose. I knuckled the glass.

"You know where this is?" I asked.

He didn't look at me. "Off Jackson," he said.

At least finding Jackson was not difficult. It appeared to be Bloughton's key thoroughfare. I passed a grocery store called Sookie's Foods, a gas station, a sewing shop, a Christian bookstore, two churches, something called the 3-D Chow Box, a consignment shop, a hardware-store-slash-pharmacy, a bank, a library, and sparse rows of aged houses. But I passed no one who might point me in the right direction. Night was falling and I had been walking for thirty minutes. There were limited ways to rearrange my heavy load, none of them good. I thought of my mother. Had she known these streets? Had she ever traveled them? How could I know so little about this part of her life, how could I have asked so few questions? I forced determination into my gait. For her sake I would find the answers.

I came upon a building larger than most. I was almost past it when I realized it was a high school. I was fully past it before I realized that it was *my* high school. I stopped to give it another look. Beige brick marred by an old CLASS OF 99 RULEZ tag above the auditorium, white sidewalks spotted with bubble gum, yellow lawns striped by the shortest distances between any two popular points: it was a school, all right. How hard could it be to walk inside tomorrow morning? I could be anyone I wanted. I could remake myself. I told myself this over and over as I passed the dark football field, two tennis courts, and an empty parking lot.

Hewn Oak arrived long after I had given up hope. Sidewalks had given way to grass shoulders. Corn had swept up from distant fields and met the road. Still I trudged down Jackson, my bags spinning, the sweat from my palm lifting the words from my father's note. Soon there would be no directions there at all, no proof of his existence, no proof that I belonged here. Then the turnoff appeared and I took it—a winding dirt path through the woods.

After a few minutes I saw a light. I kept moving, my heart now heavier than all my bags put together. A house, little more than a cabin: I could see it now, small, square, and silent. Beyond the cabin, the bright twinkling of a river. My shoes parted the long grass of an unkempt lawn. My father's home, at last—*my* home. This was where my mother wanted me.

It was full night. The stars above me, far from Boris's facsimiles, shone with a fierceness I'd never seen in the city. I made a fist, knocked on the warped wood of the door. I felt my face curling into a defensive grimace and tried to twist it into a smile. There was a long pause. I counted to one minute, then two. Time lost track of me. I listened to the river.

After a while, I pushed open the door and directly inside was a man on a chair staring at me. He spoke in a voice like gravel and hay.

"Tell me how this happened."

5.

He was broad-shouldered and brown from sun. His bloodshot eyes focused somewhere over my head while his large hands held down his dirt-stained knees. Shadows from an unseen fire mottled his skin.

"They told me a bus," he said. I was still standing outside the doorframe, the weight of my luggage forgotten.

"They told me a bus," he repeated with a wince, lifting one of his hands and pushing it through the wild gray hair that flew from the back half of his head. "But I need more information. Which way she was heading. The route of the bus. North? I always picture her heading north."

A pop quiz, my specialty. I conjured a mental map of the fateful intersection. After some calculation, I shook my head.

"South," he said grimly. I nodded. "And the bus. Eastward? It was heading along an eastward course?" His sight line changed; for the first time, he met my eyes and I felt his agony. The answer he craved—if I knew it, I would give it. All I had was the truth, so I shook my head. No, she had just stepped onto the street when the westbound bus struck her square.

He nodded slowly, as if this was the answer he had feared. He turned toward the fireplace, his face blasting yellow. I took advantage of the moment, took a half step closer, and squinted. So this was my father. I scanned for physical similarities and was taken aback: he was me, only dragged through hell. I felt a mixture of revulsion and excitement—part of what made this man so unnerving also existed within me. A quick glance around gave me only the slimmest hints of his life: a low ceiling, rough wooden floors, a creeping darkness.

Firelight flickered strangely over a multifaceted brick wall; no, not bricks but books of all shapes and sizes, hundreds of them, stacked from floor to ceiling. I grasped at it—an intellectual garbageman, that wasn't so bad. Perhaps he rescued these volumes from trash cans and brought them back here. That would explain the pungent odor.

His hands pushed down at his knees and he was up. Fully unfurled, he dwarfed me. His forearms split the flaps of his shirtsleeves. Wires of gray hair filled in the V at his sternum. Like me, he buckled his belt on an inner notch, but his thighs left little room inside the battered pants. All I could see of his boots was that they were black and big.

There were two large gray sacks at his side, and he strapped them to his shoulders. He took a step forward, halted, and focused his eyes on my chest, as if he would rather wait me out than continue speaking. Wood crackled and snapped. We stood six feet from each other, both of us planted to the ground with added weight.

He drew snot through his nose and spat, presumably into the fire. Head down, he came right at me. I stumbled backward, outside of the cabin once more. Wrenching a ring of keys from his hip pocket, he passed me, the rotten smell briefly intensifying. His fingers nimbly isolated a key as he walked. I noticed for the first time the outline of a pickup truck at the side of the house. He was leaving. I had just arrived and he was leaving.

"Dad," I said, realizing too late that it was my first word. In a way, it was also my last: it was a name I would never call him again.

He reached the truck. His right arm fell; the key ring jingled. After a moment he turned his head halfway, the fingers of light from the house barely kindling his cheek.

"You want someone to blame? Blame me. I killed her."

His chest expanded, daring me to draw out the moment. I just stood there, gnats bumping against my face and neck. Satisfied that we were finished, my father tossed the cloth sacks into the truck bed. I saw a glint of keys, a hint of his clownish hair, and the moonlight shimmering from the opening and closing door of his truck. The engine coughed and headlights gave acute dimension to the trees. Tires turned. Branches snapped. I was left in dissipating exhaust lit by brake lights of diminishing red. He was gone.

A gnat made contact with my naked eye—only this woke me from my trance. I lunged inside and shut the door, releasing my green backpack and duffel bags to the floor. I closed my eyes, rolled my aching shoulders, and took deep breaths. The odor was persistent. He was a garbageman, I kept telling myself. Stinks were part of the job. So were odd hours. Maybe right now he was picking up an extra shift in the next town over. That bag he carried was his gear: pokers for loose refuse, shovels for scraping Dumpster bottoms, sanitary jumpsuits, plastic gloves. *This is normal,* I told myself, while my heart hurt itself against my ribs. *This is exactly how a father and son interact.*

There was indeed a fireplace, and I sat down where my father had been sitting. The seat was still warm and I shifted, disturbed by his alien temperature. I looked around. The cabin was dominated by this single room, anchored at one end by the ashy hearth and at the other by a sink, a stove, and a refrigerator. Between the two ends was a random topography of cardboard boxes, half-zippered bags, buckets brimming with trash, and mountains of books. Overwhelming everything else were newspapers, stacks upon musty stacks.

From a glance I could see that each pile consisted of a different publication; I saw headers with words like *Journal, Sentinel,* and *Herald.* Mixed with the cabin's odor I could detect the ancient ink.

I reached down to remove the shoes from my aching feet, and my knuckles grazed glass. It was a bottle of whiskey. I picked it up. It was empty. I remembered my father's red eyes and imagined his hunched figure emptying this bottle while I arrived at the train station, as I stumbled helplessly through town. *Irresponsible* was the word that settled in my mind. My mother had been far from perfect, but irresponsibility was something I had never had to deal with, much less live alongside.

All at once I was exhausted. I dragged myself to my socked feet and shuffled across the cluttered floor. Behind one door were a toilet and a tiny sink shoved against a curtainless shower. Through the remaining door was a bedroom barely big enough for the mattress wedged between its walls. The sheets were knotted. Filthy clothes wove a strange carpet across the floor. This room belonged to my father.

I dragged my bags to a far corner of the main room, near the sink, and with aching muscles slid a couple of waist-high stacks of newspapers out of the way. I removed my trumpet case from my pack so that the clothes inside could function as a pillow. I put a jacket over my legs, a hooded sweatshirt over my torso. I lay back and crooked an elbow over my eyes, the popping of the firewood the only sound. I began to pray, as my mom had taught me to when I was little, but the sentences scattered and I forgot to whom I was speaking—God, Jesus, or her.

Sleep came pulling, but one thought would not let me go. *I killed her,* he had said. It was a horrific statement. It was an invitation for me to loathe him. I couldn't resist. I did. It was arrogance, his certainty that despite not having spoken to my mother in sixteen years, he still mattered enough to have figured some way in her passing. *You fucking bastard,* I thought. *You don't get to be a part of her death, no matter how bad you want it.*

In semiconsciousness I saw the wedge-shaped nicks in my mother's left ear and heard my father ask me about the direction she was walking versus the direction of the oncoming bus. She had never heard very well out of her left ear—why had it taken me this long to remember that? She had not mentioned it in years, that was true, but it had been evident every night in the cocking of her head when she watched TV, and in the way she had held the phone to her right ear, never her left. She had not heard the bus because it had come up on her left—her left ear, the one her ex-husband, my father, had somehow maimed. This direct line drawn between my parents, the first I'd ever witnessed, was startling. Their lives *did* connect, and violently; her death was along that line, too, and somewhere along the line was an intersection that was me.

6.

WHEN I AWOKE IT was morning. The taste of charred wood burned my throat. I stood with the aid of the closest block of newsprint. I needed to pee and hobbled across the floor, stubbing my toes on any number of objects and sending one tower of papers wobbling. I urinated into the shallow yellow basin of the toilet and blinked around the dank bathroom, wondering at what seemed missing. It took my splashing cold, sulfurous water over my face before I realized. There was no mirror.

I poked my head outside. The trees were bright green and lined with gold from the rising sun. The lush forest scent temporarily rinsed my body of the cloying odor of the cabin. My father's truck was still missing.

The first day of school—it was today. The realization crashed upon me. I had counted on an evening full of discussions with my father about my classes, my textbooks, my teachers, my schedule, what time I needed to get to school and how I would be getting there. Nothing of the sort had happened and it was Monday morning in Bloughton, Iowa, and I had no books, no ride, no instructions, nothing.

I checked my watch. It was just after seven. In Chicago, classes had begun at eight. Based on yesterday's trek, I figured the school would be a thirty- or forty-minute walk. I could make it if I hurried. I ripped off my clothes and dove into the shower. The dribbles fell ineffectually about my hair. There was a nugget of soap on a shower ledge and I glided it through my pits and across my neck, and seconds later I was drying with the dingy towel that had sat wadded atop the toilet. The shorts I had worn yesterday smelled of smoke, but there was no time to find an alternative. I unzipped a bag and put on the first shirt I saw, some atrocity printed on both sides with a cartoon duck in sunglasses. Textbooks—Claire had assured me that my father would have them. My eyes spun across the room: a million books, none of them likely to be mine. I tied my shoes and stepped outside, opting not to lock the door behind me, and stood on the grass feeling naked and unprotected without the usual first-day arsenal of notebooks and folders and pencils.

I wove through the twists of Hewn Oak Road. By the time I made it to Jackson it was seven-forty. I ran.

With only minutes to spare, I made the front lawn. From a distance the students could have been my former classmates. As I drew closer, though, differences became apparent. Many wore baseball caps, something not allowed in my previous school. On average they were beefier. Every single one of them was white. The boys were red in the neck and the girls were tan, their deep browns segmented by the milky negatives left by tank tops and bikini straps. One of the boys was draining a mouthful of chaw. One of the girls had a Confederate flag patch on her backpack. An actual tractor was parked in the lot.

A warning bell rang as I entered. I had a moment of panic when I realized I didn't have an ID, not even my passport, but relaxed when I saw that there were no security guards or even a metal detector. Students scattered as though they knew where they were headed. More lockers were closing than opening. I wandered until I found the designation in faded wooden letters—PRI CIP L'S OF ICE—then waited in line behind a dozen other students. A few of them looked as confused as I felt; they continually referenced their schedules and checked the clock. The two women behind the counter communicated with the deadpan cheer of store clerks during a holiday rush. Through the clatter I heard information exchanged about switching study halls, prescription medications, erroneous locker combinations. A bell rang at 8:05. Classes were beginning; I felt another surge of apprehension. I could finally read a sign behind the desk: PRINCIPAL JESS

SIMMONS/VICE PRINCIPAL ESTELLE DIAMOND. My turn had arrived.

"What's up, hon?" the woman asked. Cat's-eye glasses were wedged onto a piggy face further undermined by excessive purple eye shadow.

"I'm new," I said.

"Name?"

"Joey Crouch."

She licked her thumb and fluttered through a few pages. "Okay, hon, I got you." She glanced at me over her glasses. "You're supposed to be with Pratt in English."

"I don't know where that is."

"The room number is on your schedule, hon."

"I don't have a schedule."

"You lose it? You got your log-in? Everything's on the computer."

"No, wait." She was already glancing over my head at the person behind me. "I don't have anything. I just got here yesterday. I don't have a schedule. I don't have a locker. I'm not even sure if I have books. My dad wasn't able to tell me what I'm supposed to do."

The woman paused and gave me her first real consideration. She pursed her painted lips and looked back down at her papers, her chin melting into the gelatin of her neck. "Joey Crouch?"

"Yes."

"Parents are . . ." She looked. And blinked. Then, without looking up, she said, "Ken Harnett?"

There was the blast of an exhale from behind me, followed by a mutter of amazement: "No way."

I had no recourse but the truth. I nodded. The woman

wormed her tongue inside her rouged cheek. Then she started clicking her mouse.

The other woman behind the counter, a younger redhead, called out, "Next," and the boy behind me stepped up. He looked me up and down, a sly grin on his square and watchful face. He wore his blond hair in a military cut, and his tight shirt showed off his arms, thick with muscle and encircled with barbed-wire tattoos. His neck was irritated from a too-vigorous shaving routine.

"Woody!" the redhead exclaimed. "I swear you keep getting taller!"

"No, ma'am," said the boy, dazzling her, and surprising me, with the size and ferocity of his grin. Over this blinding display of teeth, he favored me with another glance. "Bigger, maybe, on account of weights and stuff."

"Well, I don't doubt that. We were all talking this morning how we expect big things from Woodrow Trask this season."

"Yes, ma'am."

"And did you know I just saw Celeste not two minutes ago? Just the prettiest thing I ever saw."

"You're right about that, ma'am."

I was dimly aware of the sound of a printer. With a smack, the bespectacled woman in front of me slammed a paper to the counter.

"That's your schedule, Joey Crouch," she said. She pointed a chubby finger at the first line. "That's English with Pratt. Mr. Pratt. He's in room two fourteen. That's up the stairs and to the right. After that, you have calculus and biology and then lunch. That's on this floor, but around back. You'll figure it out as you go." She pointed to where she had written in ink a few numbers on the paper. "This is your locker number and your combination. You have four minutes between classes, so after Pratt, go make sure it works. Some of those things are a million years old, and goofy. Half of them open without a combination if you just pull hard enough, but you didn't hear that from me. Now," she said, looking at me again. "You said you didn't have books?"

"I don't know," I said. "They could be at home. My dad didn't tell me."

At the mention of my father, her tongue again retreated to her cheek. She was clearly weighing her words. "Everything going okay out there?"

Without hesitation I lied. "Yeah. It's just that we didn't get to talk before he left for work. He must've forgotten to give me my books."

She took off her glasses. They dangled around her neck on a pearled chain. "It does say here he picked them up on Friday." She sighed again and rubbed her forehead. "Talk to him tonight, find those books. For the time being I'm going to give you a replacement folder. It's got some information about the school, dress code, instructions about your computer access, all that stuff. There's a salmon-colored packet in there about extracurricular activities, too. You like sports?"

I just stared at the folder she had in her hands.

"I like band," I said.

She flapped a hand. "Well, hon, it's all in your salmon packet. I'm going to give you this pen, too, because it looks like you need one." She opened the folder, tucked the pen inside the pocket, and slid it across the counter. She gave me another lingering look, then briskly lodged her glasses on her face. "You should be able to survive today. You have any problems, you come see me. My name's Laverne, like the TV show."

I picked up my class schedule. With my other hand I took the folder. It was red, white, and black, and had an icon of a plummeting bird with its claws splayed for attack. BLOUGHTON SCREAMING EAGLES was printed in a collegiate font.

"Thank you," I said. I turned away from Laverne, my face buried in my schedule. Room 214. Up the stairs. English. Mr. Pratt. I stepped into the reverberating dimness of the hallway. My forehead struck something hard—someone's chest.

"Sorry," I said. Moving aside, I saw that it was Woody Trask. The sly smile had not left his face.

"The Garbageman is your dad?" he asked.

Sixteen years I had gone without knowing my father's name, and here suddenly was a town where everyone seemed to have an opinion on him. I blinked a few times. I could not fathom why this person was speaking to me. He was big, blandly handsome, and obviously into sports—a profile that did not at all match my own. But I needed a friend, and badly.

I attempted an easygoing smile. "I'm Joey Crouch." I held out my hand. It was a risk, but also a necessary reach from the precipice.

Woody Trask regarded my hand as if it were a fly pestering his vision. His lip curled. "Must be shitty having such a shithole for a dad," he said, stepping away and heading for the stairs in giant animal lopes, two textbooks dangling from a single monster hand. Before disappearing, he cringed. "By the way, dude, you fucking stink."

7.

I DIDN'T SEE HER in English class; Mr. Pratt accepted my late entry wordlessly and gestured to a seat directly in front, so I never had a chance to look behind me, and her name on the roll call meant nothing. I didn't see her in calculus because she wasn't there. It was biology where I saw her for the first time, striding in with a pencil in her hair and the hard plane of her textbook slanting against the curvature of her chest. She was dark-lipped and black-haired with Egyptian eyes, and wore a loose yellow dress that softened the withering severity of her features. She sat down across the room from me and spoke secrets to the girls who fell in place around her. Somehow the geometric bracket of her chair made her all the more beautiful; I could see how her lower back arced away from the plastic and how the cruel flatness of the seat accented the teardrop of her rear, and as she switched her legs I could see the tender underskin of her knees unseal and reseal with sweat. I didn't want to speak to her or meet her. I just wanted to watch her for the rest of my life.

Mr. Gottschalk took attendance. Justin Ambrose's first name had been misprinted *Justine* on all the attendance sheets, and this was the third class in which I had to watch him shrug off the chuckles. The next name called was Celeste Carpenter, and she, the girl, raised her hand. A tiny woven bracelet fell from her wrist to the swell of her arm. Celeste—that name rang a bell, but how could I possibly know her? I leaned forward, trying to see around dozens of uglier bodies, but from where I sat, only the barest outline of her face was visible.

"There's no Joey Crouch? Going once, going twice . . ."

How long had he been saying my name? Seeing Gottschalk go back to his list, I raised my hand and blurted, "Here!"

Nearly everyone in the room turned. I was met with the faces of my new life: inquisitive, territorial, bored, amused. I felt the red that colored my face, remembered my stupid duck-in-sunglasses T-shirt. I couldn't help it: I looked at Celeste Carpenter. She had found me as well.

Gottschalk looked up. He was a short, thick man with a triangle of dark hair rising from the top of his head. There was something swollen about his face, as if the underlying structure had been made from tied balloons, then painted over with skin. "Mr. Crouch, splendid of you to join us!" He bent his balloon-animal face. "The name is unfamiliar. I take it you are new?"

I nodded but was so far away I couldn't be sure that he saw it.

"Stand up," he said.

I gripped my desk. It felt scummy, hard, and real—unlike this moment.

"Mr. Crouch," he said. "Do as I say. Stand up."

I slid sideways from the chair and stood. My vision rocked. Far below, students' eyes twinkled up like streetlamps.

"Ladies and gentlemen, this is what we call a teachable moment," said Gottschalk. "Observe Mr. Crouch. This is his first day here. He is ill at ease. These feelings incite within him distress. But this is not psychology class—that's upstairs with Mrs. Keaton. This is biology, and what we're interested in here is how the exercises of the mental induce actualities of the physical. So take a look at Mr. Crouch. What do you see?"

My arms hung flat at my sides. I stared at the teacher, afraid to look anywhere else. There was giggling, but no one said anything.

"I only know two of your names thus far, so I'm forced to call on Mr. Ambrose, Mr. Justin Without-an-E Ambrose," said Gottschalk. "Mr. Ambrose, meet Mr. Crouch. Tell me what you see."

There was an edginess to Justin's appearance that I had seen too many times before. It was the desperate look of the bullied finally given occasion to bully. I braced myself.

"I see sweat?" Justin ventured. The class roared as if prompted by a maestro. I reached one hand to steady myself against my chair but it was too many miles away. Justin was right, of course. The stains from my morning run still shadowed my pits. I felt a drop of perspiration clinging to an eyelash and I tried not to blink. *I see tears!* I could almost hear Justin Ambrose's jubilation.

"Very good!" said Gottschalk over the merriment. "Sweat, aka transpiration: courtesy of the good old hypothalamus, the body generates water as a means of thermoregulation, a process that cools us as the sweat evaporates, keeping things cozy enough that we can continue to hunt the savage beast or, in the case of the female, suckle the brood."

He looked down at his attendance sheet. "Miss Carpenter, I'm afraid it's up to you. Look at Mr. Crouch and kindly supply us with a description."

A low groan of pleasure gusted through the class. Dozens of smiling faces banked to Celeste, who blinked her night eyes at the teacher, then slowly turned her face to me. Distantly I heard the clock at the front of the room tick. The compulsion to specify tugged at my gut and I fought it.

"In case you need glasses, Miss Carpenter," Gottschalk said, "Mr. Crouch is the sweaty one swooning at the back of the class. Take a look and tell us what you see."

Perfect lips parted.

"I see a boy," she said.

An uneasy, possibly disappointed noise nickered through the rows of students. "Diplomatic, Miss Carpenter," said Gottschalk. "Diplomatic but also correct. He *is*—we can presume, anyhow—a boy, which enacts its own particular set of pheromonal influences when it comes to producing that sticky mix of water and solute that we can see glistening from all the way across the room. Other acceptable answers would've included the bags under his eyes or the blemishes on his skin; the origins of which, I promise you, we will get to in due time. We have, after all, all semester." He turned back to the attendance list. "You can sit, Mr. Crouch. A-plus for the day."

8.

A BOY. IT HAD sounded good coming from her, but standing in the hallway watching two hundred kids funnel into the lunch line and stream into the cafeteria coop, the two words rang in my ears as something more demeaning. Not a man, not even a young man, but a boy. I felt it, too: here was a simple human endeavor—lunch—and I was too scared to move.

After having bought snacks on the Amtrak, I had less than ten dollars left in my wallet, and much of that was in change. My mother's meager fortune, as well the proceeds from the auction of her belongings, was inaccessible to me for two more years. For now, this was it: eight dollars and thirty-three cents. I flipped through the bills as covertly as possible, but still people looked my way.

The line got shorter. I moved to the counter, accidentally ordered too much, and used almost every cent to pay for it. The woman at the register watched bemusedly while I counted out change.

Waiting until everyone else had gone first was a mistake, I saw that right away. Although this school was much smaller than my previous one, instead of splitting lunch into separate periods they tossed everyone together, grades nine through twelve. The tables seethed with feeding. There was nowhere safe to sit without impinging on claimed territory.

I wanted to flee, but my stocked tray had already been noted by too many people. *I'm too old for this,* I told myself as I began walking down the center of the room. I swept my eyes from side to side while trying to look as if I couldn't care less. There was a seat—but I'd have to squeeze in between two girls. There was another one with better elbow room—but the bleary-eyed punks who had commandeered it looked less than inviting. I was nearing the end of the room. To double back would be disaster.

Impulsively I sat. The two boys nearest me were younger. "Hey," I grunted, nodding curtly to indicate that conversation was not necessary. The kid at my elbow edged away like I had leprosy, but the boy across from me pushed a response past his pizza. I stared down at my food, recognizable shapes in autumn colors. None of it looked edible.

"Hey, Crouch!" It was a shout from the next table over: Woody Trask, smacking his lips. He swallowed and grinned, his perfect white smile marred with something green. There was snickering from the guys around him, while the girls rolled their eyes and covered their faces. My heart sank to see Celeste Carpenter sitting to Woody's right.

"Hey," I responded weakly, turning back to my tray.

"I've got a few questions I'd like to ask you," Woody said. "If you have a moment, that is."

My eyes caught those of the boy sitting across from me. He glared, furious that I had drawn such harassment to his table. I wanted to tell him that I didn't know Woody Trask and had not done anything wrong, but he grabbed his tray and left. I picked up my silverware and stared at it, feeling the bench fluctuate as two or three other boys fled the table.

"It's no big thing," Woody said. "I just want to do a little fact-checking. Now, the Garbageman, he's your dad, right?"

I could almost hear Gottschalk's narration: *The chemicals raging inside of Mr. Crouch, ladies and gentlemen, are a disgusting but nevertheless normal part of the physiology of the teenage male.* There were a number of ways this could end, all of them bad. My mind shuttled through the options. My best hope, I determined, was to say nothing at all. With luck, by tomorrow Woody would choose a new target.

The cheeriness of his voice flattened. "I'm talking to you, Crouch."

"Crotch?" sputtered a different voice. "Trask, did you just call that kid Crotch?" I glanced up. A behemoth sat to Woody's left, slobbering over a cupcake, his head the size, color, and texture of a shaved pig. I distantly recalled a teacher referring to him as Reinhart as she made her way down the attendance list.

"You heard right, Rhino," Woody replied, keeping his eyes on me. "That is exactly what I said. So how about it, Crotch, is your dad the Garbageman or what?"

The Garbageman: it was more than a job description. At Bloughton High, at least, that was his official name. All around me, the crackle of utensils against plastic gave way to a strange wave of silence. I couldn't help it this time; I began to ease into the soft nirvana of specifying—

—the marbled turtle shell of my tray—
—the braille of dry boogers freckling the table—
—an ancient and blackened Band-Aid trampled into the floor at my feet—
—the rhythmic patterns of knees popping nervously against tables—
—the mist of someone's sneeze hanging like motes in the sun—
—in the concavity of my spoon, twenty students turning synchronously—

—but their pause was mine to break. I dragged myself back to life.

"Yeah, I guess," I responded. I looked at Celeste. Beneath the flawless cheeks, her jaw flexed in a chewing motion. Her expression remained perceptive yet removed.

"That's fascinating," said Woody. "Because we were just discussing how none of us have ever seen him pick up a single piece of our crap. Rhino here, his dad *works* for county sanitation, and Rhino's dad told Rhino that he ain't ever seen your dad pick up a single McDonald's wrapper. So what we're curious about, Crotch, is what exactly does he do all day?"

If I told them that I hadn't the slightest idea, I would only sound stupid. Specifying continued its pull—

—brown flaws in each corn kernel like coffee stains on teeth—

—the unnatural shrug in the neck of my fork—

"Pop says the Garbageman's always at the pawnshop," Rhino said, interrupting my trance. "Always selling shit. Always got mud all over his clothes, and always selling shit. You know what Pop thinks?"

Woody held my eyes with minimal effort. "What's that, Rhino?"

"Pop thinks he's a thief. Who else has that much shit to pawn?"

I looked for a clock, a teacher, any excuse to get going. Instead I saw a battered old pay phone, mounted on the far cafeteria wall. The impulse to call Boris overwhelmed me. I had not bothered to reset my cell phone after Claire had suggested that I wait and see what kind of coverage was best in Bloughton. Boris's cell number, though, I had memorized, and if I'd had just a bit more change left I could have called him, explained what was going on, told him that things were taking a series of bad turns and that I needed to get back to the city as soon as he could line it up.

"Man, I'll never forget that time we were fishing out on the Big Chief and ran across that dude, and he was standing in the water," Woody was saying, "like up to his waist in water." He shook his head at the memory. Celeste's neat smile suggested she had heard this story before.

"I don't remember that," said Rhino.

"You weren't there, dipshit," said Woody. He gave his face, beaming and animated, to the table around him, and the eyes of his friends replicated his joviality until all of them, Woody included, were handsomer. "We were in a boat and came within probably ten feet of this guy, and he was like chest-deep in the water trying to catch fish with his hands. Colder than a motherfucker and this motherfucker was out there with water up to his chin, swiping at fish. I was with Gilman and Parker and we hadn't had a bite all day, but this guy, Crotch's dad, the Garbageman, he pulls this two-foot bluegill right out of the water in front of us. With his bare hands! Seriously about blew our minds."

My head was spinning. I couldn't imagine the inert figure I had met the night before doing anything demanding such bizarre resourcefulness.

Woody did not see it that way. "It's sad, man," he said, his eyes landing on me once again. "A working man like that having to fish without bait or tackle. What they're paying garbagemen these days must suck."

"They get paid very well," said Rhino knowledgeably. "*Very* well."

"Well, then you must be right, Rhino." Woody sighed. "Resorting to crazy shit like that? The Garbageman *must* be a thief."

Celeste was merciful. Wordlessly she decided it was time to go, and everyone else followed suit, forgetting me in an instant. Even without explicit violence I was shaken. The lunch period was short, only thirty-five minutes, and just when I had settled enough to seriously contemplate my food, everyone began hastening away. The room rose almost in unison; it felt as if I were the one sinking.

The day crawled. I kept my head down. Weaving through the crowded hallway during the next class break, I heard "Crotch!" called at me. By the time the last bell had rung and I was speeding for the nearest exit, I heard it from multiple sources. *Not me,* I pleaded, knowing that every school has one untouchable pariah. *Please let it not be me.*

9.

I WELCOMED THE HEAT that singed me all the way home; it dulled my anguish and hunger. I even welcomed the prospect of a second round with my father. This abysmal day and any others like it still to come were his fault, and I would not be quick to forgive.

His truck was still missing. Despite myself, I almost sobbed in relief. I broke into a run. Inside the cabin, I flung myself to the floor in my corner by the sink. I buried my eyes in my hot elbow and felt my chest hitch up and down in alarming jags. In the darkness my mother comforted me and, after a while, whispered me away.

When I returned the sun was setting. The refrigerator buzzed and my stomach cramped in reply. I got up, gripped the rusty handle, and opened it. Yellow, stained walls greeted me—there was next to nothing inside. A wad of questionable meat, a row of condiment containers crusted shut. In the lower compartment, called the crisper by my mother, whips of onion skin were trapped in a black gel.

I closed the door, turned my back to it, and slid down until my butt hit the floor. There was nothing to eat and I had no money. These were the facts, and I was prepared to shame my father with them when he finally returned. In the meantime, though, I would scour the house. There were things I could learn here; better to learn them while still alone.

There was plenty evidence of hard work—an upside-down boot healing beside a curled tube of superglue, a pair of work gloves with fresh patches meticulously sewn over worn fingers, a pyre of misshapen shovels and hoes—but nowhere did I see proof of my father's occupation. If he picked up trash, where was his garbage truck? His uniform? Pay stubs from his monthly check? Yet the more I kicked through the crap that blanketed the floor and angled up the walls, the more comfortable I became with the moniker. He was the Garbageman because of the garbage of his life strewn out all around him: piteous scraps of food, mud-matted carpets, expired medicine, spare change in a mason jar, a brush so old it still clutched nongray hair in volume.

I opened drawers and cabinets—a few plates, a plastic bowl full of coffee grains, a scattering of utensils as random as twigs on a forest floor. Beneath the sink, to my surprise, I found an abundance of industrial-strength cleaning products. The abrasive perfumes of pine and bleach unsettled my empty stomach, but at least briefly overtook the gamey odor. Given the cabin's state, I considered placing a cleaning product atop each newspaper tower in the room—who knew, maybe he would take the hint. Instead I threw open the front door and all the windows. Through the final window I discovered a small garden between the cabin and the river. Unlike the house, it was tidy, even meticulous.

Near the floor by the fireplace I found a phone outlet, but nowhere was there an actual phone. *Technophobe:* the word fit my father perfectly. No phone, no computer, no television, not even a radio. I dreaded oppressive nights spent here in this tiny space with nothing to fill the silence.

Already on my knees, I began scanning the titles of the books bottommost to the ten or twelve stacks. Most of these were quite old, and my eyes resisted their small print and faded colorings. I hopped into a squat to better read some of the spines. There were two disintegrating books rubber-banded together: *Antropologium* and *Mikrokosmographia*. I took them between my fingers, but as I did so, the floor-to-ceiling pile bulged sinuously. I left them alone. Above them, *Historical Sketch of the Edinburgh Anatomical School* and *Great Medical Disasters*. There was a pattern here, but it could be explained away: this was an unrepresentative sample, a grouping of books perhaps collected from the discards of a hospital library. I shifted to another pile several feet away. *The Confessions of an Undertaker.* An audiotape titled *Highlights About Wood Caskets*. A thick yellow brick of magazines called *Casket and Sunnyside;* a smaller stack of a publication titled *American Funeral Director*. And creating stability concerns near the ceiling, the massive *Gale Directory of Publications and Broadcast Media*. At least this title had some tie to the newspapers surrounding me.

This was the personal library of Ken Harnett. I backed away, trying to revive the memory of the colorful and reassuring books Janelle and Thaddeus let spill into the rooms of Boris and his sisters. Instead I could only see my father's dark and troubled face. Sanitary worker or not, this might be a man I shouldn't meddle with; I thought again of my mother's disfigured ear. But instead of stopping, I dove into his bedroom, tearing at his sheets, lifting coats from the floor to see what was secreted beneath.

I found myself facing the narrowest of closets tucked behind the bedroom door. Inside, a few clean white dress shirts, a black suit, even; some ties draped over a nail. Interesting, these items—but I forgot them when I saw the safe. It was large and metal and secured with a combination lock. I kneeled in front of it and gave the handle a pull just in case. Nothing. I tried 10-20-30. I tried the combination of my old gym locker, 32-0-25. Nothing. I gave the safe a push to gauge its weight. It did not budge.

Behind the safe, wedged between it and the wall, was yet another surprise. I nudged my head through the hanging shirttails and pants legs. It was a cardboard box filled with alcohol. Carefully I lifted a few random bottles. It was the cheap, hard stuff, and plenty of it. Most unsettling of all was that it was well hidden, and the only one Ken Harnett had to hide it from was himself.

It wouldn't do me any good to knock back any gin, no matter how raw my hunger. I dragged my feet back to my dusty corner and, feeling too much like a dog, curled myself up on the duffel bags that were my bed. What a strange and mixed-up misery I felt. *Come home,* I urged him. My very next thought: *Stay away*.

10.

AFRAID OF AGAIN SHOWING up to school drenched from a thirty-minute run, I kept myself alert after waking up at four-thirty. I even tried to make coffee, but the outcome was tepid and bitter, and the caffeine only upped the intensity of my hunger. I waited for him as long as I could, praying that any minute now, he would return, any minute now.

I reached school early and successfully opened my locker, though still I had nothing to put inside. My green backpack I had protectively left at home, and my books, if they existed, still hid within my father's fearful collection. I didn't want to sift through those titles ever again.

Just outside the door to Pratt's English class, Laverne stopped me in the hall. "Good morning, Joey! You find those books all right?"

Students herded past me on their way to class. Several of them shot me doubtful looks. Instantly I saw the scene through their eyes: some short, skinny new kid making friends with the overbearing fat lady who yelled at them for running past the principal's office. I needed every friend I could get, including Laverne, I knew this, yet I felt the lie coming all the way up my throat. "Yep, got 'em," I said.

"Atta boy," she said, nodding herself into a half-dozen new chins. "You read through that salmon packet?"

"What?" I only vaguely remembered the BLOUGHTON SCREAMING EAGLES folder I held in my hand. More students, class about to start, another lie I couldn't stop: "Oh, sure, I read it."

"Well, don't forget, during study hall today you can come down to the office and get all settled for band." Horrifically, she winked. "I remember you said you had a special liking for band."

I saw a girl turn to her friend and mouth in disbelief the words *special liking*. I nodded quickly in Laverne's general direction and made telling head-fakes toward Mr. Pratt's class. She seemed to understand and waved cheerfully, oblivious that half of the class waved at me in perfect mockery as I entered. Still, Laverne's information had been useful. Anything to get out of study hall, where idle, bored kids were bound to start saying, or throwing, anything.

I sailed through Pratt's class with no trouble; cautiously, I let myself nurture optimism. Calculus went just as well; Coach Winter, apparently a feared figure on the practice field, kept order with drill-sergeant authority. It was biology that I most feared, and that was where problems began anew.

Gottschalk demanded that notes be taken, and it was still early enough in the semester that students paid attention. The lights were dimmed to facilitate viewing transparencies on an old-fashioned overhead projector. I was glad for the darkness: no one could see me and I could resist looking at any faces, Celeste Carpenter's in particular. Between statements by Gottschalk, the only sound was the scratching of pencils. It was during such a moment that my stomach, empty for nearly forty-eight hours, constricted and squirted out a noise of at least six seconds in duration.

I clutched my gut and waited for the laughs. They came. "Lunch is one period away," Gottschalk sang from the front of the room. The titters died down. I clutched my gut and made frantic pleas to God, even though they were what my mother would've called wasted prayers. About one minute later, another sound, this one like a blast of flatulence. More laughter. Again, Gottschalk reined in the class; again, a few minutes later, more elongated and high-pitched squelching. If I were someone more confident and with a cooler head, I could have laughed these off, even turned them to my advantage—I'd seen guys successfully woo girls by magisterially claiming their own farts. For me, it was too late; the absurdity was reaching outrageous levels. In a twisted bit of mercy, I could not fully concentrate on my own mortification, as I was gripped by hunger pains the likes of which I'd never felt. I had to eat.

I rode out the rest of the class by taking notes so fanatically they ran off the page and onto the desk. All I could think of was food: the distasteful spread of yesterday's lunch was now my most fervent desire, if only I had the money to buy it. When the lunch bell rang, it was all I could do not to sprint for the door. I pretended to tie my shoes so I could be the last one out.

I staggered the wrong way down the hallway, applying one

hand of pressure against my stomach. Smells drifted at me from everywhere: vanilla shampoo, cherry lip balm, Cheetos breath, an underarm deodorant reminiscent of lime. My mouth swam with saliva. I heard shouts fade toward the lunchroom, footsteps, too, and then echoing around my skull was the last in a series of lockers slammed shut.

Laverne's advice about unreliable lockers came back to me verbatim. I let my steps drift to the right until I found myself at an arbitrary locker. I looked both ways. My blood felt thin.

I pulled at the handle. To my surprise, Laverne was right—the lock did not hold. Only the lower corner of the door remained jammed in place. Inside the locker I could see a hooded sweatshirt, a backpack—and a purse. Just one meal and then the money would be returned, I swore it, and I'd slide the repayment, with interest, through the vent. I shook the door and it thundered like a sheet of aluminum. Too loud, though no more so than my stomach. I kicked at the corner and it crashed like a cymbal. I kicked it again.

The door banged open against the adjacent locker. Wincing, my stomach acids boiling, I grabbed the purse and unzipped it and looked inside. I was not aware of the block of sunlight on the hallway floor to my right until it was pierced by someone's shadow.

It was Gottschalk, motionless, observing me through his thick and rippled features. I looked at the purse in my hand. It was dainty, sequined, and pink. There was no way I could turn this into something it wasn't. Slowly I put the purse back into the locker and shut the door. I turned my eyes to the biology teacher, but all I could see was my mother's shamed expression. My hands were shaking; it might have been food deprivation, or it might not.

"The ruling class at this school is not effective at applying discipline," Gottschalk said finally. "They're not effective at prevention, they're not effective at detection, they're not effective at sniffing out losers—in short, they're not effective. This is why I do not involve them unless absolutely necessary."

I found myself nodding thoughtfully. It was a pitiful attempt to win him over. I felt like a child.

"Mr. Crouch, I appreciate the difficulties of acclimation. We were all new somewhere at some time. But this, to be blunt, is quite over any line we could draw. Not that I'm surprised. I foresaw problems with you right away. It's not all your fault, of course. As you'll learn in class, genetics has a big part to play in each of us. Nevertheless, the onus is always upon the individual to overcome and transcend those genetics. Biology, Mr. Crouch, it all comes back to biology."

I was still nodding. My neck muscles, made of water and coffee, wobbled.

"So here is what happens now. You walk away from here knowing that the next time you do this, it's not suspension, it's expulsion. You also walk away knowing you have an enemy and you're looking at him. Oh, surprised? That an instructor can say such things? I am not of the new guard, Mr. Crouch. What you get from me, in the class or out, you earn by acting like a man. I suggest you brush up on your biology. Because every day from here on out it is going to be you versus me. Am I making myself clear? Any time I want an answer, it's you I'm going to call on first. Any time I feel like assigning additional work, guess what? You're the first one invited. Until I feel you have earned this back, this shameful act, you don't have a stone to stand on, a pot to poop in." The thick curds of his features straightened. "That's the whole kit and caboodle, Crouch. Get to lunch."

11.

The mettle it took to coerce my legs into action and lead me away from study hall was equal to any accomplishment up to that point in my life. I slanted my way to the office. Laverne was not there. It was just as well. I mumbled something about signing up for band. They told me that Mr. Granger, the band instructor, had a free period right now and that I could go see him right away. They indicated the direction and I slid across the wall until I was there.

Mr. Granger was a tall, thin man with round glasses and an abbreviated mustache. When I appeared in his doorway he blinked at me as if I had blood gushing out of my mouth. "I'm Joey Crouch," I rasped. "I'm here for band."

He beckoned me with a hummingbird gesture that reminded me of my mom at her most impatient. I collapsed into a chair alongside his desk. My eyes locked onto a dish of peppermint candies nearly lost amid the desktop clutter.

"Candy?" It was all I could say.

"What, you want a piece?" he asked, but before the question was out of his mouth I had three in my hand and was furiously shredding the wrappers. I sucked and crunched, closing my eyes, the sugar stinging my tongue. Mr. Granger crossed his arms and watched me.

"What do you play?" he asked after a while.

"Trumpet," I mumbled from behind the peppermints.

"You have it with you?"

I shook my head, grinding the candies to pink salt.

"My name is Ted Granger," he said. The introduction

seemed misplaced. I nodded anyway, thinking it might buy me a few more candies. "All my troops just call me Ted."

"Joey."

"Joey, you're a transfer," he said. "You don't have the Bloughton drawl. Nor do I, as you might have noticed. Even though I've been here fifteen years this semester. Ted's Army never dies—the troops might change, but the war never ends. What brings you to Bloughton? What do your folks do?"

They were questions best avoided. I busied myself with using a pinkie to dislodge peppermint from a molar. He slapped his hands against the gray slacks pleated across slender thighs. "I've got a loaner horn. Come on, let's see what you can do."

Belly buzzing with syrup, I moved to an empty chair before a lowered music stand. Ted put a trumpet in my hands and sat slightly behind me.

"Play me a C scale," he said. I raised the instrument. The mouthpiece looked like home and I brought it to my mouth. I blew, feeling the tightness of my lips lock into the C. Once I heard the note, I held it—within was the sight of Boris emptying his spit valve in the next chair over, the smell of my old bedroom where I'd practiced, the sound of my mother in the next room humming an echo to my every note. This was *her* instrument. Even dead, she could still save me. The note kept on, strong, for fifteen or twenty seconds. Finally it lost consistency and fractured. I opened my eyes and sat there panting.

"Well, we've established that you can play the hell out of C," Ted said.

I gave him the scale he wanted, ascending C, D, E, F, G, A, B, C, and racing back down. I burned through another few scales and then dodged around as Ted looked me over. "I hope you don't have braces," he said. "You're smashing your lips to the metal like you're trying to french it." He set a piece of paper before me, barred and dotted. I played through it the best I could, my fingertips sensing the instrument's need for valve oil, the minute dents that pocked its shell. "Posture," said Ted. "Your diaphragm has a purpose, you know." Vibration anesthetized my lips, but even the bad notes sounded good; I played faster. "Medium pressure, medium pressure," Ted said. "What's with the chipmunk cheeks? Keep those things flat." As fast as I wanted to play, as hard as I wanted to keep up the illusion, the song was fragmenting and my fingers were turning to butter. The dots on the page ran from me like bugs. "Firm your corners, Joey. Did I just see you breathe through your nose?"

I shook my head and started over at the first line: C, C, G, B-flat, C. My fingers—thief's fingers, now—missed some of them entirely. I circled back: C, C, G, B-flat, C—I could hold on to nothing. The cracks in the illusion were huge now: this man next to me was a stranger, my mother was dead, Boris was gone, Chicago had been wiped off the map. C, C, G, B-flat, C—

And this time I hit all of them. A moment later I realized that Ted's fingers were delicately moving atop my own, guiding them up and down with nearly imperceptible pressure. "I don't know what you're used to, but Ted's Army is very small," he said. His fingers continued imploring. "But we can use you. You missed camp, of course, but I bet you catch on quick. Individual practice is once or twice a week, depending. We meet as a group on Fridays, then for three hours every other day after school. Next week we have our first football game, though if you need to sit that one out, so be it." At some point his thin fingers had retracted just enough so that only the weight of their shadows transferred their magic. I sounded good.

I stopped and looked at him, lips stunned, throat raw, and lungs aching. Hope, the most painful feeling of all, flickered somewhere even deeper.

12.

During the break before my final class I nearly ran into Woody and some of his gang. I veered quickly, hoping he didn't see me. Too late. "Crotch!" one of them hollered.

I kept moving. The clatter of lockers buried much of the guttural laughter. "Where's the fire, Crotch?" called someone else. I stopped at my locker to dump off some of Ted's paperwork. They swept toward me, a male chorus: "Crooooootch!" A hand swatted my locker door shut; it barely missed my nose. I focused on my shoes and made them move, right, left, one foot after another. A girl's voice, now, apprehensive but bubbling: "How's it hanging, Crotch?"

One foot after another, around the corner, my unfortunate nickname chirping in my wake. From the corner of my eye I saw the wall of flesh called Rhino. I watched my feet pick up speed.

"Crotch," Rhino purred pleasantly. There was a blur of motion. Then my testicles seemed to explode. My folder dropped from my hand; distantly I saw multicolored paper, including Laverne's salmon packet, fan across the tile. Heat knifed my gut. Cold tears sprang from my eyes. My hands instinctively clasped at my balls. There was laughter but it was muted in a storm of pain. I took a shuddering step to the side and my foot landed on one of the salmon-colored papers and slid out from under me. I fell to my knees. Blood: I swore I could feel it pumping from my ruptured scrotum. My body curled in on itself like a worm.

The bell rang. Somewhere a class was beginning without me. My hot forehead pivoted against the cold floor. "Crotch"—I should have seen this coming. The rest of the week, the month, the year: the horror film of my life played out before me. I would never be safe.

I hauled myself up with help from a fire extinguisher. Not caring who might be watching, I stuck a gentle hand down the front of my shorts and checked for damage. There was only swelling. I limped down the hall and gingerly lowered myself down twenty stairs. The cafeteria, the pay phone—it took me five more minutes to get there. I prayed for enough money in the return-change slot to augment the change in my pocket. A miracle: it was there. I gripped the icy coins in my sweaty fist and almost cried.

Quarters and dimes rattled home. My finger banged through a familiar sequence.

"Boris here."

"Boris!" My voice sounded throttled. "It's Joey."

"Joey, shit. I didn't recognize the number," he said. "How you doing? You're in luck, they let us sit outside for study hall. Everyone's texting and shit. Mr. Tepper doesn't even care, it's great."

"Great," I said, my shoulders quaking. Boris *did* sound great, so normal, so happy. I knew the meager hill of sun-blasted grass that he was sitting on and could almost feel its dog-pelt texture.

"So what's up? How's Iowa?"

I snorted back tears and tried to focus on the doodles of penises and breasts that covered the base of the phone. "It's bad, Boris. I want to come home."

"Don't give me that. How bad can it be? I bet you can play circles around those Glenn Miller jackasses."

"Boris, I'm serious," I said, and something in my voice shut him up. "Things are going real bad. I don't know what's happened. It's like . . . Boris, no one here likes me." This was grossly inadequate, but I found myself unable to put it any better.

"Okay," Boris said. "Okay, take it easy. How can you say no one likes you? No one likes anyone after two days."

"Boris, you know the kind of kids . . . the kids that get tortured? Pushed down the stairs and stuff?"

"Alfie Sutherland," Boris said instantly. "Mac Hill. I haven't seen Alfie, though—I think he might've transferred."

"That's me," I said urgently. I eyed a teacher who was passing the cafeteria. He glanced at me and slowed. It had to be obvious that I was ditching class. I angled myself toward the wall. "Boris, that's me. Like Alfie, worse than Alfie. Things have gone all crazy."

There was a pause on his end. Through the receiver I heard an unmuffled car rip by and girls scream in delight. "Look, let's not go overboard here," he said. "It's been two freaking days, man. I think you're getting a little worked up."

Rage enveloped me. "Fuck off. You don't know. I haven't eaten in two days."

"Wait, what about your dad? He's not feeding you?"

"My dad? This is all his fault!" It came out loud and shot across the cafeteria. "I saw him for like two seconds when I got here and now he's gone. There's no food anywhere. I don't have any money. I don't know when he's coming back.

I'm sleeping on the floor. I tried to get money out of a purse and got caught."

I clawed the plastic handle of the phone and took a deep breath. The teacher who had passed earlier now swerved back into sight, leading a woman in a stiff blue suit. They were heading straight for me.

"Did you say a purse?" Boris asked. "Whose purse? And you're sleeping on somebody's floor?"

"Boris, they're coming, I've got to go." The two adults bore down on me.

"Wait, is this your number? I'll call you back—"

"No! Don't call this number." It was too easy to imagine Woody picking up the inexplicably ringing cafeteria phone only to find Crotch's little friend on the other end.

"Then how do I—"

"Joey Crouch?" said the woman in the stiff blue suit.

I hung up on Boris. Gears inside the phone whirred.

The woman frowned and sized me up. "All right. You need to come with us."

13.

Vice Principal Estelle Diamond was the woman in the blue suit. She sat in an uncomfortable-looking wooden chair behind Principal Jess Simmons, tilted as if prepared to pounce. Simmons perched upon the front corner of his desk in a parody of youth, his knees battling for space with my own. Laverne made a brief appearance, handing Simmons the wrong file and turning red when told to try again; when she returned with the correct file he yanked it from her hands, gesturing impatiently for her to exit.

"I happened across Ted Granger, our band instructor, this afternoon, and he expressed some concern," said Simmons, opening the skinny file and glancing at its contents. He was a wide man with a thick neck that gathered above his collar—probably a former athlete. A pen in his hand rattled as he stabbed the ink button relentlessly. "Mr. Granger's concern was health-related."

"You are also supposed to be in Mrs. Peck's class right now," Diamond added. "But instead we found you placing a phone call. From a *pay* phone." Her emphasis on *pay* made me wonder if that phone's anachronistic existence was merely a trap to catch kids up to no good.

Simmons smiled and spread his hands, still clicking his pen. "Here at BHS, we try to make the well-being of our students our business. We know most of them by name, know their siblings, in some cases taught their parents. I want to explain this because you're new. All of us in this building, we're nearly family in a lot of cases."

I thought about Woody Trask and the effusive fawning of the front-desk woman with red hair. They were family, all right.

"At the very least we're your friends," continued Simmons. "So please think of us that way. Now," he said, the clicking of his pen reaching total frenzy, "about that phone call."

"Whom did you call?" asked Diamond.

I scanned their expectant faces. There was something I was missing.

"A friend," I ventured.

"Save some time and give it to us straight," said Simmons. "Was it a drug connection?"

"Give it to us straight," echoed Diamond.

There was nothing I could do but stare at them. The only contraband I had ever touched was a few vile swallows of peach schnapps with Boris. A wave of vertigo made me look away. In my lap I found my hands. They were trembling. Suddenly I looked up.

"I'm not on drugs," I blurted. "I'm just hungry."

Simmons and Diamond exchanged looks. I commanded my stomach to go ahead, growl, just like it had been growling all day. Nothing happened.

"Hungry," mused Diamond.

"Yes, hungry," Simmons added. "How's that?"

I paused. The precarious relationship between my father and me might not withstand the truth. But an accusation about a drug connection? That was no small thing. If they thought I was using or selling, things could get worse fast, for both myself and my father.

So I told them. Even leaving out my father's assertion that he had killed my mother, the unholy stench of the cabin, and the creepy books that reached to his ceiling, there was still plenty to say. I told them about my lack of money, the scarcity of food in the cabin, the unknown fate of my textbooks. I spoke tentatively at first, but the words soon snapped with vitriol. He deserved this, the Garbageman, for mucking up the lives of both me and my mother, and the more bile I could land on him, the better.

When I finished, the rattle of Simmons's pen had stopped. He flitted his tongue across his teeth and examined my file again. Over in her chair, Diamond watched him with such intensity she seemed sexually aroused.

"The saddest thing," said Simmons, "is that this does not come as a total shock."

Diamond dove in. "We'll file charges. Doesn't this qualify as child abuse?"

Simmons lifted a hand to quiet her, but it was clear that he was pleased by her enthusiasm. "That may not be the best way to go about it, Estelle. Joey, Ms. Diamond and I know who your father is. We don't know him well, and we certainly didn't know he had any children, but we're aware that he leads a lifestyle that is, I guess you could say, atypical."

"He lives in a shack," Diamond said. "Everyone knows it."

Simmons held up another indulgent hand; in it, the pen was back, clicking away. "Joey, say it was up to you. How would you like us to help you?"

Throw him in jail, I thought. *Charge him with the murder of my mother, the attempted murder of me.* "I just want to eat" was all I said, knowing full well the endearment such a plea would earn me.

"That's not a concern of yours, not anymore," said Simmons. He hit a buzzer on his desk. "Earth to Laverne." There was an unintelligible reply, at which Simmons and Diamond rolled their eyes. "Please stop stuffing your face and get in here." I winced on her behalf, but seconds later there she was, flopping the ripples of her upper body over the doorframe. "Laverne, fix it up so Joey Crouch here gets on our free-lunch list. Think you can handle that?"

The hatred between the principal and Laverne was palpable; it crackled for a moment before Laverne bowed her head in submission and left.

"I've heard stories," Diamond said, "of Ken Harnett scrapping through people's yards, stories of outright theft." My mind moved instantly to the pink purse—like father, like son. "He lives way out there on the river, on a patch of ground that I wonder if he even owns, and if he's ever even applied for work, I certainly have never heard of it. He's been getting a free ride for too many years. It's not like he contributes anything. Have you ever seen him show up to a single community event?"

"He doesn't even come to the homecoming rally in Bowman Park," agreed Simmons, stealing an approving glance at Diamond as if she had just removed an item of clothing.

The excitement of telling my story was wearing off like anesthetic; below, the spates of dull scrotal pain had given way to general soreness. The subtext of Diamond's rant was becoming clear: it was my father they cared about, not me. I couldn't help wondering how attending homecoming rallies had any bearing on someone's value as a citizen.

"I don't know about any stealing," I said. "I think he makes most of his money picking up trash."

Simmons studied me. His pen-clicking was so percussive that I longed to join in with my trumpet. Finally he sighed and shook my file. "We're going to play this by the book," he said, looking at me, though obviously the statement was meant for Diamond, who reacted by licking her lips. "It says here your dad doesn't have a phone number, is that right?"

"Yeah."

"Fine, we're going to write up a letter. This is by the book. We're going to write it, right now, while you wait out there with Laverne, and then you take it home and put it somewhere where he will see it."

"Nail it right to the front door," Diamond snarled.

Simmons paused and shrugged. "Somewhere where he will see it. Thursday rolls around and he still hasn't come in here for a powwow with myself and Ms. Diamond?" He leaned back on his desk and Diamond leaned forward in her chair. A few inches more and they could meet in a kiss. "At that point, then, we'll talk about involving other parties."

They both grinned, but as far as they were concerned I was not there. To them I was just the Garbageman's son. I wasn't Joey. I wasn't even Crotch.

By the pen's chuckling and the zipping noise of Diamond smoothing her skirt, I knew that both of the administrators were finished, and were gratified by what they had accomplished. "We do things here by the book," Simmons said to someone.

14.

THE WOLF-PANT OF my father's truck was a sound I would one day know intimately, but at the moment its presence was jarring. It separated itself from the din of river and forest and descended upon the house. Flakes of paint tossed across the windowsill. Exhaust fumes commingled with the tainted odor of the cabin's interior. Then the noise and vibration cut away. A truck door creaked, and slammed. Heavy objects slithered from a metal surface and clucked against each other as they jostled toward the front door.

It was Wednesday night. The night previous I had done exactly what Diamond had suggested and impaled their letter on a vacant nameplate holder on the cabin door. The letter had been sealed so that my father could not hold me accountable for its contents. Laverne, making sure Simmons wasn't watching, had given me all the cash she had on her—ten bucks—and I had rushed straight down to the vending machine. Never in the history of humankind had a Three Musketeers tasted so good, and I knew that one day, if I was lucky enough to have sex, it would have that candy bar to live up to. After a lot more junk food, I went home, slept fitfully by the sink, awoke early, and made it through Wednesday without another physical attack. When I returned home, Simmons's note was gone from the door. Boot prints provided clues: my father had found the note, read it, and gone directly to the school. My blood ran cold. What if he had driven right past me as I slumped down Jackson on my way to Hewn Oak?

It was nearly ten. Footsteps paused at the door. All the windows were open; I heard a steady intake of breath. The knob rattled and a boot pushed open the door. Ken Harnett, in a sweaty work shirt and stained trousers, entered with his sacks slung over his shoulders and two large paper grocery bags balanced in his arms. He let the sacks slump to the floor. Things inside clacked and clanged. He turned his pale eyes to me.

By now I had transformed the floor space in front of the sink into something resembling the cushion forts I had made as a little kid. The dust that had velveted the area had been, for the most part, peeled away. Four tall stacks of newspapers had been arranged into a sort of privacy wall, while an overturned bucket served as a bedside table where I set my cups of coffee or glasses of water. My duffel bags had been molded into a bed. A rolled up sweater was my pillow. A water-damaged cardboard box had been repurposed as my homework table. A cracked plastic bowl I had found filled with mismatched nails, screws, and washers now held the scraps of food that I ferreted home from school.

He gave my handiwork only a moment's attention, then walked over to the sink. The rancid odor spiked. He set down the paper bags stamped *Sookie's Foods* and began slapping groceries to the counter with such force that his gray hair fluttered. I saw many things in cans: beans, soup, corn, beets, peanut butter, jelly, more beans. He gathered the few perishables and threw them into the refrigerator; I heard them bang around the cage even after the door smacked shut. Next I heard him enter his bedroom, pull open his closet, and make xylophone music with liquor bottles. Pride lifted my chin. I had done what had been needed to survive, and this odious drunkard would not make me feel bad about it.

Moments later he was back, upending a half-empty bottle of vodka. He winced and swallowed, his mad eyes sketching lines between seemingly random points of the cabin, cataloging each item that I had disturbed. He swung his muzzle toward me.

"Aren't you going to eat?" he barked. "They tell me to buy you all this food and what, you're going to let it age?"

"You're a little late," I said. The strength of my voice emboldened me. I stood up and felt acutely the lousy drape of my ill-fitting tee and wrinkled shorts. "Three days late."

"Three days," he whispered to the wall. A large dirty hand wiped itself across his face. "Three days is nothing, kid."

I had forgotten how thick the bowed straps of his shoulders were, how braided the lines of muscle in his neck, how tall he was—his twists of hair nearly brushed the ceiling. The cabin was already too small for him; we could never share it comfortably. I considered the tiny segment of floor space I had dared to claim as my own. In the plastic bowl were the orange crumbs of chicken nuggets salvaged from lunch.

"Three days is not nothing when you have no money," I said. "I was starving."

"So I heard," he said, taking another pull on the vodka. I pictured him sitting in the principal's office opposite Simmons and Diamond and realized how completely his grubby appearance must have satisfied the expectations of those preening careerists. It must have killed him to suffer their ultimatums. I felt an unexpected, and not entirely welcome, pang of solidarity.

"I didn't tell them to write that letter," I said. "All I wanted was something to eat. Is that too much to ask?"

"And where is *your* money?" He hooked a scabbed knuckle into a frayed belt loop. "Didn't Val think to leave you a little petty cash?"

Val, Valerie: I didn't remember ever thinking of my mom by those names, despite what was printed in the funeral program and the newspaper obituary, what was carved into the cemetery marble. Coming from my father's mouth, however, it sounded breathtakingly natural. He had spoken this name before, maybe thousands of times, and the familiarity of his tone made me wonder for the first time exactly how well I had known her.

"The money's in a fund," I said.

He wagged the bottle. "It's in a fund, it's in a fund. I know it's in a fund, I read my mail. What about the other money?"

"What other money?"

His free hand made a clenching-unclenching gesture. "The money, the money! The money from the auction, where did that go if not into your pocket?"

I tried to remember what Claire had said. "It goes into the fund, too," I answered hesitantly, reprimanding myself for forgetting the details of something of such importance. Impulsively I added, "And when I'm eighteen you're not getting a penny."

His eyes bulged at my insubordination. He backpedaled toward the hearth, hoisting the bottle.

"I don't want your money." He fell into his chair. The tower of books behind him swooned. "I don't want any of this, and I don't want you."

"I don't care! I don't want you, either."

"If we agree so damn much, then what the hell is the problem?"

"The problem," I said, "is that Mom wanted me here."

"But she was naïve. And so was I, agreeing to any of this."

"By law you have to take me."

He clutched at his skull. "I don't want this."

"Stop acting like a baby."

"I DON'T WANT *YOU*!" The armrests popped within his grip. The bottle fell over on his lap, and only the contour kept the vodka sloshing inside. The cabin, home to nothing but silence for days, seemed to flicker in a supernatural wince.

"I leave town," he continued in a wavering voice, his hand flapping at the door in front of him, "all the time. For work—I go out of town to work on *jobs*. Three days? Kid, three days is squat. Try five days. Try seven days. Try two weeks. This is how I make a living. I am forty-five years old—and to eat, to buy food, apparently to feed us both? Leaving town is what I will have to do. Tell me how I am supposed to carry on if I've got to be here every day to change your diaper."

"Mom managed for sixteen years," I said. "You leave me alone again, I go straight to Principal Simmons. He'll have you in jail like that."

"Jail," my father said under his breath. "Val, how did it come to this?"

I was merciless. "You should've thought of that before you got her pregnant."

The sentence twisted a knife—even I felt it. Instantly my father hurled the bottle into the fireplace. It made a dull clunk but did not break, and this impotent gesture incensed him further.

"You don't know what you're talking about. Those things are between me and Val, no one else."

He closed his eyes and locked his chin against his chest. The black and gray bristles of his three-day scruff scraped his sternum. I saw his Adam's apple hitch and bob.

"Jesus, settle down," I said. "We'll work this out. There has to be a way."

"Jesus," he echoed. "Val raise you religious? She always had a weak spot for that crap. If it'd been me, no way. You wouldn't set one foot inside those places. If it'd been me—"

Resentment shot through me: "It *wasn't* you."

"If it'd been me, you would believe in no idols but those you can see and touch and lift with your hands like dirt," he said, raising his claws before his eyes. "Val's churchgoing worked against us from day one, and if it had been *me* there, your little Jesus and your little angels—"

"It *wasn't you*!" I shouted. "You weren't there. You weren't there and we didn't care, neither of us. I didn't give one thought to where you were my entire life! I was just glad you were gone. And believe me when I say she didn't care either. She didn't miss you. She didn't talk about you. All she mentioned was her messed-up ear, and she only did that because she couldn't hide it. So you don't get a say in what I believe or what she believed, and if I want to say Jesus this and Jesus that all night long, then you're just going to have to live with it or get back in your truck. I dare you. You know what you were to us? You were nothing. Just like you are to everyone in this shitty town. Nothing—the Garbageman."

Outside the cabin, limbs flogged themselves softly with leaves. Crickets expressed their eternal agitation. My father, his head cocked as if hearing words in this nature, lifted himself from his chair and took the three steps to the door. Instead of leaving he reached up and locked us in. My eyes shifted to the drawer where, among utensils, there were knives.

With eerie languor, he maneuvered around obstacles until he was at the bedroom door. His face was scary with resignation. "The Garbageman," he murmured. "That is exactly who I am."

The door closed behind him. Barely audible were the thuds of his boots; later, the muted chimes of fingers fanning across bottles. I didn't want to hear it. I turned to the kitchen counter and interpreted the miniature cityscape of food: Marina City, Trump Tower, Hancock, Sears. Cresting from the imagined Lake Michigan was a bag of pretzels. My hunger had abated, but I snatched the bag and tore it open. I fished out a pretzel, placed it in my mouth, and leaned back against the sink, lacking the energy to chew. I reminded myself that I had faced Ken Harnett on his own turf and won. It was a victory, something uncommon for me in Bloughton, and yet I felt only further loss.

15.

ONE WEEK LATER I gave him my conclusion. "You're going to kill me," I said. It at least felt true. He did not respond, instead turning upon me the vicious emptiness I had grown to expect. There was murder in that hopeless countenance—this

I had finally decided—and perhaps it was only a matter of time before he dispatched the son he had mistakenly created.

Chained to Bloughton by Simmons's threat, he paced the woods near the cabin. Most days when I returned home from school I saw him a hundred yards away perched on the riverbank, hands in pockets, watching the water. Other days he and his truck were gone when I got home, only to return in the early evening, gray sacks jostling, clothes scored with dirt. On these occasions, he dove without a word into the shower, where the next morning I would find a perimeter of mud. We ate separately and the sleeping arrangements did not change. At least I finally had my textbooks—he stripped them from a stack one morning and tossed them in the middle of the floor.

"When are you going to do it?" I asked him one day as he shoved peanut butter across torn bread.

I did not expect an answer, but I got one. He was gazing at the setting sun through the windows above the sink. "At dawn," he whispered. The news, while interesting, did not compel me to ask which dawn. I did not want to pry.

So I expected my demise each morning as I dressed for class. The school days during these weeks passed with increasing quickness; only snared within some moment's torment did time decelerate to an agonized crawl. Gottschalk did not renege on his sentence. Our first unit was on skin and the endocrine system, and almost every day I was called to the front of the class to be used as a real-life model. He had a telescoping metal pointer and sometimes struck my arm or neck or face hard enough to make me flinch. "Notice the damage to multiple layers of epithelial tissues," he said, prodding a patch of pimples. "The sebaceous gland that surrounds each shaft produces sebum, made up of lipids—that's fat to you. Outer layers of the epidermis flake away and the dead skin becomes glued together by this sebum, causing a blockage that can produce quite unpleasant results—as seen on Mr. Crouch here. The silver lining for Mr. Crouch is that sebum itself is odorless. This is not the case, however, for *Propionibacterium acnes,* a bacterium that sebum harbors. Based on the smell coming off Mr. Crouch on a daily basis, I'll wager that his skin is swimming in the stuff. Ten-to-one odds. Who's in?"

Gottschalk paused for the laughter. I never responded. The first time he did this to me all I could see was Celeste Carpenter sitting ten feet away with her gorgeous skin, propped cleavage, and resolute detachment. As days wore on, I let my vision lose focus so that the entire class merged into a multicolored blur. Yes, it was true that I smelled terrible, though I doubted it was the fault of my sebaceous glands. It was the third week of school and I was wearing unwashed clothes for a third or fourth cycle. There were no laundry facilities in my father's cabin, and I had yet to see how he washed his own clothes, if he ever did.

In the first month of school, I was kicked in the crotch roughly once a week and faked out dozens more times. Though Woody himself never resorted to physical contact, the attacks were clearly done at his pleasure, and he still called me Crotch when the opportunity arose—though he took care not to do it in front of adoring teachers and coaches. On those rare occasions when he was caught contributing to my debasement, the reprimands were superficial and his wide-eyed apologies held up as paragons of heartfelt atonement. More than once I was encouraged to shake his hand.

Many of the kicks occurred in gym, which had proved to be life's most harrowing regular event. The class, which came two days per week in alternation with study hall, had yet to move beyond tedious but nerve-wracking preliminaries. One week we did sit-ups. The next, push-ups. This left plenty of time for worrying about my genitals. Woody and Rhino were both in my gym class—Celeste was, too—so I kept my hands at a defensive belt-level until we were sent to change out of the compulsory dark shorts and white tees.

The muffled noise of teaching provided the bridge between these more vivid events. I took notes and read my assignments, and even studied for quizzes. I didn't see any reason to let my A average slide into the trash along with the rest of my life. Around the fourth week, important tests were doled out in several classes, and I scored perfect on all of them. While handing back the exams, a couple of the teachers took a moment to give me their best imitation of approval, though it was clear they considered the accomplishments flukes. They didn't know that I was my mother's son, not my father's.

There was no official chair rank at Bloughton, but it took only one practice with the entire band to glean that Ted sat the most talented players closest to the center, while the less gifted fanned off to the edges. I was pleased to find that the dividing line for the trumpets fell directly between me and a girl named Tess. She had tight curls of blond hair, pointy features alleviated by makeup, and a robotic technique probably acquired through a lifetime of detested lessons. As was often the case with the female brass players I had known, Tess seemed embarrassed by the forceful blowing required by the instrument—it messed up her lipstick and forced her to relinquish her carefully crafted smile and posture. She could play better than I when forced, but lazed through most of the practices, absently running her painted nails along her necklace. The only time she spoke to me was one afternoon when Woody entered the room to hand Ted a note. As resident superhero, Woody was often enlisted by teachers to run errands. This roaming naturally made him even more unpredictable and dangerous, and on this particular day it brought him into the soundproofed confines of the band room.

"Isn't he hot?" Tess whispered to me, pulling on her necklace faster than usual.

In better days I would not have dignified such a statement with a response, but it had been weeks since someone had addressed me in a manner other than hostile, so I reluctantly took the bait. "I don't know," I said. "I guess, if he's your type."

"He is." She moaned through a pouty frown. "I can't believe he goes out with Celeste Carpenter." She looked at me. "You know who she is?"

Every time I turned a corner at school and saw a female, my heart leapt to my throat in the thrilled certainty that it would be Celeste Carpenter. I saw her face in my notes, in my books, in my dreams. "Yeah, I know who she is," I responded.

"Yeah, well," Tess said, shrugging. "You probably think she's hot, too. It's not like we don't all know it; she's on homecoming court every year. But seriously. She's put on a little ass-weight, I think. I mean, she's not *that* hot. Is she? Do *you* think she is? Hot like Woody Trask hot? I heard she's a prude, too. I just don't think they make sense."

"What do you mean?" I fantasized that others were watching Crotch as he conducted a perfectly normal conversation with a perfectly normal student.

"As a couple," she said. Across the room, even Ted seemed subject to Woody's charms—he was nodding and laughing as Woody patted him jokingly on the belly. "I'm not sure they're very yin and yang as a couple. You know what I mean?"

Although it was clearly difficult, she broke her gaze from Woody to look at me. Unaccustomed to such attention, I blushed and looked down at the instrument in my hands. "Not really, I guess," I answered. "I mean, I don't know them very well. Not as a couple. Or separate. They seem all right to me. I don't know. I can't comment on her ass-weight. Or his. I don't know. I guess I can't really comment."

Her exasperated expression was exactly what my inane remark deserved. After a moment Ted took up his baton and we launched into the worst dry run of "Flight of the Bumblebee" in human history. Halfway through it, Ted tossed the baton over his shoulder and gripped his shaking head with both hands. The instruments blurted to sudden halts, and the music, such as it was, was replaced by peals of laughter. The band instructor beamed at the talentless fools he called Ted's Army, and he flipped back a page of his music. "Let's not ever play that again," he said, giggling.

Individual instruction, which took up one-third of study hall one day per week, represented the only scenario in which I could speak to a friendly face without the crowding of enemies. Ted was on a tight schedule—he had a flutist right before me and a drummer directly after—so there was not much time for chitchat. That was fine. We ran through pieces, he commented on and adjusted my performance, and every once in a while he even stood behind me to use his shadow-fingers to transmit each correct depression. Often after I sat down, while he busied himself lowering the music stand to my height, I would take a moment to relish the isolation of the cramped room and everything about it: the cheesy posters of Bobby McFerrin and Yo-Yo Ma, the embouchure mirrors on the back wall, the gap-toothed xylophones in the corner, the varnished autoharp for some reason mounted above the door, and the supply closet—a shallow nook that was always open and gleaming with a million mouthpieces, reeds, drumsticks, and miscellaneous spare parts. It was the breadth and versatility of the closet that proved Ted's longevity and worth, not the buffoonery of his inept army.

Separating each of these otherwise amorphous days were my doomed dawns. That pile of shovels, the charred poker beside the hearth, my father's soiled hands: any of these would work as the instrument of my demise. Still I studied and spooned my cold food out of cans, and still my father wandered the grounds, staring into space and water as if listening for guidance.

"How?" I asked one evening.

It had been a few days since we had last spoken; the topic, though, had not changed. "A knife," he said, looking at me for a moment before going back to reading the stack of newspapers that arrived each day in the mail. But now he was too distracted to read. He looked at me again, his eyes less scarlet than in the past, less hooded with anger. "I have a knife from Scotland," he said softly, "with a blade so sharp there would be almost no pain." The wounds of my mother's ear: maybe it was the same blade, maybe it would be the last thing she and I shared.

He was chopping wood two days later at dusk, strange helices of muscle thickening across his back with each swing, when I next approached. I stood watching for ten minutes. What had been trees divided and diminished, again and again; what had been dark and armored with bark became yellow, then white, until the pure heart of the wood shone with brilliance. Flecks stood out like white freckles against the brown of his skin. He exhaled loudly and wiped his forearm across his forehead.

"Where exactly?" I asked.

He gulped for air, licked his dry lips. "The heart." He snorted and spat out phlegm thickened by sawdust. "If you can avoid ribs, the blade will move softly. Like through butter."

He glanced up at me uncertainly, as if he had said too much and needed my approval. I hastened to nod, and he seemed glad for my blessing. He faced the massacre of wood, weighing the axe in both arms, struggling to find something that could still be made smaller. It was then that I knew that he would not kill me. Our planning and scheduling of my execution had become something of worth, something that involved an increasing exchange of trust. The next day, when I asked him how long it would take to die from a stab to the heart, he was answering before the question was fully articulated, as if he had been making calculations all day and had been waiting impatiently to be asked. Murder: it was something to talk about and we embraced it, and soon other, more mundane exchanges were escaping our clenched jaws. "Here," he said, tossing me half of a steak he had incinerated on the stove. "Sorry," I said as we both banked into the bathroom at the same time. "I'll be back around midnight, okay?" he asked late one afternoon, pausing at the door with two empty sacks looped over his shoulder. I nodded once and turned back to my homework, but inside I could barely breathe.

16.

My father continued to disappear on weekends. In his absence I began reading the newspapers. They arrived every day in the mailbox located out where Hewn Oak hit Jackson, dozens of papers from towns all across the Midwest. When there were too many to fit, they were piled in a wooden crate nailed to the base of the mailbox post. Having nothing better to do, I began bringing these back to the cabin on my way home from school. Their mastheads touted towns big and small from Iowa, Illinois, Indiana, Michigan, Wisconsin, Minnesota, Nebraska, Missouri, even a few from the Dakotas. Many of these papers originated in communities so small that the papers came out four days a week or fewer; some of them only published weekly. These I found the most amusing, with their exacting chronicles of crop growth, rambling columns referring to specific pheasants and raccoons by first names, personal accounts of exciting trips to Omaha or Ames, and dishy police blotters chocked with minor fender benders and loud noises after suppertime.

Occasionally my father read something that particularly nabbed his attention, and he would hurry to the archives of one of his dusty stacks and thumb through back issues. He did just that early in the morning on the first Saturday in October, rushing to one of the piles that made up the boundary of my floor space. Directly above me, he rustled through the pages until he found what he was seeking on the inside of the back page. The paper was old and thin enough that I could see right through it and read the backward headline: SEIRAUTIBO.

Paper in hand, he grabbed his sacks and hurried to his truck. I examined the stack. It was the *Benjamin County Beacon,* published in Mazel, Nebraska. Dredging up my iffy mental map of the U.S., I estimated that it was at least a five-hour drive to the Nebraska border. I listened to the spit of stones and the snapping of twigs down Hewn Oak. He was in a hurry; I had all day.

The safe in his closet resisted dozens of combinations. I planted my ear next to the dial, just like they do on TV, to hear whether any of my numbers triggered reactions. I sat on his bed—a mattress and box springs but no frame—and tried to think of obvious patterns. My mother: I tried her birthday, 12-15-60. I tried it backward, 60-15-12. I tried it European, 15-12-60. Bereft of ideas, I cranked my wrist through the numbers of my own birth date and with a clucking sound the lock unlatched. I stared and told myself it was coincidence. Everything about me, prior to crash-landing into Bloughton one month ago, should have been a mystery to my father. Yet here was a chilling countertruth.

I pulled lightly on the handle and the door of the safe squealed open. The awful stink of the cabin had an origin—it gasped out at me in a foul expulsion of putrid air. I gagged and dove my head to the side to spit it out. Coughing, my eyes watering, I steadied myself and peered into the darkness.

The first thing I thought of was Woody and Rhino and Simmons and Diamond, and how all those bastards had been right. Ken Harnett was a thief. My ears burned in private humiliation. Stacked inside the safe were valuables of such variety that each item must have come from a different home: rings, necklaces, cuff links, antique hairpins, ornate purses, bejeweled broaches, unusual belt buckles. In the back of the safe was a burlap sack spilling forth strange coins. I reached for a rusty Planters peanuts container and tilted it toward me. Gasping, I let it fall back. It was half full of gold teeth.

There was also a discolored manila envelope stuffed with cash. My desperation for money trumped everything else I was feeling, and I removed three twenties and stuffed them in my pocket. Having thieved from a thief, I pushed myself away from the safe and its reeking cloud. I leaned back against my father's bed, my eyes darting over the piles of jewelry. Quickly I made the connection to the newspapers. My father read obituaries to see which houses were newly vacant and used his archive to research the person's background and wealth. Keeping himself up to date allowed him to drive overnight to places like Mazel, Nebraska, in order to loot the joint before the family had time to divvy up heirlooms. I thought about my mom's leftover property and whether someone like my father had rifled through her leavings. I was suddenly filled with a righteous fury. This was why she had left him, I was positive. He was a career crook, a scumbag, and I had been sent by her to make sure he was put behind bars.

I shut and locked the safe. Then I walked into town and treated myself to the lunch counter at Sookie's, hiding from teenage voices by lodging myself in a corner booth with my face to the wall. I paid with one of the twenties, took the change to the hardware store/pharmacy, found the disposable camera I was looking for, and brought it to the cashier. On impulse, I threw in a bar of soap. When my father returned late in the night and I heard the familiar sound of shower knobs twisted full blast, I imagined his surprise at finding the zesty foreign object.

Sunday morning I thumbed through the new newspapers and used homework techniques to memorize as many obituary details as possible. I ate breakfast—generic bran flakes and coffee—and pretended to do schoolwork until my father rose several hours later. He did not say good morning. We had not become that cordial, not yet, and given what I was planning to do, I was glad.

The newspapers seemed to please him. His features while he was reading morphed through a complicated gallery:

he looked enthralled one minute and was nearly laughing the next, only to fall into a grimace of grief so genuine I felt my heart beat in unexpected sympathy. Ultimately the reading seemed to excite him. He became restless. He ate while pacing. I saw him, still barefoot, take one of his gray sacks outside. He tidied the woodpile and even spent fifteen minutes picking up soiled clothes from around the house and chucking them into a large garbage bag that he set next to the door. After a while, he plucked a seemingly random book from the center of one of the towers, but paged through it impatiently, his foot wagging. He was waiting for something. So was I.

When a ribbon of pink spread across the sky, he began to gather his things. I held off until he was rooting around in his bedroom, and then I exited through the front door. I made sure to walk at a casual pace in case he saw me. The camera in my pocket pressed into my thigh with each step. Near the Jackson intersection, I crouched in a ditch opposite the mailbox. The sky was purple now, and concealed me. My stomach roiled and my chest tingled.

Even with my ears trained for the sound of his truck, it caught me by surprise. Suddenly it was leaping from the leafed canopy of Hewn Oak, moving faster than I had expected. I flattened myself against the dry grass. In seconds the truck was upon me, its tires chomping gravel right next to my head. Dirt blew in my face and made mud in my eyes. The truck was making a turn to the left, not the ideal direction for what I needed to do, but I scrambled up the side of the ditch, counting on the cloud of dirt to hide me. I ran at the truck; I felt it pick up speed and make a dizzying surge away; I ran harder, reaching outward, feeling a spray of gravel strafe my shins like machine-gun fire, and felt my palms grip the back door. With a last burst of strength, I hurled myself over the edge. I landed inside the truck bed, edges of metal intersecting with the knobs of my shoulders and the blades of my ribs. I was on top of one of his burlap bags of tools. I rolled off. The engine's thrum shook my skeleton at such a pitch that the lunch in my stomach whipped and the sky above became a vomitous swirl. I closed my eyes. Wind, bugs, and sediment razed my skin.

Then there were highways. Velocity increased. The noise enveloping me lost its caged reverberation and joined with a hundred other racing vehicles. We were moving; we were out of Bloughton, maybe even out of Lomax County. Purple light turned into the red doom of an interstate at night. My extremities were numb from vibration; the back of my skull throbbed. An uncertain amount of time passed, what must have been hours. Surely I had miscalculated—this was one of his longer trips, and I would miss days, if not weeks, of school. Any enthusiasm at such a prospect was mixed with the everlasting fear of falling irreparably behind; I thought of Gottschalk and his self-satisfied smirk as he took credit for scaring me away.

But then the truck slowed. My stomach lurched as we slung through the vortex of an exit ramp. There was the distant ticking of a turn signal, the vertiginous pull of a sharp right. More turns, these made without signaling. The roads became rougher. The sky became true black with only the periodic abatement of a moth-flickered lamp. I drew my body to the far edge of the truck bed, bracing myself for the moment of escape. Through the cab window I could see my father scanning the streets as he rolled along what looked like a sparsely populated country neighborhood. He shut off the headlights and began to inch toward the shoulder. I made sure he wasn't checking his rearview, then vaulted myself over the flatbed door.

The pulse of the engine had hammered my legs to rubber. My knees wilted and my butt scraped rock. The truck continued to creep along without me. Ten feet, twenty feet; as it took a corner the brakes tapped momentarily and colored me red. When the vehicle eventually stopped and the putter of the engine ceased, I kneeled among the tall weeds and waited. After a moment, my father emerged, a black shadow against the blacker sheet of night, and he moved with surprising swiftness to the back of the truck. Gray bags were lifted from the trunk, and then he moved away, over the slight rise in the road and down the other side.

He was out of sight. I scrambled up the shoulder and paused for breath against the side of the truck. The engine pinged softly. I moved again until I reached the crest of the hill. Beyond, I could see the distant specks of farmhouse lights. My father had vanished.

It might not have been an accident that the truck was parked beneath the arachnid limbs of an overhanging tree. I stepped carefully through the ditch, feeling gutter water sop through the worn material of my sneakers. Using the snaking root system of the tree, I pulled myself up the other side of the ditch and squatted behind the expansive trunk. I sat panting for a while, my naked knees wedged against prickly bark, an old wooden fence behind my shoulders.

Thirty minutes, tops—that was what I expected. I used the moon's glow to monitor my watch, and thirty minutes passed. Then one hour, two hours—now it was after midnight. I slumped against the fence, clicking my thumbnail across the plastic slats of the film-advance wheel. Combined with the incriminating shots I would collect later at the cabin, one shot of a theft-in-progress was all I needed, although I planned to take as many photos as possible before once again stowing myself in the back of the truck. Unrest mixed with anticipation. Perhaps kids at school would hear about this, the news that Joey Crouch was not like Ken Harnett at all; that he was, in fact, the direct opposite, a crusader, a young man brave enough to defend Bloughton against his own flesh and blood. My mother, how proud she'd be.

There are a million noises in the night, and by the time I noticed his footsteps he was almost upon me, moving fast, making less racket than seemingly possible. I sat up from the fence and coiled my legs beneath me. My fingers, instantly sweaty, gripped the camera. My father sailed toward the truck. One sack was slung over his left shoulder. An object was clenched in his right hand. The bag was swung high over the truck bed and lowered soundlessly. He opened the passenger door with his left hand, while still holding the object with his right. I leaned my upper body past the tree, moving the camera to my eye. I saw him dislodge something from under the seat; moonlight glinted on wrenches and hammers as he unlocked a toolbox. There was the soft sigh of stirring metal as he dug and found what he was looking for. He turned around, wielding the tool of his choice, and leaned against the truck.

The moment was perfect. I pressed the button on the camera, realizing a split second too late that, in all my planning, I had forgotten the simplest of facts: this was an automatic camera and it was night and cameras at night use flashes. White light shocked us. Everything was illuminated in one instant of motionless clarity: individual blades of tall grass, bugs caught in the air like thrown pebbles, the mirrored surface of the truck, my father, his stunned expression, the handheld wire cutter, the sparkle of multiple jeweled rings, and, clenched in my father's fist, wearing these rings, a severed human hand.

17.

ON THE WAY HOME I sat up in the truck bed. There was no more reason to hide. As we pulled away from the tree, I noted with dulled surprise that the wooden fence I had leaned against marked the outer confines of a graveyard. It rolled gently over the hill, the white ghosts of gravestones perishing quietly into the pitch.

My father is a grave robber, I told myself, over and over and over—the only garbage he carried was carrion. I hoped the horror of it would diminish with each repetition, but instead it overtook me. My brain spun in slow and terrified loops: disgust at such an unspeakable act, disbelief that my mother could have lived with such knowledge, the potential reactions to such revelations by Woody or Celeste or Gottschalk or Simmons or Diamond or Laverne or Ted, and more than anything else the smell—that odor invading the very fibers of the cabin walls as well as my clothes, skin, and hair. I finally knew its origin.

I ran through the last moments back there outside the graveyard: his blank astonishment, my immobility, his slow forward motion to take the camera from my numb fingers. He placed the camera in a pocket, then picked up the wire cutter again. I heard a snip and the soft chip of bone detaching from bone. I watched him remove two rings from the isolated finger, put them in his pocket, and then take the hand, as well as the finger, with him back up the hill. I followed him with my eyes and saw him scale the cemetery fence. He was returning the hand to where he found it. It was lunacy. I could barely think, hardly move. It was much later, maybe another hour, before my father returned. He had with him the other sack, which he placed in the truck bed. He seemed beyond wrath; his eyes were glazed and he spoke not a word. When he looked at me, I held out a trembling hand to stop whatever was coming next.

"Look," I said, but I had no other words.

He did the opposite and looked away. He entered the truck, slammed the door, and started the engine. It growled to life and I watched the brake lights color the exhaust. I expected him to drive away. Instead he sat motionless behind the wheel. After a minute I climbed into the back of the truck.

Now, the ride nearly over, the wheels left the relative smoothness of pavement for dirt. Here it was, my final resting spot, the place where he would fulfill his earlier promise of a Scottish blade driven with soft precision. Trees laced their fingers above me, then clenched to blot out the night. The truck shuddered to a halt. I heard the cab door open and shut. I sat up and saw that we were not in some unfamiliar thicket but back at the cabin, and my father was loping toward the front door, leaving the sacks with me. The whisper of the river was outrageously keen after the truck's guttural howl. I looked at the sacks and wondered wildly if he expected me to bring them inside.

A long time passed. After a while I stood and urinated off the side of the truck. I lay back down, accepting for a bed the graphed surface of the vehicle much as I had accepted the floor by the sink. I checked my watch: four in the morning.

The sun would be up in a couple of hours and it would be Monday. School seemed a method of escape: I could go there, just like always, and lose myself in routine as I thought about what to do. There were even people there who could possibly help me: Simmons, maybe; maybe Ted; maybe I could even tell Laverne. Though I could not imagine how to introduce the topic. All opening statements I imagined were spectacularly insane. I closed my eyes but knew I would never sleep, and then, a few minutes later, fell asleep.

18.

The position of the sun told me I had awakened at my usual time. I yawned and felt unfamiliar patterns ridge my cheek. My homework and books were inside. I would have to go in.

I hobbled to the front door and entered. My father's bedroom door was closed. I listened and heard nothing. The bathroom looked too inviting to pass up and I slid inside, closing the door behind me, and scrubbed my face with cold water, hoping to work the indentations from my face. I washed my hands and looked down at them, remembering what I had seen. It had been a woman's hand. On her third finger had been both an engagement and a wedding ring. She had been married. The hand had belonged to someone's wife, maybe someone's mother.

I grabbed my green backpack and made for the front door. Simultaneous with my opening of it, I heard the opening of my father's bedroom. I whirled around and there he was, his eyes blazing, his gray hair wilder than ever, the tufts from his chest ruffling his unbuttoned shirt. I braced for attack.

His expression, however, was pinched and anxious. *He doesn't want me to turn him in,* I realized, repulsion and anger rising once more. I slammed the door behind me and hustled across the yard. I was beneath the trees in a moment but did not feel secure until I was well on my way down Jackson, new sweat from a new day making strange perfume with the unwashed odors of the night.

People held their noses in biology. I knew I stank; I half-lidded my eyes and tried to live inside myself. When Gottschalk called me to the front of the room, I stumbled across someone's book bag and didn't care when everyone laughed. I stood there, barely conscious, raising my arms when I was told so that Gottschalk could prod my moist pits with his pointer and reiterate the miracle of transpiration. Through the slits of my eyes I watched Celeste Carpenter's perfectly inexpressive expression; through the barred cage of my eyelashes I saw her look back with all the objectivity of a zoologist.

I sleepwalked through both classes and lunch until I found myself on my way to the band room for individual instruction. When I got there, Karla, one of our four flutists, was sitting outside the door with earbuds inserted. She saw me, paused her music, and gathered her things.

"Ted's out sick," she said, letting her buds dangle. "You might as well use your time, though."

The room was eerily quiet. Two chairs before a music stand gave the impression that Ted had died in the middle of a lesson. I wandered through the space, thankful for the chance to be alone, and eyed one of the chairs, wondering whether if I sat and closed my eyes for twenty minutes, Peyton, our drummer, would bother to wake me up when he arrived. Probably not.

There was a rattling noise. I turned and saw that Ted's supply closet was closed. I had never seen it less than agape in a blatant display of its bounty. I moved closer and listened. From within I heard muffled sounds. My sapped brain did not connect them with human activity. I had only the dumb idea that if I sorted through all the stuff in the closet, I might be able to keep myself awake. I opened the door.

Woody was inside, masticating Tess's neck, her shirt up around her armpits, his hands kneading her bra. My fellow trumpeter saw me first, and her look was one of annoyance rather than shock. Woody raised his head, his lips separating from her slick neck with a smack, and regarded me with a curious sort of half-grin.

"Sorry," I mumbled. Woody's grin broadened.

"Go away?" Tess said, her brow cleaving so abruptly her curls bounced.

"Sorry," I said again.

"Shut the door, Crotch," she commanded. I saw her fingers grab Woody's hand, which had unconsciously drifted away, and secure it back on top of her breast. The knob was in my hand, my face turned away, the door shut. Muffled noises resumed but I walked away so that I did not have to listen. I watched my reflection split and scatter across the embouchure mirrors. Ted's closet—I felt bad for him. Those two making out, they would knock things from the walls and disrupt the shelves. They would not put back fallen objects. They had no respect for Ted, not either of them, and after hooking up they would mentally mock him every time they saw him: *We got it on in your closet and you don't even know.*

Exhaustion had left me hollow and dry, and the spark of anger took quickly to flame. Tess I could care less about; we would just resume ignoring each other at band practice. But

Woody, that fucker—he could get away with almost anything, but not this, not this disrespect of Ted. And not just Ted—never far from my mind was Celeste. Although she occasionally had been present as Woody taunted me, she had always seemed as if she were waiting for permission to leave that asshole and reach out to somebody, no matter their social status. Somebody, for example, like me.

I had to find her, she had to know. The final twenty minutes of study hall felt like two hours. My mind shoved aside everything that had happened the night before so that focus could be applied to this mission of utmost importance. Punishing Woody, winning gratitude from Celeste: if I pulled off these things before returning home, somehow the ensuing lightness would push away some of the dark.

Two more classes, the final bell. Students sprang from their chairs and I fought to be in their numbers. I was due on the football field for marching band practice but dismissed it. Two floors, six hallways, and exits everywhere: how would I find her? I scanned my surroundings for packs of girls, carefully done hair, short skirts, the most stylish shoes one could buy near Bloughton. I made it down one hall—nothing. Another hall, one hundred faces, none of them hers. A third wing and still nothing: I could feel, like blood from my veins, students leaving the building by the dozens.

Around a corner toward the front entrance and there was familiar raven hair tied in exotic fashion and barretted flat in crisscrossed layers. I leapt down the stairs, squinting in the afternoon swelter. I was behind her; I was at her elbow; I gave myself a final push and I was in front of beauty and grace herself, Celeste Carpenter.

"Celeste," I panted. She had to stop—I was blocking her path. I held up a hand to buy myself a moment while I gasped for air. My smell: too late, I thought of it and hoped that any unpleasant whiff would lose itself in the outdoor air.

How to begin? My brain labored for an opening statement. *I didn't think you'd be outside,* I considered. It was at least true. From what I understood, Celeste was involved in numerous activities, and was particularly noted in theater and dance. I had overheard that play rehearsals were going every single day after school. Yes, that was it—I could ask her if she was skipping rehearsal or just getting some air before they began.

Instead it came out like a belch: "I saw Woody with Tess."

The delicate shadow between her eyebrows darkened. Her expression remained enigmatic, though I sensed a slight angling of her head. At this moment I realized she was not alone. Three other girls were a half-step behind. Though farther away, their faces were much easier to read.

"In the band room," I managed, still wheezing. All I could hear was the pound of blood shooting through my ears. "I was in the band room and looked in the closet and there was Woody and Tess. They were kissing. Her shirt was mostly off. I thought I should tell you. I thought you should know."

I waited for her face to register astonishment, possibly heartbreak. If she started crying what was I obligated to do? Console her? Embrace her? I did not know if I could. Deep inside, a hardening conviction: I could.

A jet of wind swirled her hair into a halo of daggers as her arm lashed out. The sharp nails of her hand cracked against my cheek, and in that instant I knew my mistake. She already knew Woody was a two-timer—this thing with Tess probably wasn't his first—but such facts were not for public consumption. My gossip within earshot of other students was hateful and willful destruction of the persona she had so carefully constructed. My cheek blazed with pain; I felt wet pinpricks where her nails had punctured the skin. I looked down at her hand, calm again against her skirt, cutely painted and tastefully adorned, but transposed on top was the severed thing from the night before. A chilling certainty filled me that it would be that bloated dead hand that I would one day be holding, not Celeste's.

She remade herself, placid and untroubled. Her lips twitched in a smile and she and her friends flitted away, leaving me there with the new disgrace of four thin stripes of blood hardening against my face.

19.

The phone swallowed my change. My forehead felt the coins rattle all the way down.

"Boris here."

"Boris!" I cried. "It's Joey!"

There was a pause. Without planning to, I timed it. Five entire seconds.

"Joey," he said. "Hey."

"I've gotta get out of here."

There was another pause. Five more seconds, at least.

Boris sighed. "You call me right in the middle of the day for this?"

"You're not listening," I said. My voice was shaking a bit. "And it's not the middle of the day. It's the end of the day."

"And jazz band is in like two seconds. I'm just about to go in. I'm in the hallway. Hey." His voice suddenly rose with interest. "Did you know Mac Hill played trombone?"

"Mac Hill? Boris, listen to me."

"You remember Mac. He's actually pretty good, he's been blowin' the bone in private for like four years. Hey, here he is. Mac! Hey, Mac!" There was laughter, another voice close to the phone. "I told you that shit would never hold," Boris said to Mac, and they both laughed along to a joke I would never understand. I rubbed my temples. It was hard to imagine that, for Boris, life continued to move along the same track it always had. The injustice of it brought tears to the corners of my eyes.

"Mac Hill," I droned. "I remember him." Mac Hill had been an outcast, far more so than Boris or I. The idea that he had reinvented himself as a trombone player and a compatriot of Boris bewildered me—how could anyone pull himself out of such a hole?

"Yeah, well, he's kicking ass with the brass now. I think we're going to kill at state." He paused. "You could call me sometime when you're not having an emergency, you know. I'm not nine-one-one."

"Sorry."

"Just say no. Dope is for dopes. We don't need another Charlie Parker on our hands here."

It took me a long moment to unpack the jargon. "You think I'm on drugs?" It was more than I could handle, this telepathic suspicion shared by my principal and best friend.

"No." He sighed in frustration. "You just act like it. Look, it was a joke. Forget it. Just, you know. Call at a better time. The folks, they're dying for news—how's Joey, what's Joey doing, what's going on with Joey's dad? It's a broken record with those two."

"Tell them I said hi." In the short time we had left, how could I even begin telling him the truth about my father or the severity of my persecution? Nevertheless, the sound of Boris's voice was the most comforting thing in the world, and I didn't want it to stop. "What else is happening?"

"I'm walking into jazz band, that's what's happening," he said, and sure enough I heard the cacophony of a bunch of showboats tuning up. "And I'm getting looks. So I'm out of here. Call me whenever, just not during rehearsal. All right?"

20.

THE TWO-DOLLAR MIRROR I bought at the pharmacy fit well enough behind the knobs of the bathroom sink. I stood shirtless before it. The single bulb above me, already half filled with dead houseflies, was malfunctioning, causing the yellow light to flicker. I was there, I wasn't there. I existed, I did not.

It looked like four tiny bullets had nicked my cheek. I rubbed water over the surface to clear the gummed blood, and fresh bulbs began to grow. I tried to focus on which drop would fall first, and not on what Woody would do to me when he heard what had happened.

I was Ken Harnett's son. I told myself this over and over. By refusing to kill me with his Scottish blade, he had given up his right to deny my sole request. I applied bits of tissue paper to my face. Red starbursts clotted. Yes, I would ask him when he got home. Wait, no—there would be no asking. I would demand. The light strobed, failed, revived. I existed, I did not.

The next morning I was still alone. I peeled the tissue from my face. The black scabs alarmed me but looked better after a shower. The shiner, however, was impossible to conceal, and spread nearly as quickly as word of the Woody / Tess scandal. Even I heard the reports of the big man on campus seen groveling before Celeste and how she was making him sweat it out. She gracefully ignored his entreaties in gym, and afterward in the guys' locker room his glares had lost any iota of playfulness. He said the holes in my face looked like a second crotch, an asshole, a pussy, or all three. It was said with such ruthlessness that the laughter from his crew sounded uneasy. I changed and went directly home, giving no thought to my last two classes. My father remained missing.

The bruise on my cheek flowered into purples and yellows and reds. Wednesday morning Gottschalk excitedly hovered over me with his pointer—we were skipping ahead a few chapters, he confessed, but this beauty on Mr. Crouch simply could not wait. I closed my eyes and let Gottschalk's ad-lib sermon on capillary damage fade to a blather. I felt certain my father would return in the early afternoon. I left school at lunch. He was not there.

Thursday: surely this had to be the day. I skipped school entirely and sat around the house, picking at the dwindling morsels of food, poking a finger into the strange kaleidoscope of my cheek. The bathroom light had worsened. I was there, I was not. I was not. I was not.

I sprinted outside at the first sign of his truck. It was nine at night. The bounding headlights were bisected and trisected by trees. As my father pulled the truck into its usual spot and cut the engine, I realized that "all week" had not led me to this moment. It was all year, all of my life.

He stepped from the cab. A week's growth of beard swallowed his face. He had a clutch of newspapers in one hand. Without looking at me, he took both gray sacks from the bed. The larger rang with metal tools, the smaller knocked at his heels, not full, yet plenty heavy.

"I want to go with you," I said.

He did not stop until he reached the front door, where he turned.

"No," he said.

"No is not acceptable." The words I had practiced for days sounded flimsy.

"No, *this* is unacceptable." He gestured across the patchy lawn. "This whole arrangement is unacceptable. You living with me, at your age, associated in any way with what I do. Val would have killed me. Lionel *would* kill me."

I didn't know what my age had to do with it and had never heard of a man named Lionel. None of that mattered.

"I'm all alone," I said. "I'm your son and I'm all alone."

"That might mean something to you. It might not. Regardless, it isn't enough. You're not going to be little Jerry to my Jerry Cruncher."

I was even more confused. "Who's Jerry Cruncher?"

"Dickens," he muttered, kicking at the ground. "What are they teaching you at that school?"

"Nothing." I took a step toward him. "They're not teaching me anything. I want *you* to teach me."

"You don't know what you're asking." His voice quavered. "You don't know what's entailed. You think you do but you don't." He shrugged unhappily. He looked weary and old. "Lives get eaten."

"I'm not giving you an option." I took another step. "You teach me or it's Simmons and Diamond. Or worse, the police. What you're doing, it can't be legal."

"You sure have a lot to say tonight."

"You too," I said.

The night pressed in around us. October leaves were beginning to fall. Even at night you could see the vanguards, lazing in circuitous routes. In mere weeks, the yard would be covered. Footsteps would crunch. Rain would turn the dry matter into mulch. The mulch would decompose and become part of some new growth. All these miracles would occur around us in rapid succession, and in that time my father and I would remain stationary, strangers, unless someone did something right now to alter our courses.

"When you're stronger," he said. He set his jaw, decided he liked the irrefutability of his answer, and nodded. "When you're stronger, then we'll see."

I felt the slap to my face, the kicks to my crotch, Gottschalk's interrogative stabs. "I'm strong now," I insisted.

"Prove it," he said. He lifted the heavier of his two bags, loosened the drawstrings, and reached inside. It was like the unsheathing of a longsword: he withdrew a beaten old shovel and rolled it in his palm as if it were something priceless.

"This is Grinder." He caressed the beaten wood.

"Your shovel has a name?"

He tossed it across the four feet that separated us. I overreached and it cartwheeled to the grass at my feet. We looked at the fallen tool, the verification of my worthlessness. Without another word he entered the cabin and shut the door.

Inside, the usual noises: the sacks being placed in the bedroom, the kicking off of boots, the rush of water hitting drain. I reached to the ground and gripped Grinder's handle. The weight was unexpectedly satisfying. I moved into the backyard, seeing through a window my father at the new bathroom mirror, pawing his beard and peering intently at the foreign object of his face. The light above him flickered out and, for me, for now at least, he stopped existing. I aimed the shovel.

21.

Seven hours later the first light of dawn lit up my work. I stood up to my knees in an ungainly depression six feet long, four feet wide, and two feet deep, located halfway between the back of the cabin and the river. My leg hair was matted with mud. Soil had found its way everywhere: my underwear, armpits, ears, and eyes. Every time I shook my head, dirt scattered like black dandruff. Each time I swallowed, it tasted of the bitterest coffee. My arms sang in agony. I sat on the edge of the hole, using my thumbs to poke at the runny blisters on my fingers, and considered the forty-eight cubic feet of dirt I had displaced.

Eventually my father ambled around the corner, yawning and raking a hand through his hair. He stopped at the garden and pulled an onion. He peeled away the skin as he approached. I watched and waited, flexing my cramped hands, my weariness overcome by the pride I felt in my overnight achievement.

"Onions shore up the immune system, lower cholesterol, and prevent cancer," he said. Onions—this was what he chose to speak about? I was at a loss for words. He brushed off the vegetable and took a giant bite while toeing the edge of the hole, evaluating its various dimensions.

He grunted. "So that's the best you can do."

He turned and started back toward the cabin. Rage gripped me and I snatched Grinder from where I had speared her. I jumped to my feet and drove wounds into Bloughton. I did it again and again, the dirt flying, so that my father would hear the patters before he rounded the corner. I wasn't done, I wasn't even close.

Four more hours, five. I could no longer hear the river through the dirt in my ears. The sun rose to its apex and blazed; I felt my skin sizzle and wiped dirt on my neck as shield from the burn. The ground was changing. Grinder struck rocks, vibrating so hard upon contact that my teeth hurt. I fished out larger stones by hand and hurled them over the edge, where they disappeared into the till of ousted earth.

A heretofore unknown muscle that spanned from my armpit to waist convulsed. Reaching for it, I tripped and fell to my knees. The grass was at eye level. I exhaled slowly and investigated my unsteady limbs. Mud provided unexpected definition to my body and showed me, better than Gottschalk ever could, how groups of muscle worked together. The unusual construction of my father's upper body made sudden sense: I could feel knots burning in the corresponding parts of my own musculature. I fantasized about returning to the Bloughton High hallways in search of Woody Trask, my neck tapering into bulging shoulders, my shirt straining over slabs of chest, back, and arms. That could be me. All I needed to do was keep digging.

Sometime around noon something dropped into the hole. I reached over and picked it up. It was a thermos. I unscrewed the lid and poured the contents over my face, gobbling up as much water as possible—it tasted almost sugary. I shook the last drops onto my tongue. I kept my eyes closed so I did not have to see him.

"You're too slow," he said. I felt the coolness of his shadow give way to heat.

The day darkened. Hunger burned somewhere inside me

but it could not compete with the million other pains. Five feet, six. The sequence of motions that made up the act of digging became as rote as breathing. The hardest part now was tossing dirt high enough to clear the rim—when it didn't, it hailed back down on me. Around dusk I struck water. A shallow puddle gathered in the deepest corner of the hole. I fell to my knees and cupped my hands.

I woke up blinking. It was twilight. Something had just landed on my chest. I patted around and felt wax paper. It was a sandwich, crudely assembled and bound. The scarecrow outline of my father towered stories above. I tore through the wrapping. Stale crust and dry meat were pushed around by my arid tongue. I chewed and choked, then chewed and choked some more. My father's face was backlit and hidden. "You'll never finish this hole," he said.

Nighttime—a new coolness turned my hot sweat to a stinging chill. I found myself laughing and wondered what was so funny. Seven feet, eight: when did I stop, if ever? I shoveled now as if the act fueled my very heart and lungs. Far away, inside the cabin, I heard my father rustle through newspapers, piss with the door open, shut his bedroom door to sleep, but of course all I saw was a small rectangle of sky.

I tried to calculate the amount of time I had been down there and couldn't do it. Hours and minutes had lost meaning—only feet and inches mattered now. I dug. My body revolted. My aim was becoming hazardous. Grinder struck my right foot repeatedly, once slicing into my big toe. I tried to ignore it but saw a patch of canvas soak red. I reached to brush dirt over the blood so I didn't have to look at it; I lost my balance and was on my back, my head cooling in the puddle, watching a pale worm poke from the clay. I could not get up, and even if I could, I sensed that I had finally dug too deep. The walls were too sheer to climb, and what if my father left in the morning? I began to formulate a rescue plot involving the assiduous use of the shovel, but the ideas were too glorious, too strenuous. I welcomed the void.

22.

Something was tapping against my face. A clear vision of my mother waking me for church darkened into the mud of reality. I blinked into the Sunday sun and spat to rid myself of the earthen taste. I sat up. While I had slept, the thousand aches of my body had merged into a single heaviness that was somehow easier to bear. Sunburn made my forehead and nose feel plastic and inflexible. Something batted my face again. I blinked and focused upon it. It was a noose.

Here it was then, my death. This was no Scottish blade, but I could not blame him for the change in plans. It was so convenient, with me already so deep inside my grave. I leaned my head at the rope.

"Your foot," came my father's voice from far above. "Stand up and insert your foot."

Hand over hand, I used the rope to raise myself. When I was high enough I wiggled my right foot through the noose. Half of the shoe was brown with dried blood. Without warning my body jolted skyward. I snatched up Grinder with one hand and rose and spun and felt cool soil paint across my neck and face. After I was dragged over the edge, I collapsed next to my father, who panted atop of a pile of dirt with the other end of the rope tied around his waist. I felt his fingers press into my face. With a thumb he pulled open my eyelid. He studied my pupil for a moment before moving aside, apparently satisfied.

"It's eight in the morning," he said. "Go wash off. And we're going to need to cool those muscles—I've been making ice since yesterday. Then you sleep. Tonight you and I have an appointment." He stood up and leaned over, grasping my wrists in his large hands and hoisting me to my feet. Distantly I recognized victory, some claim of respect my madness had won from the mad. Even more distantly, I seized upon the importance of the mentioned appointment. My father had lifted me from one grave so he could take me to another.

23.

He moved with speed. He wore a sack across his back that he had strapped to himself with belts to quiet the noise. I carried an empty sack, the drawstrings pulled too tight around a wrist. My hand was already numb and I imagined it separating from my body, a disembodied thing that my father could one day attack with wire cutters. We kept low.

The fence was classic nightmare: lustrous, bladed wrought iron, taller than me. This is where ninety-nine percent turn back, my father told me: Halloween pranksters, homeless addicts, amateurs giddy with fantasies of gravestones used as coffee tables and skulls as bongs. The fence, said my father, is teeth to a mouth.

He looped his bag by both straps over two fence points, the shovel and hoe within arranged to lean into the fence's crossbars. The effect was like a ladder: my father stepped on the shovel heads and climbed the handles. My bag was draped to blanket the fence points. Once the toe of his boot was wedged between the top spikes, he let himself fall to the other side of the fence while taking hold of the straps of the bag. He went down; the bag on my side rose. It was complicated and impressive.

Once over, I stubbed my toes on markers hidden low in uncut grass; short stones knocked my shins; larger ones rushed me at crotch level like the ancestors of high school tormentors. I kept moving out of fear of losing my father's trail but was impeded by the things that kept appearing at my eyes' edges: faces, outstretched arms, wings, all of which were fashioned from stone. Motionless, my feet began to sink. The ground was lousy with growth.

The fence crooked and so did we. I sailed between two crypts and the entire cemetery presented itself as a sweep of white dominoes. To be alone in a graveyard is to be outnumbered; I hurried to find my father. I discovered him stationary in the middle of the yard, barely distinguishable from the angels and saints surrounding him. He told me the stones were our compass and their faces pointed east. With his toe he exposed the tiny numbered cornerstones caretakers used to identify plots. They glimmered everywhere once we resumed moving. Dark birds, maybe bats, circled in escort. I watched them, entranced, and fell facedown on somebody's deathbed. *I have no business here,* I thought frantically, inhaling the sharp, grassy odor of the too-green lawn.

A hand on my back—I barely held back a scream. It was my father, lifting me by the waist of my jeans like just another clattering sack. I brushed from my elbows grass and mud that felt more like hair and gristle. A right turn, a left: these roads were poorly marked. I knew we had arrived by the bulge of earth that had not yet settled to the depth of the connecting properties. The burial was recent, but not too.

Don't look at the name, my father said, and I listened. It's not a person, he insisted, it is meat spoiling inside a box. He ran his hands over the plot as if feeling for a pulse. The handheld spade was out and so was a backsaw. He marked out corners, a square four feet wide, four feet long. I took a step away and someone took hold of me. Oblivious, my father made an incision with his saw, then used the spade to strip the sod like rind from orange. I dared to look over my shoulder and saw Jesus gazing down at me with smooth white eyes and open arms. Three of the fingers on his right hand were missing, and I wondered if he could still bless me with those gone. And even if he could, given what I was there to do, would he?

A bedsheet was unpacked and unfolded. It looked to be a twin of that knotted across my father's bed. He slid the segment of sod onto the sheet and slid it away. Exposed now was a perfect square of dirt—skin peeled from a torso in preparation for surgery.

Thirty to forty minutes for a fresh grave, he told me; two hours for an old one. Waterlogged it can take upwards of four. There was a flashlight but he didn't use it; to prevent accidental illumination the batteries were kept in a separate bag. Come closer, he gestured. I didn't want to leave Two-Fingered Jesus. My father used his voice now. Come closer if you want to learn.

Experimental jabs were made. They were nearly silent and my father approved. Lessons began. Five feet, he said, leaning into Grinder. That was all we had to go. There was something funny about this, and it took me a moment to remember: my hole, back at the cabin, really had been too deep.

The scooped dirt landed precisely upon a bowled tarpaulin stretched across the adjacent plot. When it came time to return the dirt, I realized, we could fashion a funnel and pour it back in. The chunk of the shovel, the splat of clods shattering against tarp—the volume was excruciating. Perhaps it was due to all the hard surfaces, because everything else was louder, too: that skittering leaf, that squirrel, those branches ticking past one another overhead.

The only thing that whispered at an appropriate volume was my father. The taking from graves, he said, is the oldest profession there is. Early man took what he needed from the mounds of his fallen fellows. Egyptian masks and sarcophagi, Chinese jade burial suits, all were useless to the soil and therefore recycled back into the world. Da Vinci stole bodies from the morgue to study anatomy, he told me. Michelangelo, too, though he didn't have the stomach for the necessary dissection. My stomach lurched—two feet more and the unwilling stomach would be my own.

He was deep now, three feet. After a brief period of rest, said my father, Michelangelo resumed his studies, and this is the mark of a true artist, to have the mettle to see what truly lies inside of man. I inched forward so as to not miss a word. He was a better teacher than any at Bloughton High, better than any I had ever had. The mess of his life—maybe it was only a mess when seen from a limited perspective. The possibility suddenly existed to me that there was other knowledge of such importance that it overwhelmed the world's quotidian concerns, and such knowledge came from the inside: bodies, bones and tissues, and maybe even another layer deeper, souls.

A bullet crack threw me to the ground. It was Grinder, striking her quarry. My father knotted a swath of velvet around the blade. The subsequent sounds were muffled. I crawled near and caught glimpses of neighboring coffins peeking through the dirt—buried too close together, my father complained. At the bottom of the hole, the casket's surface shimmered through the dirt like water. I looked there and saw my reflection.

His hand reached up from the grave, startling me, and grabbed a mallet and a crowbar that had been modified with a right-angle bend. There followed a blast of metal crunching through fiberglass, and to me it was the sound of my mother's bones splintering a windshield and popping headlamps. Pay attention, said my father. Fragments of casket lid hopped through the air as he cranked the crowbar. It was amazing how cleanly the lid split in two. I was struck by the swift perfection of his motion, the exacting way he guided his tools. I was still marveling when he set aside the lid.

A green thing that used to be a woman was screaming at me, jaw slung open to the neck and eyeballs flickering with animation. She was alive—I swooned and grasped at the headstone for support. The smell was to the cabin odor what being immersed in the ocean was to tasting a grain of salt. Somewhere my father's lessons continued, narrating the horrors in excruciating medical detail. Bloat, he said, had already plundered the woman's torso; her gut, having fed on itself for too long, had ruptured right through her clothing. Brown mud leaked from the mouth and ears. Brain, my father said stoically, an early victim to putrefaction. It was with great fear that I looked into the eyes that I had taken for alive, and in a sickening moment I realized that they *were* alive, in a manner of speaking—each socket was a writhing mess of maggots.

I began specifying—

—the dress bunching around the shriveled bags that used to be breasts—

—tongue and lips inflated by bacteria into grotesque purple fruit—

—but no, please, not here, not now. I concentrated on my father. He was dealing with another ring that wouldn't dislodge from its puffy finger. He let the hand drop and it smacked into two inches of black slime. We call that coffin liquor, my father said as he reached for his wire cutter, and it's the result of bacteria in the casket's vacuum turning the corpse to mud. I watched him take the woman's left hand. Most of the skin sloughed off in a single sheet like a translucent glove—slip skin, my father assured me, nothing more. He let the skin dissolve into the coffin liquor and regripped the moist green hand. I noted with dull astonishment that the woman's nails were painted candy pink.

With a brittle crack the finger was severed and my father removed the ring and placed it in his pocket. From his shirt he removed a tiny spool of wire and set about cinching the finger back onto the woman's hand. The campground rule, he said, twisting tight the wire-ends with needle-nose pliers: leave them in no worse shape than you found them.

To finish the repair he turned the arm over. On the woman's wrist, a surprise: a gash, beaded with more maggots. It was a suicide wound; now the need to specify pounded at my skull. This boiling pile of meat that used to be a woman was not the result of natural causes but had come to be out of a belief that the world beneath the dirt was better than that beneath the sun. Not true, not true. I wished that Two-Fingered Jesus would hold me again with his ivory arms.

I was ready to throw up. My father heard the choking and

commanded me to count the stars. I felt the grass on my back and saw glimmers above but I had forgotten all of my numbers. Monks in the Middle Ages, explained my father, those who were said to have miraculous powers, could allegedly take the graves of saints and bishops and transport them from the subterranean to the celestial, and those stars you are counting are their bodies. I asked what this magic was called. Translation, my father responded, as he did something that caused the corpse to slosh noisily in its puddle. Eventually the term lost its meaning, he continued, and became just another word for what we're doing right now. Translation.

Why did she kill herself? I found myself asking the question aloud. There was no answer, of course, but my father's voice was at least soothing. Long ago, he said, suicides were buried outside of town at a crossroads, so that when the tortured soul awoke there was a three-in-four chance she would choose the wrong path home. Even now, my father continued, there are suicide corners in cemeteries, ugly and unkempt areas with bad drainage. Then his tone sharpened. Shakespeare, he said, condemned his characters to death by suicide thirteen times in his plays, and if it was good enough for him, and good enough for your Jesus, then it's hardly worth getting so riled up about, is it? I searched for Two-Fingered Jesus and wondered if his crucifixion had indeed been a suicide, and if my presence at this open grave was a suicide, too, the self-killing of something important inside of me.

She's beautiful, said my father. In general suicides are unusually beautiful or unusually ugly—come closer and see. I pressed shut my eyelids. How he could find beauty through the squirming disorder of her face confounded me—but it also humbled me, just a little. I peeked at him and he was waiting with an outstretched hand.

I would not have believed there was room enough for both of us, but somehow my father spidered his body to the woman's right while I squatted to her left. The smell down there coated me like a syrup and began shrugging its way across my tongue. I could not let this spoilage inside me; I held my breath. My father pointed. The necklace, he said. He had left it for me to remove.

It was not that different from sticking your hand into an opened pumpkin. On the way to her neck my fingertips dug tunnels through her cheek; for a second her face was Celeste's and the wounds were revenge for those she had given me. The set of my father's lips told me that we were lingering too long. I clenched my teeth and yanked at the necklace. It didn't come free. Beside me, my father patted the woman's shoulder. I don't think he realized that he was doing it. He patted her with more gentleness than he had ever shown me, as if saying to her, shh, it'll all be over soon.

The clasp, of course. I reined it in, and with each inch of progress the strand plowed deeper into the ulcerous neck. Finally I had it but felt faint and realized that I was still holding my breath. I drew a heaving, ragged gasp and contaminated air slid down my throat. It was inside me now, death was inside me. Somehow the necklace came free and I fumbled it over to my father. My knees pistoned; one foot dipped into coffin liquor. Then I was wriggling like a worm over the hole's edge, gasping upon the tarpaulin, translated to the stars.

Somehow the casket lid was put back in some semblance of order. I didn't watch. I rolled off the tarp to allow my father to refill the grave. He was still talking, but it was hard to hear him over the sickly rattle of my lungs. Decay was claiming my entrails. Over the snowy thump of dirt, I detected my father speaking of something called the Satipatthana Sutta, a passage called the Nine Cemetery Contemplations. It was one of the books in the cabin, I knew it, and I wondered if he would later assign the reading. The passage, he said as he tamped down the earth, details a process wherein apprentice monks meditate upon bodies in various states of decay until they overcome disgust and embrace the serenity of the body's ephemeral nature. I knew this was meant to comfort. But there was fetid mortality swelling inside me, I was certain of it—I could feel its long claws thread my organs.

We were up and moving. A heavy sack skipped across my vertebrae. Still my father spoke, and still I tried to listen, but my ears buzzed with the low hum of disease. He told me, and I tried to understand, that what we had done was something ancient and possibly noble, but also vilified and to be undertaken with the utmost solemnity; and that, most importantly, it was a craft passed down for generations, teacher to student, and as of tonight this group included not just my father, not just a clandestine group of men spread all across the country, but also, horrifyingly, me.

"We're called the Diggers," he said.

24.

MONDAY, SCHOOL—THERE WAS no way I was going, they would smell my sin all over me. I prayed to the placid and forgiving Two-Fingered Jesus: *Save me*. Even though I didn't deserve it, my prayers were answered. Five minutes later, I pushed to my feet to vomit into the sink. I would not suffer school today. I was sick for real.

Consciousness was sporadic. My eyes ached, so I closed them and fixated on the sweat that slopped my shirt and boxers to my skin. I had read about fevers so severe that people's brains were literally cooked, and I remembered the dark liquid pooling from the dead woman's mouth and ears. I coughed and spat until everything came up, corpse-tissue mush, coffin liquor, all dredged up from my guts and sent back through sewer pipes and returned to the earth. I glimpsed myself in the bathroom mirror and saw a corpse.

Harnett's hands were icy. I realized he was lifting me from the toilet. Then I was moving through the air and set back upon my bed, feeling moments later a rag draped over my forehead. There was ice wrapped inside, but a few minutes later it was water. My head pounded and I took advantage of the noise and hid inside. No cemetery, no woman, no maggots, just a fire in which I alone burned.

After a time my eyes fell upon my father standing at the stove within a cloud of steam, and I became riveted by the normalcy of the apparition—Ken Harnett, not grappling with graves and the enormity of death, but clanging a metal spoon against a metal pot, stirring broth. He served soup and I drank it. Later there were crackers and water. By now it had to be at least Tuesday, and wretchedly I began to fret about the classes I was missing and what it meant for the future my mother had plotted. Was I in danger of flunking out? Suspension? This was worse than risking the wrath of Woody and Gottschalk. Then my father returned from an absence and set a stack of papers on my cardboard-box desk. "Your assignments," he said.

Just sifting through the papers strengthened me. Though

sweaty, my fingers itched for my textbooks. I would show them. I would continue to ace every exam. I would turn in work so strong they would accuse me of cheating and I would welcome the challenge. I drifted off imagining their thwarted effort. Let them try.

A cool hand against my face rose me from slumber. I blinked my eyes open and saw an elderly man kneeling above me. He had sparse gray hair and a slotted, wizened face of the darkest chestnut. He wore a white clergyman's collar. My first thought was one of vanity: my smell, the stink of the grave, this man of God would recoil.

"Hello, Joseph," he said. "I'm Reverend Knox." The sonorous buzz of his voice was deep and true.

My throat burned. "Hello."

Knox smiled so widely the hairs in his mustache pulled away from one another. Bones whined audibly as he twisted his neck to look over his shoulder.

"This boy's got the boneyard blues."

Behind Knox I could see my father standing with his fists in his pockets, shuffling his feet like a scolded schoolboy. "His first time. What do you expect?"

"That's no excuse for laying him on this cold floor," Knox snapped. "Man, you ought to have your head examined."

"Stop coddling him," Harnett said. "It'll work itself out."

"Work itself out, my missing foot," muttered Knox. I gazed at the swaying fabric of his black pants and ascertained that, indeed, the lower half of his right leg was gone. I searched for his face and he waved a hand as if erasing the last few moments. "I got just the cure, Joseph. We gonna put your dad to work, amen?" Knox winked, then called over his shoulder. "Shake a leg to your garden, old man, and get me one of all you got. And not just an armload of nasty onions. We're also going to need whiskey. Don't even try telling me you got none. And two lemons, and if that means you need to drive into town, well, I don't know what to tell you besides you're running the Lord's errands now. God is good?"

To my surprise, Harnett moved right away. He lifted his jacket from the rocking chair and fished his keys from the pocket. "Don't be polluting the kid with this Lord's errand shit, all right?"

Knox took on a philosophical tone. " 'It is enough for the student to be like his teacher, and the servant like his master. If the head of the house has been called Beelzebub, how much more the members of his household?' "

My father raised his hands in surrender and exited. Knox placed a hand on his knee and with a pained grunt lifted himself into the air. He wedged a single crutch into his armpit.

"Are you one of the Diggers?" I asked.

"Just one of Jesus's foot soldiers. God is good? No, child, I don't approve of hardly a thing your dad's ever done. It's wrong. I don't need to tell you, you know it in your heart. But that's Jesus's miracle, Joseph." Knox smiled. "Two men such as your father and myself, breaking bread? God *is* good! Ken Harnett's soul is on fire, yes. But you know what that means? It means my soul is on fire, too. And the two of us, amen, we douse each other's flames." He patted his sleeves by means of illustration.

"You know? What he does?"

" 'Woe to those who call evil good and good evil, who put darkness for light and light for darkness, who put bitter for sweet and sweet for bitter.' "

I tried to bring myself to one elbow. Knox winked.

"We gonna fix you up, amen?"

It just came out of my mouth: "God is good."

When Harnett returned, Knox shoved a wooden spoon into his hand, and now my father stood before the stove, poking sullenly at vegetables. Knox clattered a number of bottles across the counter, eventually handing me a glass half filled with a golden liquid. He limped to my father's rocking chair, sat down, and set his crutch horizontally across the armrests.

Knox sighed, kneading his stump. "Forty years I been trying to knock sense into your fool head and forty years you been telling me to save my breath. Now I don't have a whole lot more breath left to give, so you best let me say my piece. Amen?"

For a moment my father stood motionless. "Don't say that."

"When God calls my name, I plan to come a-hopping, to a land where there's no crutches or dentures or medicine bottles no one can open. You, you'd kick and scream all the way to glory. Don't believe a single thing put in front of your two eyes. Don't even believe in the Incorruptibles."

"I'll give you a hundred dollars not to start this again," Harnett said. "Two hundred."

"Saint Teresa Margaret." Knox elongated each word with exquisite pleasure. "Fifteen days after death with cheeks still as pink as posies, praise Jesus. Smelled like posies, too—every witness swore it."

"I know tricks that could pull off the same thing," Harnett muttered from the stove. "Give me the right chemicals and five minutes with the body."

"Thirteen years later! They move the blessed body and upon exhumation find Saint Teresa Margaret uncorrupted still! A miracle, given unto Saint Teresa Margaret for the healing miracles she bestowed as His servant. Oh, God is good."

"This was what, the eighteen hundreds? The seventeen hundreds? I tell you what's a miracle, that you believe any of this." Harnett pushed sizzling vegetables around the pan.

Knox slapped his knee and guffawed. One of his teeth was capped in gold. " 'I am the resurrection and the life!' " He laughed and slapped his knee again. " 'I am the resurrection and the life! Whoever believes in me, streams of living water will flow from within him.' Visit the monastery chapel of Santa Teresa dei Bruni. See for yourself. Then come back and you explain it to me."

"She's been embalmed, Knox." Harnett sighed. "And I'm not going to Italy."

"What's an Incorruptible?" My voice surprised even me. Knox looked pleased that I had spoken. Harnett's reaction was less enthusiastic.

"Tell the child," Knox said. "He asks a sensible question."

My father chewed his lip for a moment. When he spoke, he kept his eyes on the vegetables. "There's two kinds of preservation," he said begrudgingly. "There's embalming, and then there's sort of natural embalming."

"Like the Iceman," I said.

"But some people," he said, pausing long enough to indict Knox, "say there's a third kind, whose bodies don't decay because of their . . . I don't even know. Their virtue."

"And we call 'em the Incorruptibles," purred Knox.

"Some of us call 'em bullshit," said Harnett.

"Saint Francis Xavier—oh, let me tell you about Saint Francis Xavier!" Knox's hands were raised at the level of his head in private elation. "Saint Francis Xavier, passed in 1552. You know what they said in 1974 when they examined his remains? They said, 'Why, it looks as though Saint Francis is only sleeping.' Or Saint Andrew Bobola, tortured and burned alive, or Saint Josaphat, who they drug up from a river! Incorrupt, each of them. Tell me now that God is good!"

There was a snapping noise as my father turned off the stove. He lifted the pan and dumped the contents onto a plate. "All of which is very interesting and none of which means a goddamn thing."

"It means that the grave is a holding pen." The gaiety of Knox's drawl hardened into something magisterial. "It is a waiting room. It is temporary housing, amen. It means that we bury our bodies at the *pleasure* of our Lord and He is *aware* of those bodies and even, amen, *possessive* of them. He be using the Incorruptibles to deliver a message, Ken Harnett, that you isn't to be down there messing around with his property. Now, put some salt and pepper on that before you give it to the child. Mary and Joseph."

A few irritated banging noises later, my drink was joined by a plate of food: roasted slices of red and green pepper, tomato, and plenty of browned onion, plopped unceremoniously onto a bed of sticky rice. I went for it with my fingers before my father pushed a fork into my palm. After stuffing some in my mouth I washed it back with a big gulp of the liquid concoction. Instantly my throat stung and my eyes screwed shut. So *this* was whiskey. It hit my belly and radiated heat, and only moments later did I taste the undertones of honey and lemon. My first thought was that it was like sucking gasoline vapors. My second thought was that I wanted more, and down the hatch it went.

Knox was chuckling. "Those blues will be gone in no time," he said. His eyes twinkled and his hands clasped at his heart. "A son. God is good. God is *real* good. 'Sons are a heritage from the Lord,' Psalm One Twenty-seven. This is a gift, Harnett. Don't you throw it away."

Harnett looked at the old man in a way that was almost affectionate, and in that moment I recognized two men with much history between them, two men on opposite sides of a battle who kept fighting despite an abiding respect.

"It's a warm October," Harnett said. "Good news for your arthritis."

There was silence for a while as I ate and drank. The sun was sinking. Unexpectedly it caught the bathroom mirror and temporarily blinded me; my eyes filled with white light and my ears momentarily rang with a sound like ravens. When I again opened them, Knox was kneeling before me, gently taking the empty tumbler from my hand and replacing it with a glass of water. I blinked; I must have blacked out. Over Knox's shoulder I could see my father outside, raising an axe at the woodpile. I could also see Knox's car, a small, battered junker that had to be at least twenty years old. The reverend's large hand patted mine, and I marveled at the pure whiteness of his palms.

"Your father," he sighed. "I save what souls that I can, but only the Almighty knows which path your father will take." He squeezed my wrist and I could feel a sinewy strength alive in the old man's bones. "Remember your Proverbs. 'Listen, my son, to your father's instruction and do not forsake your mother's teaching.' Understand? I want the Lord to have an easier time with you than He does your old man. Amen?"

I felt myself nodding limply.

"And whatever you do," he said, widening his yellow eyes and leaning forward until I could smell his musk of coffee and peanuts and minty cologne. "You stand clear of Mr. Boggs. You do not go near Antiochus Boggs."

I opened my mouth to tell him I didn't know any Mr. Boggs, but then Harnett's steps thundered inside and I heard the crash of firewood spilling upon the hearth. Knox stood, swaying for a moment before catching himself with his crutch.

"You know what my great-great-grandma would've prescribed this child?" Knox called loudly to Harnett.

"Another whiskey, probably."

"A mellified," said Knox. He glanced at me. "That's a mummy been steeped in honey a good many years. There are those who believe eating a mellified has great medicinal value. Kind of like that drink I fixed you. Mite bit stronger, though."

"Stop messing with the kid." Harnett kicked the firewood against the hearth. "That crap never left sixteenth-century China."

Knox began limping across the floor. I panicked at the thought of his exit—I felt certain that Knox and the strange knowledge he was privy to were key to explaining so much about Harnett, my mother, and me. "If you don't think they were practicing that stuff on the bayou in my great-great-grandmother's day, then I don't know what to tell you. Called it mummy honey, she did. Ha!"

His breaths were labored as he hopped to the door and reached for his things. He draped a scarf over his bony shoulders and pulled a hat so low it flattened the tops of his ears. He sighed and hesitated at the open door, fishing a small set of car keys from his pocket.

"Not sure when I'll be through again," he said. "Plenty of Diggers to see, though, and I'll keep sending along news."

"And telling us all how damned we are," Harnett said.

"That too, that too. By year's end I hope to've brought a couple more into the fold. Maybe you too?"

Harnett looked grim. "Maybe."

Knox patted my father's shoulder. "Well. I hear tell there's a relocation coming up this winter. Could be before year's end. I'll send word."

"I appreciate it."

"And I don't have any real news about—" Knox paused with his mouth open, then closed it. He shrugged. Somehow I knew who he meant: Mr. Boggs. "But what I do hear, it's not good."

"Okay. Appreciate it."

Knox pointed at me but kept his eyes on my father.

"I know. I will. I will," Harnett said, nodding.

Knox sighed again and nodded. He pivoted on his crutch and turned to face the dusk. He inhaled deeply before leaving.

"It may be a warm October," he said, "but it's going to be a hell of a winter."

25.

It was called Fun and Games. How something so innocently titled could end so badly, I don't think anyone could have suspected. With the semester nearly half over, the boring but predictable fitness tests had finally run their course. That these mindless time-killers were finite seemed to befuddle the gym coaches, Mr. Gripp and Ms. Stettlemeyer, both of whom had spent most of the previous seven weeks relaxing on the bleachers.

"Starting today, we're going to be splitting up the class," announced Mr. Gripp. He was a tall man who went everywhere in a sweatshirt and gym shorts and had the drowsy bad temper of someone who had been doing this for way too many years. "Girls are staying with Stettlemeyer here in the gym. Guys, you get your pick. You can do this unit Ms. Stettlemeyer has planned or you can come with me to the weight room and, you know. Do weights."

We were scattered across the floor. Ahead of me several feet was Celeste. A circle of females kept her sealed off from Woody, who nonetheless beseeched her with puppy-dog expressions. I kept my eyes down and repeatedly told myself the same thing: Incorruptibles existed, all right, and Celeste was one of them—nothing anyone could do could damage her. My hand crept to obscure the yellowish remainder of my bruise. *Keep your distance,* I reminded myself, but it wasn't because I feared her wrath. It was because I was afraid she would smell my cemetery reek, and that the wrinkling of her fine features would telegraph to everyone in the room what kind of monster I really was.

"Listen up, people! I'm calling my unit Fun and Games!" Stettlemeyer shouted from around the rubber-cased whistle she kept clenched in her teeth. She delivered everything in this fashion, which was funny enough when she was urging us to "Push it!" but downright hilarious when she was caught attempting to compliment someone's hairstyle. There was snickering, but as usual Stettlemeyer was deaf to it. "Here's what we can look forward to! Various light athletics! Volleyball! Badminton! Table tennis! Scooter ball! And we'll change it up almost every session! I think you'll be pleased by the wide variety!"

I certainly didn't welcome the uncertainty of a "wide variety," but the other option, the weight room, worried me even more. Located at the top of a narrow flight of stairs off the gym, it was an ominous space more or less owned by Woody and his ilk. I visualized dumbbells and weight racks and other more complicated machinery, all twisted to cruel use against me.

Gripp hitched up his shorts. "Okay, everyone who's coming with me come with me."

There was a tense moment during which no one moved, and then Woody yawned, slapped Rhino on the back of his shaved head, and stood. In seconds boys everywhere were scuffling toward the weight room door. After a moment of herding, Gripp scanned the remaining crowd until he found the straggler, me, all the way in the rear. My skin burned as every girl in the room turned to face me.

Then Gripp shifted his gaze to where one other boy sat, on the far side of the group of girls. Like me, he was short and slim, but where my features were small and dark, his were large and freckled, and he wore his blond hair to his shoulders. He looked only vaguely familiar. Was he in my biology class? English? If so, I knew absolutely nothing about him. Well, I knew one thing: I envied his ability to skate by unnoticed.

Gripp screwed up his face as if it were his sworn duty to call out such miserable pussies. Then, maybe too old for such shit, he changed his mind and was gone. "Okay! Everybody! Calisthenic formation!" Stettlemeyer clapped her hands. There was groaning and sighing and sneakers squeaking from shiny maple flooring, followed by the mechanized configuration of orderly rows. I lurched and scurried and finally landed in the last row. I noticed the blond kid choosing a spot far from me and I was glad—by ignoring each other's existence, perhaps we could escape the mirror images of our failures. Up ahead, Stettlemeyer cranked up a boom box and shouted, "Superhits of the eighties! Oh, yeah! Superhits of the nineteen eighties!" The Pointer Sisters were fading out; Kenny Loggins was fading in.

"Jumping jacks!" Stettlemeyer yelled along with the synthesized beat. "One, two, three, and four! One, two, three, and four!" She began strolling along the ranks, clipboard and pen in hand. I heard her shout, "Name!" and heard a voice lower than my own respond, "Foley." That was the blond kid's name—Foley. He glanced my way and I quickly averted my gaze, yet everywhere else I looked was even more inappropriate: ponytails swishing, boobs bouncing, the hems of shorts swishing dangerously close to buttocks. I aimed higher, at the basketball hoop, and unsuccessfully pushed away the thought gnawing like a bug on my brain: all of these bodies, young and smooth and sturdy as they were, would end up in the ground, where their bones would be sifted through by a man like my father. Maybe a man like me.

"One, two, three, and four! Nice! Nice! Keep it going, ladies!"

Giggles erupted around me. I located Stettlemeyer and she was already wincing at her gaffe. I returned my eyes to the basketball hoop: *Keep jumping, keep jumping*. But I sensed Stettlemeyer's approach and felt her tap on my shoulder. *Go away,* I willed her. *Can't you tell what I've done? Can't anyone?*

"Name!" she hollered as quietly as she could.

I halted midjump. My body parts jounced; I felt humiliatingly male. At least forty feet were pounding down in near unison. With the gymnasium echo, it sounded more like one hundred. Thundering over everything were the ripping guitar solos and computerized backbeats of superhits of the eighties. I should not have been able to hear anything over this commotion, much less a whisper, but perhaps my hours spent on alert in a desolate cemetery had sharpened my senses. Hissing through the ranks of female bodies came Stettlemeyer's answer: my name, my true name, the only one I would ever have at Bloughton High.

26.

HARNETT CAME HOME AROUND eight, long after I had eaten a wholesome dinner of peanut butter and crackers. He made as much noise as possible tossing his gear into his room and tromping around, and I shot him glares between every math problem. Soon he was at my side, throwing wide cabinets in search of food. I smirked; earlier I had gone through the same futile hunt. Eventually I heard the thud of peanut butter, the jangle of a knife, the rustling of the bag of crackers. *Bon appétit,* I thought.

Instead of slumping into his rocking chair, he took a seat across from me on a stack of newspapers. I rolled my eyes and returned to my math. Despite my many absences, I was threatening to get an A in calculus, and that was exactly what it felt like—I was making a threat against Coach Winter's insulting presumptions. The fact that he was the football coach made it all the sweeter.

Harnett began smacking his peanut butter and crackers. I gritted my teeth and faced my numbers again. Functions f, g, and h. The computation of the squeeze principal. Negative one is less than or equal to sine x is less than or equal to positive one. It was no use—his indulgent, expectant gaze weighed too heavy.

"Is there a problem, Harnett?"

"What're you working so hard on?" he said through a mouthful.

"Calculus."

"Calculus," he said, swallowing. "That's not going to be much help."

"It's going to be a big help to my grade point average, so if you don't mind?"

He stuck a cracker into his mouth and ground it thoughtfully. "Now, geometry, we might find some use for that. When will you be taking geometry?"

I tapped my pencil in irritation. "Try two years ago."

He nodded slowly. "That an important assignment?"

I shook my head in wonderment. "What? Who cares? You don't care. Why are you asking me this?"

"Curious," he said, picking at his teeth with a pinkie. "That an important assignment?"

I slammed down my pencil. The cardboard table did not give it the resonance I would have liked. "I don't know. Yes? I guess so? I've missed so many classes now that every assignment is important."

"When's it due?" he asked.

I almost laughed at the absurdity. Since when did Ken Harnett become father of the year? "For your information, it's due tomorrow morning. Second period. And if it's not handed in precisely at the start of class second period, do you know what's going to happen?"

He cocked his head in interest—a gesture I did not trust.

"What?" he asked.

"Well, I'll tell you, Harnett," I said, lacing my fingers in mock patience. "There are only so many assignments in a given semester, and each assignment is worth a certain percentage of the final grade. Each time you are late, another certain percentage is taken off the grade for that assignment, no matter how well you do. And eventually, you end up like me, looking at the last eight weeks of class with absolutely no room for error." I waved my paper. "Even if I nail this—which is more and more unlikely the longer you keep asking me questions—even if I nail it, if I turn it in any later than the start of second period tomorrow, the percentage taken off would make it mathematically impossible for me to get an A in the class."

"And this is important to you."

"What, getting an A?"

He nodded again.

I gave him a good hard stare. His eyes might have looked like mine, but the brain behind them could not have been more dissimilar. Good grades—no, perfect grades—were the only possible escape route from Bloughton. It had been my mother's dream, and mine. I couldn't expect the Garbageman to understand.

"Yes." I snatched up my pencil. "It's important to me."

He planted his hands on his knees and gave me a sharp nod as if to say "Good enough," and then rose and crossed the room, dropped himself into his chair, reached for the new stack of newspapers, and once again pretended that I didn't exist.

27.

IT WAS A TRICK. When I awoke, my calculus book was on the floor next to me—not where I had left it. I sat up and squinted at my watch. It was just past five-thirty. Harnett's bedroom door was open and the fire had long ago died. I pulled on some jeans and a hoodie, tiptoed across the cold floor, and peeked out the front door. The truck was still parked. Where was he?

The dewy grass darkened my shoes as I walked through the glossy violet of predawn. As I moved past the garden, I made out Harnett standing in the yard between the cabin and the Big Chief River, his right hand curled around Grinder.

The hole I had dug had been filled in. Indeed, its gentle rise looked uncomfortably like a grave. Harnett stood a good twenty feet to the west. It was too dark to see his face. I ventured another few steps. The water sounded like grinding glass.

"When you dig, time is against you," he said from the darkness. "Time is always against you."

Something about his tone made me think of my mother, his Val, and how time had thwarted all three of us.

"But you dig anyway," he continued. "Because there's something you want at the bottom of a hole, only it's not a hole yet, because you haven't dug it. Got it? Now. The Merriman grave up in Lancet County is just sitting there, waiting for us. We're losing time and money every day. So let's not drag this out." With alarming quickness he drove Grinder into the earth. It made a sound like a sheathed sword and stuck there, wobbling gently against the dark sparkles of the river.

I squinted and yawned. Obviously the man was nuts. It was too dark to see much of anything aside from my breath. I hid my hands inside my sweatshirt and crossed my arms tight against my chest. "Can't we do this later?"

"Start when you want." He shrugged in silhouette. "But you've got a couple hours till school and, like I said, there's something you want at the bottom of a hole."

He left Grinder and walked past me without a word. I

shivered and looked at the shovel. She still vibrated. Like a divining rod, I thought—and then it hit me. My calculus homework. Those questions about due dates.

The asshole had buried my homework.

"You gotta be kidding me!" I cried, clutching my head in panic. I whirled around and caught a glimpse of Harnett disappearing around the cabin's corner. "Are you crazy? Wait! Wait!"

In the distance, I heard the front door open and close. The bastard was going back to bed. I was motionless for a moment, resolved to freak out but uncertain of the best way to do it, and then sprinted toward Grinder and wrapped both hands around her handle. The ground below was black and wet, barely visible.

"How deep?" I shouted at the cabin. I strained to hear past my heaving breath and pounding heart, but knew it was futile—there would be no response from my father. "Oh fuck," I said, twisting the handle between my hands. "Oh fuck, oh fuck."

I grabbed Grinder and pulled. She unstuck from the moist dirt and hummed in my hands. My mind was spinning. I had asked for this. I had insisted that he teach me. This was what I got for allying myself with a maniac. I kicked aside the more delicate tools of a backsaw and spade. Harnett's rules could go to hell. I had no time for fussiness and no stake in anything beyond rescuing my calculus.

The digging hurt, but not as much as before. Four feet later I struck something and instantly dropped to my knees. I tore through the mud with my fingers and after five minutes of grappling dislodged a black garbage bag wrapped around something hard. I reached into the bag and withdrew a flat piece of wood, apparently inserted by Harnett so that Grinder did not damage the homework tucked beneath. I removed the papers and shook them in a muddy, victorious fist.

Sunlight warned me that first period was just minutes away. Fine, I'd miss first period, but not the second, not if I ran. I examined the mud slopped across my clothes and skin, the wet soil oozing from my shoes. Maybe at school I could change into my gym clothes. The idea was so inspired that I felt a tuft of grass fall from my cheek when I grinned.

One hour later, we passed our calculus assignments up the row and I watched as Coach Winter flipped through them. It was obvious when he reached mine—from the back of the room I could see the muddy smears—and for a moment I thought he was going to reject it on standards of cleanliness. He glanced at me over the top of the papers, taking in the soiled shirt and jeans I had not found time to swap with my gym equivalents, and decided that berating me wasn't worth the effort. He went back to shuffling assignments and I felt it for the second time that morning: victory.

Good luck continued at Fun and Games, which kicked off with an activity that was neither. Akin to a sack race, it involved standing back to back with a partner, locking elbows, and attempting to execute a number of ridiculous tasks, like picking up kick balls and ducking beneath a limbo bar.

Partners were switched up twice and both times I feared getting paired with Celeste or Foley. Instead my first partner was Heidi Goehring, an honor roll student with a questionable bowl cut but cool, chunky glasses. From what I had gleaned, Heidi kept her nose out of trouble and in the books; she would nevertheless appreciate the social darts that would fly her way if she mishandled her moments with Crotch. But she hesitated for only a moment before smiling and offering her elbows. We tripped around the gym like idiots, laughing a little more freely each time we ended up on our asses, and though the whole thing was too stressful to qualify as enjoyable, there were moments when I forgot everything except that only two thin pieces of fabric separated me from a real live girl. I fantasized that, for those brief moments, Heidi Goehring might have shared similar thoughts. When we finally unlocked and rubbed feeling back into our muscles, she returned my embarrassed smile. Unable to hold her gaze, I looked away and saw Celeste across the gym, somehow looking dignified even through this debasement.

Any residual sensation of contentment vanished once we had adjourned to the locker rooms. Guys gave Woody hell about Celeste, wondering how sore his wrist was getting in her absence. "Guess she's too busy spending all her time playing fun and games with Crotch here," Rhino laughed.

Woody's glare was ferocious.

"We're starting to wonder what *kind* of crotch you got under there, Crotch," he snarled.

I pulled on my pants as quickly as I could. Rhino broke the silence by smacking Woody on the back and joking about how my menstrual cycle would probably align with the girls' soon, while another guy flapped his wrist and tittered about what fun I'd have trading tampons with all of them. Usually such cracks broke the dark mood, but this time they hounded me back into the gym, where Celeste, Heidi, Foley, and everyone else got to observe the continued slurs. Retribution boiled in Woody's throat; this was just the beginning of what he had planned for me. When at last the bell rang, the abuse spread through the halls like contagion. After such a victorious morning, it was a crushing reminder that I did not and would not ever belong.

Ted had cautioned me that I couldn't miss another

practice and still play at Friday's homecoming game, but compared to the memory of my mother's take-no-prisoners tone, his warnings were ineffective. When I got home I leaned against Grinder and pretended the river was Lake Michigan and my mom was next to me, her arm angled protectively about my shoulders, her fingernails biting into my arm. Momentous sobs caught in my chest. Harnett could not protect me as she had. I missed her so much.

He arrived at dusk. After dropping his gear inside, he wandered around the cabin and approached, stopping ten feet away to cross his arms. I tightened my grip on Grinder and considered the dirt at my feet.

"Don't start," I said.

He shrugged. "It was a terrible hole and you know it."

"Don't fucking start with me, Harnett." I swung the shovel. Grinder sliced at the hard ground and rang when she hit violently off-center.

Harnett narrowed his eyes in disapproval. "If you didn't notice, our cabinets are empty. We need food. We need money. What we *need* is to get up to Lancet County and do the Merriman grave. But look at you. You're not even close to ready."

I made another frustrated stab with Grinder. Harnett winced at the clang of metal.

"You don't know what I've been through," I growled.

"You had to get up a couple hours early. You had to use a shovel. That qualifies as hard labor?"

"School!" My voice broke in half.

He paused. "School."

"Yeah, school. The place where I go to get tortured every day? Ever heard of it?"

His puzzled, almost innocent confusion drove me mad. I

brayed and drove Grinder with all my might. The flat surface of the shovel hit square and a great jolt shook through my skeleton. The pain was instant and I backpedaled. Grinder fell into the grass, her wooden handle split into three shards.

My father sped forward and kneeled. He lifted the broken wood and tenderly rolled it across his palm.

"Grinder," he said. "She broke."

"It was old," I said, trying to tamp down the horror. "It was old, it's not my fault."

He peered up at me as if incredulous that I could possess this kind of strength. "I've had her for a very long time," he whispered. "Twenty-six years."

I wiped my face with a sleeve. "Well, now you got me."

He toyed with the wood for a moment longer, pressing together the edges as if harboring a fantasy of repair. Then his shoulders fell and the pieces dropped to the grass. He wiped his palms.

"Tell me," he said.

"Tell you what?"

He blinked up at me. "School."

The river roared.

I opened my mouth but had no idea what came next.

He watched me. The setting sun colored him red.

"It's hard," I said. Without the shovel to hold me up I battled collapse. "Every day since I came here. It's so hard."

"You study all the time."

"That's not what I mean," I said. "Studying doesn't matter. That's not school. That's something else. That's . . . paperwork."

"You're unsatisfied in some way."

I laughed once. "Yeah, I guess you could say that. I'm unsatisfied. That's one way to put it." I looked out over the golden treetops. "Everyone there is against me. I don't know why. They do things to me. They embarrass me. You have no idea. You have no idea." I pressed my eyelids against the tears that wanted to return.

"Good," said Harnett.

I peeked out at him in disbelief.

"These people at your school." He shrugged. "They're not supposed to understand us."

"Us?"

He nodded. "Diggers."

I sniffed up the snot the tears had thickened. "What does that have to do with anything?"

He clasped his hands. "The world is full of pain. Everyone you see there is hurting from it. That principal I had to speak to? And his assistant?"

"Simmons and Diamond," I said automatically.

"They eat pain for breakfast. You can't stand next to them without expecting it to rub off. You're unhappy there. I'm not surprised. I don't think it's possible to be happy in proximity to such people. I've never found it possible. But beneath?" He touched a finger to the ground. "Beneath is a different story. There's no pain down there. You remember that woman. You sat next to her. You touched her. Her life was pain, too, but down there all that was gone. Remember?"

I said nothing.

Harnett fanned a hand through the grass like he was petting an animal. "There are things down there you wouldn't expect, kid. Solace. A little bit of power. There's so much to be had down there, and everyone," he said, waving a hand at the sky, "everyone is reaching up, up." His caressing fingers became a fist that pounded once upon the dirt. "They're reaching in the wrong direction."

He gathered the splinters of Grinder, the shovel he had used since long before I was born, and stood. We were an arm's length apart and for just a moment I thought about reaching out.

"That hole you dug," he said. "It was a terrible hole."

"I didn't have time."

"The hell you didn't." He walked away. Near the corner of the cabin, he looked over his shoulder. "It was terrible and you know it."

"Okay," I croaked. "It was terrible."

Late that night, as I tossed with nightmares, I thought I heard my father rustling through the forest and the halting sounds of lesser tools digging a hole; and finally, even later, the bone rattle of Grinder's pieces being tossed into a shallow depression, the great burier buried at last.

28.

AND SO THE LESSONS began in earnest. I spent the next night writing a paper for Gottschalk, only to find it five feet under at dawn. Harnett was there, nudging my sleeping body with his toes and thrusting into my hands a brand-new shovel with a gleaming silver blade. The shovel was mine to name, he told me, if and when inspiration struck. When I complained that I had no clue what one was supposed to name a shovel, he told me only that I would know when the time came. He ceased complaining about the Merriman grave in Lancet County; instead he offered me an onion from the garden as he bit into one of his own. I declined. Fifteen minutes later,

I dug for my life while he squatted a ways away, staring into the trees and eating.

"Dying is a tragedy," he lectured from the darkness. "Death, though—death is just science. When we're dead, A happens, then B happens, then C. None of it's pretty. When the embalmers, those crooks, when they get their hands on us, they do their worst. They suture our anuses to keep everything inside. Kid, I'm just telling you how it is. But they can't stop science."

Science—Gottschalk's paper. I set my muscles to the rhythm of Harnett's speech and doubled down.

"A wooden casket, six months after it's gone under, we're talking about some body discoloration, maybe some mold. An airtight job, same amount of time, and we're looking at the kind of mess we saw the other night. Those caskets are ridiculous. The inner liner's bolted, the outer liner's cemented shut, and sometimes they put the whole thing inside a concrete vault. And then they bury it five feet down? You should be asking yourself what's the point of all this nonsense. Who are they protecting the body from? It can't be rain, it can't be decay—they both find their way in anyway. It's us, kid. After all these years, it's still us."

I found better ways into the dirt, new angles of attack, cunning trajectories.

"Was a time when the opposite held true. Everyone was scared of being buried alive and wanted an easy route out. Coffins had gadgets, little rods attached to bells above the earth, mausoleums with switches inside to activate lights and buzzers. You can sort of sympathize. Medicine wasn't what it is today. Mistakes were made. Imagine disinterring a loved one and finding the underside of the lid covered with their scratches."

There were animal bones down there, graves within graves.

"Why bury them in a box at all? Good question. Why put them in clothes? Funeral directors run up bills into the millions just dressing up corpses and poisoning the dirt with chemicals. We Diggers are ecologists by nature, kid; if I could, I would remove every body and plant it naked back in the dirt. Composting is the ideal. Instead we pay three thousand bucks for a four-by-five-by-seven plot, a plot that can get sold out from under us if the cemetery gets lazy setting aside their twenty percent for upkeep. There's a funeral director in Michigan who held a body for four years while he sued the family over a late payment. It's disgusting. Disgusting. Cemeteries are more profitable than farms."

My homework was in my hands but it would not reach Gottschalk in time—I had another assignment still in progress, and had yet to erase my traces.

"It almost seems like revenge, then, doesn't it, that heirlooms are buried to keep them out of the hands of others? But it's not revenge. It's pride. It's belief in some awards-based system of afterlife. That is self-aggrandizement taken to fanatical levels. Sure, it has a historical basis. Fine. As do we. So they will keep giving and we will keep taking. It's the natural order of things. The earth should be kept clean."

He took a moment to observe how I poured dirt back into the hole.

"You would be exposed in one day," he grunted. "One hour."

It was true. I made what pitiful repairs I could and slunk off to school. Gottschalk received the paper over lunch period and he gloated over its lateness. He took out his red pen in front of me so that I would see its bloody point. Next time,

I promised myself—next time I would dig faster. No assignments were due the following day, so that evening Harnett had to get creative. After dinner I dug for my shoes by flashlight. My initial reluctance faded when I recognized that studying was studying—biology, calculus, digging, any one of them might become my future. I sank my naked toes into the cold dirt. As I labored, Harnett sat cross-legged in the grass with a bowl of noodles. He had rubber-banded a crinkled sheet of red transparency over the end of my flashlight; apparently that made it harder for human eyes to see the beam. I dug through an alien planet of purple grass and crimson dirt. My father ate and talked about the newspapers.

"The *Crafton Legion*. The *Tri-County Bobcat*. The smaller the paper, the better; details get loose, editors get sloppy. I don't fault them for this. I admire it. These are real people who know how to mourn. So. Start with the obituaries. Read the names. Go with your gut. Janvier: yes. Fitzbutton: no. Know your history. Family names have legacies. There was a fire in 'eighty-nine that killed three generations of Wilkins. It was hard to go to work that day—I had followed so many of them into so many graves. I gave them one month. When I saw them again, they did not look good. Burn victims rarely do."

Smaller shovel strokes at acute angles. Finally I saw the logic.

"Look at the spelling. Smith: no. Smythe with a *Y:* oh, yes. Look at the middle names for clues. Wadsworth. Whittaker. Middle names are what really reveal a family, what they are proud of, what they are ashamed of, how old parents were when their kids were born—an important fact if you think about it for even a second. Now look for the spouse. An entirely new surname to cross-reference. Children, too, same paragraph. He leaves behind three children. Get their names.

And be wary of exotic spellings: *Kayleigh* with all sorts of useless letters. Weigh the variations. Surviving her is her daughter Katherine. Kathleen. Kathy. Katie. Kate. Kat. Kay. Say these names aloud. You know them from school. Picture these girls. Picture Christmas morning. Picture the gifts. Notice rings on hands, how Christmas lights sparkle on new jewelry."

By my red light I passed through soil horizons I had learned about in school: surface soil, subsoil, substratum. I'd studied hard and knew what to expect.

"How old was he or she when he or she died? This one's easy. A lot easier than calculus, kid. If they died young, don't lose hope. Parents are weird with dead kids. They will weigh them down with mementos. I'm not sure why. Maybe it's an offering so that their other kids don't die the same way. And also: how recent was it? Because under most circumstances it's unwise to bother a grave people are still visiting daily. These kinds of mourners notice everything. They take pictures. They bring gardening gloves and shears. I've seen people bring their own push mowers. Be patient. Obits are like sales leads, except these leads never grow cold."

I found my shoes six feet deep and wrapped in plastic. I treated them like flesh, lifting them with utmost care.

"Obits love nicknames, get used to it. Some of them seem redundant. Robert 'Bob' Douglas. Others demand attention. Jeffrey 'The Bulldozer' Wallace. Herman 'The Monkey Man' Hansen. Laura 'Spanky' Hopkins. A girl called Spanky—do I need to draw you a picture? Do not bother with this grave. Unless she is old money, and then make haste. It's easy to get bogged down with details. The papers will tell you what church they went to. Forget it. They will tell you which local schools they attended. Forget it. Sometimes they'll tell you what their favorite book was. This is rare but helpful. Use your head. This part isn't rocket science."

I saw for the first time how soil fits back together in a kind of order. It filled me with happiness.

"Most obits don't give home addresses. If they do, sure, go ahead, do a drive-by. Also, don't forget: every story has a writer. Get to know each newspaper staff. Often rookies get the death desk, even interns. That doesn't do us much good. But true mom-and-pop outfits? You want to run an obit for your granddad, you write it yourself, mail it in, and they'll print it. This is when things get interesting. Hyperbole kicks in, or a devastating lack of it. Grale Gompers. *He ran the most successful salted cracker company in the Midwest.* Or: *He worked at a factory*. That hurts. That's not an obit, that's a middle finger. *He had three beautiful children who attended Stanford, Yale, and Princeton*. Versus: *He had several kids*. It's not whether he was loved or hated. It's whether he was loved or hated and by whom and when, and what that means about what was put under the dirt. If you need to, take notes in the margin."

The sod swathed the filled hole like a bad toupee. I still had a lot to learn.

"Last thing. The picture. Sometimes there will be a picture. It's usually a snapshot of some sentimental value. Listen up: almost never will it match the text. The text may speak of a man of means: you'll see an old geezer in pj's. The text may hint at abuse and disorders: you'll see a bow tie and champagne. So ignore it. Pictures are not facts, they are fleeting instants with little meaning. Cut it out with a scissors if you have to. Because you don't need it and you don't want to know, trust me. You don't want to know what they looked like."

That night I set my aching back against the sink and picked

at the dirt under my fingernails. My mind raced and everything came out jumbled. Was it Harnett torturing me in gym class? Was it Gottschalk thrusting a shovel into my hands? What day was it? What month? I clung to Friday because I knew it was homecoming, but that wasn't enough and the idea of a calendar disgusted me. How could I bear to see all those school days still to come, blank white squares marching forth in their patient infinity? Then I thought of what Harnett said about hatch marks left inside a coffin by someone buried alive. It was a feeling I understood. Taking a knife from the counter, I carved the first hatch mark on the side of the sink, where Harnett was unlikely to see it. This was exactly how I wanted to conceive of my new life: a past scratched down in memory of my mother and a future that could still lead me anywhere.

29.

"TRANSLATED FROM THE LATIN meaning 'carrying-away vessel,' the vas deferens, the duct that transports sperm to the urethra, is not present in all species of animal, though it is most certainly present in Mr. Crouch here. Although clothing impedes us somewhat, you can see from the indication of my pointer the location of the penis, and, slightly moving southward now, the scrotum. Now, the scrotum— My apologies, Mr. Crouch, for that tap, which apparently was a bit vigorous. As I was saying, the scrotum houses the testes, something hopefully all of you know by now, and coiled near the back of the testes is the epididymis, which connects the efferent ducts—remember the efferent ducts, class, from the quiz you all did so poorly on?—which connects the efferent ducts to the vas deferens, somewhere approximately right here. Again, apologies, Mr. Crouch. Folks, let's keep the laughter at a reasonable level. Very good. Now, let's follow the path. During the onset of ejaculation, the sperm travels from *here*—apologies—through the smooth muscle walls of the deferens in what is known as peristalsis, until it gathers *here*—once more, apologies—in the urethra, collecting secretions from the bulbourethral and prostate glands, until the flow of semen is expelled from *here*—and now I fear that my wrist has a mind of its own because it seems as if Mr. Crouch is approaching a fetal position. It is not my wish to perform an accidental vasectomy, so perhaps I ought to let our volunteer take his seat. His reaction is, however, worth noting. It is a sensitive bundle of parts, the male genitalia, certainly not anything you want someone striking repeatedly with a metal rod. Although if that person is yours truly, a teacher trained in all things anatomical, then one might hope such a teacher knows what he is doing. One might hope. Now, now, boys and girls, I appreciate the show of enthusiasm, but let's at least attempt to keep the volume to a low roar."

30.

Fun and Games continued to the superhit stylings of Richard Marx and Wang Chung. The latest game involved an enormous beach ball and a volleyball net, but I had successfully convinced Stettlemeyer to let me sit this one out on account of a "stomachache." Gottschalk had only connected two or three times, but the tip of his pointer was equal to a Rhino kick any day. I crouched against the bleachers, my midsection aching, and watched Woody on his way to the weight room. He smiled at Celeste and then at me, though the qualities of the smiles were vastly different.

Stettlemeyer blew the whistle and the game began. I leaned my head back and counted. Five hundred and seventy-one seconds later two ratty sneakers approached. It was Foley, my silent partner in this ongoing disgrace, having been rotated out of all the bouncing bullshit.

"Gottschalk got a little personal today," he said.

Foley shared my biology period, though it had taken me half the semester to realize it. My pulse raced as he sat down next to me, but I kept quiet—it was the safest course.

"Supposedly five or six years ago a kid tried to call him on his shit and sued the school for emotional damages. The whole town went ballistic. He's got like ten degrees, so everyone thinks he's God. The lawsuit got dropped and Gottschalk got a raise out the deal. So if you're thinking of appealing to the greater good, think again."

I kept my eyes on the girls. Heidi Goehring had the ball and didn't know what she was supposed to do with it, but I liked how the heat of exercise had turned her cheeks pink.

"I hear what they call you," Foley added.

"Congratulations," I said.

"No need to be a dick. I just have ears."

"Well, that's good information to know. Thanks for that."

"Dick," he said under his breath.

We sat in silence for a moment, listening to the shrieks of the girls and watching the beach ball twirl across dozens of bright fingernails.

"Ever heard of a power dump?" he asked.

I glanced at him. "No."

"It's when a whole bunch of guys sneak into your house and take a dump in a huge pile. Happened to me in eighth grade. I didn't find it till much later because my mom was driving me back from my dad's. When she saw it she cried like a baby. This was at a different school. Different kids than Woody and Rhino. But basically the same kind of assholes." He snorted. "Literally."

It took me a second but I snorted, too. The echo of that tiny noise swelled, pushing all air from my chest. Laughter—at Bloughton High. Was such a fluke possible to replicate? My brain reeled with words, jokes, enticements that could keep Foley at my side before he remembered that I was lethal. *My name's Joey.* I could at least say that. *Foley, right?* But I had no oxygen, no saliva.

"Anyway," he said, standing up. "There's always gonna be Woodys and Gottschalks. It's just a matter of making yourself so they don't see you. Right?"

And then the next girl rotated out and Foley moved to replace her. I watched him slink away, hoping he'd give me a smirk or raised eyebrow, something that said I was not alone. It was too much to hope for. I did not hold it against him.

31.

FRIDAY, HOMECOMING, AND THE white faces of Bloughton High were striped in red and black. The entire building rattled with artificially induced excitement. The morning's regular schedule was interrupted by a pep rally, during which I sat in with the band as Celeste beat the odds by stealing the crown from her senior counterparts. I found myself pounding my seat along with everyone else. She was our queen, *ours,* which meant, in some little way, she was partly mine, too.

Afterward Ted gave us our mission: bleachers, seven o'clock, fully zipped and buttoned and capped. He looked at me when he said this. I thought about that as I walked back home to grab some dinner and fetch my trumpet—his strange belief in me, his patience. Thirty minutes later I stared out the window and saw a peculiar thing, a man standing in the river.

I carried my sandwich to the riverbank. Harnett was shirtless and waist-deep, his arms floating at his sides, his face turned to the water as if meditating. Suddenly he swiped, his arm cutting through the surface and lifting two razors of spray. I stood transfixed as the fish escaped. Harnett watched it dart away through the depths.

He spoke without looking up. "You've got about two hours."

It was then I noticed the shovel rising diagonally from the rocky bank. I felt a flutter of something in my gut—not despair but the thrill of accepting a challenge. Always a step ahead, my father had buried my trumpet.

It was my first dig on slanted ground. The top of the hole gave way constantly. Rocks fought back against my entry. Principles I'd learned had to be rotated and adapted. I succumbed to the authority of my arms.

"Tell me about her funeral," he said.

"It was small," I said instantly. I wondered how long the two of us had been readying this question and answer.

"How small?"

"My friend Boris and his parents. Some of her work friends. Couple neighbors. I can hardly remember it now." In fact, most of what I remembered involved a spider dangling in the ceiling corner above the casket.

"Why aren't you digging? Keep digging."

I lifted the shovel and jabbed. Roots held possessively to the earth. I frowned and twisted the handle, my palm and fingers tingling with the sensitivity of a safecracker.

"We didn't know a lot of people," I continued. "We hardly ever went out. She had like a thing about going out. She never once crossed the state border, did you know that?"

I heard the glissando of another swipe through water.

"She made me promise," Harnett said when the music faded. "When we went our separate ways, she made me swear never to set foot in Chicago. Despite its value as a territory, I agreed." There was a pause. "I was being shut out, I knew that. I didn't know she was shutting herself in, too—shutting in both of you. Believe me. I had no idea."

Nothing was going right. The hole was eating itself so that I couldn't gain entry. I took to my knees and probed with the shovel and muttered bad words. Mud soaked through my pants, bird shit was all over my arms, and I was in danger of being late to the game. A flash of resentment shot through me. I sent a prayer to Two-Fingered Jesus and spoke.

"The cuts in her ear. That's why she wanted you to stay away. Right? When you said you killed her, that's what you meant. She couldn't hear well and that's why she got hit by the bus." I swallowed. "That's what I figure."

"Don't start figuring too much," he growled. "You've got it in your little head that I pushed her around? Or what? Slashed her with a knife? What happened to her ear—" He cut himself off and I heard a slow intake of breath. "She was right to leave me. I accept that. And I'll take responsibility for all of it. But I never laid a hand on her. You try to remember that, kid."

A light haze of rain began scattering pinpricks into the surface of the river. The impending twilight made him look cut off at the waist, and I thought of the old reverend and his missing leg.

"How do you know Knox?" I asked.

Harnett's dark eyes searched even darker waters.

"We all know Knox," he said after a while.

"But how?"

"He's an old friend of Lionel's."

"Who's Lionel?"

"Lionel taught the trade to me and Boggs."

Now we were getting somewhere. I explored with the shovel but kept an eye on my father. "And who's Boggs?"

Harnett shrugged off the rain.

"No movement can exist entirely in secret," he said. "Knox was a preacher in North Carolina when Lionel was just getting started, before I was born. They grew up together. Knox knows us, all of us, and he travels around, passes word, acts as a messenger of sorts. He doesn't do this as a favor. Quite the opposite. He thinks keeping us connected makes us want to change, like it's a support group—AA or something. He intends to save our souls, every one of us. He's persuasive, too. We've lost quite a few to him over the years."

"Will he come back?"

"Always does." Harnett flicked his eyes from the water for just a moment. "You better keep at it."

I looked at the sloppy hole, the dented shovel, my scrawny limbs, and it seemed an impossible task.

"Knox told me to stay away from Boggs," I said.

"You don't need to worry about that," Harnett said.

"Knox thought I did."

"There are territories." Harnett sighed. "The whole country is divided up. I've got the Midwest. Boggs is way out west. He wouldn't come this far. He wouldn't dare."

Harnett sounded uncertain. It was an unfamiliar inflection and I didn't like it. Quickly I tightened my grip on the shovel and tried to clear my mind. I lifted the handle high, aimed, and closed my eyes.

"This Boggs guy," I heard myself say. "What exactly did he do?"

The shovel blade whistled as it flew, cleanly severing a tree root thicker than my wrist. In that instant, everything clicked into clockwork perfection: my sweaty palms molded to the lacquered wood so that bone and tool were of one body. *The Root,* I told myself with assurance and satisfaction. *That is my shovel's name.*

Praise was what I wanted and I turned to the river, the Root raised victorious, my face askew in a grin. For a moment I saw the cresting of a slick belly and a webbed fin, and then a fish squirmed through Harnett's fingers. He put his hands on his hips and turned toward me, panting in the rain with a look more menacing than any I'd seen since the day I'd arrived in Bloughton. My elation dimmed. I made the connection.

Boggs had something to do with my mother.

I did the only thing I could. I dug. My muscles strained against the weight of the wet dirt. I gave in to it: the riverbank patting my knees, the Root's handle rubbing my shoulder, the rain mussing my hair—it was as if she were right there. I worked faster. Mud flew and my ears recorded every splat so I could retrieve it later. I was at the trumpet case in mere minutes, and as I began to shove the hole back together, I became aware that Harnett stood just behind me, struck mute by my surge of power. I finished the work, panting, and squinted up at him through the rain. His eyes glowered at me, and then glinted jealously at the Root. He jutted his chin at my trumpet case.

"Take it out," he said.

I tried to catch my breath. "What?"

"You're in such a hurry," he said. "Some great big hurry to get to some sporting event. Or else it's some practice every goddamn day after school. While we have things to do, the Merriman grave, you're busy with this piece of tin. So get it out."

"Why?"

"Because I want to hear this thing that's causing me so much trouble."

Each latch on the case weighed one hundred pounds. I scooped away the mud. Inside, the brass was tawny and water-spotted. The mouthpiece fought against insertion.

"Play," he said.

"It needs tuned," I muttered.

"Pick it up and play."

I mashed my lips in frustration; it was just coincidence that this was also the right comportment for playing. The instrument was cold against my lips. Rain made impatient noises against the metal.

"What am I supposed to play?"

"I don't care," he said. "Something easy."

All I could remember was the Bloughton Screaming Eagles fight song. As inappropriate as it seemed, it was at least fantastically easy: G, C, F, F, G, C, F, F, A.

I licked the rain from my lips and blew. G, C, F, F—and then trouble, the wrong note. I backed up: F, F—and two fingers fought for the same button. I shook the rain from my shoulders. This was something I could play in my sleep. F, F—and the next note split into octaves. Harnett's expression rested somewhere between bemusement and loathing. F, F—and here I hesitated too long, so I looped around as if to gain speed before leaping: F, F, F, F, F. Harnett openly smirked now, the black and gray bristles of his beard twisting cruelly. My muddy hands shook; cold rain streamed down my back; my lips reddened and bled: F, F, F, F, F. Now I saw what Harnett was saying—this whole thing was a farce. My lungs and lips stuttered like a child so aggrieved he can't get out his first sob: F, F, F, F, F, repeated until it was the sound of our breathing, the thump and squirm of our organs. It was the saddest of father/son theme songs, and no coincidence for either of us that the letter it was based upon stood for failure.

32.

I HEARD THE BAND before I got there. Slowly I pushed my face into the chain-link fence and gazed across the field. Moths attacked the massive lights, which scribbled white commas on wet helmets. The bleachers smelled like popcorn and ketchup and sounded like the biggest family in the world. With the exception of one garbageman, the entire town of Bloughton had turned out; I spotted the trench-coated Principal Simmons and his wife; a row back, eyeing them, Vice Principal Diamond; I found the long-suffering Laverne as far from the two of them as possible, huddling with three pipsqueak kids beneath a Screaming Eagles blanket; I didn't find Heidi or Foley, but found my mother over and over before realizing that the lips were different, the hair too short, the left ear lacking the telltale notches.

Even from a distance I could tell that getting wet was not for Ted. His conducting was stiff and fussy. *You think this is tough?* I wondered of him. *Try digging a forty-five-degree, five-foot hole in the side of a rocky riverbank.* I made the same challenge to Woody and Rhino and Coach Winter, all of whom stood beleaguered and winded on the sideline. At halftime, the band played while Celeste Carpenter and her four-woman homecoming court were escorted onto the field by a group of guys in alphabetic jackets. My view shifted and I found myself fantasizing about the dazzling green grass of the thirty-yard line, as yet untouched by cleats. My free hand instinctively flexed: the Root could cut through that turf as if it were cream.

Sometime during the second half I trudged home, my new white uniform gray with mud from passing cars, my trumpet case squeaking with each step. Harnett was waiting. With a pair of scissors he pointed to an overturned bucket. I sat and felt his rough fingers gather a handful of wet hair at my nape. I heard the snicker of metal and felt the blades slide cold against my skin, the damp segments of hair tickle down the back of my shirt. "I bet you name your scissors, too," I muttered. Through his calloused thumbs I thought I felt the vibration of laughter; he rotated my scalp an inch so that I could see the Root where he had placed it, fully cleaned, right next to the door.

33.

FOLEY SHOOK A FORK free from a thatch of interlocked utensils and tossed it onto his tray. The cafeteria smelled like overcooked beef.

"It's just the way it is here," he was saying. "People attack anything. You have to not care."

"But I do care."

"Then you have to learn to act like you don't."

We shuffled another few feet, waiting for our turn at the steaming vats. "I try," I said. "But now that they hate me, it's like they won't ever let up."

"They'll let up when you stop making it so interesting," he said. "After I got power-dumped in middle school, they all called me Feces Foley. A name like that, you'd think it'd stick, right? And for a while it did, until I just embraced it. I even wrote it on my assignments: 'Why Erosion Matters, by Feces Foley.' And bang, it went away."

"You think I should sign my papers *Joey Crotch*?"

"Why not? You gotta own it, man. You're Joey Crotch. Joey Motherfuckin' Crotch! And I'm Feces Foley! We're like a kick-ass band. Joey Crotch and the Feces Foley Experience."

I considered this. "Huh."

"Yeah, *huh*. Look, I became invisible there, and when we moved here, I just did the same thing, easy as hell. You can do it, too. You've got to. That's what it's all about—being totally nothing until college. That's where you start existing, not here." He lowered his head and sniffed through the steamed glass. "Gimme a hunk of corn bread."

I nodded at the cook. "Me too."

"And what the fuck happened to your hair?" Foley asked, tucking away a strand of his own. "Someone take a lawn mower to that bitch?"

"My dad," I said. A glance in the mirror that morning had properly demoralized me. There were patches cut so close the scalp shone. Other areas sprouted like potted plants. There was nothing I could do but keep my head down, though even that stance posed a problem—my father had carved a bald spot right into the top of my head.

Foley continued. "All those ass-hats are just prejudiced because you're not from around here. This whole place is so unfucking-believably prejudiced. You're fat, you're gay, you're skin's a little darker, you got a weird name. They'll go after anything. And it's not just the kids, either; it's the teachers. It's everyone. Look, this is exactly what I'm talking about!"

Foley pointed at a standard offering of the Bloughton High cafeteria menu, the Meat Po'boy.

"*Po' boy* is racist?" I asked.

"Goddamn straight it's racist," Foley said. He lifted his head to the cook behind the counter. "One Racism Sandwich, please."

The woman glared but served it up. Foley smiled at her. "And a Racism Sandwich for my friend here, too."

My friend. I blinked and moved my feet and lifted my tray for the food and tried to keep breathing. Foley pulled out a black wallet affixed with a metal skull and crossbones, yanked out a few bills, and stuffed the change into black jeans. Black underwear showed through a few premeditated holes, while a black Judas Priest patch dominated the right buttock. Everything Foley wore was black, every day, which I now suspected aided his power of invisibility. Slightly embarrassed by my teal polo and blue jeans, I followed with just a nod to the cashier; I was still on Simmons's free-lunch list.

"Hey!" he shouted. "Where you going?"

I had automatically assumed abandonment and had veered away to search for a seat. But Foley was gesturing me over. My heart thumped and my stomach roiled. I sat down and stared at food I was now totally incapable of eating. Across from me, Foley was already smacking his lips.

"See that kid?" Foley chewed his food and jutted his chin. "Another Racism Sandwich. They used to rail on that kid and call him a homo pretty much constantly."

Being branded as gay was the worst thing that could happen to anyone at Bloughton High. During past lunches, I had witnessed members of Woody's gang casually pause beside this kid and ask with fake earnestness how much he liked the taste of dick on a scale of one to ten. You heard this stuff ten times a day in any high school, so by itself it didn't faze me. What gave me nightmares was the kid's shell-shocked shudders.

Foley moved on, pointing in another direction. "That tall girl there, they've done crazy sexual shit to her just because she's retarded, which is hardly her fault—she's another Racism Sandwich. And that girl over there, Steffie Vick? She's a Racism Sandwich, too. Too fat." Foley shrugged, gauging Steffie's weight. "Guess she's more like a Racism Buffet. But that doesn't excuse what they do to her."

"Me," I suggested.

"Racism Big Mac," Foley agreed, nodding at me earnestly. "Goddamn Racism Happy Meal." We looked at each other for a moment and started laughing. I picked up my po'boy.

" 'Why Civil Liberties Matter to Me, by Feces Foley,' " I said.

"Dick," he muttered. But he was smiling.

We ate in silence for ten minutes, the best ten minutes since a bus hit my mother.

"I'm glad you quit band," he said at last, picking at his teeth with a pinkie.

Trying to quit had felt to me like kicking nicotine must feel to smokers. It also had the same conclusion: it didn't work. The weather had not improved since homecoming night, and by the time I had walked into Ted's rehearsal room earlier that morning, I was cold and wet and shivering. Ted had been there, early as usual, deep in his supply closet.

"I quit," I had told him.

It had been dark in there, yet light had caught his round glasses.

"You've got heaps of talent," he said.

Of course you'd say that, I thought.

"You're a good performer."

So are you.

"I hope your father didn't put you up to this."

You wish it were that easy.

"This saddens me, Joey."

You don't know sadness, I thought, remembering what the trumpet had meant to my mother. It was a sentiment worthy of someone ancient and weary. Yet my outward reactions were those of a child: I shrugged and tried to flee.

"Don't take another step."

Ted's voice had deepened considerably. I turned around at the entryway.

"You don't want to be in Ted's Army, fine," he said. "You might have your reasons, and I suppose it's even possible those reasons are valid. But I'm not going to have it on my conscience that something I did drove away a player like you. So here's what's going to happen. You and I, we're going to keep practicing."

I blinked at him.

"Nothing to say? Well, that's just as well. I'm prepared to say everything. You come in when you can make it. Most days I'm here from six-thirty in the a.m. until six-thirty in the p.m. You show up at either end of that spectrum and I'm all yours. We'll practice. You and me. Just to practice. All unofficial, whenever you have the time. If there's some peer pressure involved in your decision, forget about it—they don't have to know. If you're following some parental edict, Joey, listen to me. Parents don't always know best."

Boris would have insisted I take the offer, but I doubted that I could any longer achieve a song other than F, F, F, F, F.

Ted nodded. "It's settled, then. You come by when you can. I'll be here. And if anyone asks either of us, we just tell them the truth: Joey Crouch quit."

He raised an eyebrow and waited. It was beyond my powers to disassemble such an unimpeachable plan, so I just nodded. He made a shooing gesture, returned to restocking his closet, and then spoke with his back still turned.

"What are you still doing here? Go, go, go, go, go."

So, yes, I had quit, though only in a manner of speaking. I hated to begin my friendship with Foley with a lie. But what other options were there?

"Because, no offense, but band was part of your problem," Foley continued. "Everyone goes to your stupid football games, we're all required to attend your gay pep rallies and supergay assemblies, and you've all got those megagay costumes and big-time-gay hats. That ain't helpin'. You don't seriously like that music anyway."

"I like jazz," I said.

"I suppose you also like shuffleboard and prunes." He closed his eyes and shook his head. "You don't like jazz."

"I do," I insisted.

"You just think you do," he said. "You don't know any better. No offense. But no one's shown you what real music is. I think you're ready for something a little more aggressive. Welcome to high school, Joey Crotch."

I thought about some of the jazz players Boris and I had listened to who had sounded plenty aggressive to me, like Peter Brötzmann and Mats Gustafsson, but I kept my mouth shut. The Judas Priest patch on Foley's butt was my only clue. "Like Judas Priest?"

He shrugged. "For starters. There's a whole underworld of bands out there that will smash your fucking face in with their fucking boots," he said, his eyes shining. "Music that will rip out your rectum and stuff it down your throat."

"Great," I said.

He pointed a finger at me. "I'm gonna post you some tracks."

"We don't have a computer."

"Then I'll burn you some discs."

"We don't have a player."

He ducked his head in exasperation. "I've got an old Discman. I'll give you the damn thing. Just listen to the CDs. Keep an open mind. And prepare to kneel at the steel throne of the mighty bloodbeast." He raised his pointer and pinkie fingers, both slick with po'boy grease, and attached the makeshift horns to his thrashing forehead, his blond locks swishing about his grimacing face. I couldn't help laughing.

The laughter became a choke. Someone was tapping on my shoulder. Black shirt, brown sweater, pale skin—it was

Heidi Goehring. I choked some more, for a moment imagining slobbery bits of my po'boy landing upon her thick glasses. Amazingly, instead of flinching she only smiled politely and swished her strange bowl cut at a nearby table.

"Joey, you're the only one who could've possibly answered the bonus questions," she said.

I shrugged in wretched bewilderment.

She arched her eyebrows. "Calculus?"

Yes! Calculus! I nodded with enthusiasm. Though we didn't share periods, we both suffered through Coach Winter's shaky stabs at education, and almost daily I saw Heidi poring over her textbooks during lunch. Usually she was with a few friends, other honor roll girls with their homework fanned alongside their food, but today the seats around her were empty. And I was being summoned.

I glanced at Foley. He eyed Heidi suspiciously but said nothing.

"Okay," I said to her. "All right. Okay. All right."

As if by teleportation I found myself sitting down next to her, and out of her mouth were spilling the letters and numbers that made up that week's extra credit. She pointed and asked questions. I found myself shaking my head and correcting her. She groaned and called herself stupid. I told her not to feel bad, it was a tough one. Her thin lips twisted into a satirical smile and she peeked through the sides of her glasses.

"Okay, smarty," she said. "Let's do the next one."

As I led her through the proof, I began to get the feeling that she already knew the answer. Twice I made nervous mistakes and she was quick to fix them. I thanked her sincerely for her assistance, which just made her chuckle some more.

The whole thing was making me feel dangerously relaxed. I glanced at Foley to make sure he still existed and that this whole day wasn't a dream.

He was frowning in another direction. I followed his gaze and found Celeste sitting at a table, gabbing with friends. A few seats away, Rhino, demolishing food with his ponderous jaw. Next to him, Woody Trask, still cruelly separated from his girlfriend, cracking his knuckles over an ignored tray of food and staring directly at Heidi and me.

"What's wrong?" Heidi's finger hovered over a differential equation.

"No," I said. "I mean, nothing." I felt the focused heat of Woody's concentration. "I should probably go eat."

"Oh." She sounded offended. "It's not like Winter curves these things."

She thought I was trying to protect my grade point? That was all wrong, but my tongue was inferior to the task of sorting it out. The chair coughed as I stood.

"Who are you looking at?" she asked. To my horror, she twisted herself around to search the cafeteria. I stumbled over the chair trying to extract myself from her table.

Heidi's head whipped back to her homework. She removed her glasses and smoothed down her hair.

"Woody Trask is looking at me," she said in hushed wonder. Whether this statement was meant for me to hear, I didn't know or care. I tripped my way across the floor, my face burning, my chest stinging. I sensed something whip by my face. A mustard-slicked bun bounced off my chest. A brownie vaporized against the back of my head. I didn't bother to check which of Woody's lackeys had done the throwing. All that mattered was how Heidi's kind eyes had lost all interest in me the second she removed those glasses.

I dropped into place across from Foley and pointed my face at my cooling po'boy.

Almost immediately Foley's tray screeched from the table. I looked up and met eyes that had gone dark and guarded. I wanted to say something. He didn't know what this single lunch had meant to me—tonight when I carved the day into the side of the sink it would be more than just another line.

"What do you think you're doing?" he hissed. "You like getting kicked around? You want that shit to continue?"

"No," I pleaded. "No."

"I can't help you if you ignore every fucking thing I say."

"I'm sorry," I said. "I didn't know he was watching, I didn't know—"

"I'll bring those CDs." His formerly buoyant voice wilted with sarcasm and distrust. He peered down at me as he passed. "You got brownie in your bald spot."

34.

Nathaniel Merriman was buried in Lancet County, Iowa, just south of the Minnesota border. Harnett and I arrived at about four in the afternoon. We left our tools in the truck and wandered together onto the main path. The Lancet County Cemetery had no fence, but we paused at the sign stating the house rules: no pets, no littering, closed at sundown. Nothing at all about digging up bodies.

Just enough daylight remained to make a pass of the plot. But as soon as we crossed the threshold I was deluged with memories of the suicide victim bloating in her pool of black liquor, and within instants I began specifying—

—*golden specks of pyrite embedded in the stony path*—
—*the scabby contours of damp tree bark*—
—*shrubbery knotted in the shapes of hands, pitchforks, jester hats*—
—*ants squeezing from a hill like pus from a wound*—

—and soon swirled within a heightened reality of such absurd levels that I began to totter. Harnett righted me by the collar and told me to look about solemnly as if I were hunting for a loved one's grave. Eager for a good grade, I frowned and tossed my head in a frenzied search.

"Easy," Harnett said. "You look like you're having a seizure."

The gravestoned horizon was an exposed jaw of foul teeth. We instinctively hugged a row of mausoleums, their barred doors allowing slivered glimpses of stained glass and locked drawers. Breaking into these, I realized, would not involve any digging. I whispered my brainstorm to Harnett.

"First off," he responded in a fake conversational tone, "whispering like that it makes it look like we're planning to rob a grave or something."

"Sorry," I whispered. He glared and I tried again more casually: "I'm sorry."

He gestured at one of the crypts. "They're usually not worth the effort. You chip a lot of cement and bend a lot of iron and break a lot of glass. There's no time to repair that mess, and that's the most important thing, kid, the most important thing of all: never let them know you were there."

"Duh." I said it because I could feel the security cocoon of my specifying wear away, and beneath, waiting patiently, was the dead woman, her maggot eyes, the chasms of her slashed wrists. Quickly I scanned the cemetery for Two-Fingered Jesus and thought I saw him proselytizing to huddled stones.

"You want to spend a few years in prison?" Harnett asked with a fake cheer that emphasized his ill temper. "Either of us gets caught and it's third-degree criminal mischief. And that's progress. A hundred years ago, you'd be strung up by your neck and publicly whipped. If you think something similar isn't possible today, then you're reading the wrong newspapers."

The pathway forked. Harnett paused to gauge each path's twists.

"How old is the Merriman grave?" I asked.

"Been under two years."

"Why'd you wait so long?"

"Wasn't listed in the obits. Had to piece it together from other sources."

This meant there would be no fresh mound, no telltale bouquets. "So what, we're going to read every single gravestone to find it?"

"Open your damn eyes." He pointed at the ground. "See that?"

"Sure." I paused. "I see grass and leaves."

Harnett chose a path and charged ahead. He pointed at another seemingly random patch of ground. "Okay, there. See?"

I saw only more grass and leaves and told him so.

He pushed a hand through his hair. "New graves rise slightly. You know this. After some time, though, the opposite happens, they settle and sink." He pointed yet again. "When leaves fall, they come right out and *tell* you where to look, they practically hand you the bodies. If you can't see this then you better wait in the truck."

The subtle clue, when I finally noticed it, was repeated all over: leaves caught in gentle depressions otherwise imperceptible to the naked eye. It would be the same with thawing snow, I realized with a surge of excitement. This was what Diggers did—they used nature's clues to solve mankind's puzzles.

Encouraged, I picked up speed and unexpectedly collided with Harnett. Pain burst through my nose. He whirled around and dropped into a praying position before a random grave.

"Damn, Harnett." I rubbed my injured nose.

"Get down here," he said.

I read aloud the name on the stone. "Oliver Lunch." I snorted. "Nice name."

"Will you get down?"

I kneeled and dutifully tried to summon images of Sundays at church with my mother. Nothing came to me. Harnett sneaked a glance over his shoulder and then retreated to Oliver Lunch. "You never know what you're going to get, kid."

I took the cue to peek over my shoulder. In the fading light, at the top of a nearby hill, a woman in a black dress embraced a shiny obsidian gravestone, her posture of genuine grief putting our feigned sorrow to shame. Even at this distance it was clear she was sobbing. I blinked at Harnett.

"I thought you said it'd been two years," I said.

"It has been. To the day."

It dawned on me. "The anniversary."

He shook his head and exhaled. "Well, shit."

We quietly returned to the truck, sat in the cab for ninety minutes until the sun had sunk, and then grabbed our gray sacks and moved quietly back through the cemetery. When we reached Oliver Lunch, Harnett again put on the brakes. My hand flew to my abused nose; he gripped my arm and pulled me from the path.

"Well, *shit*."

"*Damn,* Harnett," I complained, checking my nostrils for blood. "What, she's still there?"

His shape in the darkness nodded. Nearby was a mausoleum the size of Harnett's cabin, and together we squatted against a wall. Once my eyes adjusted I found the grieving woman, still draped across Nathaniel Merriman's marker and uttering occasional soft noises.

"She can't stay there all night," I said. "Can she?"

Harnett did not respond.

I crossed my arms and snuggled my head into a thin cushion of moss. "Some anniversary."

Harnett locked onto the Merriman mourner. "Sometimes the digs go easier than you'd expect, too. Once I drove across three states to find a diamond tiara a beauty queen had been buried in. The graveyard, when I found it, was going through some sort of septic situation. Ground overrun with mud and sewage. Stones overturned and sinking. It was so bad her skeleton had floated up and she was just sitting there waiting for me, the tiara right on top of her head." His forehead knotted. "Spent all night trying to give her a proper burial, but in that muck? I was just wasting my time."

He settled back against the crypt with a sigh. "This is right where we want to be. Good sight line, a posture we can hold for as long as necessary, up against a structure we can depend on."

"Depend on for what?"

He glanced at me. "Depend on not to fall down."

I laughed once, quietly, but he was dead serious.

"You think anything in here is kept to some sort of code? You lean against a stone like that woman out there is doing, and you're gambling. Some of them are just barely nudged into the dirt. Some of them, if you haven't noticed, weigh several tons. Things of such size fall over. That's what happened to Copperhead."

"Copperhead," I said. "Was he a Digger?"

Harnett nodded and pointed at a massive twenty-foot cement monolith. "Decided to take a breather against one of those. Crushed his skull. Crushed everything. This was just three, four years ago. Knox told me the police report wrote him off as some kind of drunk." Harnett looked at his hands. "Copperhead never took a drink in his life."

The night stretched on. The clouds wore thin in spots and the thousand points of the Milky Way reflected each one of the markers below. Still the Woman in Black slumped and moaned. After a while her noises were joined by another: my stomach.

"Suck on a stone." Harnett tapped the loose rocks at our feet. "It'll help."

I picked one up and examined it.

"But it's a rock," I said. "It's a dead-person rock."

"Christ almighty." Harnett sighed. "Either your stomach or your mouth is going to wake up every corpse in this yard. Go find some food." He jabbed a thumb toward the cemetery entrance. "Get going."

The darkness in that direction was absolute. Maybe I had misunderstood. "What?"

"We passed a little place. Just around the corner from the truck." He reached into his pocket, rustled around for a moment, and then pressed a twenty into my chest. "Here."

"But, hey, wait."

"I'm serious, kid." He kept his eyes on the woman. "It's going to be a long one."

The place, when I found it, was a tavern barely bigger than the single pool table it housed. A fat man with a ponytail pocketed stripes by himself while a woman with tattoos covering her neck watched sitcoms behind the bar. I coughed to get her attention and asked if they had any food.

"We don't sell food here," she said.

"We got peanuts, Eileen," said the man.

"We don't got any peanuts, Floyd!" she yelled with surprising ferocity.

"We got pickles," he said.

"Floyd!" She picked up a baseball bat and shook it at him. "We don't got any goddamn pickles!"

He shrugged. "We got jerky."

Eileen set down the bat and looked at me proudly, gently brushing her hair back from her forehead.

"We have *lots* of jerky," she purred.

My pockets crammed with twenty dollars' worth of Slim Jims, I escaped from Floyd and Eileen and plunged back into the purple gloom of the cemetery. I was back at my father's side in minutes and together we peeled cellophane from greasy tubes of meat and chewed. Between swallows, Harnett continued his lessons. He told me about barbershops, next to newspapers the single best source of information on the recently deceased. Whenever possible, he told me, he would get a haircut in an area where newspaper coverage was thin; no self-respecting barber could resist listing everyone he knew who was ailing or recently dead. Before I could complain that I myself would've preferred a barber job to Harnett's home-salon butchery, he continued. "Barbers and Diggers have been intertwined for centuries," he said, noting something called the United Company of Barber Surgeons, begun in sixteenth-century Britain. "Together they were able to get from Parliament the exclusive right to conduct anatomical dissections."

I wagered a guess: "And the Diggers supplied the bodies?"

Harnett just smiled. "In time," he said, though I didn't know if he was responding to my question or just delaying the answer.

Harnett described other important systems, too: the worlds of pawnshops, jewelry brokers, and antiques dealers, and the risks and rewards of associating with each. He told me of brokers who routinely abused Diggers with piddling offers and veiled threats. Reverend Knox—who wanted the Diggers saved and in church, not damned and behind bars—passed along warnings of these blackmailers. The day Knox died, Harnett lamented, the road would become much more treacherous. How would they know, for example, which buyers would purchase gold teeth without asking questions? Or which curio dealers traded in vintage Bibles?

"When Knox is gone," Harnett said, "the money will dry up. And then, for most of us, there will only be Bad Jobs."

"What's a Bad Job?" I asked.

"There are things," he said, gesturing into the blackness, "that people out there will pay you to do. Pay good money for you to do. There are things people want and we are the only ones who can get them. There are other things, too, even worse."

"Like what?"

Harnett ignored the question. "Any Digger who starts down that path, he's pretty well near the end. You can't do those kinds of jobs and live with yourself. I've seen it again and again, Diggers who thought *Just this once, I need the money.* And that was that."

"Suicides?" I whispered.

My father spat out a hunk of bad jerky. "Many."

35.

Light fought rudely toward my pupils. I tasted dirt and cloth—Harnett's shoulder. I sat up quickly, wiping at the drool and tasting the sour crud of Eileen and Floyd's rations.

"Shh," Harnett said.

I rubbed my eyes; pebbles, embedded for hours within the heel of my palm, dropped into my lap. The Woman in Black was still there, curled like a dog on Nathaniel Merriman's plot. An edge of morning sunlight warmed the tops of gravestones and threw black stripes across the gentle slope of the cemetery, but churning across the sky were storm clouds.

"Don't we need to get out of here? It's light; people will see us."

"I've waited too damn long. I'm getting in there."

"But people will see," I insisted.

He looked at me. "People don't see as much as you think."

I opened my mouth to call him on his portentous bullshit, when suddenly he wrapped both arms around me and threw me to the ground. The stink of jerky from his breath filled my sinuses.

A man was walking up the path. Seconds later he glanced our way, but Harnett had successfully concealed us in the shallow ditch at the mausoleum edge. The man continued up the path, his crisp and metered footfalls sounding like Ted's metronome.

Harnett rolled off me and crouched low. I followed suit. The man left the path and crossed over to the Woman in

Black. He got on one knee beside her and shook her gently until she raised her head.

"Okay, that's more like it," Harnett whispered, nodding.

Together, the man and woman looked up at the brewing storm, then appeared to exchange words. Still kneeling, the man stretched out his arms and took the woman into a furious embrace.

"Oh, no," Harnett said.

The man and woman clutched at each other, and their backs shook with the force of their crying.

"You have got to be kidding me," Harnett said.

Moments later, they were both sprawled like toddlers, pawing at Nathaniel Merriman's grave and pushing up tufts of sod with their feet. Harnett cursed and stood, lifting me by my collar and pushing me onto the path ahead of him.

"Where're we going?" I said.

"Breakfast," he growled. "Until these basket cases get their shit together."

We left the cemetery, checked on the truck, passed the bar where I had bought the jerky, and walked down a main street even less exciting than the one in Bloughton. Harnett moved as if he could smell the bacon in the air. I yawned and struggled to keep up. Within five minutes he had sniffed out a diner, and we pushed through the door and fell into opposite sides of a booth. A waitress approached.

I recognized the tattoos instantly. I looked past Eileen and into the kitchen, where the ponytailed Floyd was jabbing a smoking grill.

Eileen's red-painted lips split to reveal two rows of false teeth.

"It's our jerky boy!" she cried. "Floyd, it's our jerky boy!"

"We don't got any jerky," he muttered over the sizzling.

"It's the boy who *bought* the jerky!" she shouted.

"We don't *got* any jerky, crazy woman."

Harnett rubbed his temples. "Two coffees. Two of everything: eggs, bacon, toast, but coffee first."

Eileen made a squiggle on her pad. After some bickering between Floyd and Eileen over Eileen's penmanship, the caffeine arrived and I sipped while Harnett gulped. The whiskers around his mouth darkened.

"Now what?" I ventured.

"Now," he said, swallowing. "Now we wait. We see what kind of rain clouds move in. Or we wait for night. She can't make it another whole night." His hand shook and the surface of his coffee swayed. "No way she can."

For a while nothing interrupted the listless sputter of the grill. No customers came in or out. Eileen and Floyd were silent and unseen.

"So." He eyed me briefly before staring out the window. "School going okay, I guess."

I marveled at his ability to avoid asking a real question. All sorts of responses bubbled to the surface. *Yeah, it's going okay. Only I get drop-kicked in the balls about once a week and an insane teacher stabs me with a metal poker on a routine basis and I've been forced to take trumpet lessons in secret and the only person who even remotely resembles a friend recently suggested that I start referring to myself as Crotch. Aside from that, yeah. It's going great.*

Instead I held my tongue as Harnett rubbed at his pink eyes. I realized that while I had slept and drooled, he had kept watch on both me and the Woman in Black. All at once I felt weak and discouraged—I didn't have it in me, this man's mental and physical stamina. But when he scraped an unsteady hand over his weary face, I also saw that he was getting old. His muscles would soon lose definition. His bones would winnow and weaken. My mother was already gone; I wasn't sure I could take another desertion.

"Yeah, it's going all right," I said.

He nodded out the window. "We'll get you back by Monday morning, don't you worry," he said. "No way she can lie there another whole night. No way."

But after another seven hours spent pacing the stacks at the Lancet County Library, wandering around a hardware store for so long the proprietor began dialing his phone, grabbing another meal from Eileen and Floyd, and sitting silently beneath a gazebo in the town square to watch the ceaseless downpour, we returned to the soggy cemetery at dusk to find the Woman in Black still there, alone and slumped against Nathaniel Merriman's stone. I didn't have to look at Harnett to feel his frustration, nor did I want to—after all, this was all my fault. If Simmons and Diamond hadn't created a situation preventing Harnett from abandoning me, he could've visited Lancet County weeks ago.

We stood against our mausoleum for a minute, our shoes submerging into mud.

"Stay here," said Harnett. "I'm getting our bags. Another hour and she'll be gone. No one lies in the rain at night. I don't care how crazy they are."

It didn't sound as though he believed what he was saying, but regardless, he took off, his narrow shape parting silver curtains of rain. I turned my attention back to the Woman in Black and after only a moment's hesitation began to approach.

She was older than I had guessed, at least my father's age. Up close her body revealed itself to be more bony than slender, and what had looked like fair skin instead was blue and veined. Her black dress clung to some sort of cream-colored undergarment that flopped from below her disheveled hem. Everything she wore was stained; even her hands and neck and face were spotted with mud.

I gripped the cold stone and lowered myself to both knees.

"Hello," I said. The rainfall made it practically inaudible.

Her eyes opened, releasing either rain or tears. Both of her hands automatically contracted, raking in handfuls of mud.

"Daddy," she croaked in a voice coarsened by days of continuous sobbing. Almost magically all the relationships became clear. Nathaniel Merriman was the vaunted patriarch; here writhing on his grave was his daughter. The man who had briefly joined her had been her brother, Merriman's son, though his sorrow had reached limits more quickly. There was no telling why she suffered as she did. Perhaps her father had been tremendously kind to her and the world was repellent in his absence. Perhaps he had been cruel and her lament was for the amends she had been denied. Perhaps he had been missing and she grieved for being cheated of shoulders to grasp and cheeks to kiss. Or perhaps she was lost in pain entirely her own and so reached for a parent as does a small child, as if physical contact, no matter how it is accomplished, will dull the knives.

I reached for her before I knew what I was doing. I withdrew her fingers from the mud and used a palm to wipe grass from her clammy cheek. I felt my heart open to her as it had opened to no one since my mother; I felt a lightness in my chest, releasing me momentarily from the death grip of my current life. Her hands fumbled to my waist, then my shoulders. I felt my lips moving and though I could not hear the words, I knew I told her of Valerie Crouch, also dead and capped with stone like Nathaniel Merriman. I told her of the wonderful arms of my mother, her infinite freckles, the red flip-flops she wore to translucence. I told her of crying on our doorstep when I was ten, afraid that I was going to flunk out of fourth grade, and how my mother had rocked me in her arms like a baby so expertly that I didn't care about the passersby who saw. I told her of pretending to talk in my sleep so that my mother would hear and peek her head in, allowing me to see her face one more time.

The Woman in Black embraced me and shuddered. We might have cried; there was too much rain to tell. When I stood, her frail body rose with me. When I walked, I felt the unsteady pivot of malnourished legs within oversized sockets. When we passed the mausoleum and the hidden figure holding two gray sacks, I held her tighter and felt the brittle cage of her ribs interlock with mine.

Together we left the cemetery. I pushed open the tavern door with my foot and for some reason was not surprised when both Eileen and Floyd glided toward us with open arms and sympathetic smiles. Eileen took the dripping woman from my arms, while Floyd pulled out a chair for her and went for a towel, clicking the coffee maker on the way. I receded until the holiday glow of the bar lights was replaced with the underwater luminosity of a rainy dusk.

My father was four feet deep by the time I returned. I followed the small rivers of water that fell in waterfalls upon his laboring back. He dug with the Root—somewhat awkwardly, as the tool was not his own—and said nothing as pound after pound of mud fell in place on the unfurled tarp. When the top of the casket was uncovered and breached my father held out a hand, which I took because the ground was slippery. We pored over the two-year-old remains of Nathaniel Merriman, a man Harnett knew everything about but wisely kept from me, only pausing to point out the valuables, which I removed, and the particularities, which I noted, like the PVC piping the morticians had used to replace organ-donated bones so that the body held up better for mourners as well as mortuary staff leery of manipulating a flaccid corpse.

Rain made soup of the coffin. Harnett said we needed to move fast. It was too dark to read his face, but I knew how to decipher his pauses: I had done something good, maybe even impressive enough to tell Knox the next time he came through so that the reverend could pass the story along to Diggers everywhere. I allowed myself only a short moment of pride before holding out my hand for the Root.

36.

My makeshift calendar continued to devour the side of the sink, each groove in the plywood evidencing yet another day of unspeakable things. Horizontal slashes finished off sets of five. I counted them. Today was Halloween.

My path to school took me past lawns ornamented with foam gravestones spray-painted with novelty names like Dr. Acula and D. Ed Corpse. I saw little kids with backpacks and lunch boxes rush out front doors and pause to straighten these memorials and I almost laughed. For one day a year, even children pretended to cozy up to the dead. What everyone forgot was that beneath those fake stones were real graves—maybe eons old, maybe fresh. The dead were below everything and everyone and that fact did not change just because tomorrow these families would whisk these decorations into boxes and put those boxes into attics. They were fooling themselves. Eventually a man with a shovel would wait them out. Last night that man had been me.

As Fun and Games began, these thoughts still seized and thrilled me. These teenagers loitering in their shorts and T-shirts were of little matter; I had lifted the Woman in Black from cemetery mud and delivered her back into living arms, the closest thing to a resurrection I'd ever seen. So I barely noticed when Stettlemeyer started shouting names. For the past two weeks, she'd succumbed to mercy and allowed Foley and me to pair off when possible, but today a tiff between two girls had incited her to assign partners based on nothing but the cruel mercy of the alphabet.

"Table two! Carpenter, Crouch!"

The Woman in Black turned into Celeste Carpenter. She was right in front of me, within slapping distance. I edged away. Her arms were crossed, and in the upper plane of her beautiful mask I sensed a lingering dislike.

"We're partners," she said.

"What?" I asked. "Okay." I blinked. "What?"

"Ping-Pong."

"Oh, okay, sure," I said. "What?"

She gestured curtly at the green table behind her. Her dark hair fanned as she made an artful pirouette and took her position on the far side. I toed into place and picked up the paddle, running my fingers over the nippled rubber. All around us volleys were crackling. I looked down the line of players and saw Foley a few tables down, slanting his eyes at me.

"She's not here," Celeste said. Her paddle was propped against a cocked hip. "Heidi Goehring. She changed periods. That's who you're looking for, right?"

For a moment I was confused, but another look around proved that Celeste was right. Heidi was gone. The memories of Lancet County peeled back like scorched paint, and beneath lay the lunchroom, calculus proofs, Foley's disapproval. Mostly I saw Heidi's reaction when she saw Woody looking at her. Although she was bright, I feared she would have done anything Woody asked. Even if it meant joining him inside a certain closet in the band room. But it was me he was interested in, not her, and such an event could not have ended happily for Heidi.

It came out of me unwittingly: "What did he do?"

She switched hips. "You don't know how much trouble you've caused."

"Me?" To avoid her eyes, I took hold of the ball resting against the net. "All I did was move here."

"Yes, and maybe they handle social situations differently where you come from. But you have to learn. Here is not there. Maybe you came from a really small town. I understand how that might be. But you need to adapt."

"Small town?" I squeezed the ball in my fist. "I came from Chicago. It was like a million times bigger. A billion times bigger."

The paddle slid from her hip. Her torso sank back and her shoulders squared, as if seeing me for the first time. Her dark eyes glimmered.

"You're from Chicago."

I shrugged. "Yeah."

"Chicago has an incredible theater scene. Dance, too."

I shrugged again. "Okay."

"Steppenwolf? The Joffrey? Hubbard Street?"

She leaned over the table and everything else was vanquished by the double swells of breast visible from her

V-neck. "That's right," I mumbled. Quickly I dropped the ball and sent it across the table. She swiped at it, missed, and ended up smothering it against her chest. It squirted away and went clattering beneath the table. Instinctively, I took to my knees to retrieve it. In the shade below I located the ball rolling back in her direction. I reached for it and instead felt lotioned skin—a hand, not severed at all, but warm and electric—and then soft breezes, hair, conditioned and combed, not the wiry tangle of the grave—because she was there, right beside me, crouching and reaching for the same object, and for an instant she filled my vision—

—the pale crescent of flesh glowing between shorts and shirt—

—Ls and Ts and Ys of a complicated bra pushing through fabric—

—the baby fuzz of hair on the swoop of her neck—

—a pinprick mole dotting the exact spot of a necklace clasp—

—regions of depth in her hair so black all detail was lost—

—three strands of hair still charged by our static and reaching—

"Oops." She plucked the ball from the floor and then smiled at me. Dazzling, even in shadow. "Nice and quiet down here, huh?"

Dozens of balls against dozens of tables sounded more like a hailstorm. "Sure is," I said.

"So, the theater scene, yeah. You know of it? Well, of course you know of it. How well? You have connections there?"

It was a bad idea, but the second I thought of it I could not pull back.

"Yes," I said. "My mom knew someone at one of them."

Her eyes widened so that I could see how the green mixed with hazel. "From which theater? Can you ask her?"

I shook my head. "She's dead."

"Oh." Her forehead wrinkled. I hated to see it that way. "You think you could still find out? I'm working on a routine for the Spring Fling. You know what that is? It's a talent show. The biggest in the tristate region. They do it right here in the school auditorium. It's no joke. People come from all over. And they give out awards, some scholarship-type stuff, but even better are the contacts you make. You wouldn't believe who they get to show up to this thing. Hey, maybe you can send your contact a tape of my routine? Maybe even get them to come down for it? This is great news."

I wanted to punch myself. Yes, my mother had known someone affiliated with some theater, but only barely. Most likely that person was a volunteer usher or just some schmuck with season tickets. But Celeste was practically licking her lips.

I forced a smile. "I'll see what I can do."

"Oh," she sighed, lacing her hands and leaning forward so that her head grazed the bottom of the table. It was like the first movement of a hug. I imagined the rest: the plump of her breasts, the push of her hips, the smell of her scalp. "After school. Today. Come to rehearsal room B just off the main chorus room. I'm practicing my routine. I've just worked out the steps. Wait'll you see it. You'll come, right?"

She dragged me—by the hand!—back up above the table and the ghostly prickles of that contact steered me through the rest of Fun and Games, around the suspicious glares of Woody in the locker room, past the remainder of the day, and into rehearsal room B when school let out, where to my honest surprise I found her there, as promised, stretching in a silver leotard. Almost immediately she resumed the chatter. The talent show, she explained, wasn't until May, but it didn't pay to rest on your laurels, not ever, not even when an event was six months away, especially when that event was the Spring freakin' Fling.

"Everyone involved practices like crazy," she continued. "Especially me. We practice all the way up until the day of the Fling and then we all go out to a movie together a few hours before it starts. You know, to relax. We bring our parents and significant others and everything. It's like a tradition, and it's hilarious, because every year a couple people leave the movie to throw up, they're so nervous. They should be. You know Shasta McTagert? She was discovered at a Spring Fling and joined the Rabbinger Theater and now she's on that TV show about the ghetto school. You probably think it's a fantasy."

"No," I protested. "Fantasies are good."

"They *are* good." She made a sound like a purr. Then she spoke as if what she said was confidential. "A fantasy world is the best kind of world to live in because if you don't want it to end it doesn't have to, and it can totally take over Mere Reality."

Her face brightened as she enunciated this phrase. Instantly I liked the sound of it. My trumpet lessons, my prayers to Two-Fingered Jesus, my specifying—all of these were escapes from Mere Reality. The only question was which half of my life was real: my fluorescent existence here in the this room with Celeste Carpenter or the dark nights spent with Ken Harnett.

"If I do something really fantastic at the Spring Fling—win top prize and all that—then there's a chance Mere Reality will become exactly what I want it to be. I can be a dancer.

Everyone says that. But I really can, I know it. I just need the right people to see."

Finally she hooked her iPod up to a stereo, crossed her ankles, and twined her arms above her head. A Spanish theme began—a trumpet. My neck burned with jealousy. She was only running through the steps, hardly giving it her all, but if anything her casual drowsiness enhanced the titillation—it was as if her slow gyrations and sleepy spirals were being performed before her bedroom mirror. With each bend and stretch of spandex she fired more questions about my hometown theater scene—the neighborhoods, the ensembles, the directors, the wages—and I mumbled and lied my way through each of them. Eventually it became evident that I was the first real big-city kid she'd ever met. I convinced myself that I had a right, even a responsibility, to foster her fantasies. There would be no Mere Reality, not between the two of us, not if I could help it.

37.

"HEY, DICKHEAD," FOLEY SAID. "You plow through those discs?"

Outside among the early-evening trick-or-treaters, he was more invisible than ever in a knee-length black coat over black jeans and a black hooded sweatshirt. His mom, he had told me, had cruelly forbidden him to dye his hair black, even for Halloween, and it was only this blondness that prevented him from altogether blending into the night. I was struck by how much I missed my own mother telling me no. Harnett wouldn't care if I came home wearing pink pigtails.

His question was silly. Since Foley had handed me the plastic bag full of dozens of burned discs, some cheap earbuds, and a busted-up Discman, I had not stopped listening. The Discman wouldn't function unless it was held shut with duct tape, but fortunately that was something Harnett had in abundance. I'd been isolated at home for so many weeks in almost total silence that the music had nearly electrified my skull the first time I pressed play.

At Foley's recommendation I began with Black Sabbath's first album. It seemed impossible to me that it had been written and recorded forty years ago. The very first line, sung with apprehensive terror by Ozzy Osbourne, a personality only known to me as a pop-culture punch line, was anything but funny: *What is this that stands before me?* Peering across the shambles of a small, dark cabin, I asked the same question of myself; elbowing into a swarm of disinterested high school students the next morning, I asked the question again; in Gottschalk's class; at lunch; during Fun and Games; considering my face in the bathroom mirror or my future of burrowing among the graves: *What is this that stands before me?*

It was a question that the rest of Foley's discs tried to answer. He had meticulously labeled each CD with artist, album, release date, and one of a dizzying array of genre variations that more than satisfied my itch for specificity: heavy metal, black metal, atmospheric black metal, doom metal, death metal, sludge metal, gothic metal, Viking metal, Celtic metal, speed metal, thrash metal, power metal, progressive metal, industrial black metal, industrial post-black metal, symphonic extreme metal, pagan folk, grindcore, goregrind, dark ambient, experimental ambient, ritual drone, noise drone, ritual rhythmic noise, and depressive rock. They included bands like Opeth, Moonsorrow, Pentagram, Motörhead,

High on Fire, Type O Negative, Hammers of Misfortune, Wolves in the Throne Room, Primordial, High Tide, Waldteufel, Ulver, Nachtmystium, and Agalloch. The musicians in these bands often credited themselves by mysterious aliases like Necroabyssious, Panzergod, Defier of Morbidity, and He Who Gnashes Teeth. When I asked Foley where these bands were from, he listed countries all over the world. My life, for so long confined to Chicago city limits and now to limits even more constrictive, suddenly felt part of something expansive. Sometimes at night I was saddened that the music of my trumpet was being replaced, but I covered up those old tunes, as well as the memory of my mother's needling, by thumbing the volume button on the Discman and letting the metal rattle me until I was numb and sleeping.

Foley was particularly passionate about a band called Vorvolakas; when he told me they were from Chicago I rushed home to listen. The album was called *Greifland,* and from the first moments of sonic wash and grinding guitar I found a fearless embrace of the dark and doomed that mirrored my present life. The chorus of the title track gripped me by the throat and I pressed back on the Discman again and again until I had it fully memorized. The words offered no escape; instead they dared darkness to do its worst. As the night overtook the cabin and the batteries ran out on the player, the words crashed through my memory over and over:

We became oblivion.
Caused our own extinction.
Ravaged our own hearts.
Damaged our own souls.
Ate our dreams of sleep.
Cried our miseries.

Darkness may await you.
But we are already there.

For the first time ever, I had not been able to wait for lunch so that I could somehow express to Foley the inspirational effect of these lyrics. My hands had trembled around my fork and spoon—I had so much to say and no way to say it. Was chanting *We became oblivion* the key to vanquishing myself until I was a perfectly anonymous nothing just like Foley? I had watched Foley stuff his face until finding the courage to stammer these important three words.

Foley had grinned, showing me the corn dog ground by his teeth. "You listened," he said. Then he'd hunched in and spun the most amazing tale—the time when his mother had taken him to Chicago to visit his aunts and he had been introduced to Vorvolakas by an older cousin who knew a doorman who didn't bother with IDs. When the band took the stage the crowd coalesced into a single rippling beast. The peal of the guitars was deafening, ratcheted along by the machine-gun fire of the drums. The front man screamed as he played, his head banging so ruthlessly that each whip of his long hair terminated in an explosion of sweat. It was astonishing and staggering; it was the only real metal show Foley had ever attended. "I'm going back sometime soon," he'd vowed. "I check their website. I know when they're playing. One of these days I'm heading back if it means I have to hitchhike. You bet your ass."

It was a delirious fantasy, this escape to Chicago, but Foley's firsthand details made such an escape seem almost possible. Suddenly there was a path back to my mother's home, only the road was treacherous and required acceptance of a frightening oath: *We became oblivion. Caused our own extinction.*

"I checked their MySpace last night," Foley said, "and they're playing up there in like six weeks. Now, driving's out of the question. And I don't have the money for Amtrak, and I know you sure as hell don't. So I was thinking Greyhound. If we can get over to Monroeville, we can hop a Greyhound. Those things are cheap as shit. You ever ridden a Greyhound?"

I'd ridden a million buses in my life but never one that went any farther than the suburbs.

"Fair warning, then, it's supposed to be pretty much the worst possible way to travel. I read that there was this Greyhound heading up to Canada and right in the middle of the night this guy takes out this knife, this big fucker of a Rambo knife, and starts *chunk chunk chunk,* decapitating the guy sitting next to him." Foley shrugged. "I bet they barely blinked at Greyhound headquarters. I mean, it's just reason number seven thousand and thirty-three why Greyhound sucks, right? Anyway, we're taking Greyhound. But you get the aisle."

"I don't know about this *we,*" I said, thinking about how many slashes I would be adding to the sink between now and then, and how many of those slashes would correspond with late-night digging—unscheduled events that didn't fit comfortably around trips out of town.

Foley turned on me instantly. "Take it or fucking leave it." He rounded his shoulders and picked up the pace. "I'm seeing Vorvolakas on December tenth in Chicago. You want to stay home jerkin' off your dad, hey, have fun."

Foley had been volatile all night. In the locker room after Ping-Pong, I had been dizzy with the perfume of Celeste's attentions; diminishing beneath those feelings were shame and fear over what had really happened to Heidi—the imagined manners of her debasement were numerous and graphic. Foley didn't give a shit about either girl. He had pushed past me out of the gym and ignored me the rest of the day. I couldn't be certain that he trailed me to rehearsal room B, but in the parking lot a half hour later he had savagely unleashed every rumor he'd ever heard about Celeste, most of them involving the maniacal measures she took to protect her triumphant future (example: she made Woody wear two condoms at once). Foley couldn't understand why I would risk my burgeoning invisibility by interacting with *Celeste Carpenter!* and courting the wrath of *Woody Trask!* I needed Foley worse than he needed me—we both knew it—and so I choked out an apology. Appeased, he suggested that we walk around that night and scare trick-or-treaters—after all, he said, Halloween was a metalhead's favorite holiday. Desperate for his good graces, I had shown up at eight o'clock in front of the school as promised, and we'd begun slouching through Bloughton, not attempting to scare a single kid.

And now I had pissed him off again. "Maybe I'll be able to go," I lied. "I'll just have to check with my dad."

A woman passed us, holding hands with two little boys, one in a Darth Vader getup, the other one wearing the forked tail and horns of Satan. Both Vader and Satan were sobbing, their night of sugar prematurely curtailed. I remembered being that young and ungrateful.

Foley hit me on the arm.

"The graveyard," he said. "Oh, man, we should go to the graveyard!"

For reasons unknown, I had never considered that Bloughton might have its own cemetery. I wanted to keep everyone at school as far as possible from my life with Harnett, and the idea that there was intersecting territory was unnerving. I opened my mouth to protest, but Foley was walking and talking too rapidly.

"If you want to be metal, hangin' in a graveyard is like a prerequisite. Oh, shit, I should've brought my speakers! Have you seen *Return of the Living Dead*? It's basically about a bunch of metalheads and there's this one part where they go hang out in the cemetery and they're blasting music and getting wasted and this one chick gets naked and starts dancing on top of the graves. It's awesome. It's like the best scene in the movie. This is before the chemical rain starts and turns all the bodies zombie."

I recognized the shapes long before Foley: the telltale trees spaced like weight-bearing columns, the banner of purple lawn speckled with stones like a sprinkling of snow. By the time Foley pointed, I was already counting rows of markers and using multiplication to gauge the property's size.

"You haven't seen *Return of the Living Dead*?" He shook his head and stopped at the edge of the chest-high fence. "I don't understand what's wrong with you." I gripped the iron with one hand and liked how it felt, cold and quiet. Beyond, the necropolis was even colder and quieter. That was good; I felt myself nodding approval. This was a place that held its secrets.

My palms itched for the Root.

I wedged my foot between the bars as my father had taught. Already I could see the Johnson grave that figured into local lore. Years ago a hit-and-run driver had killed two local middle schoolers in separate incidents; it would be fascinating to see the damage for myself. But halfway over the edge I caught Foley's expression and stopped. Now that he was faced with the reality of stone and shadow, his fantasies of grave dancers and toxin-fueled zombies were being devoured by the same fear that seized so many.

I lowered myself back down, my heart pounding. What had I been thinking? What exactly had I been planning to do? I felt Foley's hesitation burn toward shame. The next thing he'd do would be to lash out. I moved quickly to rescue us both. "I don't know about this. The whole thing kind of creeps me out."

"Really?" He looked relieved. "I guess we don't have to do it. I mean, if you don't want to."

"Yeah, let's not," I said. But my longing remained. Right there, over that gentle rise, under cover of that towering oak—the perfect spot.

He turned and leaned his back against the fence. I followed suit, grateful to cleanse my vision of the underground temptations. Even masked, children did not venture this close to the town graveyard, but we could hear them booing and giggling from nearby sidewalks.

"You watch out for Celeste Carpenter," he said finally. "She's just going to get you into trouble."

"I know."

"And you ask your dad about that Greyhound."

"I will."

He shook his head, his blond hair catching the moonlight. "Can you imagine it?" He grinned at me. "Vor-fuckin'-volakas?"

I smiled and nodded.

He made devil's horns with his fingers and shouted the opening lyrics to our favorite song. Instinctively I shrank away. Such loud noises so close to the dead—Harnett would not approve. But Foley continued and after a moment I laughed and joined in. We charged forward to find ears to hear our song, bellowing at a volume only Halloween made acceptable. "*We became oblivion,"* we screamed, managing to scare a few kids after all. The words were true: this nothing, this absence of pain, was all I had ever hoped for in Bloughton, and here it was.

38.

THE NEXT LINE: *CAUSED OUR OWN EXTINCTION*. It's the opposite of the self-esteem crap they feed you at school, but it works just as well—as soon as I embraced the fact that my existence mattered little to anyone, including Harnett and God and Two-Fingered Jesus, I stopped hurting. I walked into the cabin insensate to pain and told Harnett that the place was a dump. He swallowed down the last of his onion and started pushing stacks of paper against the wall. Moments later, I joined him, and he gestured to indicate his preferred order. It was the beginning of a great change. Day by day, the state of the cabin improved. The cleaning products under the sink were put to use. Dust was swept from horizontal surfaces. The smoky blot of the hearth was scrubbed vigorously in turns by both of us. The upside-down bucket formerly used as my barber chair was righted and filled with solvent for mopping. I went over the floor once; when I returned home from school that day my father was emptying out the bucket for what he said was the fourth time. The floor, though it was cement, shone.

I had not seen a bottle of liquor in weeks. Harnett appeared to exist on a diet of water and onions, though now when he did cook he usually made a portion for me. I still was not crazy about how he tossed me steaks and sandwiches I was expected to catch with bare hands, but it was a minor complaint. Even better, he had taken to giving me an occasional allowance, and with the money I made weekly hikes to the grocery store and bought things like Stouffer's frozen pot pies, Cocoa Krispies, and Cool Ranch Doritos. Seeing these for the first time, he slammed the cupboard in derision and grabbed an onion. That night I awoke to a crackling noise and saw him huddled by the fireplace with gutted Doritos bag in hand, licking Cool Ranch dust from his fingers.

The more he offered to me, the more I gave back. After returning home one afternoon to find him cursing about a noteworthy pawnshop that had relocated without a forwarding address, I told him that he should get Internet access. It wasn't the first time I had said it, but it was the first time he didn't sneer. He sat in his rocking chair with arms crossed while I struggled to explain the Web. Harnett waved at his wall of books and insisted that he had all the research he needed, and besides, no Digger wanted anyone to be able to trace their activities—why else did I think they relied so heavily upon an elderly reverend in an unreliable jalopy?

Somehow, though, I coaxed him to drive us to the public library, where we waited in the computer line for ten embarrassing minutes while staff and patrons wrinkled their noses. Once seated, I opened the browser and I entered the information about the missing pawnbroker. Within seconds I found the reopened location, just a couple of towns over. Harnett pulled a crumpled piece of paper out of his pocket and began plotting the theft of a librarian's pen. I told him to cut it out, then hit print. Harnett handled the Google Maps page like a rare document. I smiled to myself, reminded of how my mother had carefully stapled and filed her "important" e-mails.

Harnett's work schedule was nowhere near what it had been before Simmons and Diamond laid down the law, but it had gradually increased again to two or three digs per week. He did these digs alone, yet was always home before I went to bed. Such discipline required more time spent studying newspapers and choosing quality over quantity, and I saw the toll the routine was taking on not only his wallet but also his nerves and body—having to cover more miles more quickly, he often left the cabin long before I awoke. It was not unusual for him to go on a two- or three-day sleep bender to recover from these travels. Either he remained frightened that I would make good on my vow to turn him in to my principal or his actions were an earnest, if strange, crack at good parenting.

He didn't remember Thanksgiving but I celebrated silently as we ate our Stouffer's pork cutlet and mashed potatoes, our side of onions, and our dessert of Cocoa Krispies. I told Two-Fingered Jesus that I was thankful for being able to embrace oblivion—everything good that had happened to me, the relative equilibrium at home and school, had begun with that. I promised him I would continue to trust in my mother, who had sent me to Iowa for a reason I still didn't fully understand. I did not tell Two-Fingered Jesus about the weekend digs that I continued to do with Harnett, nor did I apologize. His stone emissaries were in every cemetery we entered, and they knew full well what went on there.

Once or twice a week, I managed to see Ted, so early in the morning or so late in the day that not even Woody could find out about it. Ted slapped down sheet music. I played. He clapped to stop me and pointed at the bungled bar or hummed a correction. On rare occasion he would use his fingers to guide mine through a treacherous passage. There was no celebration for good playing, no admonishment for failure. We rammed through it as if it were punishment, yet week after week we both came back for more. The only spoken words came from Ted at hour's end: *Next lesson, then.*

Every free minute in between was for my mom: I studied. Ignoring the smirks of Gottschalk, I dashed to class early so I could read ahead. I spent lunchtimes with a textbook opened alongside my tray, and after several days of Foley's grousing even got him to quiz me.

And all the while there were occurrences too reminiscent of what had happened to Heidi. A kid named Kyle read a skit with me in English and it was so funny that we got applause from everyone in the room but Woody. The next day, Kyle came into class wearing a bandage over his temple and a stupefied look. A week later Laverne stopped me in the middle of the hallway to obtain my proper mailing address, and while she had my attention she jabbered numerous questions about how classes were going, how things were at home, how was I adjusting to Bloughton—and everyone saw. When I left school that day I found Laverne quietly crying over the FAT BITCH that someone had keyed onto the hood of her car. I slunk by without a word, repeating the Vorvolakas in my head.

With no solid proof otherwise, I found it surprisingly easy to pretend that these abuses had nothing to do with me. Besides, my mind was on Fun and Games, where, to Foley's dismay, Celeste continued to nab me whenever there was pairing up. A couple of times, she and I were even forced to touch. As she did so, she would ask for updates on my theater connections while telling me how her Spring Fling rehearsals were progressing. I ignored the shadow of someone who might be Woody watching from the weight room doorway and convinced myself that Celeste was not repelled by my odor of onions and death. She, after all, was Incorruptible, only she.

39.

Hundreds of flies exploded from the casket as soon as the lid buckled. I shielded my face with my arms. Harnett ducked. Their small black bodies bounced off our cool skin and wiggled through our hair before they oriented themselves and dispersed. It was several moments before the buzzing noise was gone.

"Is that normal?" I whispered.

"Yes," Harnett said. He paused. "No."

There was no normal—if anything, that was what I was learning. No body decomposed like another. Some bodies bleached until they became rice-paper skin against twig skeletons; others bloomed into extravagant deformities of rainbow colors. No two cemeteries were alike, either. Each had its own challenges of scouting and approach; some had sight lines that provided a feeling of security while we were digging, though in truth there was no security, not ever, so said Harnett. This cemetery, for instance, extended flat as pavement for miles, with stones filing all the way up to the highway before resuming on the other side of the street.

We were at one of Kansas City's largest funeral grounds—the southernmost point of my father's territory—and though it was a place Harnett had visited several times in the past, it made him jittery. There were fifteen-foot fences topped with razor wire, night watchmen and motion-controlled lights, security cameras that had to be fooled with mirrors. Our pace dragged. My father had yet been unable to find a suitable replacement for Grinder, and I could see the mismatch in each swipe of his shovel, the way the handle wanted away from his fingers.

Overall it was a well-kept corpse.

"The flies." My breath made spirals in the air. "How do they stay alive down there?"

"The human body has everything," Harnett replied. "It's a world unto itself. It has pockets of air, areas of warmth and cold. Plenty of fat and meat. All it takes is one fly to start a colony."

He tore his gaze away from the highway long enough to frown at me.

"Remember what I told you about being buried alive? Things live underneath longer than you'd think. That includes people. There's a condition called locked-in syndrome—the Germans call it *Eingeschlossensein*—where the nerves, they shut down; to someone who doesn't know better it looks like brain death. You still hear, you still see, only you can't communicate. They take you to the slab and you're aware of every minute of it."

I felt a flare of irritation. We'd been over this before, and once he got going on the subject he would not stop. Sometimes his voice even rose to unsafe levels. I could see his excitement as he patted the corpse's pockets, searching for a golden watch he was certain was there.

"An EEG would tell you if someone was really dead." I sighed. I loathed hauling out a Gottschalk fact, even in an attempt to end this tiresome conversation.

"Maybe so." He had the body on its side and I could see where the man's suit had been scissored up the back by the mortician for easy maneuvering. "I'll tell you what they used to do, to make sure you were dead. They had lots of ways."

"You've already told me."

"They'd slice your feet with razors. Or use nipple pinchers."

"They put needles under your fingernails, I know, I know."

"Boiling wax on the forehead," he said. "Tobacco enemas, urine in the mouth."

"They stuck pencils up your nose and pokers up your butt. What's your deal with this stuff?"

He squatted next to the dead man. The golden watch was already rolling around his palm—he had it, yet still he sat there absorbing the odor. Finally he looked up.

"I have my reasons," he said. "Let's go through it once more."

Not far away, a heavy transport vehicle—maybe a garbage or cement truck—thundered past the cemetery. Small avalanches of dirt streamed from the side of the hole, pattering against Harnett's shoulders. My pulse accelerated. I wasn't used to digging in the presence of headlights.

"Let's *not* go through it," I said. "Come on, get out of there."

"Tell me the three things." He shifted so that his knee blocked the corpse's face from the falling dirt. Again I was struck by the strange courtesy he showed the dead.

"The three things," I repeated, thinking. "Calm? You should try to stay calm?"

"C-A-S," he recited impatiently. "*C.* Calm, remain calm."

"Right, right," I said. "That's what I said, stay calm."

"A," he said.

"Air. Conserve air."

"Which means."

"Which means," I said, pressing shut my eyes. "Don't hyperventilate. Don't scream."

"And whatever you do."

"Whatever you do, don't light a match because it'll suck away all the air."

"S," he said.

"Shallow. A shallow grave. Remember that if you're buried alive most likely you're in a shallow grave. The reason is—"

"The reason's not important," he said.

"It's important to me," I said. "The reason is that if someone is burying you alive, chances are they're probably in a hurry and doing a half-ass job. So you're probably just a few feet deep."

"Which means."

"Which means," I said, ducking beneath the flash of passing headlights, "that you can get out. If you can find the coffin's center of balance, figure out which end is resting higher. You can break through."

"This is difficult because."

"This is difficult because you can't gain enough leverage. You can't swing your arms. Why is this so important to you?"

He ignored me. "If the coffin is wood."

"If the coffin is wood, you're going to have to bust the shit out of your hands, maybe even your head. You have to use focus techniques. Find the lid's weak point, probably along the seam, and bash it in. Get ready for a mouthful of mud and remember that you can breathe through it. It won't seem like it, but you can. All right? A-plus?"

"And if it is a metal casket."

"We can go over this while we fill the hole."

"And if it is a metal casket."

I clenched my teeth. "If it is a metal casket you need to disassemble it. Sometimes there's runners on the inside you can take off and use like a crowbar. If the casket is lined you can use the fabric to protect your hand while you punch. You can also use the material for a hood when the dirt starts coming in."

"Which it will."

"Which it will," I repeated. "Right. Okay. Got it."

" 'To die is natural; but the living death / Of those who waken into consciousness.' " I was lost before realizing that he was quoting poetry. It was not the first time. " 'Though for a moment only, ay, or less, / To find a coffin stifling their last breath . . .' "

"Huh," I said.

" 'How many have sustained this awful woe! / Humanity would shudder could we know / How many cried to God in anguish loud, / Accusing those whose haste a wrong had wrought / Beyond the worst that ever devil thought.' "

"Just beautiful," I said. "Now get out of there."

"Percy Russell." He nodded at the attribution.

The casket lid was reassembled with fast, dexterous fingers, and moments later Harnett surfaced. Together we gripped the tarp and portioned it back in segments, pausing between strata to pack the clay. While Harnett stowed our tools, I replaced the sod, kneading the sutures with my fingertips until the blades of grass clung to one another in natural affect. I lost myself in the task; after a few minutes I looked at my work in some astonishment. Suddenly I yearned to show Harnett what I had done. Even more, I wanted to show him how my life was being patched back together: the new friend I had; the beautiful girl who did not seem to mind touching me; the fact that I was just a few measly grades away from getting straight As—my mother's goal, but maybe one he could care about, too.

He did care, in his own way. That night, in that cemetery, it became clear to me. He taught what he felt I needed to know in order to survive. His obsessions, then, were worth understanding.

"Being buried alive," I said. "It has something to do with being a Digger."

Harnett paused halfway through a motion of sliding the Root into one of the sacks.

"It's something they do?" I ventured. "Or it's something done to them?"

He wiped his hands against his pants and stood.

"Oh, man," I said. "It's something they do to *each other*."

Harnett turned around, one sack thrown over each shoulder, a diamond of pale moonlight shining from his eyes.

"Why?" I whispered.

He hitched up the bags.

"For punishment," I guessed, and his dire expression told me that I was right. "Punishment for what? For screwing up? For letting people know that they exist?"

We stood motionless in the dark. I was on the right track.

Ice shot through my veins.

"Me," I gasped. "It could happen to me."

Once spoken, it was appallingly obvious. Among the Diggers there was no crime worse than revealing to the world their existence, and by taking me on, Harnett was accepting the greatest risk of all. A master who was also a father might be suspected of turning a blind eye to his son's mistakes. Harnett drilled me mercilessly to save both of our skins.

"It won't happen," I said. It was a promise to my mother.

"No," Harnett said. "It won't happen." His face, not hidden soon enough, told a story considerably less assured.

40.

Foley had taped inside his locker door a picture of circus freaks. It was black-and-white, probably circa the 1920s, and featured an array of physical oddities, gathered on two levels of risers for a group portrait. In the back row dwarves in evening wear stood between a sword-swallower on one side and, on the other, a giant so tall that everything above the waist went unseen. Farther down, a tattooed lady stood next to a woman in a leopard-print dress who was covered in fine fur. In the front row, an obese woman sat next to a pretty girl missing her legs and balanced on a wheeled cart. Identical twins wearing cummerbunds, ties, beards, and what looked like white dreadlocks stood alongside two dark-skinned pin-heads draped in animal furs. At the right edge of the picture was a man in shirtsleeves whom I found far more disturbing than the rest. He stood with his hands on his hips, and his body seemed inexplicably conflicted—his chest too sunken, his belly too low, the bend of his arms and legs somehow mis-aligned.

"That guy creeps me out," I finally said.

"It's the Congress of Freaks," Foley said. He pointed to the man I had mentioned. "His head's on backwards."

From that day on, we adopted the phrase. No more did we attend Bloughton High. Instead we were but representatives of the Congress of Freaks, and moved among our fellow initiates, troubled and troubling, but no more so than anyone else. I thought of myself as the Backwards Man, always looking at the shit I left in my wake. Foley was the Manly Giant, and Celeste, when I saw her, was Legless Mite, the girl balanced atop the wheeled cart—beautiful and dark-eyed and powered with a grace frightening to those burdened by regular limbs.

It was the last Friday of the semester, and I entered the school with almost breathless excitement. It had been a tremendous week. After returning from Kansas City, I had nailed every paper and exam the bastards had put before me, and a perfect score on my closing biology test was all I needed to claim victory. The final day of classes before Christmas break was Monday, which meant I had all weekend to prepare for Gottschalk. Most kids groaned; I celebrated.

After lunch, I hurried to the final Fun and Games. I didn't expect to remain friends with Celeste, if that was what we were, when classes picked up in January, and so felt an urgency to talk to her a final time, no matter how many lies I had to make up about theatrical agents who were this very moment booking tickets for Bloughton. But when I walked through the gymnasium doors, my hopes sank. Stettlemeyer and Gripp lounged next to each other on the bleachers as they had for the first half of the semester, and students gathered in loose assemblies, not a single one of them wearing gray shorts. There were a few basketballs and Frisbees lying around for those so inclined, but clearly the coaches had decided to let the final session function as a social hour.

Stettlemeyer barked a reminder that we all needed to go empty out our lockers at some point. Half the crowd got the task out of the way immediately, including Foley, whose invisibility made him impervious to intimidation. When he returned with his sweats twisted into a rank knot, we situated ourselves on the bleachers and watched our classmates mingle. I was so used to seeing them in dismal gym wear that they seemed rather like sophisticates at a cocktail party. Stettlemeyer's superhits completed the deception.

Celeste, Woody, Rhino—I kept tabs on them for ten or fifteen minutes, then let them slide from sight. Dwelling on any of them was not going to help the next few days of intense study. But Foley's constant bitching—currently about how his grandparents always gave him noncirculating commemorative coins for Christmas, what the fucking fuck was up with *that*?—wasn't interesting enough to keep my mind off the gymnasium's missing character, Heidi. I stood up.

"Hey, where you going? I haven't gotten to the Limited-Edition Barack Obama Inaugural Series yet. Wait'll you hear what those things are made of. You'll shit a brick."

"Clothes," I said. "Locker room."

"Oh, right. Well, hurry up."

Alone in the stairwell, I paused to relax in the cool darkness. Maybe next semester I could get out of gym entirely, I thought. The locker room door squeaked beneath my fingers. I had heard of such arrangements in Chicago, of being permitted to add an extra class in lieu of gym. I passed red benches, black lockers; my nose tickled at the fog of aerosol. Yes, I would ask the school counselor, maybe even today after school—I didn't know why I hadn't thought of it before. The first number of my combination was thirteen. I smiled. Maybe my luck would just keep getting better.

Then impact—teeth rattled, cheeks and lip smashed against clammy brick. There was no air; I wheezed; great vises collapsed my lungs. The spice of armpit hit my nose. Far away I heard the skittering of my shoes and then the horrible absence of sound as they were lifted from the floor.

I went horizontal. Blood rushed to my head. There was a

splashing noise and I looked down to see two large Nikes stomp across a thin puddle of water; I was being toted like a suitcase. I wrenched my neck and saw Rhino and then there was a great blow to the top of my skull. All went black—and then I saw starbursts, tasted the blood from my lacerated tongue, and heard a chuckling from above.

"Didn't mean to hit that wall," said Rhino. "Honest I didn't."

I opened my mouth but my swollen tongue took up too much space.

"It's your lucky day, Crotch." I didn't need to look to confirm the identity of this second voice. "We're performing a public service. Free showers to anyone who smells so shitty I can smell him all over my girlfriend."

"Trask, do they still count as girlfriends when they don't even let you—"

"Rhino, you're going to want to shut the fuck up."

I was flipped through the air—my stomach lurched—and then I felt hard cement reverberate up my ankles. I blinked; everything looked green. I shuffled my feet and heard water, and then slipped and felt against my back two twists of metal, hot and cold. I slid until the seat of my pants hit standing water.

"You'll have to forgive Trask," Rhino stage-whispered. One of the metal knobs whined. Vibrating through the wall, the digestive squeals of plumbing coming to life. "When it comes to you, he gets a little agitated."

The water blasted. I gasped—it was freezing and every muscle in my body clenched at once. For a shocking moment I was the corpse and this was rain and I pleaded for my father's shielding. Then I blinked and watched the puddle turn pink: proof of life. Rhino exclaimed in a mixture of shock and glee. My eyes saw through water. Soaking pants; fingers, my own, clawing blindly at the air; my shoe heels scraping senselessly at the drain in the floor.

I caught a flash of Woody, leaning against the far wall, perfectly dry. "Soap," he said.

"Scrub-a-dub-dub," sang Rhino. "No more stinky-winky."

A terrible taste hit my bleeding tongue and I became aware of a turquoise liquid, dribbling. Then more of it, appearing in splotches across my stomach and pants. I squinted through the downpour and saw Rhino pumping soap from a dispenser and flinging it at me in handfuls. My eyes stung. Suds slid down my face in foamy tears. The hard walls of the shower made it sound as if the entire school were laughing.

God is good.

"All purty," Rhino announced. He daintily dipped his hands in the water stream to rinse them. I sensed his retreat and heard the dull thwack of a high-five.

Woody's breath warmed my ear.

"Stick to your own kind, Crotch. Or we can do this again next semester."

Footsteps splished through puddles and they were gone. I traced their progress and noticed other faces poking around the corner. There were four or five of them, their jaws agape, and not just boys, but girls, too. I scooped a mountain of bubbles from my lap and spat the synthetic tang of cheap soap. Woody and Rhino had succeeded—I was nothing if not clean.

I tried to stand but slipped in the turquoise lather. There was laughter. More voices now, too many. I reached for the knobs to pull myself up but they too were slick. It was getting darker; more and more heads blocked out the locker room lights. I barely heard the noise of someone pushing through the throng, and even when he was kneeling at my side and tugging at my arm I barely saw him. It was Foley, trying to help me up, his black pants soaking blacker, and all I felt was jealous rage that, even here, almost no one saw him.

"Joey, come on, man."

I slapped away his hands and lurched. The nearest onlookers shrank back as my shoes fanned water. I tromped through the shower and past the red rows of lockers, meeting no one's eyes, concentrating upon the squish of my socks. I had the door pushed open before I felt Foley's dry fingers take handholds of my soggy clothing.

"Joey, man, I told you to stay away from them—"

"Move."

"Joey—"

"Move." I wrestled against his embrace. He lodged himself into the doorframe for leverage.

"Joey, what the hell?"

"Move." I lowered my head and bulled forward, knocking him aside even as he tried to keep hold. I shouldered the door. It smashed against the far wall and rocketed back. Foley screamed, a high girlish noise that I instantly hated him for, and I looked over my shoulder to see blood patterned across the brick. The door had slammed his finger, and he held the misshapen purple thing in front of his face in disbelief.

Keep moving, I told myself. *Up the steps, up the steps.*

Three bounds later the stairs were history and I was through the door to the gym. While I trailed shower water across the floor, Stettlemeyer showed Gripp funny snapshots she had stored on her phone.

I made it to the cafeteria right as the bell was ringing. An excess of quarters hung heavy in my sodden jeans and I plunged the coins home, stamping out Boris's number. It rang and rang, burying the last echo of Foley's pain.

An automated message picked up. Somehow I waited until the beep.

"Boris, call me now. Right now. This is Joey." I recited the number. My voice was all over the place, wild.

Students passed on their way to the day's last classes. I eyed them, shifting my feet in a growing puddle.

Twenty minutes later, I deposited more money and called again to the same result.

"I'm not screwing around, Boris," I said. "Call me back. *Call me back*." I gave the number again and hung up.

Fifteen minutes passed.

"Boris, where are you?" Bound by the cord, I paced in a tight circle, my wet clothes clinging uncomfortably. "Don't tell me you have this thing off. You don't ever have it off. You're avoiding me. Stop avoiding me! You have the number. *Call it*."

Ten more minutes.

"What the fuck is your problem?" I shouted into the phone, my voice breaking. "You've got no right to treat me like this! I need you! I need you to call me! Pick up your fucking phone and call me!"

Five minutes later the pay phone rang. I jammed the receiver against my lips.

"Boris!"

"This better be good," he said.

"I'm coming home. Now. I mean it. Right now. I'm heading to the train station right now."

He groaned.

"I don't believe this," he said. "You need to learn how to keep it together."

"Can you wire me money? I'm heading there now and I don't have a dime."

"Wire you . . . ? What does that even mean?" He was speaking softly as if from a public place. "Of course you don't have a dime, you've spent it all dialing my number three thousand times."

"Find out the number to the Bloughton station," I said. "Call them. Arrange it. Put it on Thaddeus and Janelle's card. I don't care how you do it!"

He paused. "I'm not putting anything on anyone's card."

I could barely keep my voice down. "Why the fuck not? You've done it before! Boris, I need this!"

"What you need is help, Joey."

I heard through the receiver someone saying "Shh," followed by Boris's muttered apology.

"Where are you? You're not in school?" I was surprised at my own accusatory tone.

"What's it to you?" Boris snapped. "Last day of school here was yesterday, moron. Thaddeus and Janelle took me out to a movie. *Which* I'm missing."

The image of something so cozily privileged as the graduate-degreed Watsons escorting their well-behaved son to a subtitled movie at an art-house theater that probably sold imported beer and gourmet coffee, and all as a reward for something as mundane as concluding another semester, consumed me with envy and spite.

"Who gives a shit?" I howled. "We've been best friends for a million years and the moment I need you all you can do is complain about missing some movie? Are you kidding me? Get *out* of there."

"Were," Boris said. "We *were* best friends. I don't even know you, dude."

I closed my eyes and let the words sink in. Through the receiver I heard piped-in movie-theater smooth jazz, laughing strangers, the distant flutter of popping corn. My side of the phone was even louder—boys shouted as they bought vending machine food, girls in the hallway squealed, and their volumes increased as they pressed closer in their eagerness to confirm that Crotch was indeed hunched over the pay phone, drenched and crying.

Crying—yes, I was. The tears felt different, oilier somehow, from the rest of the water beading my face.

"Boris," I said.

"I don't think you should call me anymore."

"Boris, please, listen."

"Don't call me anymore."

"Please listen."

"Don't call."

"Please."

"Don't."

It was the last word he would ever say to me. The dial tone was deafening.

I turned to face the gawkers. Their eyes were too bright, their postures too predatory, the smiles on their faces too ravenous—they were the freaks, not me. I fumbled the receiver at the phone. It fell and dangled, but by then I had plunged into their ranks. They parted to make way, their enraptured whispers like tires through wet pavement.

My last hope: Simmons and Diamond. I didn't care about the retribution I would suffer once Woody and Rhino had been suspended. All I cared about was that the principal and vice principal acted speedily on my behalf. Really they had no choice. The abuse had been vicious and the witnesses many.

Passing my locker, I snatched my biology text but nothing else, not even my coat. Moments later I closed in on the familiar wooden letters: PRI CIP L'S OF ICE. Laverne was standing just outside the doorway, struggling to direct her second arm into a coat sleeve.

"You're wet," she said, blinking at me in surprise. "Joey, you're all wet. What happened?"

"I need to see Mr. Simmons."

Laverne opened her mouth, then closed it.

"That's going to be impossible." Her normally nasal tone was flattened with an unexpected coolness.

"Ms. Diamond, then, I don't care."

Laverne took a moment to adjust her hem before deliberately attacking the buttons, one after another. When she was fully sealed, she raised her chin proudly. I felt a twinge of distress at the smug set of her lips.

"I'm afraid you can't speak to either of them," she declared. "They have been removed."

There was motion behind her. In the office, a row of adults were exiting the principal's office, unfurling scarves and pulling gloves from pockets. Neither Simmons nor Diamond was among them.

"Why?" I asked Laverne.

"Inappropriate relations," she enunciated with relish. "Ms. Diamond should have known better. Mr. Simmons is a married man, after all. And on school grounds, no less."

Laverne's wink informed me that what she said next was just between friends. "Mr. Simmons," she whispered, "really should've done something about those scratches on my car."

I saw again the FAT BITCH scraped into metal. In a roundabout way, I had been responsible for that, and now *that* was responsible for *this*. Everything, how the world toppled like dominoes, it was all my fault.

Movement in the office caught my attention. There was one adult among the group not draped in winter clothes, someone who in fact was accepting curt handshakes from each of them in turn. When I saw who it was, everything fell revoltingly into place: an interim principal had to be appointed, someone with a reliable and distinguished tenure, someone who knew the ropes and was unafraid of tightening them.

"Mr. Gottschalk will make a fine principal," Laverne purred, patting me on the damp arm. "I bet he'd meet with you right now."

I ran. Past Laverne, through students, across the spot on the lawn where months ago Celeste had slapped me. I was on the sidewalk, my lungs scorching, before I heard the shout.

"Kid! Kid! Hey, kid!"

Harnett was behind the wheel of his idling truck, leaning over the passenger seat to yell from the lowered window. I drew to a halt, sucking in icy air with each gasp. Snow spun in dizzying loops.

He gestured impatiently. "Get in."

I stopped several feet from the truck. Gray air mushroomed from my lips.

"The hell you doing?" He smacked the seat. "Forget it. Tell me about it on the way."

I was shaking my head and hadn't realized it at first; I thought it was a trick of the swirling snow.

Harnett scrabbled through the junk in the front seat and came up with an envelope. "This is from Knox. There's a relocation in West Virginia. It's a ten-hour drive and we're already late."

The snow burned as it dissolved against my wet skin. My head continued its mechanical refusal.

"I told you about these. Kid, relocations are one in a million." He threw up his hands. "Why are you just standing there?"

At that moment he finally began to take it in: the wet hair, the lack of any winter clothing, the biology text dangling from one pale hand, the blank look of rage fixed upon my shivering face. He dropped the envelope. His expression sharpened and with each uptick of his anger I felt an ebb in my own, as if he were drawing it from me and taking it upon himself. For an instant I tried to keep what was mine—*he* did this to me, after all; it was *his* fault I stank so bad that I had ended up in the locker room shower. But at last I let it go, let all of them go: Boris, Foley, Laverne, Simmons, Diamond. The departure of such a group made Harnett my sole protector. My father, the Garbageman, Bloughton's outlaw, here at the Congress of Freaks, armed with sharp tools and an accelerating anger—blood would spill from school windows and dribble down stairs unless I prevented it.

The truck door handle was icy, the seat stiff. I tossed the biology text to the floor, picked up the envelope, and studied each palsied squiggle. Droplets from my hand smeared the ink; my vision was similarly blurred. The engine coughed and the wipers began pushing snow. Knox had been right. It was going to be a brutal winter.

BOOK II

Lamb and Slaughter

1.

SOMETIMES THE DEAD STAND in the way of progress. Perpetual-care funds are mismanaged, cemeteries change hands or become orphaned, state or government agencies rezone the land for new purpose, or private owners simply do with the property what they wish—and often what they wish for is money. New condo buildings. A bigger Walmart. So the decision is made. The cemetery ground will become something other than a cemetery. Every single casket will be disinterred from the earth and reinterred somewhere else.

My father called such an event a relocation. Old graves, new graves, mausoleums, aboveground tombs—like a going-out-of-business sale, everything must go. Aside from even rarer events (like a grave-digger strike and the resultant stacks of unburied caskets), there was no better way to study up on decomp and burial techniques in a concentrated span of time. For these reasons, said Harnett, relocations became impromptu conventions. No Digger could stay away. My stomach stirred in anticipation of meeting these men of the night.

We sped through southern Illinois; by the time we hit

Indiana I was asleep. When I awoke outside of Cincinnati, Harnett picked up right where he had left off, babbling about legendary relocations, like the six-hundred-year-old Cimetière des Saints-Innocents in Paris, which was dug up in 1786, razed, disinfected, and covered with cement while its human remains were squirreled away in underground catacombs. It was the middle of the night when we stopped for fuel and coffee near Kentucky's Daniel Boone National Forest, and over the ticking of the pump Harnett droned on about the ten years it took to relocate ninety thousand remains from San Francisco in the 1930s, and how the ground itself was then built upon by a college. Little did school administrators know that the cemetery relocation itself had served an educational purpose.

My clothes had long since dried, but I was still cold. I used my biology text to block a crack in the door and shut my eyes. Only lack of movement jolted me awake. Peach morning light textured the dusty office windows of a roadside motel. I heard a crackle—the last of several bags of Cool Ranch Doritos that Harnett was polishing off. He sucked cheese from fingertips that smelled of kerosene and turned off the motor.

"We're here," he said. "Let's drop our gear and get to town."

"Will *he* be here?" I asked. I didn't have to speak his name.

He crumpled the bag. "You read the letter."

Indeed I had. Knox's writing style was overreliant on abbreviations, but communicated well enough a greeting (*K./J.*—), the details of the relocation (*Dec. 15–24, Mt. Rgn., WV*), an apology for the letter's lateness (*lately tkn w/brnchitis*), and, in a postscript, the admission that it had been over two years since he had last seen or heard from Boggs (*B. MIA. 2+ yrs*). In all likelihood, Knox wrote, Boggs was dead (*B.—prbly.*

dec'd). Harnett's feelings on the matter were unclear. I thought about my mother's death—quick, brutal, and unexpected—and wondered if a gradual destruction was even worse.

The relocation itself seemed improper, big machines rattling crypts and sneezing black exhaust across gravesites while dozens of men stomped and hollered and crouched with their sandwiches and coffee. Harnett planted his fists in his pockets and strolled down the bordering sidewalk, his eyes bright and watchful. I imitated him and absorbed what I could. There were cranes and dozers and backhoes and dump trucks. A foreman used spray paint to mark a number on the side of an exhumed coffin. There was a cordoned lot full of caskets parked like miniature cars. Harnett's eyes spun over the bounty and his lips moved in silent memorization.

Once we had circled the cemetery, Harnett turned his attention to the neighboring storefronts.

"Here," he said. "We want to set up camp right here."

Across the street were an insurance office, a shoe store, a VFW hall, a diner, and a coffee shop.

He grimaced. "I hope you're thirsty."

In truth it was shoes I really needed—some more insurance probably wouldn't have hurt, either—but after the long drive the need for coffee trumped both. We skipped across the asphalt, entered the shop, and stood in line. Once I was enveloped within the warm and spicy atmosphere, my stomach growled and I tugged on Harnett's sleeve to point out the muffins and scones. He shrugged noncommittally and then, when it was our turn with the barista, I hid my face while she monotoned the definitions of tall, grande, and venti. "I just want a large coffee," Harnett pleaded after almost a full minute of negotiation.

"And a cranberry scone," I added. "No, blueberry."

The shop had plenty of window space, and we situated ourselves at a table allowing an unobstructed view of the excavation. On one side of us, a kid my own age moused languorously at a laptop. On the other side, an old man dominated by a beard hanging halfway down his chest looked listlessly at a newspaper while an old hound dog slept at his feet. I inhaled the scone while Harnett sipped his venti and watched coffins rise.

"They call this silt coffee," he muttered a half hour later. Nevertheless he looked longingly into his empty cup.

"You should try the vanilla latte," I suggested. "And these blueberry scones are the shit."

He considered the intimidating barista before giving me a pitiful look. I sighed, took his money, ordered another scone and drinks for both of us, and returned, sipping my Americano while trying not to laugh at Harnett's suspicious swishing of his vanilla flavoring. We settled into silence, watching heavy machinery jerk around tight cemetery spaces, tiny plumes of breath making the men themselves look like steam-powered machines. Occasionally something would happen—a backhoe would topple a headstone, a decrepit coffin would be draped with a tarp to protect sensitive onlookers—but mostly it was tedium. This, too, was school, I reminded myself, and as the hours wore on I became increasingly impressed with my father's dedication. The hiss of cappuccino steam, the ringing of spoons to cups, the piped-in acoustic rock—these sounds clamored for my attention, yet Harnett was inviolable.

We were both on our fourth cups when the bearded man with the dog spoke.

"I found a way to get corpse-stink out of hair."

I choked and spat; coffee spotted the table. Harnett, though, just stirred his cold latte and shrugged.

"That's what you said ten years ago," he said.

"True." The man scratched crumbs from his beard. "But this way involves egg whites and Lemon Pledge."

The two men sat nearly back to back, scanning different angles of the same cemetery. They did not turn to look at each other.

"Can't say that sounds promising," Harnett said.

"I didn't say you should drizzle it on your ice cream. But if you're looking to neutralize your odors, you could do a lot worse. Only problem is once I got it in, Fouler spends the rest of the week trying to eat my hair."

At the mention of her name, the old hound raised her chin from the ground, leaving behind a dollop of slobber, and swung her droopy lips in my father's direction. Harnett lowered a hand and scratched beneath the dog's paisley kerchief.

"Hey, Fouler," he singsonged. "Hey, girl." He opened his palm and let the dog lick it. His nod toward the bearded man was almost imperceptible.

"Crying John," he said.

The man lowered his newspaper so that our eyes could meet.

"Morning, Joey," he said.

I could not conceal my surprise. Tufts of the man's massive beard rearranged as he laughed. "That's right. I know you. You're the new Digger."

"Don't scare the kid," Harnett griped. "And I'll let him know when he's a Digger, not you."

"Oh, he's a Digger, all right." The man examined me as if

searching for flaws. "Knox said how you handled yourself with that woman. Now, that was something. Something like that takes a special touch."

"Kid doesn't need a big head."

"You think *you* could've sweet-talked a lady like that? I know exactly what the great Resurrectionist would've done. He would've taken his shovel and gone *bang*. And dragged her out by the hair. There's your sweet talk for you."

The man guffawed. Fouler whined in concert before dropping her chin between her paws. Harnett studied the cemetery.

"Right." The man sighed. "Well, Joey, I'm Crying John. And this slab of fat down here is the Befouler." He nudged the animal's ribs with his toe and she bared her grimy canines in a lazy display of irritation.

I didn't know what to say. I cleared my throat.

"How old's your dog?"

Crying John's voice flipped into falsetto. "Who, old Fouler here? Ole Foulie? Aw, she's just a baby. Just a big old fat baby-cakes, ain't you, Foulie?"

"Sixteen," Harnett said. "Give or take."

"No, sixteen's exactly right." He slapped the dog's flank. "Raised her from a pup. Best Digger working today, present company included. Ain't no one better than old Foulie. Ain't no one feistier, either."

Fouler's tongue curled in a yawn.

"I'm sure you've already seen plenty of things you never thought you'd see," Crying John said. "But you haven't seen anything until you've seen Fouler here run out into a mess of twenty thousand stones and go directly—directly—to the hole that needs diggin'."

"That's an old wives' tale," Harnett said.

"Then I'm an old wife. What she'll do, see, is start sniffing around the premises, over and over in smaller and smaller circles, until she gets dizzy and sits her butt down, and that right there is where you want to make the first strike."

Harnett offered an indulgent half-smile. "That's not exactly true."

"You've never seen it!"

"That's not how you've told it in the past."

"Well, that's how I'm telling it now!"

Harnett shot me a look. "Take one guess why he calls her the Befouler."

I looked at the sleeping hound. Her paws twitched.

Crying John pulled at his beard and looked out at the cemetery. "Okay, so sometimes she poops." He raised a defiant finger. "But if she poops, then we're *really* in business! Anything in Foulie's poop zone is A-one material. Pee zone somewhat less so."

"So," I said, gauging the distance between the men. "You two are friends?"

The word made both men fidget and stare even harder through the window. With a shiver I remembered *C-A-S: Remain Calm, Conserve Air, Shallow Grave*. As amiable as Crying John seemed, he belonged to a group that held to a grisly code. Harnett and I were both risking something by being here, I had to remember that.

Harnett cleared his throat. "Haven't seen John in, what?"

"Four years?"

"Four. Or five. The relocation in, where was it?"

"Texas." Crying John sighed and flexed his fingers. "It's been some time."

In the cemetery, workers were breaking for lunch, some moving in groups toward the diner.

"Why does he call you Crying John?" I asked.

Crying John shrugged. "I'm not sure it's something to talk about."

"Indulge him," Harnett said.

The man toyed with his cardboard cup. "It comes from a method. A method I haven't used in years. I don't need to, not with Foulie. But back in the day, you know, I'd do what I had to do. I don't know if I'm really proud of it."

"You should be," Harnett said. "It was genius."

Crying John shook his head. "Don't be dumb. I just ended up being good at it. I've got, I don't know, overactive tear ducts or something. Always been kind of a crybaby. When I was small I'd cry if there were too many clouds in the sky. Even in high school, when— Well, hell, I don't have to tell *you* this. You're a boy in high school and start crying, you got about ten seconds before the beatings begin, right? But the slightest provocation and bang, the waterworks."

"You turned a negative into a positive," Harnett said.

"Hey, I'm learning the trade and I've got these eyes that run like wild, so I just put two and two together. I remember the first time, I was scoping out a belly just outside of Glacier National Park, beautiful country, with these snow-capped mountains and pure, crystal lakes and skies so clear they hurt to look at. . . ." His eyes began to shine.

"John's got the Upper Mountain territory," Harnett said. "Montana, Idaho, Wyoming, some of the Dakotas."

"Anyway." Crying John wiped his eyes with the back of his hand. "I'm up there and it's gorgeous and there's a little funeral going on in the same cemetery where I'm walkin'. Just your standard deal: people in black standing around a coffin looking serious, but for some reason I keep walking toward it, closer and closer, until I'm right there standing next to them like I belong, like I know the dead person, too. Look, maybe it was the mountain air. It's so cold and sharp sometimes it feels like it just gets inside you and cleans you out, and then you feel all new like you're kind of reborn. And so I'm standing there feeling reborn and looking at this casket that doesn't mean anything to me, not a damn thing, and I blink my eyes and sure enough I'm crying, and no one takes it as weird because everyone else is crying, too—and then I think about how my whole life I been crying and how people always get so weird with it and back away like I got a knife, but for once I'm crying and people don't mind. Not only that, but some of them even reach out and tell me it's okay. And so I start crying more. It's not like I can even look away—it's beautiful country up there, beautiful, every single thing that you see. Now I'm crying louder than anyone, and no one, not a single person questions it. I'm right beside the casket when it hits me."

"You get to see everything," I whispered in awe. "I bet you don't even need newspapers."

"I do. These days I do. I haven't used that method since I got Fouler trained. But yeah. It was good work. And there's no secret to it, either. People are sad. You just don't see it until you're inside it, every day, like me. These guys out here, running these machines and pulling up these sleepers—they're sad. The young lady selling us coffees—she's sad, too, you wouldn't believe how sad. I can see it. I can't *not* see it. Day and night, Joey, I tell you, it's all I can ever see. 'Cause only a crier can really understand a crier. And it's tough, seeing all these criers wanting to cry who can't because they gotta be running a bulldozer or selling coffee. It'd be so easy for me to help. But hard, too. I'm getting old. My eyes hurt. It's hard."

The small swath of skin visible amid all his hair was creased along lines of age and sorrow. Harnett respected the silence before breaking it.

"There was the will," he urged gently. "Tell him about the will."

"It's a wake, a regular wake, some Tuesday night, some suburb of Boise," Crying John said. "The kind of thing I did all the time: pick one out on a hunch, mix with the mourners, drink from foam cups. Only this time I get there and I'm it. There's just a funeral director and me and he's asking me if I'm there for the visitation, and I say yeah even as I'm reaching for the door, but he starts nodding like he's really grateful and gestures, you know, right this way, sir, and so I go on into the viewing room and there's this fellow all laid out. Nice coffin, good suit, decent-looking old guy, but not a single mourner in sight. And the funeral director urges me to sign the guest book, which I never do, I never, ever do, but it's just him and me and I can't weasel out of it, and while I'm holding the pen and looking at the blank page I realize that there will be no one else coming. This guy is dead and I'm it. Look, I don't know if this fellow was evil or if everyone he knew just sort of died off over the years. But at that moment, I'm all he's got, right? I'm the best friend the guy has in the world. So I sign the register. I go on record saying this man will be remembered, and look. I was right. Here I am, all these years later, still remembering."

"About a month later," Harnett prompted softly.

Crying John took a great breath.

"About a month later I get tracked down by a lawyer and he lays on me a document. That fellow left me everything. It's not much—a bit of money, an old Cadillac, but also a little house, a little square of land. His instructions were to split it among his mourners. So now I got this house and land. I went out there maybe four or five times to see it, but I never really got a good look. My eyes were too blurry."

"So you live there now?" I asked.

"What? No." He narrowed his eyes at me. "I sold it, wiped my hands of it. A Digger has to keep moving. A house and land, that would just complicate things."

"But, Harnett . . ." I looked helplessly at my father, but he was cringing at my slipup and busying himself with the view. I felt doomed but blundered on. "He's, you know. Been in the same place for, like, years."

Crying John's lips thinned.

"We don't all have your father's . . . talents."

Harnett groaned and rubbed at his eyes.

"Luck, that's all it's been, and one day it will run out," he protested.

The bearded man leaned in. There were no tears in his eyes now.

"Yes. It will. For all of us. And that's why we're here, right now, truth be told. To meet the future."

2.

Real education came after nightfall, when we prowled the emptied cemetery, pressing our knees into the dirt and aiming illumination only where it was safe, down holes. Harnett used the light to point out nuggets of bone, crumbled remains of cement liners, and even filaments of wood that hinted at an older coffin buried beneath the first, an old trick of miserly caretakers. We put our hands to dozens of covered caskets, Harnett whispering words to give each texture meaning: particleboard, softwood, walnut, copper, fiberglass, stainless steel, cultured marble; six foot three by twenty-two inches, six foot seven by twenty-four. At the same time, unseen others conducted their own studies, and all of them obeyed the accord of silence.

Unburdened by takings or tools, I felt exceptionally light scaling the fence. It had been a long day-and-a-half for me, an even longer one for Harnett, and yet we did not return to the motel. Instead he led me through a sleepy downtown to a pub called Andy's. I imagined my mother's reaction to my hanging out in a bar and grinned. What else were fathers for?

We slipped inside and moved past a bar held down by lumpy men in flannel shirts, a glowing jukebox, a scuffed pool table, and various sticky-looking surfaces, finally wedging ourselves into a booth in the farthest, darkest corner of the room. A woman with a scar running down the center of her nose slung a bored hip at our table and Harnett turned down her offer of three-fifty pitchers. Instead he ordered two burgers and Cokes. We wrapped our cold hands around warm meat, feeling the drizzle of grease and blood drip through our knuckles as we bit.

My elbow bumped a bald, skinny gentleman with wire-frame glasses resting upon sharp cheekbones. He was sitting next to me; how long he'd been there I had no clue. His lips twitched at my father in a kind of greeting.

Harnett paused in his chewing and nodded at the man.

"This is Under-the-Mud," he said. "He's got the Northeast."

"Oh," I said. The man had to be nearly seventy. "Hi."

Slowly the man laced his fingers and angled his plated skull. I felt the race of his beady, bright eyes.

"Son of the Resurrectionist," he said. "That is a legacy."

I wiped my lips and pointed a greasy finger at my father. "Who, him? The Resurrectionist? He's got a name, too?"

Under-the-Mud hiked a slender eyebrow. "It's not just a name, child. It's an homage." He paused for an apology or justification. When it didn't come, the eyebrow rose higher. "To the resurrection men. Of old England, dear boy."

I didn't like his tone—it reminded me too much of Gottschalk. The urge to tell him how ridiculous these cryptic code names sounded was nearly irresistible. But then I felt an unexpected rush: if I were given one of these names, I would be part of a club. I would no longer be alone.

A new voice responded. "No sense getting your claws out already, Mud. It probably seems asinine to someone who wasn't born in the Crustaceous period. You can take that to the bank and smoke it."

I looked up and saw standing alongside the table a nondescript gray-haired man in his sixties wearing a gray cap, gray sweater, gray scarf, and gray pants, each item springing coils of gray thread. He reached out, thumped Under-the-Mud on the back, and stretched out a hand to my father. Harnett threw a look around the room to ensure we still went unobserved, then submitted to a brief shake.

The man addressed me next. Even when I stared straight at him, he threatened to blend into the smoke. "Hello there," he said. "I'm Fisher."

"I'm Joey," I said.

Fisher laughed. "That won't do at all."

Under-the-Mud thumped the table with a scrawny fist. "He withholds from the child the facts of the resurrection men, he withholds his own name. I bet he withholds his old slogan, too. *'I can get anyone.'* That's what he used to say when he was young like the child here, and proud."

"Mud," Harnett sighed. He picked up a napkin and wiped his fingers with meticulous strokes. "I never said that."

"It was your slogan. You can't tell us it wasn't."

"It was given to me, maybe." He displayed his clean palms. "I never claimed it."

Under-the-Mud addressed me in a patronizing tone. "The quote was borrowed from Sir Astley Cooper. Sir Astley was one of the preeminent London anatomists of the eighteen hundreds and friend to the resurrection men."

"The resurrection men," Fisher interrupted. He smiled at me patiently. "Body snatchers who provided bodies for classroom dissections before there was any other legal means to get them."

Under-the-Mud turned his skepticism upon my father. "We look forward to hearing your reasons for hiding this history."

Beneath snapping red neon, the two men sized up each other. The sound track switched from a caterwauling weeper to a boot-stomping ass-kicker. Barely audible from the drinkers around us, laconic chatter about sports and kids and jobs—nothing that remotely hinted at this underworld insanity. Yet I edged closer to the Diggers; there was self-confidence within this delirium, and I found myself hoping that Harnett had in fact used the brash slogan. In its own way, *I can get anyone* was just as powerful as *We became oblivion,* maybe more.

"I'll decide when he's told what about what," Harnett said.

Fisher shrugged and leaned his body weight on the table; our Cokes slid treacherously. "Look, there's more than nine ways to skin a cat," he said. "That was long ago, back when we were all green behind the ears and the Resurrectionist was still working with Baby."

"Wait, stop," I demanded from the corner. "Who's Baby?"

Now Harnett squirmed. He gestured at the man in gray and killed time with some backtracking. "Fisher here has the Gulf territory."

" 'And I will make you fishers of men,' " quoted Under-the-Mud. "Surely the child knows that one."

Fisher dismissed the comment with a gesture. "I'm sure Knox would love it if that was relevant. But mainly it's because I like to fish. Got a little jar I keep with me on digs, fill it up with worms as I go. Grave worms are primo for fishing, absolutely primo. Bet you didn't know that."

"There's a lot he doesn't know," Under-the-Mud grumbled.

"Those were the days, though, weren't they?" Fisher said, yanking off his cap and patting down the gray tufts of hair. "When Lionel was still digging and it felt like it'd never end? And every time Knox came through he would tell tall tales of the younguns, Resurrectionist and Baby, and our jaws would hit the floor. What was the number? The two of you, how many?"

"Twenty in a single night," said Under-the-Mud. "That's what I recall."

"I've always heard twenty-one," said Fisher. "Even with two men, I still can't imagine it. Was it twenty-one?"

Harnett finished off the last bite of his burger.

Under-the-Mud raised a finger for attention. "Working as a team—of course it had its benefits. Just look at us, all these years later, fawning over the numbers like they're sports statistics. But let's not forget that teams are by their very nature dangerous. Diggers work alone. That's the way it's always been. When Lionel was through teaching you and Baby, he should have forced a split. But you two stuck together, just so we could sit around a couple decades later and ask each other if it was twenty or twenty-one. And we all know what happened as a result. We all known what became of Baby."

Boggs was Baby—I had figured out that much. In the chilling pause that followed I investigated a scar that cauliflowered the skin at Under-the-Mud's elbow. The hair at Fisher's temples was streaked with an ancient white slash and he was missing a pinkie. There was violence in this life that I had only begun to appreciate.

"The Resurrectionist can't be blamed for Baby," Fisher said at last. "Nobody can."

"We just ought not to forget the danger of working in pairs," Under-the-Mud insisted, turning away from me. "That's all I'm saying."

As the men kept talking, I basked in the respect they gave my father. In Bloughton, Ken Harnett was only the Garbageman, but here he was legend to legendary men. As the room grew darker and louder and smokier, other faces manifested through the gloom—Screw (Southwest), Brownie (Lower Midwest), the Apologist (Central East), and even Crying John and Fouler—and every one of them paid tribute to the great Resurrectionist and grasped happily at the few words he offered.

I tried to hide my surprise following each introduction. They were ancient, every one. It should have been cartoonish how their storied personas clashed with the gnarled and wrinkled reality. Perhaps once they had been dashing adventurers brimming with vitality, but now they had hairy ears and liver-spotted hands and swaying jowls. They were well muscled but unhealthy-looking. Scars and disfigurements were rampant. They each smelled bad, the same kind of bad; waitstaff kept their distance and nearby stools remained vacant. They used obsolete jargon that slowly I deciphered: graves were "bellies"; tombstones were "heads"; corpses, depending on their circumstances, were "swimmers" or "risers" or "sleepers." They spoke with reverence of something called the Monro-Barclay Pact. Their smiles were genuine, but their eyes were haunted and preyed upon me at every opportunity. Uncomfortable though it was, I preferred it to the dismissive cruelty of the Congress of Freaks. At least here I was being judged as a potential equal.

Beneath chatter, Harnett would murmur asides. They were good men, he told me, but almost every one of them relied on tricks: video cameras, aerial photography, global-positioning devices, mechanized telescoping shovels, ground-penetrating radar that emitted electromagnetic pulses. According to Harnett, these techniques were risky and unreliable. Sensory awareness, memory, gut feelings, and a good shovel: these were the only tools he advocated.

Their war stories, though, were astonishing. Fisher asked me about the 1878 death of Ohio congressman John Scott Harrison, son of our ninth president, father of our twenty-third. When I admitted ignorance, everyone took turns telling the tale. Crying John set the scene: at Harrison's funeral, family members noticed the disturbed grave of a family friend named Devin; when they investigated, they found Devin's body to be missing. Brownie picked up from there: afraid that John Scott would suffer a similar fate, the family bricked and cemented the grave, laying atop it a ton of marble slabs and hiring two watchmen. Screw jumped in next: after the funeral, the dead congressman's son, John Jr., traveled to Cincinnati to search the medical college for Devin's body. Under-the-Mud took the good part for himself: John Jr. found a hidden body, all right, dangling from a rope in a hidden chute, but it wasn't Devin—it was Congressman John Scott Harrison, buried just one day earlier beneath every known armament. The Apologist, the quietest and most mysterious of the group, deferred his turn, leaving Fisher to claim the denouement: it was determined that an anatomist at the college, Dr. Christian, had worked in association with a janitor to procure bodies, and in fact, Devin's corpse was ultimately discovered bobbing within a vat of brine. The Resurrectionist broke his silence by asking me the only remaining question: the accused were tried and convicted, the bodies successfully reinterred. But who had actually done the deed? Who had found a way to break into an unbreakable grave?

"You notice," he said, while the others hung on his every word, "that no one even asked the question."

"We're invisible," agreed Under-the-Mud with audible pleasure.

Just like Foley, I thought. Maybe it truly was the key to survival.

Fisher winked at me. "Out of the pot and into the kettle," he said.

It was obvious they knew the culprit, but even huddled in confederacy they would not utter the name. Instead the exchange moved fluidly to the actor Charlie Chaplin, buried in 1978 in Switzerland. "Born in Britain, but he was America's and everyone knew it," Under-the-Mud said as he rapped his bony knuckles. Ten, twelve, fourteen eyes blinked my direction and I understood that, in this particular case, all territorial restrictions were moot. Chaplin's coffin, Fisher continued, disappeared a few months after it had been planted. Some thought it was so that he could be interred in his native England; others thought it was so that he could be given a proper Jewish burial; most, however, figured it was the work of a crazed fan. A group of mechanics, concluded Crying John, claimed responsibility and demanded a ransom that went unsatisfied. Eleven weeks later, Chaplin's coffin was found in a cornfield and placed in a reinforced concrete vault.

"You wonder what a man like that is buried with," mused Brownie.

"Yes," said Screw with a smile. "You wonder."

They all looked at their drinks for a moment and a thrill ran through me. *One of these men did it,* I thought. *One of the men at this table.*

"But the big one," Crying John continued, "was one year earlier."

"Memphis," said Screw.

"Forest Hill Cemetery," added Fisher.

Under-the-Mud mulled me over for a long moment.

"Elvis," he said.

My mouth fell open. "No."

Harnett raised a hand to calm me. "Don't get too excited, kid. Look, the guy died and things got a little crazy. They put him in a mausoleum and on the day of the funeral a drunk driver took out a couple onlookers. The kind of security they needed around his grave, they just weren't able to provide it."

Crying John offered a handful of peanuts to Fouler, popped the slobbery leftovers into his own mouth, and spoke as he chewed. "Couple weeks later, cops arrested a few guys for trespassing near there and one of them said something nutty, that he was a police informant planted to expose the plot to steal the King. Somebody—somebody who was never named—had promised these guys forty grand if they pulled it off."

"But they didn't," Harnett said.

"No, they didn't," Crying John admitted. "And four days later, at night when no one was looking, they moved the King's body to Graceland. You can see his grave on a tour if you want."

"Yeah, that's right," I said. "I saw a show that said his middle name was misspelled on the gravestone."

"The icing on the camel's back is this," said Fisher. "If Elvis had been ransacked at Forest Hill, everyone would've known. People around the world would've heard of it. Diggers know better. But if he was dug up at Graceland, different story. You think the Presleys would want that news advertised?"

"Are you saying . . . ," I started.

Fisher held up his hands. "I'm not saying anything."

I looked around at each Digger in turn.

"Whose territory is Memphis?"

Slowly all heads turned to the Apologist, a man so innocuous it took me a few seconds to remember why this kindly-looking fogey was sitting at our table. The wan smile that had graced his face all night long did not alter.

My throat burned. My eyes stung. I hailed down the scarred waitress and begged her for more water. The pub had become an asylum, a holding pen for the mad, and there was no way for someone as steeped in extra-credit practicality as I to accept such outlandish and unsourced claims. Yet I did. These men were reminiscing; they were not out to impress me.

Brownie waited until the waitress was gone. "Aberdeen's dead."

"Natural causes?" asked Crying John.

Brownie shrugged. "What's natural?"

"The Inca Prince has the Big C," Fisher said. "He won't last another six months, that's what Knox says."

"And what happened to Poe? And the General?" Screw sounded like he didn't really want to know.

"They're done," Under-the-Mud said. "Knox has them attending church five, six times a week, praying as fast as they can to make everything right. Too old to dig worth a fig anyway."

Crying John stroked the sleeping Foulie. "We're all too old."

At this, they began tugging at their sleeves and checking their watches. In almost perfect synchronicity they lifted their beers and drank, as if honoring their fallen comrades. Even Harnett chewed the ice from the bottom of his glass.

"And Baby? What about Baby?" asked Screw. "We can't sit here and pretend he doesn't exist."

Fisher raised his head from his glass and looked directly at me.

"Wake up and smell the butter, Screw," Fisher said. "We got a new baby now."

At my elbow I felt Under-the-Mud bristle.

"Valerie," Under-the-Mud rasped. Harnett's tired eyes rolled upward once more. "Doesn't the memory do anything to you? Doesn't it give you pause?"

"I didn't plan any of this," Harnett said. "Not her, not the kid."

"Because it does something to me. Goddamn if it doesn't do something to me. Of course, I never met her. None of us did. But each report from Knox—why, it thawed the midnight dirt."

To such solitary men, word of a woman in their midst must have been electrifying. It had only been a few weeks ago that Harnett had told me of the prostitution that once ran rampant in graveyards, a practice that made a kind of sense when you considered how cemeteries were both public and private. These Diggers' primary experience with females might have been with just such women. So stories of my mother's open mind, ruthless intelligence, resourcefulness, and, yes, beauty—it might have been enough to shake any underworld. I felt a desperate happiness for her. She had lived some life, at least, before I came along.

"She was something, all right," said Fisher.

"It was like she was all of ours, in a way," said Brownie.

The Apologist parted his lips as if to speak, then shook his head helplessly.

"And then she was gone," Under-the-Mud said. "You can try to place blame elsewhere, but you know where it lies. And look at you now. You're off and doing it again."

"You just want me to fail," Harnett said. "I don't know why, but you want me to fail."

"No, I want you *out.*" For a Digger, the slight increase in volume was tantamount to screaming—everyone cringed. "She could've taken you away from all this. Given you a real life. Given you your son. I would risk death for such an opportunity, even today, right now. All of us would. Life, Resurrectionist! Life was handed to you on a platter! And what did you do? You pissed all over it. Now here comes your son and a second chance. And what do you do? What do you do?"

I gripped my cranium. The dropping of mugs upon bar tops was like a stampede.

"It's late," Screw said.

Under-the-Mud rolled his tongue around his old teeth. "It's later than you think."

Screw nodded for a moment, then stood up. He lifted his coat from the back of his chair and in a single motion flung it onto both arms and was gone without a word. Brownie downed the last of his beer and dropped into darkness. Fisher stood and gave me a concerned look before nodding curtly to both Under-the-Mud and my father. The Apologist rose next, limping over to the side of the table and holding out a brittle-looking hand. With a resigned frown, Under-the-Mud took it and was helped to a standing position, both men wincing over old bones and sore joints. The two of them shuffled away, parting to take opposite paths around the pool table and ignoring each other when they met again on the far side.

Crying John slid into the booth beside me. Moments later I felt warm fur as Fouler made her obligatory rotations before settling. Crying John brushed peanut shells from his beard.

"Everyone's tired," he sighed, while Harnett picked at his dirty fingernails in the dim red incandescence. "Everyone's tired and everyone's old and everyone's scared. You just have to remember that."

"They complain about the end," Harnett said, "how the end is coming, how it's almost here. What do they think I'm doing? I know he's my son and that carries certain risks. But he's a hope. Am I wrong? He's a hope for all of us. That maybe the age isn't ending."

The jukebox track began to skip. In the jarring and intermittent silence, women's frivolity transformed into desperation and men's bluster into anguish. The normal world roared back and tried to dismantle the delirious fantasy that had been built up around our small, sticky booth. It frightened me, but Crying John seemed not to notice. He regarded my father for a long moment. The darkness made it hard to confirm the gloss that coated his cheeks.

"Maybe that's what they're saying," he said. "Maybe the age *should* end. You ever think of that?"

3.

The next day was Sunday, and when we made our morning loop of the cemetery I had my biology text under my arm. Forty-five minutes later, upon resuming our positions at the coffee shop, I opened the text but couldn't concentrate. Harnett had dug out binoculars from his glove box, and in between moments of spying he kept staring at me.

"What?" I finally demanded.

"This thing you do," he said. "Where you space out. What is that?"

"What do you mean?"

"You know," he said. "Out at a dig or when you're upset. That thing where you space out."

"Specifying," I sighed. "Mom called it specifying."

"All right," he said. "So what is it?"

"What do you care?"

"Are you having some sort of mental break? Or some kind of fit?"

"A fit?"

"It's best if you tell me," he said. "We're out on a dig and you have some kind of fit, it's both our asses."

"Dude," I said. "I'm not having a fit."

He crossed his arms and settled back into his chair, ready to listen. I checked around the shop to make sure no Diggers were nearby, and then I realized I could not remember their faces. The guy rifling through the utensils—was it possible that was Brownie? The old man outside the window hunched before the newspaper kiosk—it might be Under-the-Mud, but really I had no idea. These men were so good at disappearing that only their colorful nicknames stuck with me.

I rounded my shoulders and in low tones told Harnett everything: when the specifying had begun, the stressful situations that set it off, the near-blinding clarity. When I finished he toyed with the binoculars.

"And you remember these things," he said. "These things you specify."

I closed my eyes and let my mind shuffle through the past few months in reverse order—

—*a pinprick mole dotting the exact spot of a necklace clasp*—
—*golden specks of pyrite embedded in the stony path*—
—*tongue and lips inflated by bacteria into grotesque purple fruit*—
—*the unnatural shrug in the neck of my fork*—

—and it was as if brand-new, every shimmering, electric, frozen instant.

"Yeah, they're there," I said breathlessly. "They're all there."

"Can you do it at will?" he asked.

"What do you mean?"

"I mean, can you . . . specify whenever you want?"

I thought about it for a moment. Specifying had always been for me an unpleasant defense mechanism, never something I would willingly invoke.

"I don't know," I said honestly.

Harnett grunted.

"You might think about that," he said at last.

And there it was—an idea so simple it had never occurred to me. Despite doctors' labeling of the technique as some sort of handicap, it had the makings of a powerful tool, particularly for someone needing to memorize bits of newspaper, details of caskets, locations of graves, the contour and texture of grass before the first incision. I couldn't help wondering whether my mother, who had shrugged off psychologists' recommendations and indulged my near-photographic recall, had anticipated that one day I would find a good use for it.

It was too much to consider, and I rose from the table.

"Where you going?" Harnett asked.

"I can't study here. I'm going next door to get a snack."

"I was planning on doing another walk-by," he said, adjusting the knobs on the eyepieces. "Maybe even try cutting through the cemetery—as a local history buff, that sort of thing."

"Do it yourself," I said. "This test, I can't tell you how important—"

"Yeah, okay." He sounded a little hurt. "Straight As, I know. Fine. Go eat."

I put on my coat, picked up my book, and headed for the door. I paused.

"You want me to bring you back anything?"

He leaned forward so that the binoculars touched the window.

4.

I ORDERED A BASKET of fries and settled onto a stool at the end of the counter. Oldies were screaming from a speaker directly above my head, and the familiar melodies made it somehow easier to slip into the rote patterns of memorization. It wasn't as inspiring as Foley's CDs—not even close—but by the time the Four Tops segued into the Monkees, I was beginning to understand DNA storage in eukaryotic versus prokaryote organisms.

Halfway through the fries I shook the salt too enthusiastically and it went everywhere, dull sparkles bouncing across the book and lodging in its crevice. I pounded it against the counter, and with the side of my palm scooped up the salt. Remembering an old superstition of my mother's, I took a pinch of it, said a prayer to Two-Fingered Jesus about acing Gottschalk's exam, and tossed the granules over my shoulder.

"Devil's after you," said a man sitting on the stool to my left.

I glanced over at him. He was abnormally short. A long-tailed black coat draped to the heels of his dress shoes, yet strained against the horizontal shove of his Goliath shoulders. Beneath was a magenta vest and a ruffled shirt. Nearly everyone in the diner was wearing their Sunday best, but even among the tie clips and flowered hats this was an especially dapper ensemble. Its condition, though, was shabby. The sleeves were pilled and the elbows shiny with wear. The vest was so threadbare it was iridescent. Patterns in the black tie revealed a previous wadding, and the shirt ruffles carried similar triangular motifs.

"I'm sorry?"

"Devil. Salt." Like many of the people around me, he had a Southern accent. "Sorry, I saw you throwing salt."

Still he did not meet my eyes.

"Oh, yeah," I said. "Did I get it on you?"

"It's to keep away devils, they say."

"I didn't know that," I said. "It was just something my mom did."

"That's right." He nodded to himself. "I had forgotten."

He turned to me and offered a tentative smile. His eyes were the clearest blue I had ever seen, like glass, like pictures of Mediterranean waters. These gentle pools were captured within a face that looked edgy and exhausted, but a face that nonetheless did in fact resemble a baby's, with everything cute taken to an uncomfortable extreme: rosy flush rendered eczemic, cherubic cheeks gone saggy, hair so tangerine and fine it floated like broken cobweb. Most discomfiting were his rows of tiny teeth, mere dots of white upon red gums.

My chest constricted.

"You're Boggs."

A fly hit him in the eye; he nudged it away with a knuckle.

"I've come such a long way to meet you, son. You wouldn't believe how long."

Everything told me to run. Knox had warned me about him; Harnett had refused to discuss him; the Diggers had offered to his name their ominous regrets. But I was rendered motionless by how utterly dissimilar he was to my mental picture of him. Though muscular, he was diminutive. He was soft-spoken, well-dressed, mannered. And he looked at me with an earnest hopefulness that was heartrending.

"I'm not supposed to talk to you," I said.

He held up a nervous hand and licked lips that were dry and cracked from too many hours in the sun. "I know. I mean, I had a hunch. But hear me out, son. I came so far. California—that's two thousand five hundred seventy-five miles I came, and I had to jack a Hyundai in Missouri when my first ride up and died on me. Maybe that was wrong of me. Maybe so. But I had to get here. I been dreaming of this day so long."

He firmed his lips as if mobilizing himself for action, and

then thrust out his hand. I stared at it. The fingers were stubby, the nails purple and pulverized beyond that of any Digger I'd met. Either he was unusually clumsy or unusually busy.

Dejection flickered in his eyes. The hand floated erratically. I couldn't bear it. Limply I took it and his warm fingers curled over mine. The shake itself was minute but as firm as granite. His crystalline eyes sparkled.

"Antiochus Boggs." His voice clotted with emotion.

He had me by the hand; I shrugged and replied. "Joey Crouch."

"Joey, son, I'm not your dad. But I should've been."

I pulled my hand away. In an instant my textbook was stowed and I was on my feet. Boggs slid from his stool and veered to cut me off. He was shorter than I. I could see sunburn shine through the loose whips of his red hair. When he raised his hands to halt me, the suit strained over his shoulders and biceps.

"Apologies," he said. "That was out of line. I'm tired. Been driving nonstop for three days. Haven't slept. Barely eaten. My brain—it feels like it's busted open. Earlier on I thought I felt it dripping out my ears." He laughed once, tried to reel me back in with the admission. "I'm serious. Kept reaching up there and everything. Thought to myself, *Now, what's that boy gonna think when he meets his uncle and sees brain dripping out his ears?*"

"You're not my uncle," I said.

"Is that what I said? Lord, my mind. No, son, no, I'm not your uncle. That's true. Dammit, you're right. But I feel like I am. Your dad and I grew up close as brothers. Closer, even. There was some unpleasantness, yes, and the unfortunate result was that I did not get to make your acquaintance. Not then, not for sixteen years. But here you are. And here I am. Sixteen years later and I'm finally meeting my son."

He shut his eyes and gave his head a brisk shake.

"Sorry. Sorry. My brain's sliding right out my skull. Apologies?"

He turned upon me those spectral eyes. Specks of blood dotted his bottom lip.

Slowly I sat. Keeping his eyes on me, he again mounted the stool. It took him several moments. When he was properly seated, he straightened his sleeves and attempted to tuck excess ruffles into his pants.

"You've been given what we in the South call sucker bait. A false bill of sale." He gestured at the street. "I'm guessing those men you met sketched me out to be a monster. And you believed them, because why would you not? They're your elders. They're supposed to look out for you. But, son, look. Use your own eyes. Do I look like a monster?"

His wingspan, when he spread his arms, wasn't much. Behind him, the place was thickening with families absorbed in their own lunchtime mediations. Next to these groups of combed and belted believers, Boggs just looked remarkably unwell—and alone. I felt an unwelcome but unequivocal surge of sympathy. I, too, knew loneliness.

"No," I answered. The obvious pleasure the word gave him troubled me, and I forced an edge into my voice. "What do you want?"

"Want? Well, for starters—I'm a little embarrassed to be honest. Seeing how we've just met and all. But I'm a little low on funds since my ride up and died. If you're not intending on finishing those french fries, I'd hate to see them thrown out."

I blinked at him, then at the food. The smallest of shrugs was all he needed. He pulled the plastic basket until it was stationed directly beneath his chin. Small fingers fumbled through the salt and grease and came up with yellow slivers that he piled on top of his tongue. His shrunken teeth affected a horizontal motion to grind the food to mash.

"That's it?" I asked. "Food?"

He paused midchew. "There is something else. A favor. It's an embarrassment to have to ask it. I would've preferred to pass more pleasantries. But I feel like I know you, son. You feel it? It's okay if you don't. It's not gonna hurt my feelings."

I did not answer.

He swallowed and wiped his mouth with his sleeve. A moment later he winced at his behavior and wiped his sleeve with his fingers. Then he looked at his fingers and started searching around for a napkin. The holder was out of his limited reach and reluctantly I withdrew a napkin and handed it over. He nodded his thanks and wove it through his fingers.

"I'd like to speak to your dad," he said. "If you think you can arrange it."

I thought of the single wall that separated the diner from the coffee shop.

"I'm not sure I can do that."

He fumbled inside his pants pocket and withdrew a dingy razor blade.

"Wait." Panic hit me—the blade, chipped and pimpled with rust, was no equal to my father's Scottish masterpiece and would hurt plenty and spread disease when it cut. "Listen. Maybe I can. At least let me try!"

He looked at me in confusion and then at the blade in his hand. He laughed.

"This is my shaving razor," he said. "I ain't coming to get

you, son, relax. I just wanted to show you that I'm taking this serious. Cleaned my suit at a BP back in Tennessee. Shaved this morning in the library up the road. Got myself a haircut, too."

He licked his palm and tried to paste down the flyaway hairs. Looking closer, I could see the flushed evidence of newly shorn cheeks, as well as the survivors flitting like orange antenna in the ceiling-fan breeze. I tried to modulate my heart rate. "He doesn't know. Harnett—he doesn't know you're here. None of them do."

"That is by design, son," he said. "Why would I announce myself? So they can make a spectacle of me? Had a lifetime of that already. How they're creeping around that marble farm out there like they're playing detective, *that's* the spectacle. That fat, hairy one? The one with the rotter bitch dog? Fourteen times he circled that thing in one hour. What in blazes are you learning on your fourteenth lap?"

He leaned closer. The blue pouches beneath his lower lids swelled to prominence. At the circumference of his perfect eyes I saw root systems of broken vessels. He smelled like all Diggers smell but dipped in the faint turpentine of insomnia. The latter was a scent I recognized from my mother.

"That's all they ever do," he said. "They walk in circles. It's like a metaphor. Once every blue moon they get together and slap each other's backs and then get right back to walking"—and here he walked his fingers around an invisible track—"in circles."

Somehow I held back from nodding. The Diggers were a clique as insular as any in high school. Why I hadn't realized this before baffled me, but I felt gratitude at being trusted with such an observation. Few people since I had left Chicago had met me with anything but skepticism or outright hostility; I wanted to reward him for that, as well as exercise the feeling of maturity it gave me.

"They *are* old," I offered.

Boggs snapped his fingers and pointed at me. "My boy's a sharp one. That's right. They're geezers, ain't they? All but me and Kenny. And you too, son. I think that's why I trust you. You're not set in your ways. You've got an open mind. That's the most important thing in the world, an open mind. Your mom had one. Kenny, too. I bet that's hard to believe. He's a rule follower, that one, an order giver. Be quiet, be still, be invisible. He wasn't always that way."

I took the opportunity to resolve a controversy: *"I can get anyone."*

He laughed. "That's right! *I can get anyone*—now, that's the old Kenny. Back when he had a pair, right?"

Loyalty tugged at me. Harnett wasn't as bad as Boggs said, he couldn't be.

Boggs picked up on my hesitation. "No, see, you're right to defend him. A good son protects his father and vice versa. You were my son, no one would hurt you, not ever, they wouldn't dare. Lord, you're a sharp one. May I ask you a question?"

"I guess. Yeah, okay."

"It's kind of personal."

"That's fine."

"Okay." He took a deep breath. "You ever wondered what would happen if they knew?"

"Knew what?"

"What you do at night."

I glanced around. Just the words made me sweat. "Who?"

"I don't know. The people you see every day. You go to school?"

"Yeah."

His head bobbed with enthusiasm. "There you go. Kids at school. The jerks who shove you around. The teacher who treats you like dog crap on his shoe. The little lady who gives you a hard-on the size of Canada and then breaks it in two."

Just like that I was hanging on his every word.

"What about them?"

"Well, what if they knew? All of them." A smile fluttered the edge of his lip. "Every single last rotter."

A thrill burned through my chest and up my spine. I saw the Root dripping dirt as she rose victorious from a hole, and the awed and submissive expressions of Gottschalk, Woody, and Celeste.

Boggs slid a few inches closer. The cuff of his overlong sleeve was held back with what looked like rusty diaper pins.

"Correct me if I'm wrong. But I sense something here. A commonality. A special bond between father and son that no one else—"

"I'm not your son."

"My brain, it's my brain, I swear earlier it was coming out my ears. The point is, you and me? We're the same. Can't you feel it?"

"No," I said automatically, but even I heard the lack of conviction.

"No? Really? We're not related by blood, I give you that. But look. You don't have a mom or dad. You could make an argument on the dad part, I realize; it's an open question whether Kenny fulfills the requirements of fatherhood. That's for you to decide. Now, take me—I don't have a mom or dad either. You want to know what happened?"

How could I not? I tried to sound disinterested. "Okay."

"Originally I had both," he said. "I was born in Atlanta.

But when I came out . . . well, look at me. Surely you noticed I'm a little different."

I shook my head. It was a weak and futile gesture.

"I appreciate that," he said. "But there ain't any hiding physical facts. I wasn't born right. I guess you could call me deformed. So they sent me off. Foster homes. Nine of them. Largely unpleasant memories, if you want to know the truth. Stuff you don't want to know about, like what happens when you pee the bed too many times or accidentally kill the new kitten. You wouldn't believe how many daddies touched me in inappropriate ways. I would never do something like that to you, son."

I'm not your son—I wanted to say it but couldn't for fear that it would shatter the wide, clear glass of his eyes.

"There were good things about it, too. I got strong, real strong. I found out that there's things in the dirt you can live off if you need to. Eventually the orphanages got me, but I kept breaking out until they stopped chasing. That's when I fell in with the rotters. I mean the Diggers."

An even smaller Antiochus Boggs happening upon those strange and secretive old men—it was hard to imagine their acceptance of him until I remembered how I first came upon Ken Harnett, hostile and uncommunicative in a darkened cabin.

"The point is," he continued, "I've never fit in. Just like you. And I don't mean any offense by that. Not fitting in? In my book, that's a good thing. You can't make a mark on the world if you just vote the party line. So can you see it? How we're the same? Am I making any sense? My brain isn't exactly right."

He looked aggrieved. I felt a need to reassure him. "I guess it makes sense."

"Lord, that's sweet music." His rotund cheeks quivered. His lips made inchworm shrugs. He shut his eyes and I pictured the pure and exquisite ocean that might flow from such resplendent irises. When he regained control over himself he peeked up at me shyly. "Guys like you and me, we're special. We have talents others don't have, won't ever have. Then why aren't we happier? You ever ask yourself that?"

"Yes." If there was one undeniable truth, this was it.

"Me too. Took me a lifetime to figure it out, but I won't make you wait that long. You just have to ask yourself one question: What do we take from the rotters? Aside from trinkets and trifles, what possession of genuine worth do we win for our efforts? The answer ought to depress you, son. The answer is *nothing*. Deep down, that bothers you. Doesn't it? Sure as hell bothers me. And those old men you met, they're satisfied with nothing. With all their gifts—and I won't bullshit you, they have gifts—at the end of the day, they're satisfied with making circles. Over and over. Over and over."

With that, he tucked his small hand inside his coat, eased unseen buckles, and withdrew a large black book.

"I've taken more," he said.

A fist snared Boggs's collar and shoved. He struck the counter, rebounded, lost his balance, and tumbled from his seat. His impact sounded like a gray sack dropped to cabin cement. The vacated stool made merry-go-round circuits. A few feet away, the book slapped down and Boggs lunged for it. The rest was blocked out—Harnett was in my face, hauling me to my feet and squeezing me with one hand while he dug for a ten-dollar bill and left it wadded on top of the check.

His face was bloodless. "Your schoolwork."

Numbly I picked up my biology book and Harnett steered us away. Already Boggs was up and blocking our path, over a foot shorter than my father but, due to his fantastic breadth and the startling incongruity of his three-piece suit, just as imposing. Harnett pulled back, holding me in check with an elbow. Boggs's pink face broke into a heedless grin.

"Kenny," he said. "Lord, it's good to see you."

"Step aside."

Boggs shook his head as if there had been some terrible misunderstanding.

"This is silly. We shouldn't fight. If you could just give me a minute I'd be—"

"Get out of my face."

A burly man in chef's whites was leaning over the counter.

"There some problem here, folks?"

Oldies still blared from speakers, but beneath the music the dissonance of the diner was smoothing as families broke off their conversations and began to take note. Boggs straightened his vest and adjusted his rumpled tie. He gestured apologetically at a vacated corner booth. If there was anything a Digger feared it was attention, and the longer we stood there the more we got. With a single flex of his jaw, Harnett forced a tight smile at the cook, took three giant steps, and landed on the far bench of the booth. I wandered after and he tugged me down next to him.

Coattails rippling, Boggs slid onto the opposite bench. He pushed aside the uncleared plates and dirty utensils and smacked the book down before him. It was large and nondescript and bulged with its untitled contents. Boggs's little hands stroked the faux-leather cover.

"Two minutes." Harnett flicked his eyes at a nearby clock,

where a second hand lazed past bad caricatures of Marlon Brando, Marilyn Monroe, and James Dean. "Time enough for these people to get back to their business."

"You're getting bent out of shape," Boggs said. "There's no reason. It's just me, Baby. Do you know how far I came to see you? Two thousand five hundred seventy-five—"

"Tick tock." Harnett kept his eyes on Marlon, Marilyn, and James.

Boggs sat back and frowned. "Right. Down to business. That's how it always is with you. I guess I'd forgotten. Well, fine. We can make this a business meeting if you want. I do have some business to transact."

"That's up to you," Harnett said. "One minute."

Boggs spoke faster. "You're going to be glad we had this conversation. You're going to see that this is exactly where you belong. Right at this table with me. With me and Joey. The three of us—you remember how it used to be? With me and you and Valerie? We were family then, and the three of us here now, we can be—"

"Don't talk about her. Don't talk. I've got nothing to say to you." But Harnett couldn't resist. "Go back to your hell-hole. Your ditch. Wherever you're squatting now."

The words were like bullets. Boggs flinched at each one. He hid his face, turning to the dirty dishes for guidance. When at last he spoke, the syllables were tentative and imploring. "She's gone now. I know it, I heard. And I'm so sorry, Kenny. You don't know how sorry. But you don't need to be like this. I've done nothing to deserve it. I'm trying to make things better with us. You're my brother and nothing can change that."

"We were never brothers."

Boggs's voice shattered. "How can you *say* that? Of course

we are! All those years growing up—what was that? Did that not happen? You need to remember it, Kenny. One of us has to, and my brain is falling out my head. Did I tell you that? It's true. You're probably glad. But you shouldn't be. No one should feel that way about his brother."

"Don't worry. I don't feel anything at all." He glanced at the clock. "Time's up."

"Wait. Now you just wait. I know you like I know me. We think the same. You may not want to admit that, but it's true. We both know, for instance, that when a rotter dies, that's it. There's no fantasy land of heaven or hell. It's like that old saying we used to say: *You can't take it with you*. Except here's the thing. You ready? You ready for our business transaction? Turns out they *do* get away with something. Don't they?" He shifted his despairing gaze to me. "Don't they, son?"

"Do not address him," Harnett said. I barely heard. I could not take my eyes from the unnatural thickness of the book.

"What the rotters get away with is dignity. *Dignity*. And that's wrong. And you know it. They had their time. They had their degrees and careers and portfolios. All so they could buy themselves a diamond ring and die with it on, all so they could get themselves buried wearing it—and what's the point, Kenny, seriously now, of a diamond, which is designed to reflect light, what's the point if there ain't no light to reflect? You and me can steal that ring, sure, but that doesn't get down to the real issue, now, does it? Brother—you know I know you know it."

Boggs sank his fingers into the soft flesh of the book and with deliberation slid it across the table. It made the sound of ice being shaved. Boggs twisted his wrists clockwise and the book was suddenly facing my father and me with all the malice of a darkened cellar.

I stared at it. Harnett did, too.

"This is a gift. If you want it. I began it when I heard about our son."

I found myself drawing back the front cover.

"I started it alone but we can finish it together."

When I saw the first Polaroid it was as if I had known all along. My heart did not accelerate; rather it seemed to slow and slug thickly against either lung. I turned pages. More.

"I call it the Rotters Book, Kenny."

More. More.

"My Rotters Book. *Our* Rotters Book."

More. More. More.

"A bunch of filthy stinking rotters."

On each wrinkled page, nestled between the claws of scrapbook photo corners, were four instant photographs, each one of a corpse smashed flat by the unkind swat of a cheap flashbulb and slathered a garish green by the yellow snot of developing liquid. They were old men, their translucent skin stretched and pocked like moth-eaten fabric. They were little girls, their lips strung with purple pearls of rot, their cheeks appled with rupture. They were genderless skulls, a thousand years old, the dried jelly of what used to be flesh crusted to gray bone. Caught in explosions of white light, once-severe brows were erased, once-regal cheekbones whittled to kernels; they were pink, white, blue; they were the color and texture of afterbirth. And there were hundreds of them, these cold and bent photos, each one stamped with Boggs's muddy fingerprints—the autograph of this intruder who had come at them with chisel and shovel, smashing first their caskets and then their sanctuary. It was sickening and dazzling, this litany of trespass.

I could feel the heat of Harnett's armpits, see the sweat spreading from his hands.

"No one's ever seen anything like it, Kenny. I can promise you that. You know what this is? It's a *communication*. It's going to tell the whole wide world that we're watching. There's not going to be any more creeping around like cockroaches. No one anywhere is going to even think about dying without having to go through us first."

Page after page—it was as if someone had done my specifying for me.

Boggs's voice was bursting with joy. "I still haven't told you the best part."

Together my father and I looked up.

"Two pictures," Boggs said. "I take two. One goes in the Rotters Book. The other I leave down there with them." He beamed proudly. "Pinned right to their chests."

Harnett went over the table. Condiment bottles spun and clattered; I saw a white line of salt and felt a familiar urge except this time didn't know in which direction to throw. Harnett's hands squeezed at Boggs's throat. The smaller man gurgled in surprise and cranked his foreshortened arms as if he were drowning. His frenzied feet nailed me under the table—my foot, my shin, my thigh—and for a flash I was back within the Congress of Freaks, not son of the mighty Resurrectionist, just Crotch, and these kicks were what I deserved.

I rolled from the booth and hit the floor. Above, Boggs pushed at my father's eyes with his thumbs. Harnett twisted and tried to toss him away, but Boggs had already taken firm hold of my father's coat and they both went crashing. Harnett's head struck the hanging lamp and it whirled.

Knees knocked me; normal people were closing in. Their

hovering presence yanked me back to a world I had somehow forgotten. From my sunken vantage I saw beer bellies and holstered cell phones and practical purses, and I wanted it back, all of it. *Take me,* I begged of them, but to their eyes I had long since become oblivion. They only saw strange, faceless men wrestling on top of cheap tableware. Reluctantly I returned to my newer world and within the bedlam saw my father attempt to grab the steak knife still spinning upon the unbused table.

Blood was streaking down his forehead—the lamp had slashed him good. He tried to wipe away an eyeful and Boggs, his compact torso contracting ferociously, took the opportunity to slam him to the table. Plates vibrated and silverware floated in midair; the steak knife twirled and Harnett's hand pinned it to the wall. One second later it was clutched in his fist, the blade flashing.

Finally there were arms everywhere, pulling the two fighters apart, and in the tangle of bodies I saw faces that triggered recognition: here was Brownie, lifting Boggs in a backward bear hug; here was Under-the-Mud, prying Boggs's fingers from a bloodied neck; here was Screw, restraining Boggs's thrashing legs; here was Fisher, doing the same to Harnett; here was Crying John, already hoisting Harnett by the coat collar; and here, like a ghost, was the Apologist, gently coaxing the knife from Harnett's fingers.

Through it, the two men roared.

"Kenny! Kenny!" Boggs cried. "What did I do?"

"We should've taken care of you years ago!"

"Was it my brain?" Boggs clawed desperately at the sides of his head. "Did my brain do something wrong?"

"You're no brother to me and no son to Lionel."

"I am! I am!" Boggs shook free from his captors and

snatched up the Rotters Book. Panting, he regarded each old man in turn. The pale grief drained from his face and replaced itself with a florid loathing. "Why are all of you looking at me? I don't exist to you, remember? Don't any of you remember? You banished me. All of you agreed to it. That's how much you all loved your Baby. You banished me and you want to pretend that you're blameless. Well, go ahead. Pretend. Act like I don't exist. Pretty soon you'll change your mind. I swear it. You see this book?"

"Get out!" Harnett boomed. Crying John took handfuls of his clothes to keep him at bay.

"Yes, brother—oh, sorry, Mr. Resurrectionist, sir. Anything you say. Resurrectionist tells Baby what to do and Baby does it. Those are the rules, right?" He futzed with his suit until he recognized its hopeless condition. The tie slopped in an inebriated loop; the vest was missing buttons; the shirt was bedecked with food. The violation of this façade of respectability infuriated him. He grated his tiny teeth and glared at Harnett. "You're no different than the rest of these rotters."

"You stay in your territory," Harnett said. "You remember Monro-Barclay and stay the hell away."

"The pact?" Boggs laughed and a mist of blood painted his ruffles. "If I'm not your brother and I'm not Lionel's son, then guess what? I'm an orphan again! I'm an orphan and I belong to nobody. Any pact you rotters have ain't my concern. I plan to finish my book on schedule. And if that takes me into enemy territory, I don't know what to say. I have no enemies. I love all of you. You know that. It's you who don't love me."

Boggs limped in the direction of the door. He muttered as he passed me.

"Ask Daddy about the Rat King," he said. "Ask Daddy

about the Gatlins." He turned up the volume so that everyone—Diggers, diners, cooks, everyone—could hear. "The Rat King? The Gatlins? Your memory, old men, is selective!"

At the mention of these curious oaths, Harnett pulled against Crying John's embrace. Boggs ducked and crabbed sideways. After his stubby fingers hooked the handle of the front door, he scanned the crowd until his eyes found mine. "Your first hole, son. Remember the feeling? Now imagine it times a hundred. Times a thousand. Imagine how a gentleman of breeding raises his little Digger."

Boggs slipped the Rotters Book inside his coat and I felt a stab of loss. He pushed open the door and a sparkling cone of snow turned him into some dizzying dream. A jingle of door bells, a flare of coattails, and he was gone.

Already the Diggers were threading into the crowd and loosening from my memory. The worst possible thing had happened. They had been seen, addressed in public, and now, thanks to my father's rash behavior, would have to disperse far sooner than they had hoped. As the interlopers withdrew, the surrounding gawkers took on even finer dimension. I wanted so badly to run into their arms and join their routines of afternoon casseroles, evening board games, school-night early bedtimes. Any quiet mundanity—I'd take it and love it and never want anything else, I'd swear to it.

But even these people were scattering, half grinning with the anticipation of the stories they'd tell about the outrageous dispute they'd seen at lunch. Only Crying John remained at my father's side. He took a clean towel from a cook and placed it in Harnett's hand, then lifted that hand so that it applied pressure to the wound. Harnett shook off the man's grip and looked away in shame. With nothing but a lugubrious frown, Crying John slipped through shoulders and became just another plaid shirt receding from spilled food and broken dishes. I thought, but wasn't sure, that I heard a distant muttering: "C'mon, Foulie."

Braver legs approached. "You okay, mister?"

Harnett checked the towel. It was deep red. At his feet, blood made moth blots across the tile. He wiped his slick face and neck and tossed the towel onto the destroyed table.

"The truck," he told me.

"Good," I said, tearing my eyes from the gore and scooping up my biology text. "Let's go home."

We pushed through the crowd and were outside. Boggs was nowhere.

"We're not going home," Harnett said as we carved the cold morning air. The sidewalk behind him was spattered with red.

"What? But school. My test."

"Lionel." For once he ignored the caskets tasting fresh air across the street. "We talk to Lionel."

5.

Blue mountains, yellow forests, black miles of scorched highway—landscapes metamorphosed in ways I'd never imagined as we barreled through West Virginia, then Virginia, and on into North Carolina. Harnett drove so fast I could feel the tires battle their axles.

As we neared Lionel's home in the Outer Banks, the landscape adjusted yet again to long, shimmering inlets and grassy flatlands giving rise to tall fronded trees and spiked bushes. Houses were built on stilts. Storefronts were pink and turquoise and waved flags that looked beaten by centuries of sand. And yes, sand—it was everywhere, shifting in random patches along the shoulder, rippling across the highway, piled intentionally in front lawns and speared with novelty flamingoes. I lowered the window and tasted fish. Harnett cranked the wheel, and for the next half hour we traveled parallel to an ocean I wanted badly to see. The surf shops and seafood restaurants ebbed. Only when there was nothing left at all did Harnett turn down an unmarked path.

He killed the engine a respectful distance away from a charming, if crooked, white house with pink trim. For a moment we sat listening to the overheated engine. Then he got out and I followed, and the ground was so solid I nearly fell.

The front door squealed and a cane stabbed its way into the driveway. It was an elderly man sporting a floppy beach hat, sunglasses, and an unbuttoned shirt that revealed a gaunt torso and sparse curls of white hair. Harnett met him in the middle of the yard. They stopped a few feet from each other.

"It's Baby, isn't it?" Lionel's voice broke into octaves almost musical. "Baby's dead. Baby's dead."

Harnett shook his head. "We just spoke to him."

With a liver-spotted hand he flipped the clipped-on shades from his bifocals and examined the brown rings of blood encircling Harnett's skull.

"Must've been some conversation," he said.

"He's up to something and I don't know what—"

Lionel waved for silence. "Please. You're tired and hungry. We'll save unpleasantness for a bit." He stretched his neck toward the truck, a smile playing at his lips. "Where's Grinder?"

The remorse was overwhelming.

Harnett faked indifference. "She broke."

Lionel's face fell. There was a complicated moment of give and take between the men, hard emotions fought down and painted over with softer ones, possibly for my benefit. "I'm sorry, Ken. She was a good instrument. You'll find another, I'm sure of it."

Then he looked at me. Even swaddled in folds of skin, the brown eyes sparkled.

Harnett hooked a thumb my direction. "The kid."

Lionel took an unsteady step, poked my foot with his cane, and laughed. He reached down and took up my hand. His palm was dry and his bones, as they squeezed, felt fragile. Still I could see the ghost of his former physique.

"Don't fret," he said softly. "All instruments break. All it means is that they have served their purpose. It's all any of us can ask, really." I found myself nodding, strangely heartened by how the term instrument could refer to both my trumpet and the Root.

Lionel's other hand sealed our handshake. "My stars! He looks like Val, Ken. My boy, you look just like your mother."

These unexpected words, this warm welcome—it was all I could do not to start sobbing. As if in sympathy, his own eyes filled with tears. His arthritic hands gripped harder.

"Honored," he said. "Honored."

"Lionel, easy," Harnett sighed. "He needs that hand for digging."

Lionel chuckled. He took a step back and regarded us both. He drove his cane into the dirt.

"What a treat! Come in, come in!"

He began hobbling back toward the house. Harnett and I followed.

"I'll have Lahn make up the spare room," Lionel said.

"We can't stay," Harnett said.

"What? That's idiotic."

Harnett glanced at me and again I felt guilty.

"The kid's got school."

"Hmm." He yanked at the ungreased door. "Well, I'll have Lahn make up the room just in case."

The normality of his home was heartbreaking. There were no stacks of papers, no ash-stained hearth, no hastily assembled bedding alongside the sink. There was a sofa and end tables with coasters. There were framed pictures. There was an aquarium in which bright fish waggled. There was a TV. With a grunt, Lionel leaned over and picked up a phone. A phone! I shot a yearning look at Harnett, feeling like a little kid inside a pet shop.

"Lahn, two very special guests have arrived at my home," Lionel said pleasantly. "Would you mind terribly coming by and fixing up the spare room?"

"Lionel, look—" Harnett began.

"Oh, thank you, Lahn. We won't be here when you arrive, so just let yourself— That's right. Oh? That might be nice, too. Yes, let's plan on it. We'll see you then." He hung up the phone. "Lahn will be fixing us dinner. You remember Lahn's dinners."

Harnett swallowed his protest. "Fine. Dinner. But then, really, we have to leave. The kid's got some test he says is important."

"Then I'm certain it is." Lionel gave me another long look. "Well. We can discuss it during our walk."

"What walk?"

Lionel indicated a closet. "Joey, get yourself a good coat. It gets cold on the beach."

The ocean—it was impossible to conceal my grin. I sorted

through the coats, only for a moment remembering the one I had abandoned in my locker before fleeing the school.

"You shouldn't be walking," Harnett said. There was a note of genuine concern in his voice. "You can barely make it across the room. We'll drive."

"Hogwash." Lionel rapped his cane against the floor. "And where we're going you can't drive."

Properly gloved and hatted, we exited through a rear door, passed through a backyard dominated by off-season flower patches and a freestanding porch swing, and picked up a faint trail leading into the trees. Harnett hovered over Lionel, tensed to catch the old man's fall, but the probing cane seemed to know the location of every rock and root.

Harnett recounted the relocation, Boggs's surprise appearance, and the contents of the Rotters Book. As he spoke I tried to envision my father as a little boy, looking up to his teacher much as I looked up to mine. Lionel took the news stoically, his brown eyes squinting through the fading light.

"And he looked bad," Harnett finished. "Really bad, and he wasn't making sense. He might be on something."

"His has always been an addictive personality. It's what made him such a Digger." Lionel kept his eyes on the trail. "Part of me isn't surprised he's acting out. He blames me for a lot; blames you for even more. But the way he's chosen to go about it, it's the worst thing he could do. You know what would happen if that book got out? Or, how do you say it, computerized? And sent out through the computers?"

"He's left evidence in every single coffin," Harnett said. "Someone gets exhumed for an autopsy and they start finding these? Hundreds of years of history up in smoke."

"It's just another sign," the old man said. "You can only

fight so much, Ken. Are you going to fight the turning of time? Not sure I see the use of it anymore. How many of us are left now? Less than a dozen?"

"We need to do something. Don't we?"

Lionel paused. "What exactly would you do?"

The prospective murder of Boggs, their brother and son, hung in the air.

Harnett kicked at the ground. "I don't know."

"If you're expecting me to issue some magnificent edict, I'm afraid I will disappoint," Lionel said. "No Monro-Barclay Pact would work now, not with what Baby has become."

I interrupted. "Everyone keeps talking about that Monro-whatever. No one ever says what it is."

Lionel missed a beat; his foot landed awkwardly and Harnett was there with both arms. Lionel fought free. "He doesn't know?"

Harnett let go and dropped back. "No. But it's time."

Exhilaration filled my chest; I quickened my step, passed Harnett, and came almost even with Lionel.

"When Ken and Baby were your age," Lionel explained, "and still my students, it became clear to me that Diggers were at a critical moment. Boundaries were custom, not law. Bellies were being dug only to find they were already harvested. There were ambushes, one Digger taking from another. Even Knox had almost wiped his hands of us. And then the inevitable happened. Well. Now I've forgotten his name."

"Boxer," Harnett called out. He had fallen even farther back.

"Boxer, that's right, and he wasn't one of the troublemakers, according to Knox."

"What happened to him?" I asked.

"He was killed! By another Digger! Over what—territory,

property, money, who knows. But tragedy so often brings with it rare opportunity. So I sent out through Knox the call to meet, all of us, just once, right out in the open, where together we would set down rules, laws, best practices. And out of it came the territories. It took days to finalize. Everything was taken into account. Geography, climate, types of soil, centers of population. Valuable assets, too: the Civil War graves of the South, the pioneer and Indian burials of the West. The lines were drawn with precision and care. And we called it the Monro-Barclay Pact. You remember why, Ken? Your father was always a good student. I bet you're a good student, too."

My voice was small but confident. "I am."

Harnett had dropped so far behind his response was inaudible.

"I presume you know that Edinburgh, Scotland, was the front line for body snatchers. In 1818, two surgeons, Dr. Monro and Dr. Barclay, each of whom employed resurrection men to obtain cadavers, decided all the rough-and-tumble stuff out there was senseless and so decided to divide the local cemeteries between them. Our pact was in that spirit." Lionel smiled to himself. "Of course, Monro and Barclay's deal went south when Dr. Liston came to town. But that's a story for another time."

"Boggs said you banished him," I said. "Like he wasn't happy with the West Coast."

Lionel wiped sweat from his face; I noticed that I wasn't warm. "His predecessor did very well with it. I don't know. I tried to be fair. To Baby especially, I've tried to be more than fair. He made all of us nervous with his—I guess you could call them innovations. The rest of the Diggers wanted him out, end of story. I couldn't do that. So I gave him the West.

I honestly believed he would thrive out there. And he has, at points. There are times when he does the work of ten of us. And other times . . ." Lionel paused and unstuck his cane from the mud. "I can't help but feel I've failed him in some regard."

Harnett shouted from behind. "We should be turning back."

Lionel shook his head forcefully. "We keep going. I've got something important to show you."

"It can wait. It's getting dark."

"It cannot wait." Lionel struck a low-hanging branch with his cane. "Not this."

So we walked. With each step, I gathered courage.

"You knew my mother," I said.

"Indeed. I consider it one of the rare pleasures of my life."

"How did you know her?" I pleaded. "I don't know any of it."

"I will tell you," he whispered.

Transferring his cane to his left hand, he pulled me closer and clamped his hand to my shoulder. I felt him give half of his weight to me—the price of his story.

"There is no handbook for what we do," he began. "There is no university, no library. You cannot seek us out because we don't exist. The trade is passed down, master to apprentice. That's it. For all these reasons and more, finding a suitable trainee is nigh impossible."

"I wasn't that hard to find," I said.

"You're different. You're blood of a Digger. And not just any Digger, but the Resurrectionist."

"They don't like it," I said. "I could tell when I met them."

His breaths were becoming shallower. A squiggly blue vein pulsed at his temple. "That was the real revelation of the

Monro-Barclay meeting. We saw each other for what we really were. Not beasts, not phantoms. Just sad, lonely men. Men who knew, from the first time they took hold of their instruments, that it would consume their lives, repel any hopes they had of friendships, of wives, of children. You are the first son to become an apprentice because there have been no other sons."

"And they hated him, right? Because he had both, a wife and a son."

"But then they came to know her. Just through stories, true, but that made it all the better, made it into something like a fairy tale. She was a miracle to them, this mother of yours. She came into this world, where no woman had ever trod, and did not flinch. She didn't entirely approve, either—she was like Knox in that way—yet she understood what we did and why we did it, and she brought something to our lives that no one has ever brought, not before, not since."

He stopped. Far behind, I heard Harnett's footsteps also stop, allowing us our privacy.

"Light." The golden dusk glimmered in his eyes. "Happiness. Warmth. Hope. Diggers had never hoped. But now your dad would come home soaked with dirt and smelling of death and she would wrap her arms around him. I saw it; Knox saw it; and then he passed word of this unbelievable thing that we'd seen. And vicarious though it was, we *lived*. My stars, for a few years there we were alive. Do you have any idea what that was like for us? I imagine you do. Then you can also imagine what it was like for us when she was gone."

We were heading downhill.

"Tell me why she left him," I said.

"There are plenty of reasons to blame myself. Let's face it, somewhere along the way I got it in my head that I was special, that I could effect change. And so I did things differently. I found new ways to dig holes and made sure Knox spread the word. I organized Monro-Barclay. And, Joey, truth be told, I took great satisfaction from it. I was vain and reckless. Joey, in my own way, I was not unlike Baby."

"They say you are the greatest Digger ever," I said.

"Was," he corrected. "And the reason I quit wasn't just that I was getting too old to lift Gaia. Oh—she's my—"

"Shovel," I guessed. "I mean your instrument."

Lionel nodded. "I quit out of guilt. Guilt that what happened between Ken and Baby was as much my fault as anyone's. I took on two apprentices at once. I took them to Scotland for two years to learn their history. I treated them both as sons. That's how headstrong I was. No matter that half the stories in literature have the same plot: a king has one kingdom to bequeath and two sons, and therein lies the ruin of all three."

The dimming light lent the conversation an added urgency. "Her ear." I trembled at the nearness of the answer. "My mother's ear was all messed up. She could barely hear out of it, and that's how she died."

Lionel's chest was beating up and down, too fast. With a valiant grunt, Lionel pushed off from my side and we were moving again.

"I'm getting to that. Now, Knox was the one who found me your father. Your dad's dad, your grandpa, sold a church to a black congregation and ended up dead. Didn't pay to cut blacks a square deal back then. Anyway, Knox was starting out at that church as a preacher and befriended your father, who was hanging around services begging for food and swiping wallets. Before I knew it, Knox had me raising the kid.

Naturally I didn't tell Ken about my profession until he was fifteen."

"He figured it out long before then," I said, thinking back on my own sleuthing. "Believe me."

Lionel laughed. "You may be right. So Baby came a few years later. He tracked us. No one before or since has been able to do it. He tracked us to multiple digs. By the third or fourth time I knew we were being followed, so I set a trap. We caught him just inside a cemetery fence and he tore up Ken something fierce—broke his nose, dislocated a finger, practically sliced an eyebrow clean off. Didn't get a good look at him until after we had him pinned. Smallest little fella I'd ever seen, the strangest little body, and a couple years younger than Ken, to boot. But he wasn't scared. He didn't beg to be let go. He just begged to come with us."

"Yeah, he kind of tracked me down, too." I looked down and saw traces of sand beneath my shoes.

"I didn't know what the hell to do. I put the fear of God in him, smacked him on the ass, and let him go. Couple weeks later, we had a cat die on us, got hit by a car. Your dad was fond of this animal. Used to sleep with it sometimes. Went by some stupid name like Pookie. Or Scoobie. Something like that. Hey!" I jumped as he yelled back over his shoulder. In the distance I saw Harnett take notice. "What was the name of that cat? The one who got run over?"

Harnett's response was immediate and morose. "Fred."

Lionel shrugged. "Anyhow, we buried the animal in the backyard. Next morning the carcass was sitting on top of its grave. Understand that the reconstruction was flawed, but for someone without a day of proper instruction it was astounding. When Ken told me he didn't do it, I knew it had to be that shrimp who punched like Joe Louis. I knew it was risky. I knew that. But the boy had raw talent like I'd never seen."

I eased him over a patch of loose gravel. "It's hard to believe they ever got along."

"They were all each other had. Don't be mistaken, there was plenty of one-upmanship. Ken could set him off with the wrong word about any number of topics. Baby had a complex about his lineage; thought he belonged in high society and it was just bad luck that he'd gotten kicked to the curb. He wouldn't dress for the work; he liked to look like some kind of silver-screen playboy. He wanted constant credit, constant. But my stars, could that boy move dirt."

Suddenly the trees were behind us.

"Ah, here we are," he said.

A red gash dove through the purples and blues that feathered the sky. After a moment I looked down at the steep slope at our feet. I shouldn't have been surprised, but I was. At the bottom was a cemetery.

"Ever seen the ocean?" Lionel asked.

I shook my head.

He smiled at me. "We'll get closer," he whispered. "Let's wait for your dad."

When Harnett joined us, he wasn't happy.

"What's this?" he asked. "I don't see why we're here."

"Look at how the light hits the water," Lionel mused.

I had not been aware the ocean was already in view. "Where?"

Lionel pointed. "Through the trees there. See the motion? How the rays shoot out in all directions? Ken, what does that remind you of?"

"Harpakhrad," Harnett said. He glanced at me.

"It's a perfect example, really," Lionel said, "of the differences between my two pupils. I acquired Harpakhrad for Baby while I was in Egypt. Her stem was made of lotus, mulberry, sycamore, and something called the doom palm, braided together while the branches were still growing and then petrified—the stem alone must have taken fifteen years to fashion. The blade was beveled iron and gold; the handle was encrusted with jewels and topped with a palladium scarab. It was the most marvelous thing I'd ever seen."

"How'd you afford it?" I asked.

Lionel's dismissive shrug recalled the demurring of the other Diggers. "I was in Egypt. There are tombs in the Valley of the Kings that remain unknown to most."

Images from history class crowded my mind: priceless statues, bejeweled thrones, golden death masks, chests and sarcophagi of infinite value.

Lionel cleared his throat. "Story for another time. The point being that there was never any question whose instrument it would become. Most Diggers, they don't care if they find their instrument in a dump. The pedigree shouldn't matter—when you have the proper instrument in your hand, you know it. Baby, though, I knew he would force Harpakhrad to become his own. He would bend her to his will. And when he dug at dusk the light would hit the scarab and the legs of the beetle would scatter the sun, just like this. I'm sure it still does."

"I doubt it," Harnett said. "Boggs would've sold it years ago. Probably for thirty bucks and a hot meal."

Lionel squinted into the sky. "She's out there somewhere. I know she is. I would like to see her again. Just once more."

Harnett ran a hand through his hair and gestured back at the trail. "It's late."

Lionel turned to him. "You have to let Grinder go. Look at your hands. They're curled like she's right here."

Harnett looked at his fingers as if they were strange objects. "They're old," he mused softly, turning them over. "They can't learn to hold new things."

Lionel nodded firmly. "They will." For some reason he looked at me when he said this.

The end of Lionel's cane disappeared into the unmowed grass of the hill. His feet shuffled as he began to descend. I heard Harnett's frustrated sigh as I hurried to remain at Lionel's side.

"Just a bit farther now," he huffed. "And such a pretty time to get there."

6.

THE CEMETERY GRASS WAS neatly trimmed, yet still swayed in mesmerizing patterns cut from the ocean wind. Harnett assisted Lionel now, and the old man's hand latched on to my father's shoulder more confidently than it had mine. I had never moved through a graveyard so haltingly; between each step fell an interval of at least ten seconds.

"At the diner Boggs said something about the Rat King," I said. "And something called the Gatlins."

"Boggs and I worked together. Lived together," Harnett said. "Then I met Val."

"How?" I asked.

"It doesn't matter," he said.

"How?" I demanded. The scrunching noise of dead leaves announced our entry into the final grove of trees separating the cemetery grounds from the ocean. The tide rasped like dying breath.

"Not far from here. At the beach," he said. The vision was madness—my mother in a yellow or pink bikini, tossing away her sun hat while my father chased her through seaweed and sand castles. "We got along. We spent a great deal of time together. I felt compelled to confide in her."

"You were in love!" Lionel shouted. "Jesus Christ, can't you say it after all these years?"

"Easy now, right foot." Harnett steadied Lionel. "Boggs and I were away a lot on digs. He'd dig faster and better than me. Left foot, come on. And when we came home— It was a small place. Things got uncomfortable. Boggs would look at her. There were tensions."

"Tensions," Lionel scoffed. "He wanted Valerie for himself."

Harnett scanned the murky horizon. "We have to get moving. Right foot. Come on, step."

And between encouragements my father told the only story left to tell. Once upon a time there were two men who loved and hated each other as only brothers could. One brother did things according to tradition; the other craved glory at the expense of all else. One night while unearthing a coffin, Ken Harnett told Antiochus Boggs that he needed to go his own way. Seconds later, Boggs shrieked. He had discovered a dead Rat King. A terror most consider nothing more than myth, a Rat King is a number of rats whose tails have become tangled and sealed with dirt, blood, and shit. Joined as one, they move and think and die as a single creature and their discovery has always portended bad things: war, the plague. Boggs became agitated. He took up Harpakhrad and demanded that Harnett retract his words—the omens were telling them they must stay together forever. Boggs stomped and screamed and cried. Lights were turning on in nearby houses. Harnett did not know what to do except strike him down with Grinder.

After placing Boggs's unconscious body carefully upon a park bench, Harnett hurried home to Valerie Crouch. It was three-thirty in the morning and yet she was up. She greeted him with a strange look. *It's fine, he's sleeping it off in the park,* Harnett said, but Val said that wasn't it. She was pregnant. The first thing through Harnett's mind: the Rat King.

The second thing: panic. What did a child mean for a Digger? He was fearful and didn't like the feeling. The only remedy was to dig and dig boldly, and so he got into his truck and went to uncover a man named Phineas Gatlin. It was a tricky dig that he and Boggs had been contemplating for months. The belly was in a family cemetery just outside a bedroom window and within sight of unchained dogs. Harnett rushed and failed. Dogs barked. People awoke. They pursued him. Harnett made it back home long enough to throw Val into the passenger seat and then they were on the run.

When Harnett one day settled in Wisconsin, it was Elroy Gatlin who split his door with an axe. A year later in Michigan, it was Wentworth Gatlin who shattered his windows, hollering for justice. Then it was other sons and other grandsons, spread across vast stretches of time and geography. Sixteen years would pass until the day I arrived at Harnett's door, and though Bloughton had served as his best hiding place yet, he was confident that the Gatlins would one day be the end of him. It all made sense now: the cabin's disarray, the refusal to engage in a community. For a decade he'd expected every day in Bloughton to be his last.

No one could track like Boggs. He loved Harnett, and Valerie, too, but if he could not be part of a family, there would be no family at all. It was just a few weeks after the Rat King's discovery that Boggs was able to lead the Gatlins right to them. Harnett and Val were sleeping in a barn when the ambush came. Three attackers, shouting the Gatlin name and swinging shovels and picks. Harnett was terrified. Not because they could kill him but because they knew what he had done. Seeing the Gatlins with raised tools? For Harnett it was like looking in a mirror. He didn't think about Val. He didn't think about the baby inside her. He thought only of himself, and when one of the Gatlins swung a shovel, he ducked. The blade ripped through Val's ear. It sounded like a rubber band snapping. Then Harnett heard the blood. Even then he didn't move to protect her. He ran. When Val pulled herself up, the Gatlins, perhaps not expecting a woman, were startled and backed off.

My mother had saved Harnett, not the other way around, and now that it was spoken aloud it didn't surprise me. What did surprise me was the depth of Harnett's regret and the tsunamic force of his love, which had not only survived sixteen years but threatened to usurp even my own. Everything about him, every impressive quality, every deplorable routine, stemmed from his failure to save the one person who had saved him.

"Forgive," Lionel gasped. "Yourself."

The world had ended. The sharp salt odor made me sick. We were perched above the beach on an outcropping. I staggered to the edge. Sand coated my tongue. The bleeding razor of sun healed to smooth gray tissue. I sank to my exhausted knees and let the pounding waves become the blood in my veins. The image of my injured and bleeding mother was more vibrant than any I'd had of her in months. I stretched until I was flat on my stomach. Icy patches of grass adhered to my cheeks. Something even colder met my outstretched fingers.

It was a single tiny gravestone reigning quietly over the entire Atlantic. The engraving promised a fittingly anonymous end to the life of a Digger:

LIONEL MARTIN 1923–

Harnett's voice: "Lionel, no."

"Yes."

"Don't show me this."

"Don't turn away from it."

"You can't go through with it."

Lionel's voice was proud. "Your beliefs are not mine."

"A burial, after everything you've seen?"

Lionel managed a smile. "What a spot. What a world. Look at it."

I drew myself up and did what he said. Lionel was right; it had been worth the long and painstaking trip, and I felt a debt to these men for taking me so far. Moments later I knew how to repay it. Lionel had insisted that this spot was important; Harnett had asked me that morning if I could specify at will. So I forced open my eyes, nose, mouth, ears, and fingers, and leaned backward until I fell onto the soft blanket of Lionel's future bed, the thick ocean my sheets, my every sense dreaming with exquisite detail—

—the split oak forking overhead—

—the capillary universe of leafless treetops threading the horizon—

—cursive alphabets invented by our footprints—

—the fibula of beach lying hard and gleaming below—
—the bilious curdle of surf—
—rock scatterings that drew invisible pentagrams between points—
—the shape of the outcropping itself: a fallen maple leaf of stone—

—all of it fading now, fading, darkening, darker, dark.

7.

LAHN WAS MAYBE TEN years younger than Lionel and said very little. Words, however, were unnecessary—the older man knew by the rap of knife against cutting board which dish Lahn was fixing. Despite his exhaustion, Lionel rhapsodized about Lahn's Vietnamese cuisine, and made us partake in his sweet-and-salty noodles despite Harnett's suggestion that we just grab a couple of onions for the road. Lahn declined an invite to join us, instead smiling and bowing and leaving the room.

Harnett looked different to me, especially when the dinnertime conversation veered back to my mother. With each word I saw cords of pain pull at the corners of his eyes and carve at his forehead. These markings, previously unnoticed by me, lent his features a startling vulnerability. For the first time, I felt the urge to put my hand to his back and feel how similar his shudders were to my own.

"You hold her too high," Lionel said. "You've made her out as an ideal, and that's dangerous, Ken. Dangerous to you."

"What am I supposed to do?" he said. "I remember how I remember."

Lionel pointed a knotted finger at me. Under his nails, dirt. *Grave dirt,* my mind thought automatically. *His own.*

"The world's foremost authority is right here! I bet he knows stories that would make you think you never knew her at all. All you have to do is ask. Go ahead."

Harnett narrowed his eyes. "Why would I want to do that? Think that I never knew her? That makes no sense."

"No, what you're doing now makes no sense." Lionel scooped up rice and tucked it inside his mouth. "Tell us something about your mother, Joey."

"Like what?"

"Something not-so-good. Even bad."

Harnett clanged his fork to his plate. "The kid doesn't want—"

"And what's with this 'kid' and 'Harnett' business? It's not natural."

Harnett shut his mouth and chewed. Lionel nodded at me in encouragement. Various scenarios presented themselves—my mother elbowing with unrepentant force a parent who was talking during my trumpet solo; unleashing a cyclone of expletives when refrigerator magnets succumbed to the weight of A-plus papers—but none of them fit.

"See, he's got nothing," Harnett said.

"No!" I opened my mouth and waited for words to fill it. "When . . . before seventh grade . . . I was just about to start seventh grade." The details of the story were foggy, but I kept going, uncertain of where I was leading myself. "And she took me to the store to buy school supplies. Folders and pencils and that kind of stuff. But I was starting gym that year—"

I broke off. This was an embarrassing story. But Lionel was waiting, and even Harnett was unable to conceal his curiosity. I took a breath and continued.

"And we had to buy a jockstrap. For gym."

Harnett swallowed. "You needed a jockstrap for gym?"

"Well, no," I said. "Not really. But I didn't know that. It was my first year in a real gym class. A jockstrap was on the list. I thought I'd get in trouble or something if I didn't have everything on the list. So once we got done buying folders and stuff, we got to the jockstrap part and she goes back to the sports section and finds them, except she doesn't know what size to get. So she takes out a size small and stretches it out in front of me."

Harnett was looking at me like he didn't get it.

"I mean, there were kids everywhere! We were right in the middle of a store! People were staring! She flipped off like three of them!"

Tears were brimming from Lionel's eyes as he tried not to choke on his rice. Harnett, meanwhile, knitted his brow. Finally he nodded curtly.

"She had to gauge the size of your manhood," he concluded.

"My *manhood*?" I appealed to Lionel. "Who talks like that?"

Lionel pounded the table with a fist, flecks of rice shooting from his lips.

Harnett squinted at me. "And you found this embarrassing."

"You are an alien!" I shouted. Harnett frowned. I shook my head helplessly at Lionel and found that I was laughing, too. I gave in to it and laughed until my back hurt. Lionel groaned and wiped his eyes with a napkin. Harnett shrugged, picked up his fork, and resumed stuffing in noodles as if the two of us weren't there.

"Sounds like Valerie," Lionel sighed. "Just as soon kick your ass as say excuse me."

We adjourned to the living room. Lahn toyed with a power strip and I caught my breath: Christmas lights. Bulbs of red and green and gold gave the otherwise shaded room a cozy holiday hue. Moments later I heard the unmistakable tinkling of the only Christmas album my mother could listen to without pretending to retch, *A Charlie Brown Christmas.* The combination was too much; still weakened from my laughing fit, I had no defense to the tears that smeared my vision. I rubbed my face and looked away. Lionel pretended not to notice and extended a hand so that Lahn, squatting upon an ottoman, could massage his knotted digits.

"If what you're asking me is should you do something, like go to California, try to steal the book, my answer is no," Lionel said. He gave Lahn his other hand. "You know how Baby is. He might have already tossed the thing in a fire."

"Not this time," said Harnett. "And the book—Lionel, it was *thick*."

Lionel flexed his fingers and smiled at Lahn. "You're a godsend," he said. "You'll come by tomorrow morning as usual? There's a ham we might as well cook."

Lahn nodded to Harnett and me before exiting. Lionel watched him go and sighed.

"Baby calls me, you know," Lionel said. "Somehow he got the number. Sometimes he'll call, on my birthday or Father's Day, even, and he'll sound so happy. He'll be laughing like a little boy."

Harnett leaned forward. "He calls you? Here?"

"Then other times, it's tears. Crying so bad I can't make out a word. Not that I need to—it's always the same few things. He wants compliments or attention. Sometimes he just wants money. What he really wants, of course, is forgiveness, but that's one thing I can't give."

Harnett was practically out of his seat. "What else does he say?"

Lionel relaxed his limbs and closed his eyes. "It's hard, raising boys. They want to become you, but also they hate you. Those are competing desires. Put them together and you have a form of suicide. Think of it. Generations upon generations of men killing themselves over and over, and for what? Because love and hate, both are too powerful, and no boy—and no father, for that matter—can live up to either."

The music was melancholy. I heard the faint slap of palms to thighs.

"Well," Lionel said. "Some of us are ancient."

The cane was dragged across the carpet. Veins in his neck articulated as he brought himself to his feet. Harnett stood but did not approach. The cane gingerly tested the floor as if the carpet might conceal quicksand, and then Lionel proceeded across the room until the two men faced each other.

"Can't you stay just one day?"

"The kid," Harnett said. "School."

Lionel's eyes took on a faraway look, as if only now recalling. He winked at me.

"Test on the last day of school," he said. "Must be a tough teacher."

I cleared my throat. "He is."

They looked nothing alike, these two men, but I could see how the mighty bow of my father's back might one day collapse into Lionel's stoop. There were other similarities, in their arms and hands and in the web of lines spiraling from their eyes. Harnett was becoming Lionel and Lionel was becoming oblivion.

"So long, then," the old man said.

My father had carried this man from the ocean, across the

cemetery, up the hill, through the woods. Now he could not touch him.

"Ice those muscles," Harnett said. "Stay off your feet."

"Will do."

"We'll be back." Harnett looked at his feet. "It won't be long."

"Sure, sure," Lionel said, nodding. He inhaled sharply and struck out with his cane. Briefly a hand clutched Harnett's shoulder.

"You drive safe, now," Lionel said.

The shoulder was released. The floor shook with the minute trembles of two feet, one cane, two feet, one cane. Gentle ripples disturbed two cooling cups of coffee. Christmas music continued. A distant bedroom door clicked shut. Moments later came the sounds of water hitting a sink, medicine-bottle clatters, mucus risen by a series of violent coughs. In his absence, the colored bulbs revealed everything.

8.

THE CAB LIGHT HAD long since been disabled, but Harnett let me rig the flashlight so it burned directly onto my textbook. The letters of each sentence scattered like insects.

"All those phone calls Boggs made, I know what he really wanted." Harnett had been edgy since we left. His left knee bounced incessantly. I could see perspiration drying upon the steering wheel. "He wants the treasure."

As determined as I was to study, some lures are irresistible. "Treasure?"

Harnett smirked, but kept his eyes on the road. "A career

like Lionel's, he could be living in a mansion right now. Two mansions. It's just not his way."

"He kept it all?"

"Remember who we're talking about. The man used to own the East Coast. You heard him talk about Scotland. His time in Egypt. He could fill a museum."

"Where is it? Did you ever see it?"

Harnett shrugged. "Occasionally I saw things. Where it all went to, I have no idea. But everyone knows it's out there somewhere."

"So he's just sitting on it?"

"What would you expect him to do?"

"Give it to someone, at least."

"To who?"

"You."

"Me? Why me?"

"Because you're practically his—"

The word hung unspoken, tossing in the chilly air like our breaths.

Harnett's expression, troubled for so many miles, loosened with a mild amusement. "Even if that were true, you're forgetting that there were two of us."

The pavement thumped beneath our tires with lulling regularity. Through the windshield, the enduring procession of painted road dashes. Beyond my window, the vacuum of night.

"I took your mother to a drive-in once. The movie happened to be about a cemetery caretaker. We thought it was pretty funny at first. This guy found out that if he put black pins in his cemetery map, the people who owned those plots ended up dying in freak accidents. He's got all the power in the world: a black pin means death. I didn't think much of it, it was just some stupid little movie. But afterward Val was quiet, like it really shook her up. She said, 'Didn't you see the white pins?' I didn't know what she was talking about. She said, 'There were white pins. He had white pins, too. If the black pins killed them, what do you think the white pins did?'

"She wanted me out of digging. It took some dumb movie for me to see it. If she could, she would give me a million white pins and I would just go scattering them like Johnny Appleseed. After we got away from the Gatlins and got her ear fixed, things were different. She started to not hear things. That included confessions and apologies. There are things I tried to tell her, I swear, only now she couldn't hear. Or wouldn't. The injury seemed rather convenient.

"You were too perfect when you came out. It was like you had nothing to do with me. Like you were something molded from the stuff I brought home on the bottom of my boots that somehow got mixed up in our bedsheets and that's what impregnated her—a million dead men, not me. I know I'm not making any sense. But when I saw you it was like you were a white pin from that movie. You were life.

"She knew it, too. She packed her bags and wrapped you up. She just had that one demand. 'You give me Chicago as a gift.' That's exactly what she said. What else had I ever given her? Or given you? I had to be happy I could give anything at all."

Boggs had confirmed *I can get anyone* as my father's slogan, but this, as much as anything, was proof of its falsehood. I could see her so clearly now, alone in an unfamiliar city, clutching a bawling infant and hobbled with a disfigured ear. Why had it taken me this long to recognize the tragedy of her solitude? She had been young and pretty and brilliant, yet to protect me she had gone into hiding. And not just from Antiochus Boggs and the Gatlins; she couldn't risk landing another Ken Harnett, either.

As we sailed from one interstate to another, the words of the biology text imprinting themselves into my brain like grit into eyeballs, I began to think that my mother's final act had been something inspired. North Carolina, Virginia, West Virginia, Ohio, Indiana, Illinois, Iowa: by giving me to Harnett, she had released me from our shared reclusion, and now each state I passed through became my home, because home was anywhere with grass and dirt and stone, and my compatriots, my family, were those who waited beneath to greet me.

9.

Back in Bloughton, I felt physical whiplash. Here, once more, was the cruel reality of a shabby two-room cabin off Hewn Oak Road, even smaller and quieter now beneath three inches of unblemished snow. It was Monday morning; we had made it back in time. Harnett collapsed into bed. While I changed clothes for school, I stared in disbelief at the calendar on the side of the sink. I had imagined millions of hatch marks and thousands of slashes, but it had only been three days since the incident in the shower room, not several lifetimes.

There was no point in bothering with first and second periods. I sat and washed down an onion with two cups of coffee before finally making that long walk through the snow. I waited until I heard the third-period bell ring and then entered the Congress of Freaks, keeping my head low to avoid the sight of anyone who had ever hurt or been hurt by me, and slipped into the classroom, where the celebratory mood of the rest of the building gave way to last-minute cramming and general disgruntlement. There was only one villain to grapple with today. I took my usual seat near the back.

Gottschalk, the new acting principal of Bloughton High School, bent his rubbery features into a smug leer as he passed out the tests. I set the paper in front of me and watched the characters rattle across the page. My body surged with caffeine and adrenaline. An absurd confidence settled over me. I picked up my pencil and began.

Some of the questions made me flinch: I felt the sting of Gottschalk's pointer as it struck various points of my body. Other questions seemed totally foreign and yet I found the answers spilling from the graphite in quick, neat letters. The giddiness that overtook me was so unanticipated I didn't know if I was about to laugh or vomit.

Fifty questions, fifty minutes. Gottschalk clapped and there followed the cracking of a dozen pencils hitting desks. Not mine, though—I was done, and had been for a long time.

We passed our tests up the rows. Gottschalk took them, pounded them into order, and took his seat as the bell rang. Cheers erupted; the real party could now begin. As the class left, whooping, I thought I saw the raven hair of a beautiful girl. No matter; I turned my gaze to Gottschalk. He had on his glasses and was already scratching away with a red pen. He glanced up. Our gazes met.

Very slowly I approached. As I passed each desk, my heart leapt at the prospect of never again entering this room. I arrived at Gottschalk's desk and stood silently as he ran a finger across handwriting I recognized as my own. I glimpsed red ink on the previous page, but not much. His pen stood poised to mark, swaying like a rattlesnake.

Page two: no red marks. Page three: his fingers regripped the pen, but nothing. Page four: a red circle and *-2*; a crossed-out sentence and *-4*. Page five, the final page: his plump finger smudged lead as it tracked each line. Finally he flipped through the pages in reverse order, adding up the tally, and marked the final count upon the front page: *-8*.

By his rubric, it was an A. I was too stunned to react.

Gottschalk set down his red pen and removed his glasses.

"I appreciate, Mr. Crouch, your powers of memorization. It's possible you possess a savantlike ability in this regard. It's also possible, I suppose, that you actually gave time and effort to the task. There are certainly many correct answers in these pages. Yet I find myself curiously unmoved. Allow me to explain. On Friday I was asked to lead this school, and over the weekend I spent a great deal of time pondering that responsibility. Those now under my purview are teachers. Teachers, in theory, teach. As acting principal, I am charged with ensuring that, at the end of the day, lessons have been learned. I cannot cut my own teaching any slack in this regard; to the contrary, I must hold myself to the highest standards. At the beginning of the semester you walked into this room unwilling to learn. I was adamant in involving you. Countless times I have pulled you to the head of the class to immerse you in the lessons to the best of my ability. The results have been discouraging. Oh, you've managed to regurgitate well enough. It's a trick you have learned. But I do not condone trickery; I demand engagement. And this is where my meditation over the past weekend has brought me. Teaching is not about facts, it is about the building of character, and facts are merely the tools, as a dumbbell is a tool for building muscle. You have been the teacher today and I the student. You have taught me that an A on this test is not what you need. What you need is the maturity that will come only from engaging with that which you have so flippantly tossed aside. This, what you have handed me, was intended as a slap in the face, and I take it as such. I'm afraid I cannot turn the other cheek, Mr. Crouch. The previous principal, perhaps, but I am of different quality."

With that he raised the salvation of my grade point average, my mother's pride, the sole hope of my future, and tore it in half. He put the two pieces together and tore again. Again. Again. Ragged rectangles fluttered to the desk. I thought of scooping them up in my hands and rushing to the principal's office to reassemble and prove my score, but behind that door, too, was Gottschalk.

"You will repeat the class," he said, gathering the scraps in a tidy pile and lifting a trash bin. With a flick of his wrist the remnants of my exam disappeared. I wanted to reach out but my limbs were completely numb. "I look forward to starting anew with you in January."

Muscles in his face screwed and snaked and I imagined his smile rotted by decay into a ghastly shriek. Gottschalk replaced his glasses, straightened his papers, and picked up his pen.

"Merry Christmas," he said.

10.

We kept close to Bloughton. We chased a tornado and picked through the upchucked coffins. We graphed the smaller proportions of a pet cemetery before going after the remains of a dachshund. We turned up several uninhabited plots in the same graveyard before discovering a mass grave some fifty bodies thick, where the dead—mostly the city burials of welfare cases and unclaimed cadavers—had been moved to free up real estate. We struck an unmarked water pipe and by the time we patched it our corpse was floating. We peed in plastic bottles, unwilling to cease our motion. We had just three weeks before the new semester began. When we did sleep, it was in the truck.

Everywhere we went we found Polaroids. At first it was an anomaly, then it was a scattering, and by the time school began we were finding them everywhere—an impossible amount. There had to be a horrible toll to such an effort; I remembered Boggs's whiff of sickness and wondered if it would soon overtake him. Freed from his territory, Boggs took over southeast Iowa, not just beating us to digs but repairing the ground so expertly he fooled even Harnett. When we reached the caskets, everything of value was already gone. What we did find, meticulously pinned to each body, was a recent photograph of the corpse. Harnett ripped off these portraits and mangled them in a fist, and together we imagined the matching photograph carefully pasted into the Rotters Book. As we filled in the grave, our pockets empty, Harnett seethed with fantasies of destroying the book. Me, though, I just wanted to see it one more time.

We shared tools, but I had some of my own. When something was misplaced, even in the black of mud or white of snow, I knew it. When something broke, I fixed it. The Root never broke. I was careful. I was responsible. I was stealthy. I wore appropriate clothing. Calluses built up on my hands, huge and flat and dry as sand. I knew when to hold back. I knew when to take a risk. I could work entirely by moonlight. I modified a junked DustBuster to vacuum flakes of leftover dirt from turf and used a barber's comb to sift the rest. I used a battery-powered hair dryer to fluff patches of grass matted by our shoes. I created a rainproof undergarment made of trash bags and duct tape and stood in the shower for ten minutes to test it. Harnett watched and grumbled that he wanted one, too. My mother would have been proud.

Snow made an issue of footprints. We monitored weather reports and dug only before snowfalls. If the snow was thick enough, we dug in broad daylight. New graves were easy to find; heat from a corpse's decomp could melt a blanket of snow in two days. For older graves we brought along a tin trash can and lit a fire inside and rolled it across the plot until the ground was weeping and soft. The bodies, when we reached them, were cold and less smelly, their evolution of decay momentarily halted. There was something innocent about how snowflakes touched their oblivious faces, as if they were children extending tongues to the first fall. This innocence was gutted with each flash of Boggs's camera.

The snow stopped falling on New Year's Eve. By the first weekend in January it had already melted, and every Iowa lawn looked like the site of a Christmas massacre, strewn with the toppled bodies of Santa and Rudolph and Frosty. We dug faster than ever before—we were coming up empty too often, and Harnett was nervous. A few nights before the first day of school, Harnett dropped to his knees in a cemetery outside Meighsville and jabbed his finger at a scattering of rocks in the grass, insisting that Boggs had arranged them so that he would be able to tell if we dug up his Polaroid. To avoid touching the rocks, Harnett carved a slanted tunnel some fifteen feet from the headstone that allowed him to drag the coffin to the surface with ropes. It took all night and left us dangerously exposed. I watched the horizon impatiently. Harnett pried up the lid. There was no photo inside. The scattered rocks had just been scattered rocks.

Back at the cabin, we studied newspapers as hard as I had once studied Gottschalk handouts. Harnett's paranoia grew. There were reports from surrounding communities of sullied cemetery lots, busted padlocks, skewed headstones, muddy tracks. In his attempt to infect the earth with hundreds upon hundreds of photographs, Boggs was getting sloppy, maybe intentionally. Eventually, Harnett fretted, regular people would start noticing commonalities in police reports. Once that happened, it was just a matter of time before a disinterment led to a discovery of Boggs's project.

"I can't dig up every single grave he's dug." Harnett's chair barely contained his rocking. "I can't remove every single picture he's buried."

Even as he said this, I could tell that he was wondering whether, in fact, he could. Without its being expressly stated, our mission had changed. We would dig, and use the spoils to buy the necessary staples, but our primary objective was to erase the Rotters Book and hold accountable its author. More than ever before, Harnett would need a good shovel. He brought home dozens, some purchased, others found in landfills and alleys, and riddled our backyard with them before tossing the unfit instruments into the river.

11.

The sweatshirt and hoodies I had previously worn to school had gone stiff and black. Despite the cold, I donned the duck-in-sunglasses tee I hadn't worn since my first day at BHS. I wasn't sure why I even showed up to kick off the new semester—some remnant of decorum or habit?—but when I took a seat in my first-period class, the desk knocked against my knees and pinched my lower back. As I crossed my arms defensively, the duck in sunglasses pulled tight across my back. *I'm taller,* I realized. *I'm bigger.* Other students hastened away their gazes as I rolled my shoulders and correlated each strap of muscle to those I had seen on the Diggers. I was like them now, except that they grew weaker each day while I grew stronger. The teacher frowned when I laughed to myself. *Maybe it was all those goddamn onions,* I thought.

Biology, once again, came third period. I paused outside the room, dazed by how much smaller the hallways looked, how juvenile the students, how inconsequential the faculty. I wandered inside after the bell and took the only remaining seat, right in front. Gottschalk began by introducing himself as the new principal before praising himself for keeping his teaching gig, too. Then he began a spiel so familiar that I knew what came next—attendance, along with some mockery of people's names—and I waited patiently through the alphabet for him to call me to the front of the class. He did.

"No," I replied.

His thick lips swelled in anticipation of triumph. The words he used did not surprise me. *Don't be greedy with your talent, Mr. Crouch. You were so useful last semester, Mr. Crouch. Come help me illustrate the various units we will be covering this year, Mr. Crouch.*

I refused in silence until a curious thing happened. I heard snickering aimed at Gottschalk, not me, and in that instant I saw a flash of panic in the teacher's eyes—if he didn't wrest victory from me right away, his control of the entire semester might teeter. He banked by my desk and muttered to me in a low voice.

"Get up here and we'll let bygones be bygones."

Gottschalk was sweating. It was magnificent. He shuffled backward until his ass hit the chalkboard—more laughter.

"With or without the assistance of Mr. Crouch," he shouted, his voice ringing with alarm, "we will be taking a journey from the beginning of our existence to the very end. It's a long journey that will become ever longer the less you are able to control yourselves—quiet down, now. We'll begin with sperm and egg. From there we'll move to systems, in order: the integumentary, skeletal, muscular, nervous, cardiovascular, endocrine, immune, respiratory, digestive, excretory, finally ending with the properties of decomposition."

"You know nothing about decomposition."

It was my own voice. Perhaps emboldened by all my noes, I let these five new words escape in a snort. Gottschalk was left goggling, his arm floating in some half-finished gesture. I could see the flicker of deliberation: send me from the room or take me on in hopes of winning back his class? I never doubted his decision.

"If, Mr. Crouch, you're referring to the fact that I am not yet dead, I'm afraid I have some relatives who would disagree." Chuckles from the spectators, more polite than anything. "But I believe that even you, with your knowledge of biology so vast that you're taking this class for a second time"—more chuckling—"will learn an item or two about the factors affecting decay rate, how body mass affects the process more than environment, and so forth—"

"It's not true," I said. "Body size barely matters."

"Thank you, Professor Crouch. Now if your lecture is complete—"

"Temperature is the biggest factor." I could hardly believe it was my voice that was speaking, but I kept moving my lips and the words kept coming. "Second is access by insects. Third is burial conditions, and fourth is access by animals. Body mass is maybe seventh or eighth on the list."

A purple color was creeping up his neck. I'd never seen his teeth before, but there they were, sharp triangles of yellow rising like shark fins. "Disruption by carnivore is hardly a major concern to burials in modern-day America, Professor Crouch."

"You didn't say burials," I said. The tightness and heat that usually accompanied my public speaking had been replaced by an icy calm. "You said decay rate. These are well-known forensic results. Carnivores affect decay more than trauma, humidity, rainfall—"

"We will not be covering *carnivores* in a biology class," he hissed. "We will be covering only natural decomposition, which does not involve fauna of any sort, with the obvious exception of bugs. Now, if you'd like to continue your lesson in the principal's office—"

"Necrophages," I said.

His threat to expel me from the room had given him away. He was losing and knew it. To everyone else it must have been a comic delight, but I was locked into the kind of focus Woody must have felt when the entire season was on the line. Gottschalk stood with his bottom lip quivering, trying in vain to recollect a definition I had read a dozen times in Harnett's lurid library.

"I . . ."

"Necrophages," I repeated. "A species of arthropod that feeds on body tissue."

Gottschalk blinked.

"Oh, sorry," I said. "Arthropods are bugs."

A whoop went up from the back of the class—*Oh, damn!*—and a thrill of laughter ripped through the ranks. Gottschalk looked suffocated. I rose before he had the chance to order it and met his beady eyes on my way out. There would be no more debasing me before my classmates, no more striking me with his wand. Perhaps there would be no graduation, either, but that was a possibility I was quickly learning to live with.

I celebrated by skipping the next two classes. Somehow Ted found me pacing a rarely used hallway and with a look directed me to the band room. Was Ted why I had returned to school? I wasn't sure. I was too preoccupied with the steely coldness that had taken hold of me, and wondering if it had come from the Diggers, Lionel, or Boggs, or if it was simply the natural extension of my oblivion and extinction. Ted pointed to my trumpet case; it sat exactly where I had left it a month ago. I just stared at him—such things were no longer part of my life. To my surprise the dorky conductor had twice the grit of Gottschalk; he won the staring contest and our covert lessons continued. As usual we exchanged no words save his parting remark: "Next lesson, then."

I stuck around for lunch because I was hungry. Gottschalk had wasted no time purging me from Simmons's free-lunch list, so I paid cash. Foley was a few tables over and his presence threatened to disrupt my strange tranquility. I made a silent promise to skip lunch from here on out—he was better off without me. Like Harnett, I knew when it was time to break from my partner. A tiny part of me mourned. I pretended it was a cockroach and did what you do to cockroaches.

There were other recognizable shapes at the edges of my vision—Heidi, eating with one hand, paging through textbooks with another; Celeste, tiptoeing through suggestions of her dance routine; Woody and Rhino, no doubt recounting the shower incident to the requisite rapt faces—but to me they were as inanimate as something at the bottom of a hole. They were, I was pleased to note, only rotters.

12.

Harnett was shaking newsprint in my face as soon as I crossed the threshold.

"Peter and Paul Eccles." He followed me with the page as I pulled off my shoes. "Twin frontiersmen hired to protect the last stages of the First Transcontinental Railroad. You know what that is?"

This was my father lately: red-eyed, jumpy, implacable. I turned away from him and stripped myself of my coat. "I'm in school, aren't I?"

"It was the first railroad to connect the country," he raved. "When the Central Pacific and Union Pacific lines met at Promontory Summit in Utah in 1869, they drove in a ceremonial spike to mark the final tie."

"Big deal." I moved toward the sink and he kept right at my elbow.

"It *is* a big deal," he snapped. "They actually drove in four spikes that day to commemorate various rail lines, but the last spike, the so-called Golden Spike, was seventeen-point-six-karat gold, engraved on all four sides by various bigwigs. This was a major event. Do you understand the significance? The conquest of the West. The annihilation of the Indians. It's huge, monumental."

There was nothing in the refrigerator. I threw the door shut in irritation—Harnett's erratic behavior meant that once again it would be up to me to fill the shelves. Distantly I recognized the unjustness of such an arrangement. In my former life it had not been up to me to plan the menus of two people. I threw open a cabinet.

"The Golden Spike's in a museum," I muttered. It was about the only thing I remembered about the story and I hoped it would shut him up.

Harnett's eyes blazed. "Right. But read here. Right here. In the last months of construction, Peter and Paul Eccles were hired—hired by President Ulysses S. Grant himself, who'd just taken office. You know why?"

I banged through empty cupboards. "Because they were cute?"

"Because Grant had gotten word of an Indian uprising that was going to bloody up the completion of the railroad. The Eccles brothers had fought with Grant about five years earlier at Shiloh, and they'd been living out West with the Indians ever since. When Grant hired them to keep the peace, they took the job—he was their friend and their president—but they didn't know what taking the job really meant. You know what it meant?"

Slowly I faced him. I had some idea.

"It meant they had to kill Indians," he said. "Lots of them.

Hundreds, maybe. These Indians were their friends. Men they had hunted with, passed the pipe with. And now they were turning around and raising their government rifles and slaughtering them."

I slumped against the counter, waiting for the inevitable grave at the end of the story. My hand crept to the side of the sink, where I could feel the scars of my calendar: five days, ten days, one month, two, four, six.

Harnett lifted the newspaper. "This is Thursday's paper from Dundee, Iowa, and this here is an article about the town's links to the Civil War. It talks about how Grant showed his gratitude by giving both Eccles brothers a replica of the Golden Spike with his personal thanks carved into the gold. Each spike was worth a small fortune then; what a museum would pay for them today, I don't even know. Peter Eccles is buried in Dundee, and the town rumor is he took that spike to his grave."

"Just Peter? What about Paul?"

Harnett snatched up some crumbling newsprint from the counter. "This is an issue from October 1988, from Miller's Field, Illinois, where Paul Eccles is buried, just across the Mississippi, and it repeats the same rumor. That's independent confirmation, kid. It's true, all of it, I know it is. After the railroad was built, after they'd killed all their Indian brothers, after their president had given them these spikes that, in their eyes, were soaked in blood, they gave up on life, both of them. They put the length of Iowa between them and never spoke, and never, ever displayed the spikes, but they both kept them until they died, or so go the stories. *Both* the stories."

He stood with the two papers in either hand, gloating over his discovery. My anger was dimming; I felt a familiar tingle of excitement and my eyes found the Root where she waited pensively in a darkened corner.

"Which one do we go for?"

"If Boggs is doing his homework, he could be reading the same article about Peter. But he won't have the Miller's Field story to cross-reference. He'll suspect it's just rumor; he'll hesitate. We won't. We go now, to Dundee, and we get President Grant's spike."

Harnett was nearly slavering. The fact that my new semester had just begun didn't even enter his mind. It was just as well.

I fit my fingers over the Root. Harnett kneeled to lace his boots.

"We got him on this one," he whispered to the floor. "We got him."

Hours later he was proven correct. There was no picture pinned to the patchy remnants of Peter Eccles's burial coat, but sewed into a hidden pocket beneath his left armpit was the spike. As Harnett funneled dirt that was no different from any other dirt, I fondled the two-of-a-kind artifact; it made white lines of the moonlight. In my hand it felt as lethal as Gottschalk's pointer, as rigid as the faucets in the boys' shower room. Even here, miles away and half buried in history, I could not escape Bloughton.

My father was still bursting with pride when we got back home. Without killing the engine, he ran inside with the spike and our bags of gear. I followed and heard him lock his safe. He emerged a couple of minutes later with some extra clothes stuffed into a garbage bag.

"Sensitive stuff." He scratched at his beard and took a quick look around the room. "Requires a special buyer. Got a man in mind, but he's a full day away. He's just the right guy, though. Knows how to unload something like this, wash his hands so that it can't be traced." He paused and looked at me. "That okay? It could be Saturday until I'm back."

He was abuzz with success, and little I said would stop him anyway. I shrugged. "You don't want to take the spike?"

"No. No way. Terms first. Always terms first, get that through your head."

He slapped his pockets and nodded.

"Okay, then," he said, and left.

Five minutes later I had the spike out of the safe and was turning it in my hands. President Grant's inscription, done by hand if the penmanship was any indication, was short and somehow ominous:

GOOD FEELING.
WITH GREAT RESPECT,
U. S. GRANT

Hundreds of Indian carcasses—I pulled my covers to my chin and pictured their brown and feathered bodies strewn across the desert before they were eviscerated by scavengers or buried by surviving kin—and all that was left in memorial was this block of gold no bigger than my forearm. Part of me was glad that it would soon rest beneath temperature-controlled glass for tourists to reckon with. Another part of me wondered if it had been better off where it had lain for over almost one hundred and fifty years.

When I awoke the spike was gone.

At first I didn't believe it. I rolled over, patted the ground beside my bedding. I looked under my duffel-bag pillow, wondering if I had unconsciously stashed it there for safe-keeping. I bunched my sheets and flapped them. I ran my hands between nearby stacks of Harnett's archive, wondering if perhaps the spike's golden hue was similar to yellowed newsprint. I stood up and the smell hit me.

Like a Digger, but dipped in the faint turpentine of insomnia.

I swiped a paring knife from the counter and backpedaled into the wall. My heart hammered. He was here. His stink was over everything: the sheets I had escaped from, the knife I wielded, the wall behind me, my clothes—*my clothes*.

Mixed in with his scent was a malignant sweetness. Harnett had been right when he had told Lionel that there was something unwell about Boggs. For the first time I wondered if Boggs was actually rotting, and if it was from the outside in or the inside out.

The bedroom and bathroom doors—both were just barely ajar. Boggs would emerge running, or perhaps sauntering with predatory sloth, and the ice of his blue eyes would freeze me in place as he did what he needed to do before he could photograph me. My body arrested and I began specifying wildly, senselessly—

—shadow shards black spider ribbons—

—glaze of floor smacking for fallen flesh—

—cricket hiccups snake rattle frog croak door hinge—

—downward upward downward twist gush gush gush—

—gleeful dust suckling for a bloody soak—

—and I had to grip my skull to stop it, the paring knife clattering to the floor and somersaulting perfectly in place before the bedroom doorway. Tiny fingers reached out and seized it. No, it did not happen, but nevertheless I witnessed it repeatedly, until its hundredth repetition transformed it to fiction. Boggs was gone. His smell was melting into the morning thaw. I pushed open Harnett's door and then, braver, kicked open the bathroom. There were no signs anywhere.

Except for the missing spike. I threw open a window and let gusts from the Big Chief numb me. I retreated to the hearth and only then dared look back at the sink. Boggs was not just in Iowa, not just in Bloughton, but had been right here, in our home. He had stood over me as I had slept. He had measured my exhales, gauged my hypnagogic twitches. I wondered if this man, who had repeatedly misidentified himself as my father, had watched over me as if I were his baby boy.

My eyes found and drew strength from the Root. I'd lost the spike, yes, but there was a twin. If I acted decisively, the second spike could beat Harnett back to the cabin. I looked for the newspaper that had the details of its location, but I couldn't find it. All I remembered was that it was close—just across the Mississippi, Harnett had said. I grabbed some of my father's maps. I would have to figure it out as I went. Everything else I needed was here: digging gear, the tarp, the spade, the pickaxe, the Root. I had everything but the truck. Well, then I would steal one. I dressed warmly, packed my pockets with emergency gas money, took up the sacks, and stepped outside.

Parked on the front lawn was a car. I felt the fleabites of my hysterical specifying return—*shadow, spider, flesh, snake, twist, soak*—and fought them back. Slowly I swept my eyes over the gently swaying trees. I circled the vehicle. It was a Hyundai. Key in the ignition. Backseat brimming with fast-food detritus. Dented fenders. Rusted rims. Mud-splashed doors. Missouri plates.

The memory came slithering back: Boggs at the diner in West Virginia entreating me to grant him a moment's conversation: *That's two thousand five hundred seventy-five miles*

I came, and I had to jack a Hyundai in Missouri when my first ride up and died on me. Just another foreboding clue that made no sense until I saw the newspaper rolled up and poking from the steering wheel.

I winced as I opened the driver's side door and tossed my gear in the back, the maps in front. I lowered myself inside and pushed the seat back from where it had been ratcheted to dwarf proportions. I slammed the door and retracted the locks. The newspaper was warm; even before I unrolled it I knew what it was. It was the October 22, 1988, *Miller's Field Journal,* opened to the story featuring Paul Eccles. Boggs was guiding me as surely as if there were strings tied to each limb.

Placing my hands at three and nine, I inhaled a concentrated blast of his stink and then watched my gray exhalation adhere to the windshield. *He's watching,* I thought. The engine spat but turned over with more juice than Harnett's truck. Trying to summon driver's ed, I buckled my seat belt, adjusted the rearview mirror, and put the car into gear. There was no way to measure this fear against that I had once felt while skirting the halls of BHS. But I reminded myself that just one day ago I had beaten Gottschalk at his own game. Maybe I could win this game, too.

13.

It took me too long to find the grave. It felt as if the entirety of Bloughton were watching and judging. I had to repeat to myself my father's teachings, remember how cemetery quadrants were arranged old to new. My hands shook and dropped tools. The first incision was ragged and I blamed myself until

I peeled back the grass to reveal the sickest patch of earth I'd ever seen, spongy and irregular like healing skin. I took a handful and could smell the sour lumps of coffin wood commingled with the muck.

Digging it proved to be like scooping manure—it was heavy, wet, stringy, and smelly. One hour became two, then three, and though brutally trained, my muscles screamed in complaint. When I reached the vessel, I found that decay had turned the lid into mulch. I squatted and extracted the remains that slivered the dirt. Thankfully, Paul Eccles had been interred within a shroud, and I unwrapped it, fully expecting to find the golden spike gleaming among bones dull as kindling.

There was nothing. I unraveled the sheet and a rib or two shook free. I pulled the flashlight from my coat and turned it upon the grave. In the yellow spot of light I saw that the bottom of the coffin had long since cankered as well, and several more nubs of bone nosed from the soil like toadstools. My shoulders sank. I would have to keep digging, and there was no telling how far.

And then I saw a flash of gold. I moved the beam to the head of the coffin and noticed movement. I shrank back against the dirt. Rats—lots of them. I steadied my hand and looked again. My stomach lurched. They were everywhere, fifty, maybe a hundred of them, churning through the dirt like maggots, their wriggling feet capering upward, their red eyes flashing from inside the very walls of the hole. The ray of light alarmed them and they hurtled toward a burrowed tunnel that ran directly over Eccles's head—I could see the yellow dome of his skull beneath their frantic feet.

Whiskers tickled my neck; I gasped and swatted with my flashlight. The swirling beam caught the rats as they streamed away, their motion inadvertently carrying the golden spike straight into their tunnel.

"No!" I shouted. A rat, shockingly heavy, landed on my shoulder, and I felt its dry pelt slide past my ear before it tumbled and raced across my feet. I dropped to my knees. The tunnel was nearly two feet across and sloped downward. The spike balanced upon the precipice. I shuffled forward, my knees pinning to the dirt several fat and screaming bodies, and reached with my free hand. A cold current of rats slid down my arm.

Dozens of tiny feet scampered and the spike spun farther into the tunnel. An image of my father flashed through my mind—by now he had probably finished sealing a deal to sell the artifact and was en route to Bloughton, radiating with a pride he had not felt in years. I had lost Peter's spike; I had no choice but to bring home Paul's.

I lunged and struck the pulpy dirt so that I lay atop Paul Eccles, our elbows interlocked, his pelvis pressed against mine, his skull lodged snugly beneath my chin. I muscled my head through the cavity. The rats were up my shirt, nuzzling my armpits. Another raced up my pants leg, shuddering against my thigh. I locked my jaw and heard the thump of tails against my bared teeth.

It was a tight fit but I forced the flashlight to the level of my chest. The sight inside the tunnel was dizzying: swarms of rodents ran in loops, defying gravity. The spike was just ahead, and I squeezed my free hand into open space. The darkness flexed; three dozen rats hissed at the intruder and leapt, tussling and tangling into my hair, sinking their tiny yellow teeth into my fingers. I shrieked but could not recoil—I was stuffed too firmly. The entire weight of the cemetery pressed down.

My fingertips touched gold. I heaved forward and my

shoulders crashed against the winnowing tunnel. Dirt began to crumble. I made a fist and clubbed rats out of the way, left and right. A thick pink tail got caught between my fingers and the rat screeched and spasmed. My mother would not have hesitated, either: I squeezed the animal until I felt the convulsion of death. I tossed the body and snatched the spike. Nearly laughing, I brought it close to my body. Then I tipped the flashlight beam and saw stars twinkling from the underground night—eyes, hundreds of them, approaching, furious, and in their numbers unafraid.

Moving backward through a tight enclosure is a slow process. For a surreal moment I weighed the alternative: continuing onward to explore this subterranean city, learning the strategies of the rat, and dying down here with my kind. Yet I removed myself from the tunnel inch by inch, shutting my eyes against a torrent of rats so dense I could feel each racing heartbeat against my eyelids and throat and lips. They did not give up on the spike, even when it was clear that I was going to win. It was as if the rats had become spirit animals, invincible where the Indians of the Old West had been sadly mortal, unwilling to let this symbol of their destruction be taken anywhere other than hell.

I filled in the hole and watched the dirt drop heavily upon their tiny, obstinate faces. It was nearly dawn when I found myself once more behind the wheel of Boggs's car, and when I checked the rearview mirror I recognized the look that greeted me: it was the glazed and sunken stare of the Diggers I had met only weeks before, men haunted by the inability to tell anyone of the dreadful things they'd seen.

14.

I DROVE STRAIGHT THROUGH the morning, the bone-crack of gravel waking me each time I started to swerve, and only when I had parked Boggs's car in front of the cabin did I take a good look at the golden spike. It was indeed the mirror image of the one belonging to Peter Eccles, only Paul had possessed either less restraint or more self-loathing and had furiously scratched out whatever message President Grant had inscribed. Numbly I wondered how much this decreased the value of the artifact. I scratched my own shames into the side of the sink and collapsed.

Harnett's reaction to the new spike and the violation of his safe was overwhelmed by his reaction to the news of Boggs's intrusion. The Hyundai had disappeared long before he came home, but he did not doubt the veracity of my tale. Instantly his fevered gaze sought out the cabin's many weaknesses: the door, the windows, the world of darkness contained within the surrounding forest. Instead of delivering the spike to his buyer, he took off to the local hardware store and lumberyard and returned with a truckload of raw materials. The rest of the day was a calamity of windows nailed shut, iron bars slotted over each pane, new locks screwed onto the front door, and photoelectric yard lights mounted on all sides of the cabin. Cables were secured to the roof with industrial staples, and while up there Harnett used binoculars to search the surrounding acreage. The afternoon was spent gutting as much underbrush as was physically possible. While he hacked and hauled and incinerated, I was given the task of disassembling the woodpile so that no one—not even one very short of stature—could hide behind it.

Eventually there was nothing more to do. It was time to deliver the spike. Harnett's heart was no longer in it; it was sad to see. His victory in finding it had led to the loss of a bigger battle, and now he had to leave me to this new and untested fortress. Stress carved every angle of his face. He was thinking of running away from Bloughton, I knew it, but with a kid in tow such an escape was less viable. As he drove away I turned my eyes to the trees. I wondered if Boggs was still close and if he was watching with frustration or amusement. Mostly I wondered what he thought of my performance. Part of me still hungered for straight As.

15.

WEEKS FLEW BY. SCHOOL was worthless. I showed up on occasion just to spar with Gottschalk, absorb Celeste's hints about the approaching Spring Fling, and wait for Ted's *Next lesson, then* to notify me of the day's end. Then came night and the Polaroids. We tracked Boggs by boot prints and finger smudges and gossip and intuition, and shoveled with ferocity. Each morning Harnett sharpened his Scottish blade.

Our task was becoming increasingly hazardous. Police patrolled cemeteries, sometimes on foot with flashlights. Too often we returned empty-handed to a cabin filling with newspaper accounts of Boggs's activities. Harnett's neurosis became uncontrollable. Everyone was a Gatlin, materialized from the ether to chase him from his home for the seventh or tenth or fifteenth time, depending on how many photographs we had found that night.

He barely ate. Sometimes I had to put the food in his hands. It was on the way home from two consecutive digs—the former unsullied, the latter ornamented with another of Boggs's portraits—that we passed Sookie's Foods and I impulsively turned into the lot. The area buzzed with routines of such harmlessness that it seemed a perfect cure-all. Ambling past the bakery and shuddering in the frozen foods aisle would fix us, I just knew it.

Harnett was too distracted to put up much of a fight. He came into the store with me, a rare event. To push my luck I made him steer the cart; I hoped the task might steady the hands that had been shaking for weeks. It was prime shopping hour. People still wore work clothes and ruthlessly sought out milk with preferable expiration dates. Kids picked up from school were dragged along. Those recognizable from the Congress of Freaks offered beseeching half-smiles. Maybe it was the pitiable presence of the Garbageman; maybe it was my heroic sparring with Gottschalk; maybe it was the cumbrous burden of their culpability. I didn't let myself care. They were not the kinds of friends I needed, not anymore. I dawdled by the Doritos but Harnett did not reach for a bag of Cool Ranch. Not a good sign.

We were in the checkout aisle when a man asked if he could go ahead of us—he only had one item, a bottle of whiskey. Harnett wouldn't look at him. I shrugged and said it was fine. The man squeezed past. We all stood quiet for a moment, the bleeps of scanned items the only interruption of the piped-in Muzak. At last Harnett sighed in irritation.

"Just put it in the cart," he said.

The man didn't respond.

"Something tells me we'll need it," Harnett said. "Put it in the cart."

As the man did as he was told, I felt a twinge of recognition. The large frame, the long beard, the burly forearms—it was Crying John. He smiled a smile so sad he didn't have to say anything. I knew what had happened. Twenty minutes later he was in our cabin, on the overturned bucket, his bawls ringing metallic against the concrete floor.

"She was old," Harnett said.

Crying John cried harder. "She waited until I'd dug a hole so I didn't have to dig her one special. I would've gladly done it. Gladly. But that's not what she wanted. She circled and lay down and breathed real heavy and then—and then that was it. My little Foulie was gone. My little Foulie was dead. Oh, god, my little baby Foulie is gone!"

Great sobs shook the momentous shoulders. Harnett reached over and poured him another whiskey. Then he poured one for himself. They were the first drinks I'd seen him pour in many months; I squatted in my safety zone by the sink. The late-day light stretched the barred windows into a cage.

Crying John wiped at his cheeks. "So I did what she wanted. Wrapped her inside a blankie. Kissed her on her nose and told her I was so sorry I couldn't've been a better daddy. And then I put her in the dirt. I did it because that's what she wanted. She's buried in Wyoming. In a grave with someone else's name. No one will ever know my doggie's there. No one will ever, ever know."

"We'll know," said Harnett. "You, me, Knox, the kid—we'll make sure everyone knows. They'll talk about that dog forever."

"What's forever?" Crying John snarled. Spittle swung from his bottom lip. "There is no forever anymore and you goddamn well know it!"

Harnett took a sip of his drink. I looked away.

"Don't bullshit me, Resurrectionist. You've seen them. Don't sit there and tell me you haven't seen them."

My father took another drink, this one a bit larger.

Crying John plunged his hand into his pocket and withdrew a handful of Polaroid scraps. A few of them fluttered to the floor, serrated triangles of flesh and bone.

"I've found ten or twelve now. Even Foulie knew we were done for. That's why she gave up. She could smell the son of a bitch all over the graves."

Ten or twelve? Harnett and I had uncovered forty or fifty. Both of us kept quiet.

"I've tried to keep going. I even gave the old routine a shot. Went to a wake, the funeral, the whole business. It was a disaster. An unmitigated disaster." He appealed to us with swollen eyes. "Did you know they bury people with their phones now? I don't know why. They must be somehow meaningful. But at this funeral I'm looking down at this sleeper and his phone keeps going off. It's on mute but you can hear it vibrate, see it light up inside his jacket. He's dead, and people are still calling him, leaving him messages. When we're dead, Resurrectionist, who's gonna call us, huh?"

Harnett looked into his glass. It was dry.

"Him?" Crying John pointed an unsteady finger at me. "Is that what you really want? Look at us. Look at *me*. I've got no one, nothing. No one to tell me everything's gonna be okay. And this will happen to you, too, any day now. You'll wake up and you'll be old and alone, too."

Harnett cleared his throat. "Knox will help you."

Crying John stamped the floor. "Knox is a vulture! He circles until hope is gone and then swoops in and bites our heads off with salvation. And we listen to him, because what else choice do we got, huh? If you're seriously suggesting Knox, then I know I'm through. We're all through."

Bottle rang against cup as Harnett poured.

"Now, listen." Crying John wiped his hairy cheeks. "I came here because I got something to say. After Foulie . . . after Foulie passed, I packed it up, went to the Northeast. Wanted to show Under-the-Mud the pictures, see if he'd found any, too."

"Under-the-Mud." Harnett blinked. "Why didn't you come to me?"

Crying John paused but did not respond. "I found him. Took me a while, but I found him. In Buffalo."

Harnett's throat hitched. "Why didn't you come to me first?"

"Or I should say he found me. You know Under-the-Mud. The man did not make mistakes. Sixty years without a slip-up. I'm walking around Buffalo one morning and I hear my name. 'Crying John.' I'm halfway down the sidewalk before I realize. First thing I see are feet sticking out of the alcove of some boarded-up store. Shoes all worn through, frostbitten toes. The man himself I don't recognize. I'm telling you, Resurrectionist, I don't recognize him. He's a vagrant, all huddled up. He's got a KFC cup with a few pennies in it and a sign, one of those cardboard signs—"

He gnashed his teeth as if fighting through the tears that assailed him.

"I get down there in the slush with him and he says, 'I knew it was you.' Kind of holding his head to the side like he hears music I don't hear. And he smiles. Every other tooth is gone. Drool's falling through the gaps. This can't be Under-the-Mud. But it is."

I tried to reconcile this vile depiction with the aristocratic gent who had scoffed at me in that long-ago pub. Harnett's harshest critic, Under-the-Mud was nothing if not erudite, exacting, and neat. Debased to scrabbling for change on a grimy sidewalk—it just didn't seem possible.

Outside, the automatic floodlights hummed to life.

"Next thing he says is *Baby*. Says he knows it's Baby. He heard about cemeteries being disrupted, everywhere he went, like someone was following him and trying to get him caught. He wasn't afraid—sixty years, not so much as a single complaint. But it happened." Crying John winced. "They took his eyes, Resurrectionist. When he opened them there was nothing underneath."

Despite all I had seen, my stomach seized. It was too brutal and much too close to home. If Bloughton made a similar discovery, there was no telling what would befall Harnett and me.

"He'd asked them to take his hands instead, but they didn't listen. Not that there's much left of his hands, either. All frostbitten and broken. He says other street people kick him down and steal his pennies. When I gave him everything in my wallet he stuffed it in his underwear. And you know what he said?"

Harnett did not respond.

"*Historical precedent*. He kept saying those two words. There is *historical precedent* for this, he said. The original resurrection men, their time ended, too. We're next. We're done. It's our turn. Historical precedent."

Harnett's cup clipped the arm of the chair. The sound was irate.

"You should've come to me first."

Crying John's disgust was brazen. "That's what you say? That's your response? Come to you, you arrogant prick? Why? This whole thing's your fault. What happened to Foulie, what happened to Under-the-Mud. The end of the Diggers?"

"You don't know what you're saying."

"The Apologist? You heard about him? Stroke. Waiting to die in a hospital somewhere with tubes in his face and down his throat."

"Give me your glass."

"He's killing us." Crying John's eyes blurred with angry tears. "One way or another, he's cutting our throats."

Harnett lowered the whiskey bottle and searched out the other man's eyes.

"I'm doing what I can."

Crying John ground the heels of his hands into his sockets. "I know. I know that. I'm sorry. I didn't want to come. I didn't want to have to tell you any of this. It's Under-the-Mud, he made me promise. He made me swear that I'd find you and let you know. I'm sorry."

Harnett licked his lips and looked at the bottle.

Crying John took to his feet so fast the bucket he was sitting on went spinning into the hearth. I flinched and stood. Harnett rose, too, the rocking chair groaning. Crying John swiped his winter coat and had it on in two curt movements. He swayed on his way to the door. He attacked it with clumsy fingers. It was locked and wouldn't open. He threw one lock, but there were three more, still gummy with price tags.

"John," Harnett said. "Where are you going?"

"The mountains." Against the door, his tone was flat and clipped. "I'll vanish. You could come with me, you know. Both of you could come with me. We could vanish into the most beautiful mountains."

Harnett's expression was filled with such yearning that it was all I could do not to shout my opposition. Frantically I thought of the Rotters Book. Maybe Boggs was right and it did mean our salvation, the only way for us to survive in a new century. I could describe it to Crying John, try to make him understand.

"You go," Harnett said. "I can't."

"I know, I know, the kid."

Crying John twisted and pushed at the locks but they were foreign to him and bit at his fingers until he laughed. It was a loud and unfriendly noise.

"Locks, bars. You think this crap is going to protect you?"

"John," said Harnett.

Crying John turned on him. "You were never this stupid! What's happened to you? Can't you see what's in front of your face? Do I have to spell it out?"

Harnett spread his arms, helpless.

Crying John winced. The tears fled from the corners of his eyes into the escape channels of his wrinkles.

"He told me to tell you. He made me swear. But I lied to him; I wasn't really going to do it."

"Who? What?"

"Under-the-Mud. He said you deserved to know. See? Even at the end, he praised you. He thought more of you than any of us did. Hell of a lot more than me."

Harnett was shaking his head. "The end? Wait. Is he—"

"You still got your eyes, but you're every bit as blind. So, fine, I'll tell you." Crying John gasped down his tears. "Anyone can see where Baby is leading you. Anyone can see where he wants you to go. I swore that I'd tell you, so, all right, here it is. But just because I tell you doesn't mean you have to go there. You don't have to do what Baby wants you to do. When are you going to understand that?"

Everything became clear. I covered my face with my hands.

Crying John saw me and his beard moved in silent apologies.

"Oh, god," Harnett said. He reached for the door. "Get out of my way."

16.

We drove like we were somersaulting down a hill. Cars honked and semis wobbled as we swept into their lanes, and still we rolled faster and faster. When the sign welcoming us to Chicago passed overhead, Harnett sideswiped an Oldsmobile that subsequently chased us for half an hour. Once spat out by an exit ramp, we were lost and it was all my fault. Landmarks had rearranged in my absence. Road signs had redirected. With every U-turn Harnett toppled more kiosks and cut off more pedestrians. We squealed into three different gas stations desperate for direction. Denizens who would have never noticed me one year ago now skirted away, sensing danger. Somehow the Pakistani with the baby stroller, the Haitian with the cab, the Mexican with the food cart, they *knew*.

It was just a few hours to daybreak when we found Evan Hills Cemetery. And only when I touched the casket did I realize that I had done so once before, at her funeral, moments before walking away from the tarp-covered plot, so that now, eight long months later, my fingers recognized it. It was like touching anything else familiar from home—a doorknob, a banister.

It was undoubtedly the worst digging of Harnett's life. He was crazed. Each particle of dirt was like a speck of his sanity tossed away. It rained over me, the dirt and the delirium, and I swallowed too much of both. There existed in the cemetery a vague impression of spaciousness and cleanliness, stones kept clean from weeds. For this small favor I was thankful. Night crashed down.

Two feet, three feet—misplaced excitement over the role reversal of checking on a mother tucked into bed. Four feet, five feet—would her grin at seeing me again be wide enough to eat her face? Six feet—the clang of shovel meeting casket. Don't be noisy, Daddy, let Mommy sleep.

I sat cross-legged at the edge of the hole, facing a dark, icy cemetery I had last seen on a bright summer afternoon. Below, Harnett slaughtered the lid—it crunched like broken bone. There followed a moment of silence the length of a single breath, and then the sounds began. I shut my eyes and covered my ears. His throat had burst—it was the only explanation for the whirling, splattering sobs that tore around like cyclones.

A hand groped for the grass; I saw bloody knuckles and snapped fingernails. A second hand joined the first and this one held not one but a fistful of Polaroids, and as Harnett floundered over the edge and writhed through the cold mud, several of these pictures fluttered free. My eyes were too well trained. I saw an image of a body, nothing I could yet recognize as my mother, lying inside a coffin; in another photo, she was outside the coffin; in another, sprawled aslant next to her plot; in another, doing the splits across the stone that bore her name. She was positioned like a bloated rag doll in dozens of ridiculous and impossible poses—I cataloged each image as Harnett, still screaming, peeled them from the mud—and in several photos she was joined by the man who had lusted after her while she was alive. In these photos Baby held her body to him and kissed at her puffy face and more—but Harnett had peeled these last photos away and before I knew it was tearing them to pieces and chewing them and choking as the sharp corners split him down his insides.

He squirmed in the mud until every last piece was ingested, and then he clutched his gut and screamed. I winced as something inside me smothered. Coldness took over. All at once Harnett's behavior struck me as unseemly. "Stop crying," I said. He didn't listen. I stood and walked over to him. "Stop crying," I said again. He wailed and banged his forehead against the frozen ground. It was so loud that it scared me; then I became angry that I was scared. I kneeled and poked him in the side. "Stop crying." I pushed him. "Stop crying!" I kicked him in the hip, in the knee, in the neck. *"Stop crying!"* I shoved at him until he was faceup and then I punched, knuckles into open eyes and streaming nose. *"STOP CRYING! STOP CRYING! STOP CRYING!"* He screamed until my face was covered with his blood. I wiped it away with an arm. I would act properly even if he wouldn't. I stood, leaving him snaking in blind circles, and tucked in my shirt and patted down my hair.

"Hi, Mom," I said, kneeling beside her.

Boggs had at least returned her to a funereal pose. I searched her swollen and purple face for signs of the woman I had known, and after a minute or two I smiled in recognition. There: the broad cheeks, the longish nose, the disfigured ear.

The ear—I leaned over and took a closer look. Typically ears were one of the first features to deteriorate, yet her left one was miraculously intact. I examined the old wound, imagining the Gatlin shovel strike that had so crudely carved it. Harnett had undoubtedly seen it, too; above, he was still blubbering in the moonlight. I knew he was upset about what Boggs had done in this grave. I knew he was rabid that a copy of each picture was safely nestled inside the Rotters Book. Still, I wished he'd shut up. He was just jealous that another man had touched her, no matter that it had been his failures that had denied her any man's touch for sixteen years.

I was the only one in that graveyard deserving of Valerie Crouch. I remembered the soft fuzz of her cheeks; I reached out and touched taut and mealy skin. I nuzzled into her neck in search of her scent of wood and milk; I smelled only the grave's usual potency.

Why was she withholding herself? I felt a flash of irritation. I had come too far, across two states, down six feet of earth, for her to ignore me. I put an arm around her shoulders and threaded another around her waist. Carefully I gathered her in my arms. Her head rolled against my cheek. Before I knew it she was in my lap, her body blue and turgid and squeaking like rubber. I said *shhh* and rocked her and petted her cold straw hair. One arm was missing and one of her legs was just a sleeve of skin, and the amount of PVC pipe inside the coffin brought home just how catastrophic her injuries had been, how hard the mortician had slaved in his effort at reassembly.

She sank from my clutches. I became frustrated, first at her, then at myself. I muttered bad words she would have cuffed me for when she was living, and followed them with solemn apologies. I turned my face to the stars and cursed the Incorruptibles, those so-called saints who had so greedily soaked up all the miracles for themselves. If anyone had been a saint, it had been my mother, yet here she was, as grossly moldered as the worst of sinners.

I tucked her in. I put my lips to her tumescent ear and whispered good-night. For a few minutes I fell asleep at her side. Yet morning beckoned. My fingers found the long, cold length of a leg bone among the PVC piping and I plucked it from the coffin and used it to help myself to the surface. I set it safely aside and took up the Root.

That night I was a Filler, not a Digger. All that I had excavated from myself since my mother's death I would now fill with expertise beyond that of the Resurrectionist or Lionel or any Digger who had ever lived. I would raise bodies like a hard rain sucks worms to the surface. I would become hero to a few; to everyone else I would be the whip of flame flickering through feverish nightmares. I would become the Son, and I'd take the name in her honor, not his.

The Son's first act was to fix what Harnett had broken. I repaired her mangled grave as the mortician had repaired her body. The Root was my scalpel, the dirt her muscle fiber, the grass her skin, the graveyard her body.

17.

Almost overnight the cabin lapsed into squalor. The whiskey bottle that Crying John had left was polished off within seconds of our return. I curled on my bedsheets, my mother's stolen leg bone tucked beneath my pillow, and divorced myself from the man who now shambled about the room, kicking things and belching liquor. There were still some things I could learn from the bastard, and I would learn them, but I would not allow Ken Harnett to destroy another Crouch.

Trapped within the bolts and bars of his self-made prison, he rumbled about accepting disgraceful deals from disinterested pawnbrokers, then drank away the disappointment, as well as the measly profits, in a single sitting. He slept at unusual, random hours. I would hear the *crick-crick* of the rocking chair and the weak sizzle of the fire in the middle of the night and try to block it out with convoluted melodies I used to play in band; conversations I'd had with Boris; imagined dialogue from his new friend, the trombonist Mac Hill. The very word *trombone* dazzled me, and I fantasized how I might splice the leg bone beneath my pillow with my trumpet in time for Ted's next lesson. I would fall back asleep with these bizarre delusions swirling through my brain, confident that the soul, if it existed at all, was located in the skeleton—after all, that was the part that persevered, long after the rest dissolved to dust.

What happened next was probably inevitable. It seemed like lifetimes ago when we had both huddled next to the crypt in Lancet County waiting for the Woman in Black to end her vigil, and Harnett had condemned "Bad Jobs." His description of digs-for-hire had haunted me ever since: *Any Digger who starts down that path, he's pretty well near the end,* he had said. *You can't do those kinds of jobs and live with yourself.*

It was the nearest thing there was to suicide, he had suggested, and because he was the proudest Digger with the purest of standards, none could have predicted his rapid slide toward such work—none except me; I had seen all hope and reason leave his eyes the night he beheld my mother's corpse.

Once the first Bad Job was completed, a second was waiting. Harnett retained enough of his faculties to forbid me to go along, yet derived a self-loathing pleasure from supplying me with posthumous details. Example: a family of religious fanatics in Maine wished to enact what they referred to as a "miracle resurrection" of the clan patriarch. The entire dynasty gathered at their large country estate to luxuriate in the charade, praying over a giant feast before retreating to their guest bedrooms while Harnett watched through binoculars from the nearest field. While they slept, Harnett took care of business. He removed the dead patriarch, returned the dirt so that it looked untouched, then arranged the body in prayer formation against the headstone. The envelope of cash waiting as promised beneath the back steps of the house was labeled *Miracle Money.*

Another example: an anonymous party desired access to an Aurora, Texas, grave that supposedly housed the remains of the pilot of a UFO that had exploded against Judge Proctor's windmill in 1897. As explained by newspaper accounts of the time, local residents helped Proctor toss the refuse down a well—from which subsequent residents drank and grew terribly deformed—before burying the humanoid beneath an innocuous stone in the local graveyard. Though the stone itself had been stolen in the 1970s, Harnett used old photographs to triangulate the location. When he returned from the trip he headed straight to bed despite my interrogation. His eyes were haunted and he said only one thing: "Never ask me about it again."

For a while he resisted the worst jobs of all. While it was true that the original body snatchers had stolen cadavers for medical use, the nabbing of bodies had become a Digger taboo. I tried not to think about the leg bone beneath my pillow. That had been a one-time occurrence. I was sure of it.

Harnett, on the other hand, at first excused himself with quasi-humanitarian reasoning. Most medical skeletons were shipped from India, he said, where young people were kidnapped and murdered to meet the demand. By stealing bones for profit, he was simply helping to counter that atrocity, he claimed. We turned away from each other at the blatant lie. Plastic skeletons had been adopted a long time ago. Even Gottschalk had one.

That was just the beginning. At the request of museums or private collectors he dug up carcasses of the hideously deformed, sufferers of rare and fabulous diseases. He sliced slabs from fresh remains for someone who desired to make candles out of body fat. He nabbed a selection of hands, feet, and genitals for a famous experimental artist in Brooklyn. He stole the skull of a supposed saint that a church wanted as a holy relic. When this last group refused to pay, Harnett cackled mirthlessly and resorted to something he called the Brookes Method—piling a stack of bones on the doorstep of a defaulting client. A book in Harnett's library suggested to me that the grisly technique was named after Joshua Brookes (1761–1833), a surgeon who refused to pay his resurrection men five guineas, only to wake up one morning to find bones piled at each intersection bordering his college. The scare tactic still worked. Harnett might have lost everything else, but he got his money.

While he jetted across the country, I proved his theory. Specifying allowed me to refill graves with an accuracy possibly unrivaled in history. The dead, witness to my successes, became my friends, teachers, and confidants. The more I handled dead flesh, the more my own felt alive. Where once there had been no growth, I grew thicker, stronger, hairier, as if I were soaking up remnant life forces still swirling within each carcass. My broader shoulders required a new coat; I found one to my liking just an hour away from Bloughton beneath a Polaroid. My old shoes were flimsy jokes; I found a pair of boots six feet under a small memorial park just north. I didn't need a brimmed hat but took one anyway off a body I dug up east of town; I thought it made me look mysterious and maybe even a little dashing. All of these clothes I chose with Foley in the back of my mind. Though they reeked, they were about as heavy metal as it gets.

One balmy late-April evening I found myself back in Lancet County. After resurfacing from a new belly with three thick bracelets of glittering gemstones, I ambled over to pay a visit to Nathaniel Merriman. There I found a fresher grave to Nathaniel's left: ROSE MERRIMAN, LOYAL DAUGHTER. Here lay the Woman in Black. Guiding her from her father's grave was the first act that had gained me notoriety among the Diggers, and I felt a twinge of sadness. I sat between the two plots and brushed my hands through the grass. Soon the remains of father and daughter would mingle. I envied them. On my way out of town I stopped by Floyd and Eileen's bar for some beef jerky, just for old time's sake.

It was the first day of May when Harnett dug up the body of a teenager and plotted to ransom it to the family. I was appalled. He tried to assure me that the family had done something evil enough to deserve it, but I wouldn't listen. He had become a monster; the fact that eighteen hours later he changed his mind and returned the body to the grave did nothing to convince me otherwise. He mumbled about the almost-successful 1876 plot to steal Abraham Lincoln's body in hopes of exchanging it for the release of a prisoner, about how sometimes you had to do bad things for virtuous ends. I told him to get his shit, we had work to do.

"We" was a generous way to put it. His inebriated fingers no longer functioned properly. He made a mess of the sod. His tarps weren't level and dirt ran like rainwater. Repeatedly I saved us from imminent disaster, often having to wrench some crappy shovel from his blundering hands. I was usually the one to crowbar the casket, and when I found Polaroids I did my best to keep them to myself.

His humiliation became suffocating. He had gone through maybe two dozen shovels since the New Year. He acted out perilously, digging in broad daylight or during the traffic peaks of Memorial Day and Mother's Day. I called him stupid. He called me a chicken. It was after one of these fights that I returned from school to find him sprawled across the hearth. He had shit his pants. I dragged him to the bathroom, stripped him of his soiled clothes, and shoved him beneath the freezing shower. Moments like these shucked him of all leverage. He agreed to any deal I offered. Yes, he'd sign that F-filled report card or write a note fabricating an excuse for my continued absences—anything I wanted, as long as I did not speak of what he had become.

In mid-May, as I cased a memorial park two hours down the interstate from Bloughton, I came upon a funeral in progress. One of the mourners was Claire, the caseworker who had prepared me as best she could for life in Bloughton. To get a better look, I edged within twenty feet of her. In her simple black dress and dark lipstick she looked even prettier than I remembered. I thought about saying hello. Maybe I would look to her like a man now, maybe we could go out for coffee. Mere Reality was swept away with the breeze. Then the last invocation was spoken and the crowd broke apart and for a moment she looked right at me. There was no recognition. She looped her arm through that of a man who was probably her husband and walked away. I forced myself to laugh. Such warm, live flesh was not for me.

18.

TED POINTED AT THE bar for the third time. Beyond his manicured nails the dots and lines made weeds and thorns. I blew but my lungs withheld, knowing better than my brain they would need all their strength for the evening's dig. My fingers, too, reserved their strength. The notes that I emitted dribbled like blood.

I yawned behind the mouthpiece and glanced at the clock. It was nearly six, time to get home and suit up for work. Ted frowned and stood up straight. He reached over and shut the sheet music. I was grateful. I rubbed the notes from where they had embedded into my eyes.

When I looked again, he was still standing there staring. I waited for *Next lesson, then*. It didn't come. I cleared my throat. I set the trumpet in my lap. For whatever reason, dismissal still seemed compulsory.

"We have an understanding," he said finally. "I know that. But I would like permission to speak freely."

I shrugged. "Okay."

He crossed his arms. "Why do you keep coming?"

I shrugged again. "I don't know."

"Classes, you don't attend. Trumpet lessons, though, you come all the way here for. Why is that?"

"Like I said."

"You can't continue this way," he said. "Eventually they'll flunk you. You already know that. One day soon you won't be a student here anymore."

"All right." I pulled off the mouthpiece.

"And I'm going to tell you something else. I don't care. Flunk out. You don't like something, stop it. You don't like going to school, stop going. But don't you stop these lessons. Whatever you do. We'll meet somewhere else if necessary. We'll play outside, on weekends if it comes to that. But one thing we'll not ever do is stop. Am I making myself clear?"

I stared at my lap, incapacitated with a feeling of inevitable abandonment.

"Why?" I asked.

"Because it's all you have." He said it with such confidence that I recoiled. "Someday when it's over, whatever it is that's got you, we'll play together, you on trumpet, me on clarinet. I'll lend you albums to listen to that will inspire you. You can lend me some, too. Just think of that. Picture it. Imagine it as often as possible and one day it will happen. We'll go to an opera. You ever been to the opera? I go every year. *Faust* is my favorite. They play it at the Metropolitan all the time. You know what it's about? It's about a man who makes a pact with Lucifer in exchange for knowledge. Imagine seeing that. Picture it. Just keep picturing it and one day we'll be there, both of us at the Met. Just don't stop the lessons. Don't stop. Do you understand?"

I nodded and tears fell from my chin.

"Okay," he said. He flattened his mustache with his finger and thumb. "Well. Next lesson, then."

19.

The exact day of the accident is lost to me. After hours of sullen invectives, I had relented and allowed Harnett to join me on a dig. Just forty-five minutes from the cabin, I knew it would be a job so easy even he couldn't derail it.

But he was drunk, not stupid. He was offended by the simplicity of the dig and griped at me the entire way there. I kept my mouth shut and drove. Once we were at the location, he snatched the Root from me. I sighed and watched him murder the earth, trying to keep track of what went where so I could put it all back together again when he was through.

"You're so eager to get rid of me," he spat between strikes. "One of these days you'll get your wish. I'll be dead and you'll finally be happy."

"I'll never be happy," I said. "Keep digging."

"Don't do me like Lionel. That's all I ask. Don't stick me in a box and shove me down a hole. At least have that much respect for your old man."

I pictured Lionel's plot, perched so magisterially above the Atlantic. "You'd be lucky to have what he has."

"Hell with that. You burn me. Incinerate me. Toss me around so I'm scattered in the wind."

"Strewn," I said, remembering a fact from one of Harnett's books. "The church prefers *strewn*."

"Think I give a damn what the church prefers?"

A thunking noise—he was at the casket already. Graceless as he was, his strength and speed were undeniable.

He muttered from below. "Even better: excarnation. Will you do me the kindness?"

The term was familiar, but I couldn't immediately define it. Harnett, desperate for ways to trump me, pounced.

"It's Tibetan tradition. Celestial burial, sky burial, excarnation. Same thing. It's perfect. It's beautiful. It's more than I deserve, but maybe you'll take pity and give it to me anyway."

I heard the skipping thumps of the crowbar slipping from his hands. Reluctantly I moved forward and peeked down the hole.

"Three days." He wiped his sweaty palms on his pants. "You let me sit for three days. Don't bury me, don't do nothing. Just let me ripen for three goddamn days. Then take my clothes off, take me out to the country. If that's too much of a goddamn hassle for you, sit me out in the backyard, I don't give a damn."

I kneeled down at the edge. "Let me help you."

"You want to help me? Then dismember me first, if you got the stomach for it. It's Tibetan tradition." His lips curled in resentment as he tried again to pry the lid. "Forget it. You don't have the stomach. Just toss me out in the grass."

Part of the problem was that the Root was down there with him, getting in his way. "The Root," I said. "Hand her up."

"Not a lot of vultures in Iowa," he said. "But plenty of birds. They'll come in, one or two of them at first, and pick at me. You just stay back and let them. Pretty soon they'll be there by the dozens. They'll eat me, part of me, every one, and they'll carry me into the sky. And then when they shit, I'll be everywhere. It's goddamn beautiful and more than I deserve, but maybe, just maybe, you'll do your father the kindness."

He was visibly wobbling and slumped to the dirt wall for balance.

"Get out." I tried to be firm. I held out a hand. "You're going to hurt yourself. Get out."

"Don't forget to bring a sledgehammer," he slurred. "When the birds are done, you gotta shatter my bones to bits. Tibetan tradition."

"You're wasting time. Get out."

There was a pause and then he moved with alarming speed, snatching the crowbar and the Root in either hand and clambering up the hole. I remained crouched at the edge, unwilling to give him the satisfaction of cringing. At the top he tripped and fell on his face.

"Sooner than you think," he fumed, hauling himself to unsteady feet. "Sooner than you think I'll be gone, and then you can dig these goddamn holes however you goddamn like and toss me down one of them like a dog." He snarled. "You can go to hell."

With that he drove the Root into the ground. She made a meaty slicing sound as she impaled the earth. Even wasted, Harnett knew the sound wasn't normal. I became aware of a tingling coolness.

I raised my right hand. The top halves of my index, middle, and ring fingers were gone. Together we looked at the Root and saw three white nubs nestled to one side of the blade. In unison our eyes moved again to my outstretched hand. An eternity passed. At last blood as black as oil began slurping from the holes.

"Harnett." I held my hand higher as if he hadn't already seen. Blood twined down my wrist and arm and heavied my sleeve.

There was a blur as Harnett moved. I felt disconnected from my body. I pushed myself away with my heels until I ran out of breath and let myself fall back against the cool grass.

Above me was a gorgeous canopy of stars. Each one of them, I marveled, would correspond to a piece of Harnett's body after his celestial burial. It was beautiful after all.

At no time did I entertain illusions of reattachment. There was a grave to be filled, and Diggers have priorities. Back at the cabin, Harnett ransacked the sink cabinet until he found a dusty bottle of peroxide. He shoved a handful of aspirin at me and a glass of lukewarm water, then unwrapped the bloody cloth from my hand and dumped the peroxide. I screamed, then laughed at the girlishness of the sound, then screamed some more. My other arm toppled books. My legs sent newspapers flapping like descending gulls. I barely noticed when the front door opened and a man tossed his crutch to the floor and dropped to his knees in the sizzling lather of water, blood, and disinfectant.

Knox cupped my cheek with a cool palm.

"Jesus wept," he said. "Jesus wept. Jesus wept."

20.

As he had during my bout of boneyard blues, the one-legged reverend nursed me back to health. He sutured my wounds with a white-hot needle and kept me afloat in liquids. Somehow he found time to make coffee on the stove. He had to wrap Harnett's fingers around a mug before he would take it. My father sipped the stuff while perched near the sink, refusing to look at either of us. For once I had the rocking chair, although it felt all wrong—it was all I could do not to insist Harnett come take it back.

Knox's arrival had not been coincidence. He had heard of

the maiming of Under-the-Mud and the suspicious disappearance of Crying John and was on his way to Virginia to visit the hospital where the Apologist hovered just north of demise. To this already crowded list Knox added Brownie, who had suspended all digging to undergo an intense three-month religious study in hopes that Jesus Christ might save him. Knox had been guiding Brownie's studies when word of Harnett's Bad Jobs had finally reached Texas.

It was not like last time. There was no conversation between the men. Their wordless exchanges said it all. Knox was angry and distraught. Harnett was consumed with shame and self-hatred. Though overwhelmed with pain, I felt like the one in charge. These two could fight their little fight all they wanted; regardless, the Son would continue digging even faster and better than before, just wait and see.

The secret smiles Knox had shared with me during his previous visit were similarly absent. I wanted to attribute it to his fatigue and the long drive still ahead of him, but I knew that wasn't it. I had changed. Knox could see it in my every sound and movement. Only occasionally did he ponder me in a way that stirred sensations of hope. While I had no desire to be a part of Bloughton or the wider world, Knox's approval still meant something.

The reverend sent Harnett out for firewood, and after my father had returned and retreated to his corner, Knox spent the next few hours whittling away at the choicest log. I watched him from where I was curled up on the chair. Soon he was sanding three wooden pellets. His total absorption was itself absorbing, and I rearranged myself within the blanket that swaddled me. He winced as he adjusted himself on the bucket; it was a difficult balance to maintain with only one leg.

"You want the chair?" I asked.

He frowned at his sanding. The repetitive whisper began lulling me to sleep. Knox's voice was of the same soft and shifting quality; at first it was difficult to differentiate it from the noise.

"Hundred years old I am," he said quietly. "Sometimes feels like two hundred. Two thousand. Feel it most at times like now, when I'm not movin'. I'm *always* movin'. Made my life out of movin'. You folks name your shovels; I name my cars. Bethany, there was a beaut. Jacqueline, strong as a tank. Patty—Patty didn't last long, but she was fast. Back when I had hair it would crunch flat when I was drivin' Patty. And where do I go? Where do all these fine ladies take me? I ask the good Lord each and every night: 'Where you takin' me, Lord?' Feels like a hundred years I been askin' that question and a hundred years I been gettin' no answers. Now I'm tired. But I keep movin'. You want to know why? Because I'm scared. Me too, hallelujah. I'm scared if I turn off that engine for good, my ears will finally hear and then I'll know for sure there aren't no answers, not for me. Because I've done Him wrong. That's the kind of silence I don't know if I've got the strength to bear. That's a forever kind of silence."

The pellets of wood were fingers. He placed them in the crease of his thighs and picked up an old glove and pair of shears. He gathered three of the leather digits between the blades and began to saw.

"There be a woeful darkness out there. I see it every town I pass through. I see it on the sides of the roads. I see it real strong when I visit any of y'all. But I see it most in the rearview mirror, in me. God is good. Least I think so. I pray 'Talk to me, O Lord' and there's quiet. I pray 'Show me, O Lord' and there's darkness. These old eyes have cried buckets, so many buckets I feel like a child, younger than you. 'It's not fair,' I cry. You think God is fair? 'I've worked so hard,' I cry. You think Jesus checks my speedometer? Boxer, Under-the-Mud, Resurrectionist—I've watched so many of you pass, your names are like dust. But my life—this is *my* life. I've crossed into the most woeful darkness to bring y'all into the light. Maybe I've gone too far. Maybe I'm lost in the dark. Maybe this isn't the story of your descent, Joey Crouch. Maybe it's the story of mine."

Briefly he held greasy bolts in his lips while he traded the shears for pliers. He fitted the wood into the newly fingerless glove and clamped it in place. A knobby old thumb pressed the first bolt against the leather. He spat the rest of the bolts into a palm and began twisting the corresponding nut.

"The number of sins I've let come to pass, it's far too many to atone for. Did I assist y'all for the right reasons? I don't know, He won't tell me. When I look in the mirror, it's black. When I press my ear to the ground, it's quiet. That's blindness and deafness. That's hell. And every day hell nudges up a little closer. It's in the tollbooth on the interstate. It's in the backseat of my car. It's in my glove box, it's in my hip pocket. It's my missing leg. Father, Son, and Holy Ghost. Sometimes I feel like I'm one of them, and you're one of them, and Ken's one of them, too. Can't be true, though. Look at me. I got a deflated lung. I got issues with my prostate. My knee aches so bad some days I can't press the brake. By the way, my new car is named Priscilla Beaulieu. You know why? Because I'm hopin' she'll take me to see the King."

He frowned and raised the glove until it was a mere inch from his nose. His face was a maze of lines spiraling from a point between his eyebrows. He flipped his handiwork and inspected the reverse side. A glimpse of teeth, the hint of a smile—it was like a wedge of light thrown into a darkened room by the cracking of a door.

I reached out. He fit the apparatus gently over my hand and persuaded me to make and release a fist one hundred times. With each clench I imagined these new fingers gripping the Root. It would be different, but not necessarily worse. What I would lose in sensitivity I would gain in imperviousness to pain. I flexed my new fingers until Knox began snoring and the window bars segmented the morning light.

The snores snagged. Knox coughed and sat up. He stoked the fire and checked his pocket watch. He looked incurably old. His clergyman's collar was yellow and wilted with sweat. Coils of silver hair glistened against his scalp. He rubbed his eyes and took in the rankled state of the cabin as if in disbelief that his long life had led him to such a place. Then he arduously stood upon his leg, hopped three times, and lowered himself to my side.

From some depths his voice found an orational energy.

"Ken, join us in prayer."

The man in the corner shuffled his feet.

"Ken Harnett. Join us in prayer."

The reverend's eyes were yellow and ringed in fire. Harnett did not move, his stubborn expression making clear his expectation of reaching the same end as Crying John and Under-the-Mud. The difference was that he didn't care.

The stalemate took us through daybreak. The yard lights shut off and the silence was filled by the whistling of robins and the shushing of the river. The standoff reminded me of nothing so much as when Harnett and I had stood outside the cabin while I demanded lessons and he insisted that I wasn't ready. The reverend had probably never looked so obdurate;

his ability to outwait my father was never really in doubt. Harnett finally shambled across the room, dropped to his knees in defeat, and jerked his chin into the requisite posture. Without a second's pause, Knox began.

"Lord, hear our prayer. We have a young boy here who is injured; help salve his wounds. We have a man here who is lost; help find him his way. Out there in thy world is another man who lives in anger; help tamp his fury. Show them, O Lord, that there is light even in the darkest night. Remind them, O Lord, that though they may walk through the valley of death they should fear no evil, for thou art with them and thy rod and thy staff comfort them."

Thy rod: Grinder. Thy staff: the Root. Comforts, indeed.

"Most of all, Lord, counsel to us thy servants that there is yet time. Time for us to confess what we have seen, to repent what we have done, to ask for thy help as well as thy life everlasting. Sacrifices for us have begun and they shall continue. We know this, Lord; in our deepest hearts, we know it. But please, Lord, show us that God is good—do not demand too harsh a sacrifice. We are thy lambs; lead us yet from slaughter, I pray."

Tears ran down Knox's cheeks in two straight, dark lines. One of his hands pawed at Harnett until it found his forearm. The other reached out blindly until it snared my wrist. He held on with such ferocity that his thumbnail pierced my skin.

"This I beg of you, Lord: 'The Son of man is not come to destroy men's lives, but to save them.'

"This I beg of you, Lord: 'He that shall endure unto the end, the same shall be saved.'

"This I beg of you, Lord: 'He that hath suffered in the flesh hath ceased from sin.'

"This I beg of you, Lord: 'There is no man that sinneth not.' "

The wrinkled pouches of his eyes unknotted and a curtain of tears washed clean his dusty face. His cheeks twitched and birthed a smile, a huge one, shocking and glorious, shattering the gloomy certainty of disaster that had clouded his countenance. It was as if a heavenly hand was upon his heart—perhaps he had finally broken through the darkness and silence. He dropped our arms and lifted his palms to the sky. A great weight of emotion struggled against his voice.

" 'I send you forth as sheep in the midst of wolves: be ye therefore wise as serpents, and harmless as doves.' "

Harnett choked on what sounded like tears of his own. He rose and turned away and wove through spinning bottles and littered newspapers until his unsteady groping came upon the bedroom knob. He swayed. I held my breath; Knox inhaled softly. The whole house seemed to tilt.

21.

NEWS OF MY FINGERS spread fast. Ted pulled me aside in the hallway before third period, pushing back the sleeve of my black duster—despite its fetor never for a moment dreaming that I'd stripped it from a corpse—to gape at the contraption Knox had fitted to my right hand. Ted was just the first of several teachers and even a handful of curious students. The strange thing was that none of them asked how it had happened, as if they suspected and feared that something they had done, or hadn't done, had led to this sorry fate.

Fuzzy memories existed of a promise I had made Ted, but

all vows were void when I wiggled at him my three abridged fingers—the exact three fingers needed to play the trumpet. The last tangible connection to life with my mother had been cleanly and literally severed, and Ted was just some garbage that had gotten sliced away with it.

"You can't play anymore, can you?" He looked comically doomed.

"No," I said.

He gasped and I swear I saw tears.

"I'm sorry," he said. "I'm so sorry."

"Don't be," I said. "The trumpet's for pussies."

Every treasure in Lionel's legendary stash—that was what I would've given to have a picture of Ted's reaction. Or Laverne's reaction when I told her to eat shit, preferably her principal's. Or Heidi Goehring's reaction when I told her to cram her condolences as far up her ass as they would go. It was somewhere between sickening and amusing, how three small nuggets of sanded wood were all it took to turn me into a celebrity.

I pretended not to see Celeste in the lunchtime blitz, but her bright nails lanced my shirt and reeled me into a side hallway. The walls and floor and ceiling popped with the prim backpedaling of her heels; the students rushing past us sounded like the Big Chief River. For a few moments I avoided her expectant eyes, just as I had avoided her for weeks, banking down random corridors or even fleeing the school when her approach made a confrontation inevitable. Now I forced myself to meet her gaze. If my new fingers proved anything it was that I was made of sturdier stuff.

"Poor baby, is it true?" she whispered.

When I didn't respond, she carefully cradled my elbow and crept her fingers down my arm until her warm hands encircled my wrist. Slowly she turned over my hand and lifted the gloved apparatus to the level of her breast. Her circulating thumbs kneaded the prostheses. Body conquered mind; my breath caught in my throat; it should have been the sexiest moment of my life. But the deadness of wood and leather prevented me from feeling her touch.

"Look at you," she said. "Just look at you."

My head dipped back. What was this feeling? Was it ecstasy? If so, wasn't that what I had always wanted from her? Couldn't this be an alternate, less deadly escape route from Mere Reality? Above me, a spectacle of marvelous fluorescents and breathtaking water spots.

"I'm worried about you, Joey."

"I know."

"Maybe you should get a physical therapist."

"Definitely."

"This thing on your hand doesn't look all that sanitary."

"You're right."

"Have you thought about seeing a counselor?"

"Uh-huh."

"Teen suicide is an epidemic."

"Yes. Absolutely."

"You wouldn't ever do something like that, would you?"

I felt myself shaking my head—*Anything you say, anything at all.*

"Good. Because I'm still counting on you, you know."

My hard parts softened; my soft parts hardened. My eyes eased open and my head rocked back into place. Funny—the movement of her fingers now recalled the death spasms of a rat I'd once crushed in a grave. I smelled something burning and it wasn't cafeteria food. It was lies, both hers and mine. It was a bad smell and I wanted rid of it.

"The Spring Fling," she continued. "It's on Friday. Poor baby. Probably the last thing on your mind. But you said you'd make some calls? See who you could get to come down? You can still do that, can't you? Poor little thing."

She was beautiful on the outside, yes, but I had learned that true beauty had nothing to do with outsides. I gave her a once-over and wondered, *How are her innards?*

It was funny. I began to laugh.

The coaxing pressures against my hand ceased. Her fingers drew back like cobras. I didn't care. My laughter bounced off the surrounding brick surfaces until it was swallowed by the cafeteria thrum. Her filed nails nicked away from sanded wood.

"You haven't called anyone." Her words were torpid.

My hand still hung elevated between us. It looked like a slap and she recoiled as if feeling the sting. Fury bloomed across her cheeks. Although I'd never been brave enough to attend one of her plays, something told me that these were not the exaggerated clownings of stage emotions, nor were they the controlled modicums of feeling she parceled out to teachers and friends. These were emotions, real ones created expressly for me, and they made her look, for a moment there, naked—a sight not exactly erotic, but nonetheless exciting. Her erect posture telescoped down, the encouraging angles of her face puddled, the youthful smoothness of her eyes and lips crimped into sour whorls. It was a horrific unmasking for sure, but for me "horrific" was a concept long since depreciated. Like the return of the boneyard blues, laughter spewed from my lips and got all over her.

"Fucker," she said. "I'm glad you ended up in the shower."

I only laughed harder.

"You know what? It was my idea. I told him you stunk."

I wiped away tears with leather.

"I was glad Woody did what he did to Heidi, too."

Reflected in her eyes was the hallway door and daylight behind me, an infinite and tempting channel. I exercised facial muscles to work out the soreness of hilarity and tried to refocus. It did not shock me that Celeste had been complicit in Woody's persecutions—she had only been too prissy to dirty her hands—but I could muster little more than impatience. At the same time, her livid disfigurement rang inside me a note of caution. She was an enemy now, and there was no greater enemy to make than that of progress.

"Freak." Her red lips shone. "I don't need you, freak."

"I have to go," I said. I sniffed at the lunchtime odors and started away. There was a person of much greater importance I needed to see. When I reached the end of the hallway I looked over my shoulder. She looked good, even hunched in anger and panting with defeat. I nodded at her. "Hey, the Spring Fling—knock 'em dead."

22.

"You know who else is missing fingertips," Foley said, crashing into the chair across from me. After my months-long absence from the cafeteria, my appearance was a deliberate invitation. If I had learned one thing from the shower incident, it was that Foley had my back. He deserved my loyalty if he still wanted it.

I weighed my po'boy and didn't respond until I could do so through a full mouth. "Who's that?"

"Tony Iommi? Lead guitarist, Black Sabbath? You know that song 'A Bit of Finger'? That's about what happened to him. He lost the tips of his middle finger and his ring finger when he was seventeen." He peeked at my hand, hidden beneath the Racism Sandwich. "Just like you."

"Except I'm sixteen," I said.

"Your birthday was last month."

Tap tap tap: wood against lunch-tray plastic. The only calendar I used was the side of a sink, so I wasn't surprised that I had forgotten it, but Foley's ability to pluck this fact out of the air was impressive.

He shrugged it off. "You mentioned it once in gym. To tell you the truth, I'm a little jealous." He held up the crooked finger that I had smashed in the locker room door. "When you broke this sucker that's the first thing I thought—after they took me to the hospital, I mean. I thought, *Damn, I'm livin' Tony Iommi style.*"

I set down the sandwich and we compared damages.

"It's like destiny," he said. "We almost *have* to start a band now."

I smiled. "Joey Crotch and the Feces Foley Experience."

He busied himself tucking away his blond hair to hide his delight. And that was that—broken fingers and months of silence were forgotten. Together we left Mere Reality and returned to our fantasy journeys to see Vorvolakas live. Of course, I had already been back to Chicago the night I had dug up my mother, but some details were best kept to oneself.

Lunch ended with one of Foley's brutal assessments: "You smell like you washed your hair in shit." Half of the things I was wearing had been peeled from sacks of rotting meat, so the news hardly rattled me. I twisted my lips and waited for the long-overdue invitation. *Tap tap tap.*

"My house, after school," he said. "I'll swing by your locker."

True to his word, he came by zippered into black leather, and together we made the fifteen-minute walk to a peach-colored house at the corner of two streets dappled with geraniums and snickering with lawn sprinklers. Foley kicked off his shoes inside the door; barely recalling such rituals, I yanked off my boots. We padded silently over clean white carpet, around plush furniture, past frilled doilies and framed prints.

"Foley?" A woman's voice hollering from another floor.

"Momma, my friend Joey's here," Foley called back.

"Oh, hello! There's coconut cookie bars in the tin if you want."

"Sweet," Foley whispered, making a sharp right into a sunny kitchen.

Momma? Cookie bars? I had chocolate and coconut staining my finger-glove before I could make sense of it. Foley caught my tense expression and briefly held up his bowed finger. "Relax. I told her it was my fault. Wouldn't be the first time I wrecked myself."

Moments later we were down a flight of stairs and in his room. Metal was everywhere—a Sabbath tour poster, a clipped magazine photo of Vorvolakas, an Agalloch LP cover on display—but displayed with unflagging neatness, the poster framed, the photo sharply scissored, the album cover tacked above the exact center of his bed. There was also a TV, an Xbox, a stereo, a record player, and a computer hooked to several external drives. It wasn't until Foley opened his closet that I saw the hundreds of burned CDs, all obsessively labeled and arranged alphabetically within steel towers. Foley paused and shrugged as if to say, *Yep, here it is, my room,* then grabbed his iPod and portable speakers and headed out the door.

He slapped a drawer on his way out. "Change into something and meet me in the laundry room across the hall."

He had a band called Sig:ar:tyr wailing from the speakers when I walked barefoot into the laundry room wearing Hawaiian shorts and an old T-shirt advertising CHRISTIAN YOUTH CAMP 2005. Foley took the stinky wad of black clothes from my hands and held it for a few moments like he was weighing it. He tossed what was machine washable into the washer and dropped my coat into a large sink. My brimmed hat he set on a counter. He arranged before him an array of soaps and cleaners.

"You learn this shit when you have like four thousand little sisters," he said. "Now get in the bath."

Against the dryer: *tap tap tap*. "I'm sorry?"

He pointed upward. "One floor up. You're gonna have to scrub that stink right out of you."

The bathroom was crowded with women's toiletries, so many pink, yellow, blue, and lavender containers that I found myself backing away until my knees struck the rim of the toilet. I fell onto the seat and tapped the porcelain until Foley showed up, sighed, ran the water, and picked out five or six products, repeating more than once which bottle was for which part—skin, hair, face, hands, body. I emerged a half hour later smelling like a rose garden and dressed again in Foley's castoffs, and tiptoed downstairs, where Foley, his mother, and three of his sisters buzzed around the kitchen table munching on cookie bars.

Foley barked through the ruckus. "Momma. Hey, Momma! This is Joey."

"Nice to meet you, Joey," she said while trying to wipe chocolate from the face of a pugnacious five-year-old.

I felt paralyzed. Thankfully Foley kept things moving and soon I was dressed again in my own clothes, only now with every twitch I smelled flowers and fruit instead of sweat and putrescence. As I stepped out his front door, Foley handed me five burned CDs for the road: High Tide, Godspeed You! Black Emperor, Minsk, Sleep, and Witchfinder General.

"Metal up, bitch," he said.

Spring had overthrown Bloughton. The colors bewildered me. On the way home I banked to examine the extraterrestrial monstrosity of a sunflower and push the toe of my boot at an impenetrable berm of marigolds. Bees emerged and nipped at my fruity flavors. I let them escort me down the road. The BP's sign read GOOD LUCK SPRING FLINGERS, while the McDonald's shouted SPRING FLING 4-EVER TREASURE THE MEMORIES. Hewn Oak at least provided respite from this farce. The bees traversing my exposed flesh felt not unlike Celeste's sly tickles. I shook once. They flitted away.

Seconds after I entered the cabin, Harnett emerged from his room sleepy-eyed, his nose twitching. I made for the sink, hoping that a quick dousing would drown the cocoa butter and mango. But it was all over my coat, too, my shirt and pants, even my underwear. Somehow this pleasant odor was part of me.

Harnett wiped his nose with his fingers and leaned against the wall. He emitted a smell of his own, the metallic funk of cheap liquor. "Is it a girl?"

"What? No." Desperate for something to do, I picked up the Root and the whetstone.

"Because you know the danger."

"Harnett." I felt twice as strong with my instrument beside me. "There's no girl."

He tried to cough up the mucus clogging his throat. He looked skinny and ill. I made for the front yard.

"Smell like a cadaver," he muttered.

I whirled around. "What was that?"

He pulled his lips from his teeth like a cornered dog. "I said you smell like a cadaver."

"No, I *did*. Now you're the only one who smells like a corpse around here. You look like one, too, by the way."

I had the door open when he muttered again.

"I said cadaver, not corpse."

All I wanted was to leave. But it was not a day for letting anyone get the best of me. I cracked the Root against the floor. Harnett regarded me with despicable patience and spoke slowly. Even drunk and haggard, he was still the professor, still full of himself.

"A corpse is something in the dirt. A cadaver is something on a slab. By now you should know the difference. By now you should know what happens on that slab. The embalmer doesn't just fill you with gunk. First he bathes you. He swabs out your orifices with disinfectant. He combs your hair. He applies cologne. He gives you one last shave. It's the most careful shave you'll ever get, kid, because any nicks, this time they won't heal. And when you're done, you smell like you smell right now. Like a cadaver."

He would not talk down to me. Not ever again. The Root pendulated and knocked the front door wide in a single swift strike. I did not look back. "We both smell like dead men, then. Sounds about right to me."

23.

Annoyed by the multiplying bouquets at the front of every classroom and hallway, the gifted corsages and boutonnieres clipped to every participant, and the hysterical schedule updates blaring from the PA, I was relieved when Foley faked sick the day of the Spring Fling so we could escape. I wanted nothing more to do with the event. Foley was more concerned with me. He said I had him worried. He said he didn't want me flunking out. What was more, he said, I had a look about me that made people nervous.

So while Harnett slept off a bender, I swiped his truck and let Foley drive us a couple towns over, where no one could collar us for ditching. Once there, we weren't sure what to do. Foley had brought a Frisbee, but my coordination was meant only for shovels. Around noon we walked a woodland trail, but I lost track of the conversation each time I saw an interesting root system. In the afternoon we tugged at chained bikes and flipped through magazine racks, but in both bicycle chrome and store mirrors I was drawn to my strange reflection: the pale blue blotch of my face, the squinting of someone unaccustomed to day. I nabbed a pair of chintzy shades and wore them out without paying.

On the way back home, Foley pulled off at Bloughton's nearest neighbor, the slightly larger town where Bloughton residents went to do serious shopping or commemorate their anniversaries and proms with fancy dinners. It was also the location of the nearest movie theater. Foley parked and checked his watch.

"It's only five," he said. "We got time for a flick."

I adjusted my shades. At least it would be dark.

I don't remember the movie at all. All I remember is Foley's elbow bumping against my own as he laughed at inappropriate spots. His laughter was loud and nervous; I didn't attribute it to anything until much later, when considering what happened next.

The movie was over and we entered the hallway, blinking. Vaguely I sensed something awry; Foley was quiet and looked nauseated. I told him I needed to piss and he only mumbled. After I was done I found him hunched miserably on a vinyl bench at the end of a dead-end hall. It was his day, he was calling the shots, so I sat beside him, feeling beneath my boots the low-frequency rumble of the action movie behind the nearest closed door.

Stupidly I attributed the silence to the exhaustion of a long day.

"Celeste all ready for tonight's thing?" he asked.

The question caught me by surprise. "I suppose," I said, flexing my right hand, enjoying the pull of the leather, the bite of the buckles.

"You guys still getting along okay? I saw you two talking in the hallway." His voice, enthusiastic all day, now trembled.

I shrugged. "I guess so."

"Good," he said. "I'm glad. Really. I am."

"Okay."

"I'm happy about whatever you do," he said. "I just want to be part of it."

"All right."

"Is that okay?'

"Sure."

"Are you really sure?"

"I guess."

"Because I'm afraid when you flunk out I'll never see you."

"You will."

"You'll disappear like you did the last couple months."

"No."

"I'm afraid I'm running out of time."

"Time?"

He sat up and slid his arm around my waist. Live flesh—I jerked away. He crumpled and shrank. I felt his arm retract and then his face was in his hands, his long hair sweeping forward to hide him.

"I'm sorry," I said.

His hair danced about as he shook his head violently.

"I didn't know," I said.

"Didn't know what?" His voice was muffled and teary.

"That you're gay." Quickly my mind caught up. I couldn't believe I had never seen it. The fantasy trips, the CD gifts, the bath at his house—our entire friendship, when seen in hindsight, smacked of courtship.

He muttered a rehearsed line: "No one's gay or straight anymore."

"Okay," I said. "Look, I don't care. I really don't care."

"But I've ruined it," he moaned. "I've ruined everything!"

I winced and looked up. Far in the distance a theater employee gathered spilled popcorn.

"You haven't ruined anything." There was more I wanted to say—that being gay might be seen as a crime against humanity inside the Congress of Freaks but was hardly reason for despair in the wider world—except I found myself strangely numb. In a way, Foley was as trapped as I was. We both kept secrets that others, if they knew the truth, would exploit. I could hardly in good conscience suggest he hang a gay-pride flag from his locker.

Instead I recited a platitude. "Telling the truth is healthy."

"It's not! It was a huge mistake!"

A cold flash of nerve, a truth for a truth.

"I dig up graves," I said. "I dig up graves and rob the bodies. That's where I got these clothes, that's why they smelled."

"Stop it!" he cried. It was with a plummeting feeling that I realized he didn't believe me and never would. Not all secrets were of equal weight.

The leather of his jacket squeaked with each sob. Digital explosions vibrated our bodies as in the adjacent theater the bad guys were vanquished. The soft chuckling of a corn popper folded its way through the darkened halls.

"Hold my hand?"

He blinked excessively. Loops of blond hair clung to wet cheeks. Five thin and tentative fingers, one of them crooked, quavered.

"Just for a second," he pleaded. "Just once, just for a second."

His pale hand swayed over the carpet's faded paisley. Like one of the movies behind these walls, this moment might replay in his memory forever and, like it or not, what I did next would always be part of the plot. There was no reason to hesitate. This guy had guts, real guts, and it was the least I could do to show some guts in return.

I took his hand. His knuckles wiggled until they alternated with my own. For a moment the sight transfixed both of us—the silver buckles, the red leather, the brown wood, his white flesh. Then he closed his eyes and let his face drop into his free palm, his back shuddering.

Credit music blasted from an opened door. A gray-haired couple scuffled past us, positioning respective hats. Instinctively I wanted my hand back but I felt his grip tighten when I made the slightest pull. Doused with mysterious panic, I grimaced at each exiting moviegoer. Some of them didn't look our way. Others did, taking quick note of the two high-school boys holding hands before averting their eyes. Laughter trilled from inside the theater and rose in volume as the laughers approached. Feet kicked open the swinging door; hands made slapping noises against the glass.

They were turning on phones and already bragging about how many messages they'd received during the movie. They were speaking in giggles. They were excited girls with yawning boyfriends and vice versa. Some of them were towing what looked like parents. There were even a few beleaguered grandparents limping in pursuit. The strange thing was that I recognized them. They were from Bloughton High, which was confusing until I remembered what a certain budding thespian had told me as she had stretched the limits of her silver leotard: *We practice all the way up until the day of the Fling and then we all go out to a movie together a few hours before it starts. You know, to relax. It's like a tradition.*

I could not move, not even when they emerged. Rhino came first, trailing by the hand a fragile-looking redhead popping lozenges into her mouth—most likely a singer concerned about her voice. Woody was next, flicking popcorn bits from his shirt. The redhead was the first to see us, and she clawed at Rhino's simian arm. When Rhino saw, he reached over and shoved Woody. Celeste was smacking hand sanitizer when she felt Woody's nudge, and she was able to return the small green bottle to her purse without taking her eyes off us. The sanitizer went in, her plaid pink BlackBerry came out.

The details were easy to improvise. See, one of the homos was crying because they'd just watched a sobby romance. And see, they were sitting there in the dark because where else can two fags make out? Foley was unaware of being watched until the flashes made him lift his face. It was Celeste, her smart, open-toed, special-day shoes planted directly in front of us, snapping picture after picture—*flash, flash, flash, flash.* Her eyes gleamed. *Flash, flash.* She looked hungry. *Flash, flash, flash.* As if documenting this tawdry vignette from Mere Reality would excuse her from it forever.

She winked at me over the phone and it was like the drop of a guillotine. Panic severed as easily as fingers. A tingling calm settled through my bones, allowing me to see with a clarity usually relegated to specifying. Woody and Rhino: their gestures flew only at Foley. Celeste: her camera flashed solely in his direction. The noses of the Incorruptibles were trained to detect fear, and in my metamorphosis to the Son I had lost that musk. A new target, therefore, had been chosen.

I could taste their blood. I lapped at it like a kitten at milk.

You can't change a rotter's upbringing. Gottschalk—revenge—had been bred to humiliate, Woody—revenge—to dish out punishment, Celeste—revenge—to devour anything that stood in her way. Now I realized that I had been bred for a cross purpose—revenge, revenge. There would be no circulation—revenge—of these photos—revenge—on Monday. There would be no spray-painting—revenge—of vulgar words upon Foley's locker. Revenge—revenge—there would be no beatings in locker rooms and—revenge, revenge—in parking lots. In the dim—revenge—movie theater hallway—revenge—I lost—revenge—all feeling—revenge—in my body—revenge, revenge—yet was somehow—revenge—

aware that my face—revenge, revenge, revenge—had stretched into a smile.

24.

This is the day Woody Trask dies. I can taste it right off: the burning away of bile from the back of my throat. He doesn't know it yet. That's what makes it so exquisite. His death will not be physical, but it will be death nonetheless. He will never think the same way; he will never do the same things to others; it will be years before he is able to wake up without screaming.

Corruption of the Incorruptibles. I dug all night. You should have seen it.

I have planned it so carefully it's like being there to see it. It's like specifying so hard I can cut across time and space. He wakes up late. It's Saturday, a day he hates because there are no built-in crowds to cheer him on. He plods around home in bare feet and stops for a moment to stare at a photograph under a refrigerator magnet. He scratches his balls and picks his nose. He doesn't recall its being here before.

I put it there. I was in his house and found it at the bottom of a drawer. I couldn't resist. The photo, you see, is of Woody as a child, maybe six or seven years old, squatting in a sandbox with other children. It's amazing how some faces retain their basic elements over time, and I'm sure that two of the sandbox boys are now kids Woody torments at every opportunity. There's a chance that he will gaze at the picture until he drifts into a remorse so deep that he hangs himself from the workout machine in the basement. But that's unlikely. He is too lost in arrogance to see anything in such images except weaker children deserving of their pitiful lots.

He doesn't notice what's written on the back of the photo until after he's showered, shaved, and dressed. Unable to get the picture out of his mind, he flips it over. At first he thinks it's a joke.

weight room
6pm tonight
see you there
A FAT BITCH

But it can't be a joke. Rhino's too dumb to arrange this. Pranks are not Celeste's thing. And who knew he had Laverne's car scratched except Crotch? It takes until he is stuffing pizza-for-breakfast into his mouth for him to realize that whoever left the note has been inside his house. He feels something he hasn't felt in a long time. He doesn't know what it is. I do. It's fear.

He goes about his day. He's got meals to eat. Bros to hang with. Maybe a blow job later if he plays his cards right. But it continues to prey upon him, this note. It's not something he can bring up to his father; it would generate too many questions. It's not something he really wants to bring up to his bros, either. Because what if Crotch, even for a second, gets the best of him?

So he worries. It's beautiful—you can see it in his face. He doesn't relish his meals. He finds no joy in his bros. He's not invested in angling for that blow job. All he can think about is six o'clock and that weight room. It's killing him. It's really killing him and it's beautiful.

At five o'clock he heads to school. He figures he'll show

up early, get the drop on whoever awaits him. It's something he's learned from sports. Get up earlier, train harder. It's Saturday, so he doesn't know which doors, if any, will be unlocked. Turns out only the back door, the one nearest the parking lot, is slightly ajar. The walk takes him past the trophy cases, where his name is engraved in multiple metal plates. This is by design. Soak it up, Woody. Enjoy the feeling one last time. Because guess what engravings remind me of?

The halls are dark. He's a big guy, he's not scared. The gymnasium is darker. Okay, he's a little scared. The stairway leading up to the weight room is a total void because I've unscrewed the bulbs. He's scared. He's scared now. His heart is hammering like a little birdie's. There's the door. Anything could be behind it. But he can't stop moving. He's never hesitated inside Bloughton High, he doesn't know how.

Woody won't get it, but I've chosen the weight room for its symbolism. Without the weight room, there's no Fun and Games, no Celeste, no Foley. Maybe none of this would have happened. I owe this weight room a lot, and now it's time for repayment.

He pulls open the door, enters, and is blinded. All the lights are on. He throws a hand over his eyes. His feet tangle in barbells. He's down, hands and elbows and knees knocking against ten-, twenty-, fifty-pound weights. They're scattered everywhere just inside the door. That's not where they're supposed to be. It's so careless, what kind of jerk—

A cloth over his mouth.

This is also the day Celeste Carpenter dies. More precisely, this is the day she becomes like Joey Crouch, forever fearful and humiliated. Such a fate would seem preposterous to her at this moment. At last night's Spring Fling, her routine was flawless. No, I wasn't there. But this is how Celeste's life works. There was riotous applause. An award or two was won. People who don't know shit about dance swore it is their favorite art form. I can't blame them.

There is a note waiting for Celeste, too. It is sitting outside her bedroom door in a sealed envelope. At first read, she is alarmed. After several rereads, though, she finds it surprisingly easy to convince herself of the number of legitimate routes the note could have taken to her door. Anyway, it doesn't matter. The news contained is too exciting.

Dear Celeste,

I'm sorry about the other day. To make it up to you, I've pulled some strings. Representatives from a theater company in Chicago are here. They missed your show last night but would like a repeat performance at 7:30 tonight. I hope this is all right. Come to the stage at seven. I'll meet you in the greenroom.

Congratulations.

What she feels is not surprise. Not even close. What she feels is irritation that it took this long. After all, the crowd response last night was so forceful. After all, wasn't TV's Shasta McTagert discovered at a similar event? Celeste carries out her morning with exaggerated calmness, holding her teacup daintily, lingering with her loofah in the shower, taking time to inhale the scent of pollen sweetening the breeze. She acts like someone who believes she's being filmed.

Throughout the day she wants to call me for details but can't. It's not because I don't have a phone. It's because she can't remember my last name to look up my number. As hard as she tries all she can remember is Crotch. And that can't be a real name. Can it?

The note said be there at seven but she's a pro. She's there at six-forty-five. She doesn't see Woody's truck because I have moved it. She tries various doors, including the entrance Woody used, but they are all locked. Eventually she examines a side door leading directly to the stage, and to her surprise it is ajar. This search has taken way too long and now she's late. She goes directly to the greenroom and finds a second note.

Dear Celeste,

Wait here for me and I'll introduce you to the representatives. If I'm not back by 7:30 please begin the performance on time. They're already seated. I'm sure they'll want to meet you afterward.

Congratulations again.

Oh, the agony! Thirty minutes she waits, clutching her cued-up iPod, dying to ask me questions about the setup. Will it be stage lights or house lights? And what about the music? She's not expected to do the routine without music, is she? But she's a pro. She keeps it together. This is what she's trained for, after all. This is why she put in the hours. It all comes down to this.

Seven-thirty comes. She takes a meditative breath and heads out. From the wing she can see that the Spring Fling decorations are still in place. Pink and yellow dominate. Flowers festoon the curtains. It's only when she walks onto the stage that she realizes the lighting is all wrong. Every single spot is lit to full wattage. Black spots swim before her eyes. She turns away and sees a portable stereo near the center of the stage. As gracefully as possible, she hooks up her iPod, then springs to her starting position. Squinting is ugly, she knows this, so she accepts the temporary blindness. It's all right. She's a pro. The music begins and she makes her first move.

Twirling, she notices that the flowers have begun to wilt. That must explain the sickly smell.

Finally, this is the day that the most important things in Gottschalk's life, his so-called career and so-called reputation, prematurely expire. He will vanish from the lives of the students who endured his narcissistic orations and unjust policies. It has been my experience that high school students are quick to forget the absent. When Gottschalk is gone, he'll be as good as dead.

No notes are necessary. Instead I wait until after I have dealt with Woody and Celeste and then I call him. By now it is almost eight. He picks up on the fourth ring and only gets to say one word—*Hello?*—and I wish I didn't have to allow him even that. I don't want to hear any voices tonight or see any faces. Not live ones, anyway.

"There are students in your school," I say. "Right now. Two of them."

I hang up and prepare. There is never any doubt that he will arrive alone. In a town this size every dispatched unit gets written up in the paper. For a new principal, that doesn't look good. Besides, the idea of sending cops to his school affronts his sense of sovereignty.

Sure enough, he finds two vehicles in the parking lot; I have moved Woody's truck and Celeste's car. Both vehicles are parked in the handicapped spots by the front door. Such audacity is infuriating. He shuffles his keys as he stomps toward the main entrance, but it is unlocked. Now he's angrier. He moves to unlock the next set of doors, but they're unlocked, too. Now he's livid.

Mostly, though, he's vain and arrogant. He heads right for his classroom. Of course he does. If someone has broken in to the school, naturally they have done it to attack him personally. He can see the cracked door, the blade of light. He moves so fast he's waddling. His massive key ring jingles like chain mail. The bulbous contours of his face look ready to rupture. He grabs the knob and throws himself inside. Silently I step from the locker in which I'm hiding, close the door quietly behind him, tighten a length of rope around the knob, run it twenty feet, and then loop the other end to the adjacent classroom's doorknob. He doesn't even notice he's trapped. The thing lying on top of his desk has him mesmerized.

25.

SOMEDAY IN THE FUTURE when furtive men gather to swap stories of the Diggers, they will talk about that night. They may not like what the Son did, but they cannot deny it was the work of a master.

When I dropped Foley at home after the movie theater debacle, I promised him I'd come by the next day to talk. In truth, I didn't plan on seeing him ever again. It was a brutal thing I had to do, but I'd do it to protect him, and once it was done there would be no future for me in Bloughton.

Before setting out for the school, I had put the necessities into my green backpack. A few items of clothing, my trumpet, and the bone taken from my mother's coffin. Harnett was packing, too. He was leaving for another Bad Job and couldn't even get his tools into the sacks. Tarp pegs clattered to the floor. He gripped a bottle to steady his hands. I zipped my bag and considered offering him some kind of goodbye or good riddance. It was too easy to imagine how that would go. Instead I just looked on silently as he fumbled things like an old man and stooped to retrieve them.

I left in a hurry. Pity was not an emotion I wanted to feel, not that night. I focused on the task. There was much to do and the timing was crucial. I was not worried. In fact, I was happier than I had been in a long time. I even sang. *We became oblivion* was my song for a while. Then it was Sabbath: *What is this that stands before me?* But as I unscrewed the lights in the weight room hallway and left the greenroom note for Celeste, I realized that that song wasn't right, either. What I settled on was a lyric from Sabbath's fourth album, sung in a plaintive moan by Ozzy, one of the band's most moving choruses: *I'm going through changes.*

I wasn't the only one.

When Woody awoke he felt softness—the room's wrestling mats. But that was only part of it. His fingers felt softness; so did his toes; so did his legs. His *legs*—his legs were bare. They shouldn't be bare but they were. He opened his eyes and saw breasts and hips and maybe for a moment thought that this was a typical Saturday night and he had gone to a party, gotten beered up, and fallen into bed with a girl or three. Only this time, the muddle of their faces did not clear when he rubbed his eyes. That was because their faces were in fact muddled. One girl's eyes were hanging loose from their sockets. Another woman's nose had been entirely eaten away. Woody jerked and another woman's lips brushed his, or they would've if her face hadn't long ago peeled back from its skull. He screamed—I swear I could hear it miles away—and thrashed about in an attempt to dislodge himself from the bloated and purple embrace of three naked female corpses. He was naked, too; the dry, cold genitals of his harem pressed against his own. I hoped he thought about Tess while he screamed. I hoped he thought about Heidi. I hoped he thought about Foley. I hoped he thought about me. I hoped he thought about everyone he had ever fucked over.

After Celeste adjusted to her blindness she became aware of another lack—there was no crowd noise. Then again, it made sense. The theater representatives were probably few in number and, after all, they were captivated. She was a pro, so she kept on dancing. Somehow her eyes began to adjust and she was encouraged by the smiles shining white through the darkness. The end was near now and she tried to concentrate on her routine. She became aware of a sound, a strange whirring and clicking. Applause? Could it be applause already? She executed the bravura ending, falling to the stage like a cut flower, and convinced herself that, yes, that crackling sound was applause, it had to be. She stood and bowed and, receiving no further instruction, shaded her eyes and stepped forward out of the spots. The white she had seen was indeed teeth. The noise, though, was rats. A gang of skeletons sat in the chairs, their skulls and rib cages wired shut so that each had a rat for a brain and a rat for a heart. The sound was that of the animals chewing for their freedom. Some had already escaped and, fat with marrow, slugged their bodies up the center aisle. She did not scream. She met her audience head-on. Maybe I mentioned it before, but Celeste Carpenter was a pro.

My revenge on Gottschalk did not have the tawdry exuberance of my other efforts, but in its relative subtlety it was my favorite. His desk, from behind which he had unfairly butchered my A and beside which he had whipped me with his wand, had been cleared. Upon it sat a tombstone. Chipped into it was his name and the date. Gottschalk was not dumb. He knew right away it was over. There was a fucking tombstone in his fucking classroom. The clinging sod and clay proved it as the genuine article. After registering the sound of the door locking behind him, he squeezed himself into one of the student desks and speculated on what other horrors laid hidden in his school and what kinds of disgrace they would herald. When he heard the faint reverberations of a young man's screams from the direction of the gymnasium, he began to cry. Against his sobbing gut the chair hurt and so he stretched out on the floor, right under his tombstone. Even that close, he probably didn't recognize how much it smelled like the student he had tormented for months. He bawled until his body ached. Eventually he felt like a medical school cadaver, or even one of those pictures in his textbook, flayed open to show his undersized heart and oversized lungs and stringy intestines. He felt eviscerated, dissected, and alone. Finally he knew how it felt.

He didn't have to wait long. I had already called the cops. It had been a risk, but Harnett had said it the first time he buried my homework in the backyard: *Time is always against you.* He was right and I wanted it no other way, because for me that was how it had always been. I hitched a ride from the highway, took a bus west—that was the direction the most recent Polaroids had suggested—and began to ask questions of the homeless people who hung out near bus stations. Over the next few days, I moved from town to town, reading local papers and, when the trail felt hot, following Harnett's old advice of getting a trim from a local barber. There had been incidents, I learned, just a couple of towns over. I investigated those cemeteries in person. As I boarded another bus and crossed the Missouri River on the state's western border, I could feel him like knives in my gut.

As I approached the highway underpass, I thought of my mother. I told her that I was sorry I had left Harnett, I was sorry her plans for me had failed, but at least she would be avenged. Up ahead, I saw a shabby lean-to lit by a paltry fire. My veins pained me with each heartbeat. My muscles convulsed in expectation. I had taken care of Woody, Celeste, and Gottschalk, but I was not done.

I stood at the edge of the fire. I felt as if I were standing at its center. A man used his fingers to scoop baked beans out of a can, sucked them clean, and then motioned his head at another can.

"There's beans," Boggs said. "Just don't eat too many."

26.

Stalactites bit down from the overpass above us like teeth, salivating when semis thundered overhead. The clammy corners seemed to squirm toward the fire like slugs, craving the heat of the wan and ribboned flames. Boggs passed another finger across his lips. The tongue that licked at the gloppy residue was red and suppurating.

"I don't mind sharing." He shrugged. "You look hungry."

He leaned and his half-grin tipped from shadow. Something was horribly wrong. His face, merely ruddy when I had met him back at the diner in West Virginia, had progressed through some calamitous change. Patches were eaten away as if by acid, revealing layers of abraded flesh that winked wetly in the changing light. His thin hair had receded unevenly in all directions, leaving isolated crests of orange silk that flapped with every breath of wind. His nostrils and lips were crusted over and pulled so tight at the surrounding skin that it looked as if he were inhaling his own face. Worst of all were his eyes. The left was still a thing of pure and cerulean beauty. But the veiny tendrils that had threatened months ago had taken full hold of the right, and the infected orb poised on the edge of its lids. It moved not at all while his good eye whirled, taking in my fists, my larger and stronger biceps, the explosions contained within my bearing.

The brutal motions I had been ready to execute caught in my joints. This was not the man I remembered. From the look of things, he was barely alive. My pause was lengthy; his grin widened, and among his miniature teeth I saw absences—two, three at least.

"You look mad, too." His Southern accent seemed to have thickened. He still wore the three-piece suit, only now it was a lattice of tatters, and he pulled the flimsy lapels across his chest as if he was cold. "Not that that's a bad thing. You need that mad-as-hell feeling. The rest of the rotters don't have it, but it's pouring off you like sweat. I knew it. From the moment I laid eyes on you."

Cheetos bags, yellowed ad sheets, and condom wrappers melted into a wad that stank of burning rubber. My mother, my mother—I forced her back to the forefront. She was why I was here. As weak and infected as this man looked, he had done awful things to her.

"I only wish I could've spruced up a bit before you came. Still got my suit, but the rest of me—I'm ashamed. I know I don't look so well and I'm ashamed." He leaned back so his face slipped from the light. "There, now. Does that make it easier?"

Minute cusps of light still caught flaps of skin and lumpy growths.

He shook his head, scattering a minor constellation of sparks. "You're not here to talk, that's plain as day. You're here to kill me. That's really—I guess that's really interesting. I guess I'm interested to see how you go about it."

The words felt repugnant to me. Kill him? Never had I admitted such a thing. Killing had never been part of Harnett's teachings, or Lionel's, or any Digger's of the modern age. But what else could I be doing here?

"Take your time," he said. The throaty buzz of his voice, doubled and tripled by the concrete chamber housing us, felt like warm blankets. He leaned back against a shopping cart piled with indefinable objects. Blissfully the carnage of his face lost all definition. "It's a big moment. You want to make sure you do it right."

This was not at all the same as facing Woody, Celeste, and Gottschalk—as facing Bloughton itself. Those people and that town knew nothing about any underworld and could not possibly hope to defend themselves when that world overtook their own. Antiochus Boggs, on the other hand, *was* under the underworld; he moved in the shadow of shadows, in the margin of margins. There was nothing I could envision that the twists of his mind hadn't already considered.

"Don't feel bad. It's hard. I know it is. It won't be easy. And I can't guarantee success. You gotta figure you're going to at least lose a chunk or two. Might end up looking a little more like Uncle Antiochus than you planned. But what's a chunk or two? Already down a few fingers, I see. What's a few more?"

Even in the darkness, even reduced to one eye, he had not missed the wood supplementing my right hand. I imagined those impervious new fingers pushing into the rotten skin of his neck, past the supple perimeter of his extruding eye. Oddly there was no joy in the fantasy, only the disparaging sense that I was doing exactly what a dying animal wanted me to do.

"Did I make it worse? Son, forgive me. I'm new to this—having a son and all that. My brain and I are doing our best, I swear. Let's make it real easy. Just follow my instructions and we'll be under way. You want to have at me? Raise your hand. That's all you have to do. Just raise your hand so I can see."

Before I could stop myself I heard my wooden fingers scrape against the slanted ceiling of the underpass. Settling into my gut was an uneasy feeling that by following this simple instruction I had somehow fallen to distinct disadvantage.

"Excellent. Good. Now take a step. All right? Take one step forward if you want this to happen right now."

Following these orders felt wrong, all wrong, and yet it was direction in a directionless moment. My foot came up and forward. I took a step. He was suddenly much closer. The blue ghost of the heart's fire tickled my toe.

Boggs clapped once. "Look at that. You have expressed yourself, son. Now we know where we stand, you and I. That's teamwork. That was satisfying to me. Was it satisfying to you? That's fine, that's fine, don't answer. There's no tricks here. No rotter bullshit. I'm all yours, son. Come and get me."

Now, it had to be now, one second longer and I would be crippled with the fear of movement that had marked my life before becoming the Son. I swooned in a long, slanting step around the fire. I heard the distant note of a wooden finger ringing off of a shopping cart. The distance closed halfway; I raised fists.

"One thing." He spoke quickly. "My brain's got just one thing to say."

The organs in my body continued forward and for a moment pushed against my ribs and belly. I swayed drunkenly and clutched at the air to keep from falling on him. Boggs was a small, dark creature scuttling somewhere below.

"That whatchamacallit," he said. "That golden spike. I'd be remiss not to mention the spike. Oh, son. That there was a mighty difficult test. I'm sorry I had to do it—I'm sure you get plenty in school. But lord. Joey. Son. You did not disappoint. No one I ever known could've done that any finer. You probably didn't even think of it that way. It was just a rotter you had to dig, some rats you had to rearrange. But there's beauty in labor done right. I just want you to know that. Before we tangle. You're a poet of the dirt. That's what you are, son. A poet."

It wasn't the many-clawed feet of Millers Field's rodent army that I felt. It was other hands, absent ones, my father's, perhaps, that had been withheld from me after every dig. A distrustful glare—that was all Harnett had deigned to give me after I handed him the replacement spike.

"One night," Boggs was saying. "Just a crazy thought, hear me out. I wonder what would happen if you gave me one night. The things I could teach you—I wonder if it'd be worth your time. Hard to say. Interesting thing to ponder, though, ain't it?"

I shuffled sideways until I had a grip on the cart. For months, all those digs done without my father; for a sleepless weekend, my extravagant revenge; for days on end, the traveling and tracking that had led me here—I had worked so hard for so long, and had been so alone. An adult guiding my way again, it was all I wanted.

A swollen palm entered the firelight. "Easy does it, now."

My collapse obfuscated the fire with dirt. Tiny embers melted upon my slick skin. A cockroach scampered over my knuckles.

"I'm not going anywhere, son. You have at me whenever you're ready. But anyone can see you need rest. You look right tuckered."

Crushing fatigue fought against the craving for revenge that had powered me so far. I would sit for a moment, fine; I would rest my muscles for a stretch, all right; I would crouch here and keep watch by the flames that reflected differently in his live eye than in his dead one. When both reflections dimmed, he would be asleep, and that was when I would strike.

A strange question came to me.

"What did you do with it?" I asked.

"What did I do with what?"

"The spike. The first spike."

I heard the slither of a slow smile. A scabbed finger gestured at a battalion of generic canned foods. The glowing discs of their lids appeared to float.

"What do you think funded this feast?" he asked. "You get hungry, you just help yourself."

27.

White light—shuttling closer—the sensation of floating—this was heaven and I had lost, fallen asleep first, and though I had failed my mother at least I would see her soon.

A jolt ripped my eyes open. Sunlight. A rusted satellite

dish. Shreds of plastic bags straining from barbed wire. Graffiti tags. A sky, cloudless and blue. A *squeak, squeak, squeak, squeak.*

Another jolt and I looked around me. I was moving. Bars on either side, the earsplitting shriek of an ungreased wheel—the shopping cart, I was folded inside the shopping cart. I tried to stand but my knees and elbows exploded into the pinpricks of sleep. My head was crammed beneath the push-handle, my body deposited atop various grungy bundles. My knees popped above the top of the cart like those of a child too big for his stroller, and my feet fought for room with a tall pole of some sort propped at the end of the cart, swaddled in a stained quilt and cinched tight with twine.

Above the incessant squeaking, there was music. Boggs's Adam's apple made paroxysmal patterns as he hummed a jaunty tune and pushed me down the alley. From this angle I could see his scraggly black tie snug against his neck. Below, the ruffles of his shirt were sharp and hardened with filth.

His left eye rolled downward.

"Top of the morning, son," he said.

An insistent pulse pushed against the spongy underside of his jaw. My gut cramped as I felt a nearly uncontrollable desire to strangle. I pistoned myself a few inches and reached forward with one claw. Then the cart jounced again—another stone passing beneath the wheels—and I dropped cruelly against the metal grate.

"Relax—doctor's orders." He hummed with renewed vigor and chuckled as the cart crunched through some sort of grit. "This ride is complimentary. Just my way of saying thank you for allowing me and my brain to enjoy one more resplendent day."

I clutched the sides of the cart and tried to tell myself that it was okay that I had crumpled into sleep last night, okay that he had not in fact taken the opportunity to kill me. That had been his choice, not mine. One night was what he had asked for and, all right, I would give him that. Only that. There was an orange hue to the horizon; night was coming soon, and when it was through, so was Boggs.

With rubbery legs I rolled myself out of the cart. Boggs watched with some amusement as I hobbled and tried to parade feeling back into my extremities. I didn't like looking at him. His stature made him look too much like a child suffering a full-body burn. It had to be drugs, or disease, or the corrosive cocktail of both. I didn't have time to think it out—that unbearable squeak told me he was moving. I tried to keep up, but the waving of his coattails revealed the disquieting speed at which he traveled. I limped along, almost losing him in the gray mist of dust. We exited the alley, crossed an unmarked two-lane, and entered another alley. His lead on me grew. He steered his cart through the parking lot of a housing development. With no regard for the safety of his hands, he ripped aside planks before forcing the cart through a gap in a fence. We kicked through the mangled remains of a chain-link fence and booted aside dismembered chunks of easy chairs and TV sets. The wheels shimmied over gravel. The bent and beaten shovel that lay on the cart's lower tray thrummed with pretend life. We were lost in some netherland maze. Caught between the long-forgotten inner walls of structures built too close together, gusts of wind twisted themselves into miniature tornados, and piles of refuse levitated.

It was twilight before we emerged again into open space. A large graveyard awaited us. Boggs tucked his cart into the sheath of a drooping barn and emerged from it with the rusty shovel. From far away, the tool looked like a cane, and when he paused at the cemetery gate to beckon me, the darkness momentarily turned him into Fred Astaire—cane tapping, vest peeking smartly from the slant of his suit, playful grin anticipitating the fancy footwork soon to come.

I followed but kept a distance. I didn't trust myself to get too close. Once the dead had us surrounded, Boggs pirouetted and motioned to a line of small stones. They were as identical as school desks. Carefully I perched upon one while Boggs rushed forward to wipe the cobwebs from the side of a crypt the approximate size of a chalkboard. He tapped the board with his shovel to call the class to attention. I flinched—he was going to call me to the front of the classroom, I just knew it.

"Pop quiz." He sniffed the air. "Tell me what you smell."

Keeping my eyes on him, I raised my nose. I smelled graveyard—treated grass, tilled soil, wilting flowers, the mildew of stone.

Boggs nipped at his lips with tiny teeth.

"High school's over, son. You're going to need to work harder." He stuck the shovel into the dirt and lifted his nose to the air like a starving dog. "That's ZadenScent. That's a name-brand grave disinfectant. I'm not placing blame, but you ought to know this. There's also Garden Fresh, Chitterwick Original, and Poloxy Plus. Each one has its own special bouquet. ZadenScent always smells to me like apple pie and ammonia. You can't smell that? There's probably a million gallons of it pumped into this mud. They use it to tamp down odor. Folks at funerals don't tend to like the smell of corpses. Of course, once it gets in the groundwater it's worse than embalming fluid, but that's not our concern. That's fine by me. Rotters don't deserve much better."

Apple, ammonia—could I detect the hints? With a start, I realized my eyes were closed in concentration and I shifted from my gravestone desk, half expecting the shovel-edge to be at my throat. It remained plugged in the dirt; Boggs remained at his chalkboard. I admonished myself for taking my eyes from either of them. Never again.

"Lord, son. You don't smell it. You honestly don't smell it. What kind of trash has that brother of mine been teaching you? ZadenScent? *ZadenScent?* Son, you should've smelled it a half-mile away."

I blinked at him, an unexpected feeling of shame creeping up my neck.

His compact body paced the front of the makeshift classroom. His live eye flashed at me with every quick lap. Without warning he wrapped both hands around the shovel and began pounding it against the crypt. Sparks dove into the grass, chips of stone flew; I recoiled. The clamor shot through the cemetery, stone to stone, as the shovel contorted and dulled with each strike.

He lowered the tool, the ruffles of his shirt spreading with each massive inhale. His eye found mine and mirrored my shock. He patted his free hand over the twitching muscles of his neck, the slobbery rim of his mouth. One finger found its way to an ear and probed as if expecting brain.

"Apologies. Lord. That ain't right. That ain't no way to teach. So you don't know your ZadenScent. There's worse crimes. I'm not mad at you. Honest I'm not. It's that rotter I can't forgive. He's put you in danger. At risk. Those are rotter ways that I shall reverse. Mark my words. You've spent too much time tiptoeing through the tulips when you should be tearing holy hell through the mud."

Partially settled, Boggs resumed his lesson. The

concentration of grave disinfectant can tip you off to the caliber of any marble farm, how tightly the bodies are stacked, how packed the soil, the overall level of decomp. The brand is instructive, too; any caretaker worth his salt is using Chitterwick Original, which bodes well for the pedigree of the clientele. If you detect the lowly Poloxy Plus, the night might still be fruitful—the rotter who runs that marble farm clearly don't give a flying fuck. Dig like a wild man because varmints will shoulder the blame.

Boggs was far more impassioned than Harnett. I couldn't help it; I was thrilled. When he demonstrated how the different brands of turf could be judged by plugging them into your cheek like chaw, his animation was intoxicating. Behind his enthusiasm, however, awaited mania. When an idea wasn't easily articulated he raged, usually at Harnett, sometimes at me, but always ultimately at himself, raking at his head and tearing loose petals of dead skin. He tried to tell me about using backhoes and I balked. Noisy machinery? On a dig? He bounded at me, staying just out of arm's reach, and spat about how this was exactly what was reducing the Diggers to obsolescence, this unwillingness to make use of a machine when it *just happened to be sitting right there,* keys in the ignition. He raved on about "dynamic loads" and "impact loads," terminology having to do with how much weight a typical casket can bear before it buckles. When he saw that I still wasn't going for it, a flash of panic arrested his infantile features. Maybe he was as bad as they said, maybe his methods were offensive, maybe he was a rotter among rotters—all of these insecurities and more in a single twinge of his bulging red eye.

By the time he tackled etymology—why Shadygrove Eternal was a better bet than the Garden of the Holy

Crusader—he was trembling in the glowering dawn, barking brilliant but half-formed theories through a nonstop muddle of accusations and self-incrimination. He was crying and shouting and laughing, and the storm from which it all came seemed to push like tumors against his waxy flesh. My mind raced to catch the nuggets of knowledge before they were doused in the stew of his affliction. Then he abruptly quieted. He stood straight and lifted his chin. The rustle of the trees and the ringing of the crickets became as noisome as the din of a cafeteria.

"This is no fun. That's the problem. This is no fun at all." The blazing blue of his good eye resisted the warming dawn. "War medals? Rosaries? Toupees? Those aren't why I dig. Those aren't why you came to me, either. It's because of that other thing. My purpose. Your purpose, too, maybe. You want to see it?"

He took hold of his lapel. Through the frowzy and time-worn fabric I recognized the rectangular impression of a book. My heartbeat accelerated. It was with abstract disappointment that I felt the nodding of my head and the dryness of my lips. Perhaps just a glimpse of the thing would slake my thirst.

The lapel settled flat. He smoothed it back into place.

"Not tonight," he said. "It's getting late. Maybe tomorrow. You think it's worth it? One more day? How about it. One more day. Then you can have me. Fair trade, even steven. What do you say?"

Even then I knew that my revenge would wait. If I wanted to be the greatest Digger of all time, I could not be like the others, terrified of what Lionel called Boggs's innovations. My head was already nodding as if yanked by a noose. He had me.

28.

Time passed like labored breaths: two days became three became four. I didn't know when Boggs slept—his blue eye put me to bed and greeted me each morning. This unblinking sentry never faltered; I continued to bide my time until time got lost. It became progressively easier to forget Bloughton. Like any writer, I was completely absorbed in the creation of a book. Everything else paled in importance.

During our time near the Missouri River, no holes were dug. It pained him; I saw him press the book into his chest as if it were his failing heart. When it became clear that each of us would extend the other's life a little while longer, the first thing we did was return to his home base of California. The instant we left we eliminated the possibility of Harnett's hunting me down. In his disheveled state, he wouldn't be able to track me past Iowa's borders. I tried not to care. Harnett was a lost cause; Boggs was the only Digger alive who sustained the same degree of passion as I.

Our Hyundai ditched on an L.A. freeway and our various bundles transported to a new shopping cart, we took to the streets. Geographical separation from his brother affected Boggs in unpleasant ways. He became more irascible with each push of the cart. He sneered so hard his lip split up the center. He rushed around as if he were keeping us to some set schedule, disappearing sometimes for hours and coming home adrenalized and red-faced, coat pockets rustling with what I suspected were drugs. The only items he showed me, however, were frivolous. One afternoon he returned with a top hat he'd found rolling around a parking lot. He described how he had chased it for twenty minutes. He screwed it onto his pink and flaking scalp with obvious relish, his costume completed at last.

Thus attired, he hastened us to his favorite marble farm and demanded from me a demonstration of what I had learned. It was our first dig. The western dirt was unfamiliar, but it didn't take long to make adjustments. Nevertheless I longed for the Root. I hoped Harnett was getting some use out of her. I hated to think of an instrument of such quality sidelined.

So I worked in the balmy California night with Boggs's battered piece of junk. He squatted several feet away, tearing through my backpack in search of food. He pulled out the trumpet and with it blew a few flatulent noises.

"I hope you're not counting on morning reveilles," he said. "I sleep late."

I was deep enough to not have to see his face when he withdrew the femur.

"Now, what in the world is this?" He moaned softly. I imagined him stroking it with his small, dirty fingers. "That's some leg, and I've seen my share. That's a starlet leg, there. A runway model leg. No wonder you tote it with you. A leg like that could make you feel less lonely on a cold night, I bet."

The truth was that it did, but he was already chuckling enough without my helping out. Murderous throes gripped my shoulders, but I told myself one more day, one more day, and then I'd have learned enough. I sank myself in the soothing repetition of shoveling and was nearly four feet deep when a fist tangled itself in my collar.

I spun and saw the surly mug of a toddler centered within the darker globe of a top hat. His tiny fingers channeled the iron strength of his entire physique. "What in creation are you doing?"

I wasn't shy about my skills. "I'm digging a hole, and a damn good one."

"A hole? As in singular? Son, I could dig three while you monkey around with this one. Come on. Out, out."

He lifted me by the collar. It was as if I weighed nothing. My legs pinwheeled and at last found footing enough to buffer my landing. I heard the distant thump of his feet, the sharp noises of his tunneling. I leaned into the hole with visions of hooking his throat with my arm but was stilled by the unparalleled frenzy of his motion, how speedily he sank into the earth, how his boxy shape expanded from a core of muscles even more grossly exaggerated than Harnett's. Within moments he was obscured in a hailstorm of dirt, and all I could perceive was the surface of his top hat and the pig snorts of his breath.

All at once he stopped. Soil still suspended in air came down in an orderly pattern. He pressed his palms into either wall. The muscles of his neck and torso thickened and he raised from the hole as if by hydraulic lift. He stood toe to toe with me and pointed downward. The brim of his hat tipped loam onto my face. "Destroy that dirt, son. Fuck it up. I know you can do it."

He pressed the tool into my chest.

Once inside the hole, I expected attack. It didn't come, and I was glad, for his furious descent had inspired me. I held the shovel as he had held it; I set my feet in his bowlegged stance; I worked my elbows in his curious star pattern. Nothing, no good, failure—and then powerful arms encircled me. I tensed for death but that wasn't the plan. Ten thick fingers strapped themselves over my own and he moved his stubby arms atop mine. I resisted furiously; this man who had touched my mother could not be allowed to touch me, too.

But then I began to understand his rhythms. They were the opposite of what I had learned from Harnett—these fitful movements felt as though we were trying to surprise the dirt with each attack. It was only when I saw the incredible results that his touch reminded me of Ted's magical fingers. When Boggs backed off, I continued as if he were still there, gasping with excitement and hating myself for it.

"You're a gem." His whisper was strangulated with emotion. "My boy. You're a jewel."

But when I started to crowbar the casket and frisk the body for valuables, his proud humming constricted into shrillness.

"The rotters were right," he whined. The dirt walls around me jarred and crumbled from the impact of his pacing. "I've lost too much brain to be teaching. Son, look at you. It's like you're making love to the damn thing. It's like you're removing lingerie down there. Give me the instrument. Son, hand me the instrument. Now watch. Watch how I do it. You just got to be a man about it, that's all."

I did a poor job of hiding my shock. There were two more graves that night, three the following evening, nearly two dozen by the end of the week, and it took every single one of them before my disgust changed to something like a grudging respect. Boggs didn't bother uncovering the entire top third of a coffin. Instead he'd burrow a small shaft all the way to the head and use a noosed rope to garrote the corpse and reel it in. If the body got stuck along the way, Boggs had another tool: a long stick topped with a meat hook.

"Abra-cadaver," he'd say. "Apologies—was that in bad taste?"

Once they were aboveground it got worse. California was filled with beautiful people who crossed the street when they saw us coming with our cart, and everything Boggs couldn't say to these rotters with their boob jobs and hair transplants he said to their buried counterparts. He slung bodies so carelessly their extremities broke off. It was not rare for him to throttle the body lying defenseless before him. He'd punch it. He'd kick its teeth out. He'd yank out the transplanted hair and rip free the silicone breasts.

"There's a famous blonde," he jabbered during one of these tantrums. "She's about as famous as blondes get. I'm not going to name names, that's not my way. But she's not far from here, in a pink crypt that's discolored from all the rotters who come to kiss it. Inside this pink crypt is a hell of a casket. Antique silver-finished bronze, champagne-colored satin. And if you were to peek inside you'd find that this blonde's mortician had, well—how's a gentleman to put it?—*enhanced* her for her funeral so her fans weren't disappointed. Took me a while to get in to see it for myself. Took me years. But let's just say that that blonde has been *unenhanced*."

During such routs, Boggs tore through shirts and coats and dresses with such fervor that he often came away with hunks of fetid flesh. It hadn't always been this way—I could tell from the surprised look on his face before the expression curdled into something like glee. These handfuls of gore he'd whip scornfully into their faces, and I'd step forward to strike him down. Because what he did to the dead was too much like rape, too much like what he had done to my mother. This was a Bad Job, his whole life was a Bad Job, and he was no better—or no worse—than Harnett. The shovel, if I had it, went up.

And then he would haul out his camera.

The camera—it took my breath away the first time I saw it. When he fumbled the rickety device to his dirty face it was all I could do to not grab for it. The button would click and the bulb would flash and moments later I'd be hunched in the grass, breathless over the developing image. Half the weight of the shopping cart was dusty old canisters of Polaroid film, and the sheer magnitude of his stock made clear the epic ambition of his project.

It gave him great pleasure to see my interest. He'd stand above me curling his chapped and bleeding lips, and rub my shoulder with his little hand. "All the rotters, son, who piss on us and shit on us and expect us to ask for seconds? Me and you will take their bones and their meat. Their skin and their juices. Every last drop of their noxious effluvia. And we'll make them look at it, won't we? We'll shove it in their faces. And for once they'll see what they really look like. Isn't that right?"

In these moments I would forget his graveside atrocities and practically salivate. *The book,* I'd think. *Show me the book.*

He rarely removed it from his coat, and he never removed the coat from his back. But if I hid my hatred and was well behaved, there were rewards. Sometimes while we huddled around a makeshift fire in some abandoned warehouse after rifling through a bag of restaurant trash, he'd lick his fingers clean and withdraw the bulging volume from its hidden pocket, always caressing its stained and misshapen cover before handing it over. Paging through it was like seeing both my past and future: the many dead faces Harnett and I had met while chasing Boggs, as well as the empty pages I would help fill, the legend I would help create.

Too frequently the moments of thrilled contemplation were ruined. Near the center of the book were pictures of someone I recognized. Sometimes it took several seconds for her identity to sink in. Boggs would observe silently, the fire flashing on his remaining teeth, as hate rekindled inside me and the ache for revenge brought me to the verge of tears. *One more day,* I'd tell myself. I'd repeat the words of another teacher: *Next lesson, then*. When that didn't work I would snake my hand into my backpack and pat the smooth bone as Harnett had once patted a corpse's shoulder: *Shh, it'll all be over soon*.

29.

It was the fever of madness met with mundanity. California was cinder-block strip malls and cars inching down interstates like glittering bugs and airbrushed faces winking at us from blockbuster billboards. Movies were everywhere: acting workshops, head-shot studios, camera rental shops, costume warehouses, independent film sets with their crews of baseball-capped hipsters. Nights took on the wild hopefulness of entering a darkened theater; days took on the disoriented surrealism of exiting back into a misplaced matinee sun. The metaphor gave me the only logic to grab hold of—it was only a movie, only a movie, although the makeup was too good and the lead performance rapidly losing continuity.

Combat dragged on. Nightly I tried to outlast him. But too many hours were spent laboring, too few calories went ingested, and without fail exhaustion weakened the key joints that kept me upright. He'd smile and twirl his top hat in his hands as I began to dip into sleep. For weeks he waited until I was unconscious before reaching for his hiding places—certain crossbars of the cart, secret crevices of his coat, the inner liner of his hat—and removing his slavish array of drugs.

It was how he bested me each night and got the drop on

me each morning. It was how he had outdug Harnett and me for so many months. It was also how he obscured the anguish of failing me as a teacher, an inadequacy that reaffirmed yet again his status as the lesser son. His damaged brain rearranged its purpose. So what if he couldn't teach me? He could still use me.

"Twenty-one graves, one night." His tongue poked experimentally at the sores that outlined his lips. His face was puffy and damp with the expectation of binging. "Barely past jerk-off age, and that's what me and Kenny did. But me and you? Me and you are going to demolish that. Twenty-five, easy. Thirty, even. Son, we're gonna dig until our fingers fall off. Oh, apologies. I guess yours already did."

Electrified as he was by the sour steroids that coerced his innards, the dead had no chance. We broke twenty-one in little over a month. We got stuck at twenty-nine, and the prime number aggravated Boggs to no end, but after he upped his illicit intake eventually we broke that record, too. Such milestones fall easier when you don't care about bodies—the dead, yours, anyone's. All that mattered was the book. We never stopped working.

Ultimately need overwhelmed discretion and Boggs let his drug routines unfold in full view. He went from grave to pawnshop and from pawnshop to street corner. He smoked substances with improvised paraphernalia and injected junk into his body with bent needles and wire coat hangers. Some pills he dry-swallowed, and others he crushed and snorted. He huffed poisons from Wendy's bags and swiped cough syrup when that was all he could find. Elements of his personality loosened until they unraveled to nothing; other facets were isolated with a cruel and unexpected vehemence. He emerged from these druggings wild-eyed and licking at the blood that came dribbling from his nose, and without warning he would clobber me and grab me by the throat with his midget fists.

The first time he did this I almost killed him. It was nearly four in the morning. I was beyond tired. The beat of a nearby dance club made my heart palpitate. That night's underpass was dribbling water and turning our fire into steam. I looked longingly at the oblong parcel in the cart wrapped in its cozy quilt and asked Boggs if we could unroll it to keep us dry. Without warning he palmed a pellet of busted cement and threw it at me. I shot it aside with an elbow, but behind it came other things—rocks, cans, broken bottles, his knobby thumbs over my trachea.

Kick, I urged myself. *Punch, scratch, bite off his cheek.* The objects he had used against me were close, and I could probably grab one and bring it to his skull. Deaths, his and mine, competed with each other for a few torturous seconds, but instead of welcoming the oblivion that would now become us both, I found myself despairing for one more day, one more lesson—I was a valedictorian to the end. As I began to black out, I felt a distant sorrow that I had forgotten the original reason for seeking out this monster. Something to do with a mother, maybe my own.

"You're watching me." His face was as pink and moist as uncooked meat. "You think I'm doped up. You think I don't see. But you forget, son: my brain's out, it's everywhere, and it's watching from a hundred angles. You know what it tells me? That you talk rotter. You think rotter. That when I turn my back you're the rotter there ready to stab it. You try. Hear me? You go ahead and try."

He let go. I tasted pavement. My hearing sealed off and my vision tripled. I saw three Boggses crouched near the road screaming at passing cars, three of him slapping themselves against the head and sobbing that they were the ones, they were the rotters. The entire incident was shocking. Less so the next time it happened. By the fourth or fifth of his abrupt assaults, I knew just to nod as best I could within the throttling. If it was during those moments that I felt most superior to this raving junkie, it was also when I most shamed myself with blubbering. *No, I'm no rotter, I'm with you all the way. You're going to be famous; all the rotters out there, they will bow to you before it's over. You're going to be the most sought-after man in the world and I want to be there to see it.* Two-Fingered Jesus forgive me, I said all of this and more.

One night after such an onslaught, I woke up to find myself inside an abandoned Burger King. A meager fire burned from the wreck of a napkin dispenser. Boggs was gathering scattered condiment packets for dinner and looking remorseful. When he saw me blinking he hunkered down close and tidied his gift of mustard and salt. He straightened his hat, fluffed dirt from his coat, and with great humility brought from his coat a grubby syringe.

"Go on, son." He brought it closer. I tried to look grateful but shook my head. He gritted his teeth; he forced a smile and tried again. "I realized it ain't fair, me taking all this for myself. Of course you can't keep up. Apologies, straight from my heart. You're my boy. My brain reminded me that. So go on."

I mumbled a distraction about Burger King, the smell of the grill, how I could still taste it in the air, couldn't he? Embers flew as he swept his foot through the fire, took hold of the front of his cart, and sent it crashing into a barren soft-drink dispenser.

"I can't figure out what it is you want." In the darkness I could only see his dwarf outline weaving through the remnants of conjoined plastic chairs, the dual pennants of his coattails, the jaunty slant of his hat. "You want to be like me? Able to dig ten holes, yourself, in half as many hours? Lift out big fat rotters with one arm? Or do you want to be like Mr. Resurrectionist—pushing around rotters like he's planting daffodils? I give you everything, son, everything. Told you secrets I've never told anyone. Try to remember that. Won't you? Won't you try to be thankful? You know there's nothing stopping me from leaving you behind."

One more abandonment was something I could not take, not so close to the book's notoriety and our fame. I nodded in meek apology and made a show of enjoying a packet of mustard. The formerly backlit menu was still visible, and in my head I added up the meal deals, paid with cash, made change, and outlined a family scene starring a mother, a father, and a son—what a wonderful fantasy. Smiling, I curled up beside what used to be the fryer and feel asleep. An unknown amount of time later, I felt someone kneel beside me. I tensed for an injection from that filthy needle, but instead felt the tentative stroke of a thumb across my temple.

"Don't leave me." His whisper was hoarse. "I'm trying so hard. There are things wrong with me, I know it. I think I told you about my brain, but, lord, it's gotten worse. Something's crawled in where my brain used to sit. It's him, maybe. Both of them, maybe. They're mad at me. I can tell because they're holding on real hard. I don't want them mad. I don't want you mad, either. I just want to be their Baby, and you be my baby—see? See how it can be? We just need to stick together, do our job. That way we can show them what real love can do."

Love or hate: I couldn't decide which I feared more. After these bizarre nights of tenderness I would often receive apology by way of gift. Boggs would stash the cart, march the two of us to an upscale Beverly Hills eatery, and wave a wad of cash in the maître d's face until we were seated, usually as far away from other patrons as possible. There we would bask in the splendor of a dim dining room's live pianist or an outdoor veranda's warm Pacific air. Instinctively Boggs would dial back his persona just enough to fool diners into believing he was a garden-variety meth-head. Even I'd be fooled. Sitting there with my ranks of silverware and heated towels, I would look around at the businessmen with their PDAs and the shiny newborns in beechwood high chairs, and I would fancy myself one of them until hearing the slurps of Boggs licking the inside of his wineglass. One meal we'd be eating decadent dishes like candied bacon suspended from piano wire and the next we'd be crapping ten feet from where we wiped the ants from our pizza crusts.

His grudge against the Monro-Barclay Pact began to make sense. The West Coast had indeed quickened his corruption. These furloughs among the very rotters he most despised—actors, agents, celebrity chefs, even snooty waitstaffs—proved how nevertheless desperate he was to gain their attentions, which was precisely the larger purpose of the Rotters Book. Each time he turned his camera upon a Californian corpse, it was as if he were a paparazzo taking unauthorized and unflattering shots of unsuspecting subjects. But such was the tabloid photographer's charge—to expose how everyone looked the same once the makeup was off and the lights were out.

Five-star restaurants were not the only strange places he took me. At least once a week we'd visit a public library. Like Lionel and Harnett, I, too, suspected that the ultimate distribution of the Rotter Book would be online, and Boggs was indeed a savvy user of the Internet. He'd lock his shopping cart to the bike rack or book drop and weasel his way in front of a monitor along with myriad other homeless patrons. Sometimes I would look quickly enough to find him salivating over the website of some Iowa newspaper. I didn't need to read along to know that the aftershocks of my revenge were still being felt.

It was while he was in one of these libraries that I made an important discovery. Not wishing to be party to his inevitable expulsion, I sat against the cart beneath a palm tree. The twine used to secure the quilt over that long-hidden cargo scratched at my sweaty neck until I impulsively pulled it down, ripped free the bindings, and unrolled the blanket. Beneath was not the termite-riddled lumber I had expected, but history's finest instrument: Harpakhrad.

Everything Lionel had said was true—the multi-beveled blade of iron and gold, the braided handle of petrified branches, the fantastically bejeweled scarab—but no poetry or paean could convey such splendor. If Lionel's mythic stash of riches truly existed, nothing in it could rival Harpakhrad. The only indication of wear was a delicate shading where Boggs's hands had once fit. It wasn't difficult to guess why he no longer used it. This was a tool of the gods. Even Boggs, in his delirium, questioned whether his current work fit that description.

Yet Lionel and Harnett had been wrong about Harpakhrad's fate. Boggs had resisted selling it. Instead he clung to his master's greatest gift. Suddenly I saw Harpakhrad and the Rotters Book as two halves of the same whole, the former exemplifying what Boggs could have been and the latter epitomizing what he was. I concealed the instrument with the blanket and twine and slumped into its shade, covering my face with fingers of both flesh and wood. I, too, had two halves and this was the one I had chosen.

30.

Despite the absence of my sink calendar, I knew that I had been with Boggs for a long time. It was summer—even in California, I could tell the difference. The bikinis got smaller, the convertibles went topless, and the grave dirt sweated loose to such a degree that it seemed to leap out of our way.

And just as I became inured to the textures and temperatures of the West Coast, it was over. I awoke to the sputtering of a rusty hatchback filling our alley with exhaust. My discombobulated brain scrambled to make sense of the threat. We were near Colma, California. Located about twenty minutes outside of San Francisco, it was well known as a place where the dead outnumbered the living thousands to one. Known as the City of the Silent and slapped with the ironic slogan *It's great to be alive in Colma,* the town was home to eighteen cemeteries, and the celebrities buried there ranged from Wyatt Earp to Joe DiMaggio. Boggs, in one of the fugue states that typically followed a frenzied night of digging, had ranted all night about his many adventures in Colma, despite the fact that we had spent the evening in an anonymous corner of one of the lesser grounds. But perhaps we had taken photos of someone famous, after all, because here was a person, maybe a relative, gunning his engine for revenge. Vengeance: it gave life purpose. Something about this rang familiar to me, though I didn't know why.

Then washer fluid squirted from the hood and the wipers fanned sludge. Boggs grinned through a crescent of cleared window—another stolen car. He honked the horn in a pattern probably intended to be recognizable and tipped his top hat out the window.

"Let's get a move on." He honked some more. "Move it or lose it."

A trash bin helped me up. My legs shook and I looked down at the emaciated bones, the emphatic bands of gristle. They did not look ugly to me; rather, I took pleasure in my increasingly whittled shape. Day by day I looked more like the characters in the Rotters Book. It felt very Hollywood, this desire to be shapely and famous. Everyone out here felt this way. At long last, I was normal.

"Giddyup, son. We're already packed." I noticed in the car's rear compartment the rickety shovel, our sacked belongings, the canisters of film, the quilted cradle of Harpakhrad. "Me and you, we got a book to finish."

Light-headed with equal parts unhealth and excitement, I stumbled to the driver's side window. Boggs had already crawled aside so that I could take on the role of designated driver. He patted the seat. Flakes of dead skin salted the stained fabric. Boggs brushed it away and chuckled.

"Dig the Diggers." His voice gurgled with the sludge of meth. "Final chapter. What do you think? Ain't that poetry for a poet?"

I followed orders. Miles peeled away like meat from bone. There were as many variations of landscapes as there were colors of decay. A wasp zipped into the car as we crossed the Columbia River and Boggs let it bite him twice so he could suck out the poison and rub it into his gums. Mostly he hummed and stole one-eyed glances that I didn't like. There was one Digger, after all, whose inclusion in the Rotters Book had not yet been discussed.

Our first stop was near a military training center in the

state of Washington, and as I dug Boggs curled himself against a nearby tombstone and paged through a battered Ray Bradbury paperback that he had peeled from the bottom of a Dumpster. I didn't protest; after overindulging on the drugs he'd stockpiled for the trip, he looked worse than ever. Half of his face had been swallowed by a raw-looking rash erupting with yellow pustules, and he mumbled incessantly as he pushed his nose into the book. My impression of Bradbury was that he was not a humorist, yet Boggs chortled until his blue eye gushed water.

I unearthed a Digger named Aberdeen. Boggs was too preoccupied to operate the camera, so I took over those duties, too. Aberdeen looked bad in the photo, the leathery hood of his head shriveled in defeat. In Utah, I looked upon the remains of Copperhead and my finger paused over the camera button, hazily recalling the photo I had taken long ago of Harnett and the severed hand. That photo had never seen the light of day, and this one shouldn't, either. Its alignment in the book ended up crooked; I couldn't bear to look when pasting it in. This was not right. Something about this was not right.

Next we went to Texas to disinter the man known as Boxer. Standing above his grave with the shovel, I started coughing and continued until I choked. Boggs looked at the tears the coughs brought to my cheeks and laughed until he too was sputtering. Only a day away was a man called Wolff. His grave was well fortified: a steel casket sheathed within a concrete vault. I chipped at the caulking with a fastidious patience I did not feel. Behind me, the flipping of Bradbury, page after page. While I coughed, Boggs vomited, and I smelled the familiar scent of urine when he became too absorbed in his reading. Yet his good eye danced, and he laughed even while sleeping.

With Wolff's photo pasted into the book, we took after a man called the Dragon. Pennsylvania, however, was a long way away. My cough turned into a phlegmy hack that lived deep in my lungs. It was soon joined by diarrhea. It felt like the return of the boneyard blues, and we had to pull to the shoulder repeatedly. Days were spent flinching from the imagined threat of Harpakhrad, nights were defined by the size of the headache that crowded my brain. Sunlight scared me. Human voices threw me into a panic. Hallucinations of hideous beasts resolved themselves to be people on bikes, dogs on leashes, kids on swings. When I cried out at some macabre vision I saw racing up to the side of the car, Boggs raised his head from his book and nodded as if it were progress.

There wasn't much left of Bradbury. Boggs had used most of the pages to light our fires and wipe his ass, and all that remained was a single story printed on just nine pages. The story was about a man who begins believing that his own skeleton is plotting against him. I knew this because every day in the car and every night in the cemetery Boggs read it aloud. At first he mocked it as he did everything else, but after a while he read it with the piety of the reborn, marking paragraphs with a thumb as he flipped and compared them to previous passages. I began to notice him prodding his torso and limbs with his fingertips, pushing aside muscle so that he could feel the skeleton beneath.

One day he found a knife inside a half-empty bucket of fried chicken.

I've got to get out of here, I told myself.

At first he only used the point. He bunched his pant leg at his knee and made tiny perforations up and down his shin.

"It doesn't hurt," he whispered to himself. "It doesn't hurt, that's incredible."

A few nights later I was pulled from sleep by squealing noises. I rolled over and squinted through the fire until I saw the flash of flame on steel. The knife waved hello from where its point was inserted between two of Boggs's ribs.

Each tiny tooth was a spark.

"Look, son." He breathed quickly through his nose and further peeled back his ruffled shirt. "It doesn't hurt. You know what that means?"

I squeezed shut my eyes. Day by day the shocks dulled into nauseating routine. He read his nine pages and bled all over them. Brown wreaths of blood stained his clothes as well as the car's passenger seat. Meanwhile he became impatient for the rest of the Diggers to meet their ends. The Apologist, who remained in a vegetative state in Virginia, irked him the most. "Maybe we can help him along," Boggs suggested often enough for me to know he wasn't kidding. We could aid the downfall of Brownie and Screw and Fisher, he enthused, by raising the suspicions of their local coppers, just like what happened to Under-the-Mud. Harnett and Lionel he appeared to be saving for last.

At last we reached Pennsylvania and photographed the Dragon. We set up camp nearby and waited for the Diggers to die. I waited for Boggs to die. He kept both eyes on me, too, until one night he popped the lame one out with his thumb. I saw it bounce once and land sizzling in our fire.

"Oh," he said. He leaned forward, withdrew the organ, and set it in his lap in order to waft away the smoke. After a while, he became very sad and held his face in his hands, crying softly. It was nearly an hour later when he heaved a brave sigh, stood, and buried the eye in a shallow hole at the edge of the woods. There was something about the ritual that reminded me of Grinder's burial. It wasn't something I was supposed to see; I rolled over and told myself that none of this could be happening. But then daylight came and his right socket was like a child's mouth, happy and cavernous.

31.

It was the basest cruelty that led us to Wyoming. Crying John had long ago disappeared into the mountains, probably to die, but defiling the corpse of his mutt was still within our power. The idea of the camera's flash documenting her transformation from beloved companion to thing of grime and bone—it was too much. Upon entering the alleged graveyard, I wondered if my heart would hold out. I prayed for cardiac arrest, that simple biologic state that should have claimed my mother instead of a city bus. While I looked for a Two-Fingered Jesus to hold me, Boggs got down on all fours. He wasn't sure where Foulie was buried, but he gnawed the grass of a hundred graves and made educated guesses. Each one was incorrect, but we photographed bodies all the same.

He read, I dug. I had mastered his hook-and-pull method, but when he wasn't paying attention I still liked to do things the old-fashioned way. I pried the casket lid in a method one part Boggs, one part Harnett, and leaned in to examine the body.

A Rat King—right there in front of my face. I only barely held in the scream. This could be another delusion. I leaned forward. It certainly looked real. The corpse's face and upper body were entirely obscured by gray fur, yellow claws, russet tails. Breathless, I leaned closer and tried to count the number of intertwined bodies but got lost at twenty-two. I saw razor teeth larger for the decomp that ate their faces. Hundreds of ribs like lace. Dozens of claws like embroidered fringe. It was complex and magnificent and monstrous.

Somewhere above, I heard a page turn and a roll of chuckles.

It had been a Rat King that had foretold the destruction of Harnett and Boggs's partnership, the wrath of the Gatlins, and all else that followed. What annihilations did this uncovering portend? I lowered my head to its many faces. My heart seized when it spoke.

Whispers, whispers, of things and people I had forgotten.

One thing was for sure: if Boggs saw, there was no telling what he would do. I used the crowbar to try to push the omen toward the foot of the coffin, but the tails and legs were too ensnared in clothing and flesh. Clamping my teeth, I took hold of the network of creatures with my hands, but it held fast. Its whispers grew louder.

"You fixing each other's hair?" Boggs shouted.

"There's nothing," I heard myself croak. "Nothing here worth taking."

"Then take the shot. Climb out. Refill the dirt. If you want, I can hold your pee-pee later when you whiz."

Another page turn, another giggle.

I tore my eyes away from the Rat King and checked the Polaroid camera hanging by a strap from my neck. There was no way to take this photo without revealing to Boggs the presence of the many-tailed monster. Somehow I knew that would mean the end of me, and then I would never be able to respond to the whispers, whispers, whispers.

I heard the paperback smack the ground.

"Lord, son." I heard him struggle to his feet. "Here I come."

It wasn't something I thought out. I lay down on top of the corpse, obscuring the Rat King, slung my face to the side, and closed my eyes. Boggs only glanced at the photos anymore; maybe he wouldn't notice. The camera's flash was hot against my skin. Seconds later I pocketed the photo and was replacing the casket lid, bursts of phosphorescence fading from my field of vision.

As I filled in the hole, I was surprised to find that I was crying. I scooped away the tears but they kept flowing from some mystery reserve. It wasn't until I was mounting the evening's Polaroids that I recognized the tears from the days following my mother's death. They were mourners' tears, only this time I mourned myself. It was my own face that I was pasting inside the Rotters Book. Joey Crouch was dead.

The Rat King didn't believe it.

I continued to weep while Boggs wheezed through the delirium that passed for his slumber. I didn't want to be dead; I wanted to live. The realization came as gently as the dawn. Boggs's ultimate mission was one of suicide, and now that I had the blade poised upon my wrist I found myself unable to slash. I couldn't go all the way with him. And if I couldn't go all the way, what was I doing here?

The Rat King beseeched in multitudinous tones.

I said no. It was persuasive. I said fine, all right. I flipped the pages of the Rotters Book until it fell open to the woman I recognized. *Yes,* the Rat King whispered, and I nodded through my tears and replied: *Yes*. How deep I had buried the truth. How rapidly I had reduced myself to another bullied coward. My mission had been so simple: find the photographer and punish.

There was only one means to do it, and it was not by his knife nor my bare hands. There was a code enforced by the very Diggers whose old bodies I now photographed. These men themselves were the Rat King, come to correct my path, their tales eternally intertwined for my benefit. The sacrifice of it stirred more tears. It was their voices that whispered, whispered, whispered, to the misplaced Son that they had found.

It was difficult to veil my excitement. We rose as usual during the sun's highest point. "Iowa," he said, dropping his inflamed and alien body into the car. The command told me all I needed to know. He was ready to skip directly to the book's climax. I felt sorry for him that he wouldn't live to see his project completed. Then, in the rearview, I glimpsed in his eye the insolence of new secrets. Had he heard the whispers as well? Did he know what I was planning?

We made our way. We did not speak. He readied syringes on his lap, licked crushed powder from the dashboard, sizzled himself in uncut substances until his last nerve endings were cauterized. He bled and choked. The car smelled of burned hair. Yes, the end was coming. Together we retreated to the remains of an Akron, Ohio, roller rink and sat gauging each other across a fire fed with grubby tinsel and collapsed limbo bars. After a time, Boggs resumed poking at his skeleton. When the knife reappeared I was only mildly surprised. For the first ten minutes he wept, but when that was over he made a sound like he was soaking in a bath.

"There's a rotter." His voice was coarse with heroism. "Inside me."

32.

A BALEFUL LULL DRAPED over the two of us as we closed in on Iowa. My muscles were weak from expectation. Boggs, though, no longer acknowledged me. He was too busy re-learning to breathe and walk in concert with the intruder wrapped inside of him. He seemed amazed by his ability to persevere and blinked down at himself in naked awe.

Harman, Indiana, was the last stop before Bloughton. I kneeled at the edge of the night's opened grave. I tightened the green straps on my backpack: tonight I wanted the pieces of my past as close to me as possible. I scrutinized the gravestone for the umpteenth time. The carved name was so pedestrian I couldn't get it to stick in my head for more than a few seconds. It concerned me; I wanted to be able to remember. Once Boggs was at the bottom of this hole beneath five feet of clay, it was the name, after all, that would make visiting his final resting spot so satisfyingly simple.

I peeked over the edge of the hole. Boggs was ten yards away, his back to me, completely absorbed in his Bradbury. I lowered myself and began to open the lid. Plenty of space would be needed for him to fit inside. Sadness nagged at me as I made room alongside the coffin's bones. Boggs's life had been one of unending tragedy. Even now he just wanted to be remembered. Instead he would be buried in a grave so anonymous even I doubted my ability to specify it.

It was time. I lifted myself from the hole and held the shovel like a club. Boggs was not there. I squinted my eyes and listened for the guidance of the Rat King. There was nothing. I set down the tool and explored the surrounding hillside.

With each step I felt the cold certainty that he was gone. Whatever entity he felt was inside him had marched him away through the headstones. The warm breeze cooled my perspiration as I searched for footprints, a discarded top hat, the wet residue of blood. Back near the grave I saw something nestled in the peeled turf. I crossed over, kneeled, and lifted it. It was a brown twist of something dry and swollen. I turned it over and saw letters. Bradbury—he would never leave it behind—oh, god, he was still—

The clang of the blade rang off my pelvis. I sprawled and caught myself over the abyss. I tried to scramble away but I felt small hands draw tight my clothing and flatten me to the ground like a tossed gym bag. The trumpet and leg bone inside my backpack crushed against my spine. Above, a dry wind snapped the pages of Bradbury that had been pasted with blood across Boggs's face and arms like a form of armor. His top hat blacked out the moon. The knife was raised and bloody.

"There's a rotter in you, too, son." He nodded helpfully and crouched down. "Let me help you get it out."

He drove his knife at my stomach. Only my churning legs kept the point from landing. I wrapped the small man in a bear hug and bucked, expecting each second an impalement. Instead he pulled away from me. Panting, he stood and with his remaining eye cataloged me: knuckles, pelvis, clavicle, skull.

"Don't overreact, now. I ain't trying to kill you." He moistened his puffy lips and zeroed in on my sternum. "I'm trying to save you."

He cavorted toward me with mincing steps. I leapt across the hole and while airborne revisited what I had seen earlier: it had not been Bradbury he'd been paging through while stumbling away. It had been the Rotters Book, and he'd finally come upon my photo. Physical laws meant little to him, but books were truth. If the pages said that I was dead, then I was dead.

Within arm's reach of where I landed was our pile of belongings, and I dove for the swaddled Harpakhrad and lifted her as if she were mine. Though she was still wrapped in a blanket, the perfection of her weight and balance transfixed me. I was lost until a knife came out of nowhere to notch my shoulder blade. I felt the blow in my teeth.

"Rotter! Rotter! Don't you touch her!"

I lashed out with Harpakhrad. Boggs was too short—she sailed over his head, the blanket unfurling as she twirled. The effort sank me; I collapsed to the grass. Boggs kicked me in the nose and, when I rolled again, the ear, and, when I rolled again, the teeth. Blasts of blood and pain clouded me. I couldn't move and yet was moving: it was Boggs, toting me exactly the way Rhino had eons ago in the boys' shower.

I opened my mouth to a foul taste—ZadenScent, I was sure of it. Then gravity compacted my guts and everything green and blue swapped places. I dropped. Ancient bones splintered against my chest. Oxygen shot from my lungs. Minutes were lost, many. I opened my eyes only in time to see the first shovelful of dirt swarming at me like a cloud of bees.

It hurt when it hit my face, a million little bullets. I used my elbows as cover and shouted for him to stop. Dirt caked my tongue. It kept coming, insanely fast, blotting out the sky. Already the weight was crushing. I corkscrewed and found myself face to face with the skeleton beneath me and wondered for an instant if it was my own—maybe the fall had knocked the rotter right out of me.

Up I went, taking hold of the edge, but the flat bottom of the shovel cracked against my knuckles. I collapsed but was right back up, taking two holds in hopes of being able to maintain one of them. It was no good: two strikes and I was at the bottom again. My arms and shoulders were numb. I feared losing more digits. But still I came, pedaling my feet up the dirt walls and elbowing back to the surface. This time the shovel connected with my left ear, just like my mother, two ear injuries, two deaths.

When I landed there was no sound. Dirt fell about me, mute as snow. Deafness then reversed itself and my skull shook with an ascension of noise so great it blew tears from my eyes. Hiding from the clamor was the only hope. I drew up my legs and burrowed inside the casket. I pulled on what remained of the lid, but pounds of dirt impeded the hinges, and the bulk of my backpack got in the way. Both of these problems were solved in a few frenetic seconds and then I was sealed off from weight and light. The dreadful ringing shifted to the left side of my head. Brittle hisses of dirt broke through the bulwark of sound. Somewhere within was the whisper of the Rat King, telling me that I should've seen this coming, I'd had so many chances, I should've taken him down first.

Terror whipped in black fragments. The anonymous name on the grave, it was mine. Hard surfaces pressed against my elbows and hips and knees. My lips kissed the casket lid and ate dust. Scattered points of light shone through the blackness and I mistook where I was dying: beneath the falling stars of Boris's bedroom, the cage of the band room closet, the breathless box of rehearsal room B, the cold dungeon of the locker room shower, the filthy crevice of the cabin sink.

Where I least expected it—from the barren throat of the skeleton—came a voice so patient it slid through the din. Words we had gone over a hundred times, I recognized them. His locked jaw and persistent repetition, I remembered them. I hugged cold bones and pretended it was him and pleaded for just one more go-round: *Teach me one more time, I swear this time I'll listen.*

The bones spoke in my ear and told me to repeat.

"Calm, remain calm."

Within the airless vessel my voice was inharmonic.

"Air, conserve air."

His fear, my dismissiveness. None of it had been easy on him.

"Shallow, shallow grave."

High above me the dirt was packed, the sod sewn, and Boggs was limping away in temporary truce with his internal rotter: one Digger down, next stop Bloughton. But despite how the Rotters Book might read, I wasn't dead. The Resurrectionist had already performed his resurrection. Heart rate was steady. Rank air issued through my sinuses in fixed time. Even five feet down, I realized, I had every advantage. The lid was already broken, I knew the center of balance, and most importantly I had a tool. It took five minutes for me to remove the femur from my backpack. I would have to break it in half to gain the necessary leverage, but nothing lasted forever.

Through it all, even ascending through dirt, I made my apologies.

The cemetery balanced on my back. I shouldered it off and ran. I was made of earth and pieces of me fell off and shattered as I escaped. Inside the backpack the trumpet fought musically with the remaining dagger of leg bone, a duet that superseded the fading ringing. I was over a fence, down a road. Boggs's hatchback was gone, but he was half blind, his body no longer tuned for the operation of machinery. There was still time, though I could not falter. I could beat him back to Bloughton, back to Hewn Oak, back to the tiny cabin on the Big Oak River to save the man who had brought this boy back from the dead.

33.

It was early morning before I found an unlocked car. I had watched Boggs hot-wire plenty and was still a good student—just thirty minutes of tinkering before the asthmatic sputter. I put the car into gear and swung it around on the quiet suburban street. Tiny birds squeaked on their wires; public radio listlessly relayed the weather through an open window. These soft surges overtook the last residues of ringing. I felt light and quick. It was as if the hole I'd emerged from had held me for months. Sounds were more salient, physical objects finer. The landscape solidifying about me was manufactured but beautiful: the queues of identical homes, the columned porches, the husbanded lawns baubled with dew. So tempting, these trappings, that it was hard to drag my eyes back to the front.

A man with a shovel. In the road.

I swerved. The windshield exploded into cobweb and I saw Harpakhrad's silver and gold blade ricochet away. I stomped my foot and my forehead scrunched glass. Tires screeched. Somewhere nearby a shovel clanged to cement. Too fast, it had happened too fast—he could not have tracked me down, not already. I spat windshield. My skull hummed. My lungs stung from the steering wheel. I blinked and more glass fell from my lashes.

Harpakhrad scraped across the cement.

I kicked the windshield until I had blown away a fist-sized hole, and in that hole I saw Boggs advancing, top hat twisted low, his instrument twirling acrobatically. He was real. He had tracked me, probably followed me all night. If I hadn't found a vehicle, how long would he have toyed with me? I hit the gas and cranked the wheel. Rubber squealed and the driver's side window shattered.

Wailing enough to match the screeching tires, I glanced off the side of one parked sedan, then another. Somehow I found myself bouncing down the center of the street. A water sprinkler turned on. A man stood motionless at the end of a driveway, holding a distended garbage bag. Shit—a cul-de-sac. Dead end. I fumbled for my seat belt and secured it. I checked the rearview. A block away, Boggs was still advancing.

A delirious three-point turn later, I was turned around and barreling. All that road and it only took seconds to reach him. He didn't budge. He swung Harpakhrad like a samurai sword. Though I was the one inside a car, I was afraid. I jerked the wheel. I felt two of my tires leave pavement. The wheels landed and hurdled the incline of a front lawn, and through the hole in the windshield I saw Boggs tossed noiselessly by the front left fender. An instant later the hood crumpled against an SUV. The windshield disintegrated into my lap. The diagonal sash of the belt burned my throat.

Smoke sat in the air and the SUV's alarm was going crazy. I unbelted and reached for my door but it was already hanging ajar. I took hold of my backpack, put one foot outside, then another, and then swayed as if an earthquake were twisting the planet. I hurt everywhere. The car was totaled. Across the metal carnage of the hood, I saw daubs of blood. But I was okay. I was okay. I walked, felt old like Lionel. Right, left.

One more step. Right, left. Over freshly trimmed grass and past a novelty mailbox in the shape of a tractor. Behind me metal crackled and plastic sizzled.

"Rotter. Rotter."

I teetered in the middle of the road. Dimly I was aware of white faces appearing at windows, men with ties in their hands and women with sleep-tousled hair. With reluctance I faced the disaster I had made of someone's front yard. Boggs was hobbling from the wreckage, using Harpakhrad as a crutch. The bones of his left foot and ankle had been detached, and the dead weight drooped heavily in its fleshy sack. He took another hop and the foot flapped so freely I could see the outline of a snapped bone poke curiously at its soft container.

"Rotter, rotter, rotter, rotter."

Maybe the drugs had roasted the pain receptors of his brain. His suit smoked, his vest sizzled with motor oil, his hat was dented and oblique. He kept coming. Pages of Bradbury remained crusted to his skin but now popped as they were incinerated by razors of heat. He kept coming. His face was knotted and blackened except for the one perfect eye beckoning as beautifully as my first glance of ocean through trees. I felt my knees buckle in submission. Harpakhrad could split me in half, even if swung by a man as broken as this one.

Tiny puffs of air plumed his shredded lips.

"Rotter, rotter, rotter, rotter, rotter, rotter, rotter, rotter, rotter, rotter, rotter."

As he hobbled over a manicured stripe of flowers and past the tractor-shaped mailbox, I took a single step away. I didn't even mean to do it. Surprise flickered across his face. I tried it again—I took a second backward step and he pooched his lip in consternation. Soon I was backpedaling with considerable speed. The blue eye burned. To me it was a signal: keep moving. No car, maybe that was true, but there were always more cars. For now I would run—yes, my legs were running—and take every advantage of his injury. Hinges squeaked as people retreated to call 911. They would arrive too late, at least for me; now I was sprinting. Down the block, through the alley, and across side streets, his mutter chased me long after he had dropped from sight.

"Rotter, rotter—"

34.

OVER FIELDS AND FENCES, barbed wire catching my cuffs and cow patties baking to my soles, I kept myself aligned with the interstates by the stink of melted rubber. In Swenson, Indiana, I seared my fingers hot-wiring an early-model Skylark and in that tin oven crossed the Mississippi. I broke down in Tedrow, not fifty miles from Bloughton. I ditched the heap on the shoulder and made tracks through the ditch and the woods.

It took me nearly three days to make what should've been an eight-hour trip. I felt woefully late, yet made myself wait until dark before walking the last ten miles. To kill time I rifled through trash cans for food. It wasn't until I noticed the inordinate amount of popcorn in one of these that I recognized the building as the movie theater where Foley and I had held hands. I squatted against the brick and munched discarded Mike and Ikes and relived the atrocities that had begun there.

The clock tower rang ten as I passed the Amtrak station where I had first landed, the store where I had bought an instant camera and a bar of soap, the library where Harnett and I had researched pawnbrokers. Bloughton now seemed preposterously puny, the corners too sharp and the streets too clean for it to be anything but an unoccupied replica. Life was proven only by living room windows flickering with evening programming. Unconsciously I began to slink. I was a criminal here, in all probability a wanted man.

The town square was lit with too many lights and I hugged a line of storefronts. Hurrying by was the only sensible course, and yet I paused. For so late at night, there was an unusual amount of people milling about. Upon closer inspection I made out several loose groups of children playing in the grass and a few teenagers threading among them. A few steps closer—I had strayed into the middle of the road now—and I discerned several large objects resting in the central pavilion. Aside from the yearly Christmas display, the structure usually sat empty. I could not resist; I went closer.

The objects were coffins. The receptacles had become so prevalent in my life that it took me several minutes to appreciate the abnormality of their presence in the center of the square. People of great significance must have died. I reached the edge of the grass and stopped cold. Gottschalk, Woody, Celeste—what if what I had done had driven them to suicide and this was their ongoing elegy? No matter how bad they had been, I was worse. Self-disgust choked me. Three boys looked up and backed away. I wiped my mouth and edged closer to the pavilion until I realized that these could not be the caskets of my former tormenters. Not only was the workmanship and style of a different era, but I recognized the evidence of tampering. The markings were more than familiar. They were my own.

A girl of six or seven stood next to me. Her curly black hair was split into pigtails. She wore pink shorts and a rainbow shirt further colored by the dribblings of long-gone ice cream. A Bratz doll dangled from her hand. Her teenage guardian, bestowed with the same curly black hair, was occupied with what looked like very meaningful texting. I forced a smile at the little girl and pointed at the coffins.

"Why—" My voice was wild and I coughed it down, fighting for stability. "Why are these here?"

"So they can catch the bad man." She seemed grateful for the opportunity to flaunt her memorization. "And so to remember the bad things he did. And also to punish the bad man for the bad things he did."

I spoke so carefully the words hurt. "What did the bad man do?"

"He took them out of the ground, silly."

My intestines knotted.

"That *was* silly," I managed. "Did they catch the bad man?"

"No, but they're going to. My daddy says they're going to."

"When are they going to catch him?"

"Right now, silly," she said. "They went down the road. That's why my sister is playing babysitter."

I strained to control my pulse.

"What's your name?" I asked.

"Blood," she said, pointing at my hip. Next she pointed at my shoulder. "Blood."

"That's right, I have an owie," I said. "What's your name, sweetie?"

"Hazel," she said. "Hazel Geraldine Gatlin."

She held out her hand but I was already running down the same roads that had guided me to and from my reckless revenge. Now the revenge was theirs. This was what Boggs had been laughing about each time he had read Bloughton's online news. What I'd done at the school had led to a manhunt, which had likely stagnated until yesterday, when a family by the name of Gatlin had shown up in town muttering an accusation that local citizens were all too ready to believe. It was not difficult to guess who had finally tipped off the Gatlins.

The blaze was evident before I hit Hewn Oak. I hurtled through woods made rapturous by the red glow and burst into a clearing where everything was rippling with fire—the woodpile was on fire, Harnett's truck was on fire, and flames shot from the cabin with waterfall velocity.

The yard lamps, the nailed windows, the extra locks—every feeble attempt to keep out the world's dangers now melted and stewed. I shot through a wall of men made mute by their own savagery and slung aside a stranger who held in one loose palm a container of gasoline. Seconds later the hot gusts became scorching and my own hair felt like searing tendrils of steel. With a shoulder I rammed the door and it exploded inward and I went tumbling into a fortress of burning books. I felt fire biting like ants across my arms and brought myself to all fours. Black smoke churned like the fur of a thousand beasts being pushed to slaughter. The molten lead of sweat rolled down my back.

Direction no longer existed. I kicked through flaming books, shoved past smoldering bundles of crackling newsprint. I was at the window, the glass bubbling and slopping over my wooden fingers; I was at the counter, where fire poured upward from the sink; I was at the fireplace, where, strangely, there was no fire, just a noxious cloud of embers pouring down the chimney's chute.

My toes, blistering. Boiling liquid smoke, pouring down my throat by the pint. I lurched through a ring of flame and bounced off the side of a mattress that was partially engulfed, and there was a shape curled up near the wall, the Resurrectionist, in position for the cremation he'd always wanted. I fell upon him and hauled him up the way I had hauled so many Diggers over the past few nightmarish weeks, only this one I treated with far less care, slinging him over my shoulder while I made for the window.

The bars, the ones we had foolishly installed, blocked my way. I took hold of one and immediately drew back—it was white hot. I dropped Harnett and spun around but there was no escape. The doorway through which I had entered was a stream of liquefied ceiling. I felt Harnett spasm against my shin and I crouched to protect him from the firestorm that was coming.

A red flash of light caught my eye. On the bed, where Harnett must have curled next to it in his sleep, was the Root. I had her in my hands in seconds. She felt wonderful; I felt whole. I pressed her warm metal to my cheek and laughed. I hurried back to the window and lodged her between the bars. Harnett had installed them well, but this was no regular shovel and I no regular shoveler. We worked together in a sublime madness. I saw one bar snap from its lodging. I heard the Root cry out as she irreparably warped. Another bar was knocked loose. The instrument's handle fractured; the wood began to grind into shavings against the head. A cloud of fire licked at my neck. My laughter turned to the sobs of goodbye. I had destroyed the Root, but the bars were gone.

Her gnarled remains disappeared into the smoke. I struck

the window glass with my fist. It detonated on contact. I lifted Harnett and crammed him through the opening, heedless of shards, and punched at his shoulders and hips and knees until he slipped from sight. Behind me half of the house collapsed with a sound like a massive felled tree, and the blast of fiery air tossed me to the wall. Things all over me were ablaze. I looked up and saw the suck of poison air coursing through the busted window. I followed its path.

It was no cooler outside. I landed on top of Harnett. The cabin shuddered and leaned over us. The roof began to slide. A thousand nails pinged as they snapped in two. My hands took Harnett's shirt and hair. I felt his hands moving, too, and his legs cycling senselessly. We ran. The cabin flattened somewhere at our heels and hot shrapnel glued itself to our skin. I was still on fire. But running. I steered us over the tumorous terrain of a backyard hollowed and filled a million times over. Random patches of grass were burning. There was a slope; we stumbled. There was water; we clawed our way into it.

The Big Chief River, where Harnett had once caught fish with his hands, now caught two new wiggling creatures. Knees, waist, ribs, neck—suddenly the water was over my head. The fires on my clothing turned to gray clouds. A mouthful of wet soot, the weight of my backpack dragging me down. We were moving. A current now pulled us. I wrapped an arm around Harnett's shoulders. He had me by the neck. The sinewy ripples of the water were black, red, gold, blue, purple, yellow. Somewhere behind us an inferno drew white outlines around the faceless men gathering to see us drown. In their fixed postures I saw not just the horror of what they had done to us but what we had done to them, the befuddling inhumanity of what we'd done to those they'd loved. It hit me like loss. No other loss compared. The Root, reduced to cinder. The irreplaceable archive of newspaper and books, now ash. The scores of Foley's metal CDs, now puddled plastic. The locked safe containing our every last asset, now dividends for bickering arsonists. The sink calendar, all those days made irretrievable. And the garden, the beloved onion plants, shriveling to wire, the pungent white smoke weaving with darker threads.

35.

SCOTLAND WAS A GIANT cemetery. Each patch of grass was a plait of knolls—filled holes, that was what it looked like to me, an entire country seeded with bodies. We were just two more, moving above the ground but just as dead.

And then we came back to life. I saw it in him first, the way he looked to the skies in the morning astonished as an infant; the small smiles of genuine pleasure as he purchased pasties from a bakery and self-consciously murmured "Cheers"; the bottle after bottle of water he gulped down and peed out, as if flushing all venoms from his system. We spent the first week in Glasgow, walking slowly through streets smelling of rain, and with each day the creases in his skin loosened and dirt fell out. Sometimes I'd brush it from his coat while he slept.

We had little money. After escaping from the Big Chief we had spent a silent night shivering under thorned bushes, huddling against each other and holding our breaths each time we heard a distant noise that might forewarn men or dogs. When morning came, Harnett led us south. By dusk we were at an isolated intersection somewhere near the Missouri border, digging with our hands exactly fifteen paces from the base of a giant, three-forked tree. Four feet down was a metal box, and inside, wrapped in a towel, was a secret reserve fund of nearly five thousand dollars.

I had never been on an airplane before, but forty-eight hours later I was on the last and longest leg of an overseas flight. The passport I had kept updated my entire life finally found use; I peeled it from the bottom of my green backpack and presented it to the agent sopping wet. The backpack and trumpet were our only carry-ons, and the surviving half of my mother's bone I hid inside my pant leg before cruising through security. The plane was full and I sat in J, he in M, each of us wearing XXL tourist tees we had purchased from an airport gift shop in Detroit. A flight attendant gave me headphones and I watched sitcoms I'd never heard of. I fought to control a urine stream in a tiny, jostling lavatory. I fell asleep wrapped in a thin flannel blanket, luxuriating in the safety of knowing my father could see me from where he sat.

The cash wouldn't last. We both knew it. Discussing eventualities would get us nowhere, so we didn't bother. That first week in Glasgow we slept in hostels and ate at pubs, filling our bellies with jellied breads and mushy peas. Harnett looked like a drinker and they never stopped offering him pints. He smiled and waved them off and the silence continued.

We tended to our wounds. My cough wasted into a sore throat that left its mark in a new coarsening of my voice. The cuts on my hip and shoulder probably needed stitches, but we survived with storebought pharmaceuticals. Miraculously I had no serious burns, though every inch of skin that had been exposed during the fire went pink and peeled. Harnett's smoke inhalation had left him with a bronchitis that would not quit, but day by day his cricks and limps resolved. With time, our worst traumas scabbed over.

The stories didn't begin until we were on the train to Edinburgh. Harnett craned his neck to watch exhaust pump from industrial columns. From the scrap metal lining the rails to the mongrel dogs lifting their legs against funny little shrubs, everything seemed to delight him. Even more vitality returned to him when we stepped onto Edinburgh's cobblestoned streets. He pointed at the castle looming catastrophically at the top of the hill and laughed at my amazement. We ducked into a door among the zigzagging storefronts and bought cups of soup and carried them to a side road, where Harnett exclaimed happily upon finding an underground bookshop still in business. He rummaged among the dusty stacks and haggled with the portly owner and finally handed to me a clothbound stack of pale yellow pages: *The Diary of a Resurrectionist, 1811–1812, To Which Are Added an Account of the Resurrection Men of London and a Short History of the Passing of the Anatomy Act*.

"If you're going to start a library," he said, "that's book number one."

It had cost the equivalent of three days' worth of food, and I metered the words out as if they were equally as essential. *The complaint as to the scarcity of bodies for dissection is as old as the history of anatomy itself,* it began. Harnett spoke aloud these words as I read them, and there was a pride in his expression I had never before seen. Maybe the Diggers were finished and maybe they should not have existed for as long as they did. But they had come from noble stock, and this was what he wanted to show me.

We traveled by foot to Greyfriars Churchyard, where

Harnett showed me the giant barred mortsafes erected to keep out the resurrection men, or sack-'em-up men, as they were also called. These cages, as well as wrought-iron coffins, cemetery watchtowers, and buried barbed wire, proved the mettle of these men—despite the unsavory work and the threatening mobs, they risked it all, for money, yes, but also for the snatching of life from the jaws of disease and injury. Their bravery was matched by those surgeons who hid the illegal remains in their flower gardens or beneath their floorboards. We were not the first victims of mob violence—that was what Harnett was trying to tell me.

"And that's how it began." Harnett tested the mortsafe's strength. "The sack-'em-ups over here became the Diggers over there. A few generations later you have Lionel, and one generation after that, you have me."

"And then me," I added.

Harnett stood and brushed his hands on his pants.

"But it's over now," he said. "You have to know that."

I tapped my wooden fingers and surveyed the necropolis.

"Just because there's not as many of us anymore? That's your reason?"

"Because there's no heroism," Harnett said. "Not anymore."

So this trip to the beginning was really the end. I read my book and tried to come to terms with the feeling of emptiness. We slept in parks and took remainders of food that locals and tourists seemed only too happy to give us. One day Harnett led me to a farm and made me watch the cows eat from their trough until I couldn't take the mystery any longer.

"I give up."

"The trough," he said. "Look closer."

We moved near enough to feel the heat of the bovines and hear the flies that zipped about their tails. The trough was coffin shaped. Further investigation proved it to be one of the legendary iron coffins, repurposed as a feeding bin so long ago that the farmer probably had no idea of the relic's consequence. There were other examples: a former "putrefaction house," built to allow bodies to fully rot before burial, was now a confectionary; those nicks in the side of the church were bullet holes from a gunfight between competing sack-'em-ups; those red stains betrayed a parking lot's former life as a slaughterhouse before it was shut down when the overcrowding of graves led to pestilence.

The mysteries of the past were solved in our every waking moment, and Harnett hoped that the knowledge might make giving up digging easier for me. As we walked away from the farm, I realized that my sense of loss could not possibly compare to his.

"I only wish," he said one night as we sat at a carnival erected in the shadow of Edinburgh Castle, "that I could've seen the pyramids. Dug there like Lionel. Now, those were tombs."

"Well," I said, "we are in Europe. We could start heading that direction."

He shrugged. "Little low on funds."

"That's nothing new."

We bought another corn dog and split it.

"When the anatomy laws were finally passed here, common knowledge was that it marked the end of grave robbing."

"It was kind of the beginning," I said.

"That's correct," he said. "It was the start of the real work. But ours is a chapter they'll never know how to write. We were the reason things were missing or misplaced. Lionel used to say we were the thieves of stillness." He took a deep breath. The lights on the rides began flashing.

"Can't we ever go back?"

"Kid, look at us. We're down to nothing. So no," he said. "Well, that's not entirely true. You can, if you want. What happened at the school—you know they're pinning that on me."

Seen from Edinburgh's serenity, the boy who had wreaked such repugnant vengeance was a stranger. Giant waves of shame shook through me. It had been I who had chased Harnett from Bloughton, I who had burned down his home. Harnett let me twist in silence for several minutes, yet I felt no malice. If anyone was inclined to forgive Bad Jobs, it was my father.

"So what about the Gatlins?" I finally asked.

"Until they have my body, they might come after you."

"Let them."

"That's easy for you to say."

"I know how to run," I said. "I know how to fight."

"The fighting has to end sometime."

"It will," I said. "With me, I'm the last one."

Harnett stretched and leaned against the rock ledge at our back. Pink clouds held back the rain and the air smelled like sugar.

"Everything we learned from Lionel, this is where we learned it." He scanned the sky and looked more placid than I had ever seen him. I knew instantly that if I returned to the States alone, this was how I wanted to remember my father. "What Boggs said was the truth. We were brothers. We were." He looked at me, then at his feet. "I should have come for you. I should have found you."

Regret hurt so badly that my fingers, those that remained, went numb.

"I'm sorry." As insufficient as it was, it was all I could say. "Harnett, I'm sorry."

"Hey, kid," he said. "Call me Ken."

36.

We drank our tea on the front steps of an old church after awakening from a night in the park and laughing at the patterns the grass had left on our faces. Fog hung close to the ground, smearing the morning streetlights, and so it was a great surprise when a young man emerged from the haze. With his shoulder bag and secondhand jacket he looked like a student, but it was his American accent that all but confirmed it.

"One of you Ken Harnett?" he asked.

We glanced at each other over the steaming rims of our paper cups.

"Oh, that's awesome," the man said. "I've been looking all over for you."

Harnett was instantly suspicious. "Really?"

"Really! I'm an American!"

Harnett and I shared another glance.

The guy laughed a little. "I guess that's probably obvious," he said. "Anyway, I'm with the Study Abroad program. Engineering. That's not at George Square, unfortunately. It's over at the Kings Buildings, couple miles south of city center. You know it?"

Harnett nodded.

"Awesome, awesome. It's always awesome to meet a countryman! I'm from North Dakota! But anyway, anyway. I have something for you."

He reached into an inside jacket pocket and withdrew an envelope. It was stained and wilted, as if it had traveled a long distance to reach us.

"I've got a little job-type thing at the mail center and a few days back this thing came in, inside a bigger envelope, and it had these special instructions. It said it was for an American guy named Ken Harnett who was over here with his seventeen-year-old son. And it had a list of the places where you might be hanging out. And here's the craziest part. There was money. Fifty bucks. I'm not kidding, like a fifty-dollar bill just taped to the bottom of the letter. Most guys maybe just would've pocketed the cash but I was thinking—"

Harnett's hand was out. "Give it to me."

"Oh, right." The guy looked down at the letter somewhat forlornly. "I've been to every hostel and park within like twenty miles of here. The cemeteries, too, for some reason."

Harnett snapped his fingers. "Give it."

The guy shrugged. "Not that the British guys wouldn't have done the same thing, but a fellow American—"

Harnett swiped the letter from the guy's hand and went about tearing it open. The student was too surprised to be offended.

"I wish we could give you something," I said. "But you got that fifty, at least."

"Yeah, hey, no, that's cool, it's just awesome I found you, you know? Now I got a story."

A few more niceties were offered, but it was clear that the conversation was finished. Eventually he made an excuse about classes and scooted away.

Harnett looked like a dying man just informed of a cure. He pushed the note into my hand. In a familiar elderly squiggle, it read:

K./J.—
Msg. fr. Lahn—Lio. dec'd. No funeral. Have arr. flowers.
URGENT: at Lio.'s request, epitaph added: Job 20:15. Alerting
Dggrs. Burial: 29th. Tix at EDI. Godspeed.—Kx

"He's dead," I said. "Lionel's dead."

Harnett was shaking his head.

I felt my heart pound with hope.

"He's not dead?"

Harnett swiped the letter back and shook it.

"He is. He is dead. He is dead and I am sad." Then, to my surprise, his face broke into the gladdest smile I'd ever seen. "But he's left us a gift."

When a pastor in street clothes arrived ten minutes later he chuckled at my agitation, unlocked the church, and ushered me inside to a large Bible parted upon a pulpit. I paged forward and back. The man nudged me aside and licked his finger. After a moment he pointed at the relevant verse.

" 'He will spit out the riches he swallowed; God will make his stomach vomit them up.' " I repeated this to Harnett seconds later. He grabbed my elbow and began pulling me down the sidewalk.

"The treasure," he said.

"Wait. You mean it's real?"

" 'The riches he swallowed.' "

We were heading in the direction of the bus station, which would take us toward the A8 and the Edinburgh Airport, where Knox had plane tickets waiting.

"It's with him." I slapped my head. "It's inside his coffin."

" 'God will make his stomach vomit them up.' "

"He wants us to dig it up. That's why he showed us the plot."

Harnett glanced at the sky and up there I saw what he saw: a way out for both of us, enough money for him to live out his vagabond days in Europe and for me to follow whichever path I saw fit. He whispered, "You crazy bastard."

"But Knox sent the same note to all the Diggers," I protested. "There's no time, we'll never get there in time."

"The note said the twenty-ninth. That's two days. There's time." Harnett picked up his pace. "But you're going to have to shut up and get moving."

By midday we found ourselves at Glasgow International Airport, nearly one month after we had arrived, once more with nothing but the clothes on our backs, an old trumpet, and one backpack held together by threads. Heading for the security checkpoint, I again slipped the segment of my mother's leg bone into my pants leg and glanced at a mounted television monitor. There was a storm system heading for the Southeastern U.S. that they were calling Tropical Storm Gilbert, but it was expected to weaken before landfall. The weatherman sounded confident. I didn't give it another thought.

37.

We flew into Washington, D.C., under slate skies. The first spots of precipitation I saw were against the windows of a rental car that we had no intention of returning. By the time we hit Richmond, Virginia, the rain was battering us like machetes, popping against the hood and windshield with such force that I kept seeing Harpakhrad sailing toward the glass.

The radio told the tale. Tropical Storm Gilbert was now Hurricane Gilbert and was bearing down on the Outer Banks at Category Five levels. Winds were expected to reach 150 miles per hour. Anything within five hundred yards of shoreline was doomed. Massive evacuations were widespread. You couldn't buy bottled water. By the time we hit North Carolina a caravan of cars clogged the interstate, heading in the opposite direction. We never considered stopping. In mere hours we could call our digging days done and Valerie Crouch could at last rest in peace.

We were forced to pull off for gas about two hours from Lionel's. Vehicles idled in crowded lines for a chance at the pumps. Rain moved horizontally, ripping hoods from people's heads as they watched their words being stolen into the sky. There was a feeling of impending apocalypse; men were giddy with the threat. Harnett spent five seconds in the rain to enter the store and came back soaked to the skin. He threw a cheap shovel and flashlight into the backseat. He tossed me trail mix, evidence of a tragic lack of Doritos. Outside, an armoire bungeed to a pickup bed was disassembled by the wind. We lost thirty minutes, an hour. And the radio station kept the bad news coming: Lionel's house looked to be ground zero.

Fueled, we rolled back out into the street, the gusts fighting us for every inch. The car shuddered and creaked. Harnett pulled over for a moment and cowered as if even the effort of steering was too much. When we moved again we couldn't exceed twenty-five—anything faster and we felt our wheels begin to leave the earth.

Thirty miles from the coast the two-lane road disappeared

beneath a lake. There were abandoned cars stranded in water up to the door handles. We paused at the edge of the water. Harnett looked at me and then pressed the gas pedal. Our motion sounded like the removal of masking tape. Two fans of brown water sprayed. The tide shouldered us repeatedly like some mammoth underwater monster. Water began pooling at my feet.

Somehow we made it. We risked two more floods and crawled around scores of fallen trees. Five miles from Lionel's house we put the car in park and ran outside to pull a length of fence from our path. Immediately the car door crashed shut on my fingers. I waited for the pain, but it didn't come because the fingers were wood. Staying low, I scrambled after Harnett. Twigs and rocks audibly assailed our bodies. Trees on either side of us broke one at a time. Harnett gripped the far end of the fence, I took the near. He pulled and I pushed. I saw him yell something. He waved his hands and lay flat against the pavement. I looked over my shoulder and saw the giant yellow sickle of a broken McDonald's sign sailing through the air. It capered above us and then dove. I dropped and felt runners of water twitch as the object swooped over us. There was a crunch, muffled by the coarse bellow of the storm, and when we dared look we saw that the top of our car had been smashed in. We could still hear the mumble of bad news from the radio.

Harnett took the shovel and the flashlight. I took my backpack. We ran but it felt like walking.

Downed power lines snaked miserably. Road signs somersaulted, sparking against the pavement with each revolution. It took us twenty minutes to cross a small bridge that was sloshing and treacherous with spill. We came upon a traffic light hanging just a foot from the ground, and we fell against it, clutching it and panting. It was huge. I ducked my head against the dead red lens and for a moment the sucking howl of the storm diminished. Night was coming fast.

Lionel's charming, pink-trimmed roof had crumpled sideways into the yard, collapsing the living room wall into a smear of rubble. His tasteful furniture and framed pictures had been yanked into the sky. We staggered through the unprotected clearing and made it to the aperture of the path through the woods. Trees beat at the trail like two endless rows of fists. The light was fading. The danger was palpable.

Harnett pressed his teeth against my ear. "YOU CAN STAY HERE."

I shook my head.

"STAY HERE." He nodded. The rain thrummed from his skin.

There's no heroism, not anymore—in Edinburgh, that had been Harnett's justification for letting the Diggers expire. But I could see from the mad glint that shone from his eyes that there was one last chance for heroism and it was now.

I grabbed him by the collar and shook my head. He set his jaw and, perhaps, suppressed a grin, and then threw an arm around my back. Joined, we plunged into the screaming whorls and hurtling torrents. Wood fired like thunderclaps and heavy branches pushed against our shoulders. Harnett fought them off with the shovel, and in those courageous strikes I thought I saw something happen between the shovel and him, an accord between man and wood, but I couldn't be sure.

Trees gave way and there was the hill leading down to the cemetery and the ocean beyond. Only the hill had become a pulp of debris and the cemetery was gone. That couldn't be right. I kneeled and tried to see through the silvery thrash.

Harnett pointed the flashlight but it only lent definition to the layers of rain. He shut it off and we stared, and after a while we understood.

The ocean had surged to such levels that it had not just overtaken the cemetery but gutted it. Now it was a churning swamp crashing with coffins and boiling with bodies. Headstones tossed like leaves. Bones rolled white like surf. Geysers of mud erupted at the collision of gruesome things.

We stepped, then slipped, then fell. I splashed down in flowing water up to my chest. I wrapped my fingers around the buckled remnants of a fence and whipped my face through the storm until I found Harnett pulling himself upright a few feet away. I drove my legs through the water until I was at his side. He took hold of my arm and we moved along the fence, looking for the easiest path inward.

Harnett froze at the point of entry and tried to turn me away. It was too late. A man was impaled upon the dull square pegs of the fence. Rain beat upon his open eyes and filled his mouth. It was Fisher, the garrulous old man who had spoken in mixed metaphors and preferred grave worms to all other kinds of tackle. We had underestimated him—he had been the first to reach Lionel's cemetery, and the first to die.

Harnett brought me close and stepped into the vortex. Invisible hands yanked us into the vile stew. I raised my chin above water, pushed my feet through mud, felt my toes tickle a coffin that rolled beneath my sneakers. I reached for a headstone but it bobbed away from my grasp.

I saw black water flash off Harnett's teeth as he shouted, but his effort was useless under the ocean's continual detonations. The storm surge kicked up corpses to block his path. He fended them off with the shovel. I tried to follow. My arm plunged through a rib cage; I flapped furiously to dislodge it. Lightning flashed and I saw coffins jumping like pistons. Harnett was balanced against a towering tombstone that leaned dangerously inland. He motioned me in. I collapsed against a Jesus with even fewer fingers than I.

"I CAN'T FIND IT!" His face sparkled with moonlit salt. "I CAN'T SEE, I CAN'T REMEMBER!"

There was desperation in his voice—he was lost, as was all hope. I leaned in and our foreheads sealed with mud. I tried to tell him it wasn't true. There was hope and that hope was me. In a flash I remembered—

—the split oak forking overhead—

—the capillary universe of leafless treetops threading the horizon—

—cursive alphabets invented by our footprints—

—the fibula of beach lying hard and gleaming below—

—the bilious curdle of surf—

—rock scatterings that drew invisible pentagrams between points—

—the shape of the outcropping itself: a fallen maple leaf of stone—

—everything that I had specified the day Lionel had brought us here. I squinted and saw the lighter, brighter, softer hues of that day transposed against the seething tumult. Landmarks revealed themselves. Through a hundred bodies and the dirigibles of caskets and stones, I saw the way. I sent a silent thank-you to the mother who'd fostered this ability, and then took my first step. I grinned and looked back over my shoulder to tell my father the good news.

Harpakhrad cut through the rain as if it were fabric. Harnett's neck was struck with such force that I recoiled, lost my footing, and slithered beneath water. A bloated white face rolled past me and I batted at it, knocking the bottom jaw loose in a plume of gore. I rocketed back to the shattering planet above—Harnett, Boggs, I couldn't see them, didn't know where they were. A casket collided with my elbow and I scrambled atop it and waited for lightning. I was floating away.

There—a shocking distance behind me, Harnett clawed through the muck on his belly. Boggs followed, teetering. The remnants of his three-piece suit slopped to his body in muddy lumps. Somehow his top hat had not sailed away; the brim curled downward and I felt the sick certainty that he had sewed it into his ears. Slicing through the rain was Harpakhrad as she alternated between weapon and crutch. I realized with horror that Boggs had not amputated or repaired his foot. The dead appendage still hung in its pouch of black, gangrenous skin.

There was nothing I could do to reverse the tide. I saw Harpakhrad flash and Harnett's tool meet it across an emptied grave. The blades locked and twisted; Boggs slid away and struck again with a looping sidearm. Harnett shucked left and trapped Harpakhrad with an arcing stab of his flimsy tool. The men's bodies came close—and that was all I saw. The current spun me and the two men were lost, though I heard their instruments' thin whistles and shattering collisions before they, too, became part of the storm's texture.

The casket I was riding struck something hard and I spilled. I took another dive and was paddling toward the locomotive roar of the ocean even before I surfaced. I pushed through squalls, blinking furiously and craning my neck to note each specified landmark. I confused the storm above with the one below. I mistook floating scraps of flesh for fish. It was a black march that I half expected to kill me.

The ocean, which had once been fifty feet below, now overtook the land, leaving only a tiny island of mud at its highest point—the outcropping that jutted over the beach, the forked tree, the humble headstone. I dragged myself from the ferment and walked with my elbows and knees until my hands took hold of the stone. With shaking fingers I wiped mud from the engraving: LIONEL MARTIN. JOB 20:15.

The water glowered with a cruel green light. I embraced the stone and laughed against the cold rock. I had done what no other could do. I had found Lionel's treasure.

Harnett, though, would never find me. I raised my head into the blinding deluge and screamed; the sound was unfairly stolen. I slapped my hands into the mud; it was as soundless as a stone tossed into a frothing sea. I stripped off my backpack and prepared to beat it against the ground when I recognized the weight that shifted inside.

I pushed aside the serrated edge of my mother's bone and withdrew the only other cargo. The trumpet was warm in my palm and the rain spiraled across its golden curves. My knuckles bent comfortably around it, but I hesitated when my wooden fingertips met the buttons. There was no sensation. Nothing. There was no song my maimed body could still play. And then I raised the instrument to my lips and found that I was wrong—there was one song I could play, the Harnett family theme, and blaring through the storm was our single note of failure that, just maybe, just this night, would not fail:

F, F, F, F, F, F, F, F, F, F, F, F, F, F, F, F, F, F, F, F, F, F, F, F, F, F,
F, F, F, F, F, F, F, F, F, F, F, F, F, F, F, F, F, F, F, F, F, F, F, F, F, F, F,

F, F, F, F, F, F, F, F, F, F, F, F, F, F, F, F, F, F, F, F, F, F, F, F, F, F,
F, F, F, F, F, F, F, F, F, F, F, F, F, F, F, F, F, F, F, F, F, F, F, F, F, F,
F, F, F, F, F, F, F, F, F, F, F, F, F, F, F, F, F, F, F, F, F, F, F, F, F, F,
F, F, F, F, F, F, F, F, F, F, F, F, F, F, F, F, F, F, F, F, F, F, F, F, F, F,
F, F, F, F, F, F, F, F, F, F, F, F, F, F, F, F, F, F, F, F, F, F, F, F, F, F,
F, F, F, F, F, F, F, F, F, F, F, F, F, F, F, F, F, F, F, F, F, F, F, F, F, F,
F, F, F, F, F, F, F, F, F, F, F, F, F, F, F, F, F, F, F, F, F, F, F, F, F, F,
F, F, F, F, F, F, F, F, F, F, F, F, F, F, F, F, F, F, F, F, F, F, F, F, F, F,
F, F, F, F, F, F, F, F, F, F, F, F, F, F, F, F, F, F, F, F, F, F, F, F, F, F,
F, F, F, F, F, F, F, F, F, F, F, F, F, F, F, F, F, F, F, F, F, F, F, F, F, F,
F, F, F, F, F, F, F, F, F, F, F, F, F, F, F, F, F, F, F, F, F, F, F, F, F, F,
F, F, F, F, F, F, F, F, F, F, F, F, F, F, F, F, F, F, F, F, F, F, F, F, F, F,
F, F, F, F, F, F, F, F, F, F, F, F, F, F, F, F, F, F, F, F, F, F, F, F, F, F,
F, F, F, F, F, F, F, F, F, F, F, F, F, F, F, F, F, F, F, F, F, F, F, F, F, F,
F, F, F, F, F, F, F, F, F, F, F, F, F, F, F, F, F, F, F, F, F, F, F, F, F, F,
F, F, F, F, F, F, F, F, F, F, F, F, F, F, F, F, F, F, F, F, F, F, F, F, F, F,
F, F, F, F, F, F, F, F, F, F, F, F, F, F, F, F, F, F, F, F, F, F, F, F, F, F,
F, F, F, F, F, F, F, F, F, F, F, F, F, F, F, F, F, F, F, F, F, F, F, F, F, F,
F, F, F, F, F, F, F, F, F, F, F, F, F, F, F, F, F, F, F, F, F, F, F, F, F, F,
F, F, F, F, F, F, F, F, F, F, F, F, F, F, F, F, F, F, F, F, F, F, F, F, F, F,
F, F, F, F, F, F, F, F, F, F, F, F, F, F, F, F, F, F, F, F, F, F, F, F, F, F,
F, F, F, F, F, F, F, F, F, F, F, F, F, F, F, F, F, F, F, F, F, F, F, F, F, F,
F, F, F, F, F, F, F, F, F, F, F, F, F, F, F, F, F, F, F, F, F, F, F, F, F, F,
F, F, F, F, F, F, F, F, F, F, F, F, F, F, F, F, F, F, F, F, F, F, F, F, F, F,
F, F, F, F, F, F, F, F, F, F, F, F, F, F, F, F, F, F, F, F, F, F, F, F, F, F,
F, F, F, F, F, F, F, F, F, F, F, F, F, F, F, F, F, F, F, F, F, F, F, F, F, F,
F, F, F, F, F, F, F, F, F, F, F, F, F, F, F, F, F, F, F, F, F, F, F, F, F, F,
F, F, F, F, F, F, F, F, F, F, F, F, F, F, F, F, F, F, F, F, F, F, F, F, F, F,
F, F, F, F, F, F, F, F, F, F, F, F, F, F, F, F, F, F, F, F, F, F, F, F, F, F,
F, F, F, F, F, F, F, F, F, F, F, F, F, F, F, F, F, F, F, F, F, F, F, F, F, F,
F, F, F, F, F, F, F, F, F, F, F, F, F, F, F, F, F, F, F, F, F, F, F, F, F, F,

F, F, F, F, F, F, F, F, F, F, F, F, F, F, F, F, F, F, F, F, F, F, F, F, F, F, F,
F, F, F, F, F, F, F, F, F, F, F, F, F, F, F, F, F, F, F, F, F, F, F, F, F, F, F,
F, F, F, F, F, F, F, F, F, F, F, F, F, F, F, F, F, F, F, F, F, F, F, F, F, F, F,
F, F, F, F, F, F, F, F, F, F, F, F, F, F, F, F, F, F, F, F, F, F, F, F, F, F, F,
F, F, F, F, F, F, F, F, F, F, F, F, F, F, F, F, F, F, F, F, F, F, F, F, F, F, F,
F, F, F, F, F, F, F, F, F, F, F, F, F, F, F, F, F, F, F, F, F, F, F, F, F, F, F,
F, F, F, F, F, F, F, F, F, F, F, F, F, F, F, F, F, F, F, F, F, F, F, F, F, F, F,
F, F, F, F, F, F, F, F, F, F, F, F, F, F, F, F, F, F, F, F, F, F, F, F, F, F, F,
F, F, F, F, F, F, F, F, F, F, F, F, F, F, F, F, F, F, F, F, F, F, F, F, F, F, F,
F, F, F, F, F, F, F, F, F, F, F, F, F, F, F, F, F, F, F, F, F, F, F, F, F, F, F,
F, F, F, F, F, F, F, F, F, F, F, F, F, F, F, F, F, F, F, F, F, F, F, F, F, F, F,
F, F, F, F, F, F, F, F, F, F, F, F, F, F, F, F, F, F, F, F, F, F, F, F, F, F, F,
F, F, F, F, F, F, F, F, F, F, F, F, F, F, F, F, F, F, F, F, F, F, F, F, F, F, F,
F, F, F, F, F, F, F, F, F, F, F, F, F, F, F, F, F, F, F, F, F, F, F, F, F, F, F,
F, F, F, F, F, F, F, F, F, F, F, F, F, F, F, F, F, F, F, F, F, F, F, F, F, F, F,
F, F, F, F, F, F, F, F, F, F, F, F, F, F, F, F, F, F, F, F, F, F, F, F, F, F, F,
F, F, F, F, F, F, F, F, F, F, F, F, F, F, F, F, F, F, F, F, F, F, F, F, F, F, F,
F, F, F, F, F, F, F, F, F, F, F, F, F, F, F, F, F, F, F, F, F, F, F, F, F, F, F,
F, F, F, F, F, F, F, F, F, F, F, F, F, F, F, F, F, F, F, F, F, F, F, F, F, F, F,
F, F, F, F, F, F, F, F, F, F, F, F, F, F, F, F, F, F, F, F, F, F, F, F, F, F, F,
F, F, F, F, F, F, F, F, F, F, F, F, F, F, F, F, F, F, F, F, F, F, F, F, F, F, F,
F, F, F, F, F, F, F, F, F, F, F, F, F, F, F, F, F, F, F, F, F, F, F, F, F, F, F,
F, F, F, F, F, F, F, F, F, F, F, F, F, F, F, F, F, F, F, F, F, F, F, F, F, F, F,
F, F, F, F, F, F, F, F, F, F, F, F, F, F, F, F, F, F, F, F, F, F, F, F, F, F, F,
F, F, F, F, F, F, F, F, F, F, F, F, F, F, F, F, F, F, F, F, F, F, F, F, F, F, F,
F, F, F, F, F, F, F, F, F, F, F, F, F, F, F, F, F, F, F, F, F, F, F, F, F, F, F,
F, F, F, F, F, F, F, F, F, F, F, F, F, F, F, F, F, F, F, F, F, F, F, F, F, F, F,
F, F, F, F, F, F, F, F, F, F, F, F, F, F, F, F, F, F, F, F, F, F, F, F, F, F, F,
F, F, F, F, F, F, F, F, F, F, F, F, F, F, F, F, F, F, F, F, F, F, F, F, F, F, F,
F, F, F, F, F, F, F, F, F, F, F, F, F, F, F, F, F, F, F, F, F, F, F, F, F, F, F,
F, F, F, F, F, F, F, F, F, F, F, F, F, F, F, F, F, F, F, F, F, F, F, F, F, F, F,
F, F, F, F, F, F, F, F, F, F, F, F, F, F, F, F, F, F, F, F, F, F, F, F, F, F, F,
F, F, F, F, F, F, F, F, F, F, F, F, F, F, F, F, F, F, F, F, F, F, F, F, F, F,F,
F, F, F, F, F, F, F, F, F, F, F, F, F, F, F, F, F, F, F, F, F, F, F, F, F, F, F,
F, F, F, F, F, F, F, F, F, F, F, F, F, F, F, F, F, F, F, F, F, F, F, F, F, F, F,
F, F, F, F, F, F, F, F, F, F, F, F, F, F, F, F, F, F, F, F, F, F, F, F, F, F—

Blood gushing from his nose and a chunk of flesh missing from below his ear, Harnett came. The gas-station shovel was still clenched in his convulsing hands. He coughed mud and he walked as if one of his knees was broken. But he was there, he had heard and followed my call, and now he held my head between his hands and smiled. He was missing teeth. I pressed my hands over his and laughed.

The hurricane whipped us as we dug. The shovel was a boon, but the earth was so loose that I did nearly as well with my bare hands. I dug as never before. I burrowed into it headfirst like an animal. And even in the pitching storm Harnett's aim was true: he lifted away piles of earth bigger than either of us.

Lionel's coffin was a simple wooden box. Together we dragged it to the island and fell across it in an exhausted embrace. The rain washed away our fatigue, our pain, and our blood, until we were two men cleansed of all misdeeds. For this moment only, we were incorruptible.

He looked at me. I nodded. He jammed the end of the shovel beneath the lid and then looked at me in surprise when it opened without a fight. Perhaps considering for the first time the man who laid inside, Harnett hesitated. He peeked at me again as if asking permission.

"Open it," I said.

He pushed the lid partway aside. Even in the blackness it shone. On top was an urn—Lionel had been cremated after all, the liar—etched with an inscription from Lahn. This wasn't for us to read, and we rolled it to the side. Beneath were the first few inches of unearthly glows and galactic sparkles. Gold, priceless jewelry, artifacts of unbelievable origin—it was all here in an ordinary box, a self-contained Digger museum. If only my mother had been with us to see it.

"Father and rotter, rotter and son."

Grappling from the mire was Boggs. Mud plopped from his empty socket like a deranged wink. He drove a small fist, then Harpakhrad, into the earth and pushed until his raw face and ruined frame rose from the depths, dripping obsidian. His top hat was gone, his ears notched and bleeding like a dark mirror version of my mother. He was giggling, spewing things he'd chewed from the floating dead.

He stood; he fell. Snarling, he stood; again he fell. The festering bulb at the end of his left leg bent like a water balloon with each step. Even with Harpakhrad as a crutch he could proceed no farther up the unreliable bank. Frowning, he stuck out the dead foot as if to merely observe it and then plunged his shovel with brutal precision.

The cut was clean. The lopped appendage landed upright, then slid until it touched the lapping waves. Boggs scowled at his new stump, as if the sight of exposed bone reminded him of the rotter living inside him, but instead of extracting the invader he raised his head and beamed through the quilt of rain.

"LOOK WHAT BABY'S BRAIN MADE HIM DO!"

His dangling suit coat tripped him. Easily he shrugged out of its tatters and let it smack wetly into the mud. Beneath he was shirtless and emaciated; the scrawny wreckage of his chest muscles twitched like subcutaneous slugs and his arms were blistered by the blast marks of hypodermic incisions. A single object bounced from a strap around his neck: the Polaroid camera, loaded for its final shots. Harpakhrad whirled in his hands and the sharp edge was aimed at us. He hopped and the edge was closer.

Harnett raised his own shovel and tried to stand. His knee gave out and he crumpled. I rushed to assist him but suddenly panicked. Lionel's coffin, where was it? I turned and peered through the storm. There, three feet away, four, five—it was gliding down the muddy embankment and heading for the cliff and the waiting ocean.

Monstrous winds lashed me for my indecision. Boggs was hopping toward Harnett, who had forced himself to a sitting position against Lionel's stone. In the other direction, the casket of treasure was still sliding.

Boggs swung. Harpakhrad came down like a missile. Harnett raised his shovel like a crossbar. The Egyptian instrument was too powerful and split Harnett's tool in half. I lunged at Boggs but instantly he jutted out with the scarab handle, which thumped me in the chest and sent me skidding down the hill on my ass. I found myself within reach of Lionel's coffin and instinctively gripped the edge. It was heavy, so heavy, and began to tip into the ocean.

More lightning—we were spattered with the butchery of the cemetery's dead as well as our own. I dug my feet into the slick earth and pulled at the coffin. I heard a war cry—even through the cacophony I heard it—and turned to see Boggs strike once to the left, knocking away half of Harnett's shovel, and once to the right, knocking away the rest. A third strike Harnett managed to fend off with a cunning twist of his elbows. Panicked, I lugged the coffin a matter of inches up the incline and prayed that it would hold. I tumbled into battle but was too late.

Harpakhrad was buried in my father's chest. Boggs took the handle of the shovel beneath his armpit and squirmed down its length until his nose touched Harnett's. The downpour shredded like metal against his rigid scream.

"I LOVED HIM!" Boggs bashed his fist against Lionel's tombstone with each word, crushing his knuckles into gristle.

"I LOVED HER! I LOVED YOU! IS THAT SO HARD TO UNDERSTAND? ALL I WANTED WAS ONE OF YOU, ANY ONE OF YOU STINKING ROTTERS, TO LOVE ME BACK! ME! ME, YOUR BABY! YOUR BABY BOY!" Boggs raised his face to the black sky and bellowed, the gales funneling his tears back into his eye. *"AND THEN YOU, YOU GREEDY ROTTER, YOU WENT AND TOOK HIM FROM ME, TOO!"*

He waggled a mangled finger in what he thought was my direction. But I had moved.

Boggs collapsed, his wet face grinding against Harnett's, his small, sharp teeth scraping down my father's flesh. The mud and blood and tears flowed from one brother to the other. Harnett's hand fumbled over Harpakhrad and cupped his brother's cheek. Boggs tightened his fingers around the slippery twists of his instrument's stem.

"I GET THEM NOW, ALL RIGHT? ALL OF THEM! OKAY? GOOD NIGHT, BROTHER, MY ONLY BROTHER! AND FORGIVE ME, ALL RIGHT? OKAY? WILL YOU PLEASE FORGIVE ME?"

Harnett's lips: *I will.*

Boggs reared back for the fatal shove.

He never made it. I struck first. His cherubic face distorted. He opened his mouth in complaint and a bucket of blood splashed across his chest. He groped with one mutilated hand and found the sharp fragment of my mother's leg bone driven into his neck. Boggs stood up on his one foot and spun. I could see the end of the bone through his open mouth. With a harrowing yowl, he tottered toward the ocean. I followed on my knees.

I found him lying on top of Lionel's coffin, his head ducked deep into treasure. When he lifted his face there were diamonds embedded in his socket, gems sunk into his spongy cheeks, gold lodged in his gums. He chuckled and some of it disappeared down his throat. Leaning forward again, he embraced all that was left of Lionel, the modest urn, and cried and blubbered and sang.

The coffin tipped over the edge and dove into the ocean. Waves the size of worlds devoured him. Salt flooded through my sinuses and pushed me back. I wiped at my eyes and saw Boggs once more, peaking at an oily crest, still locked to Lionel's coffin in undying apology, glimmering with riches, his mouth torn into an unnaturally oversize grin, his laugh the sick whistle of the busted sky.

The winds began to lessen. The placid eye of the storm was approaching. I tunneled through the ooze and flopped myself next to Harnett. His eyes were locked on the incandescent sky. His fringe of gray hair was matted into a crown of mud. Harpakhrad still extended from his chest; I reached for it. Bubbles of air sizzled from the wound.

"Wait." The word flew inward.

I misunderstood his concern. "No, look, I have it," I said. I patted the soupy ground until I found Boggs's coat. Inside the coat pocket, as always, was the Rotters Book. It shook free from its buckles. "It's here, look, see, we can get rid of it."

Harnett's eyes closed. Inadvertent tears squeezed out and went blasting upward.

His hand clutched at the air. I snatched it and his fingers crushed mine. With unexpected strength he pulled me in until my head fit into his shoulder. His lips were at my ear. I felt his face's harsh bristle. I waited for words. Nothing. But there were fingers in my hair. His rough hands, stroking, stroking. I grabbed his hair, too, and pressed my cold eyelids into his warm neck. The hands continued to stroke and they were like my mother's hands. His body began to fold and I guided him so that his head rested against Lionel's stone. He fell asleep. I sat up. Rain pressed him into the earth. At some point he died. I didn't notice, I was busy measuring the stone. The Garbageman, the Resurrectionist, Digger, Rotter, Kenny, Harnett, Father, Dad: he had been called so many names, but only one of them would fit.

Next Lesson, Then

They came in maggot numbers. The bravest crawled through the cemetery in cars, while the others pressed their faces to the same fence where once Foley and I had spent a Halloween planning trips never to occur.

I zipped up my coat and adjusted my sunglasses. There was a rustle of excitement when they saw my wooden fingers. I tried to focus on the scripture being read. The local pastor seemed to struggle with the telling; the gathering crowd, larger than any he saw on Sundays, was throwing him off. I threw a glance at Reverend Knox, who shrugged at the performance as if to say, *What are you going to do?*

Knox and Ted were the only ones fearless enough to join me graveside. Everyone else was there for another reason. They wanted to see if Ken Harnett would go down in an ordinary coffin into an ordinary grave.

I had to fight down a grin. Who could forget his Tibetan fantasy of being picked apart and crapped out by birds? Instead I was burying him and having a pretty good time doing it. Childish of me, perhaps, but I know the guy would've eventually admitted that he had it coming.

Five years had passed since his death. But it had only been yesterday morning that Knox had shown up at my rented apartment. It was November and his jacket was insufficient. Feeling like Lionel outfitting houseguests, I demanded he take an old coat of mine and sat him down in a chair while I fixed coffee. The hand that gripped his crutch was gnarled and his single leg shook with uncharacteristic weakness. I considered the similar disfigurement of Boggs and my own missing fingers and wondered if for some reason God wanted Diggers so badly that sometimes he tore bits of them off.

Knox was very old. His ceaseless travel would soon end. I gave him his coffee and listened to his melancholy epilogue. With the demise of Lionel, the Resurrectionist, Baby, and Fisher during the hurricane five years ago, the disappearance of Crying John, and the passing away of Under-the-Mud, not to mention the Christian rebirth of Brownie and Screw, Diggers simply no longer existed. Only the Apologist lived on, his comatose survival funded by an unknown benefactor. He had always been the quiet and crafty one. I entertained a vision of him escaping each night to dig only to creep back into the hospital each morning to reattach the tubes, the perfect crime.

"You did the right thing, getting out," Knox said. "God is good?"

I nodded and took his rheumatic hand. He had written me periodically over the years in an increasingly illegible script, but we had never talked about the days directly following my father's death. He eased the information from me as a good master can loose an object from his dog's jaw. While the eye of the hurricane had provided cover, I had abandoned my trumpet and backpack and had tried to carry Harnett's body away. Somehow I made it through the swamp and up the slippery hill but no farther. Instead I sought the highest ground I could find and buried him in a shallow grave that I specified until it was as familiar to me as my own reflection.

A military vehicle picked me up a few miles away and I spent the next two days in an emergency shelter, sleeping on a canvas cot and washing myself in a portable shower. When the water levels had sufficiently receded, I accompanied a sheriff's deputy to Harnett's burial spot. He was still there. Over a dozen had died in the storm; there were few suspicions. I filled out questionnaires and consented to the interment of his remains in a local graveyard. I didn't give it much thought. My mind was on my future.

Eventually I traveled back to Iowa. I contacted Ted and he arranged for a hotel room and visited me the night I arrived. I explained my intent to return to Chicago. He didn't try to dissuade me but suggested I take a few weeks to decompress in Bloughton. I told him he was crazy. Bloughton was where terrible things had been done to high school heroes, where arsonists had nearly killed both me and Harnett.

"You realize they blame all that on your father," he said. "And your father is dead. You understand what I'm saying?"

There was something in Ted's eyes that I couldn't quite figure. Did he know the truth?

"You're saying they don't blame me."

"That's what I'm saying, yes." His mustache twitched. "But what I'm also saying is there exists here a sympathy for you and your . . . situation."

"What, they feel bad for me?"

The mustache twitched again. "There is sympathy."

Maybe because he, too, had once lived in a big city, Ted had the necessary distance to divine the patterns of small-town behavior. At any rate, he was right. As eager as the town had been to ostracize me when I had arrived, they were twice as eager to take me back into their arms. It was surreal. Ted took me to lunch as an experiment and the waitress put her hand on my neck and looked like she wanted to cry. We went to Sookie's Foods next and the manager himself met us in the cereal aisle and squeezed my shoulder and told me he had a stock-boy position open if I felt that would help get me back on my feet. Everywhere we went, the same thing.

At night, in front of the hotel room's television, I reported to my father how the entire town was granting me a forgiveness I did not deserve. "Look," I whispered. "People aren't as terrible as you thought they were. As I thought they were. They want to be good."

Even in death, Harnett was cynical. I pictured his exasperation at my undying naïveté. He told me to look more closely at their pinched and sweating faces. See the shame? They are ashamed at how they treated us. See the desperation? They are desperate to salve that shame with generosity. Their swift acceptance of you, said Harnett, has nothing to do with you. It's about them.

"Whatever," I said to him. "I'll take it."

And I did. I took that stock-boy job, and within six weeks I had moved up to checkout clerk. The first day at the register I was trembling. Conversation was the latest ritual I had to relearn; I'd already tackled how to wake up at dawn instead of dusk, how to wear bright white shirts and khaki pants without fearing exposure. For so long I'd angled my face so that people couldn't memorize my features and mumbled so they couldn't identify my voice—old Digger tricks. This didn't fly in the checkout lane. Soon I discovered that nothing normalizes a person faster than seeing him scan your pudding cups and economy-size diapers. Everyone in town patronized Sookie's, and people would wait an extra ten minutes just to go through my line, just to be able to impart two or three words of sympathy or understanding. I'd smile and nod my thanks and ask them cash or credit, paper or plastic?

There were challenges. For a while it was hard not to calculate the post-mortem value of their earrings and watches and cuff links. But eventually I learned to quit the habit, or at least stow it away. The forced conversations became less forced. I found myself inquiring about ailing spouses and troublesome pets because I honestly wanted to know. Without noticing the moment when it began to change, I started valuing each person's life rather than their death.

Ted helped me find the cheapest one-room apartment in town, a former office space over Fielder's Auto that stank of oil and cigarettes. I loved it. I worked forty or fifty hours at Sookie's and paid my rent proudly. Ted didn't let it go at that, either. Soon he was insisting I get my high school diploma.

"You're psychotic," I told him. "They're not ready for that. I'm not ready for that."

"After everything you've been through, you're going to let a few little high schoolers scare you off?"

"You're goddamn right I am," I said.

This was one battle he could not win. How could I shut out the phantom screams coming from the weight room, the theater, or the biology lab? Instead I agreed to take my GED. Ted brought me study materials. It only took me a few hours of review to realize I was going to ace that thing. I hadn't been a straight-A student for nothing. Twitching somewhere deeper now was another notion, one regarding a career, a real one, one involving the higher education so prized by my mother, one having nothing to do with the sacking of milk and eggs and produce.

The day before I took the GED was my eighteenth birthday, and the bank opened to me the contents of my mother's savings account: $11,375.02. To me the figure seemed more than substantial, numerical proof of my mother's noble squirreling of her every spare cent. I would not let her down. This sum, right down to those last two goddamn cents, would deliver me my future. This job of mine, it was just training. A few more thousand groceries and my emotions would be caught up with my mind. I folded up the bank statement and told my mother to hang on. I told myself the same thing. It wouldn't be long.

Never would I have guessed that there were lessons to be learned not by fleeing Bloughton but by staying put. By the end of October I was happy. It was a feeling I distrusted and I was careful not to embrace it too heartily. There were lives I had almost destroyed, after all, and that was something still requiring atonement. Gottschalk had not been fired after the gruesome events at his school—he had resigned immediately. My coworkers at the grocery—enthusiastic gossipers, all of them—told me that there had been a farewell dinner for him at the local Elks' hall and that many people had attended to toast his years of service. He and his wife—he had a wife, a fact that shook me up more than a little—moved to Florida and were gone before the Gatlins ever came to town. His portion of my revenge, the tombstone on the desk, was the only part incorporated into Bloughton record. What had happened to Woody and Celeste had been obscured by authorities, either because the victims were minors or because the acts were simply too gruesome, and survived now only as wild and specious legend.

Woody Trask did not return to Bloughton High. If I had

hoped to end his reign as the school's alpha dog, I had succeeded. That fall, his family sent him to live with an aunt and uncle in a neighboring state and I never heard of him again. In optimistic hours I imagined his senior year as prosperous, his natural athletic abilities purchasing him instant acceptance. But in my darker moments I found that scenario unlikely. I pictured him crying himself awake at all hours of the night, wetting the bed, phobic about touching female skin. What was more, I was sure that he knew I was the guilty party, not Harnett, no matter what the authorities had assured him. There had been a certain smell in the weight room that night, and he must have recognized it as the odor he himself had rinsed from me in the locker room shower. I couldn't expect Woody to vanish entirely. He was too strong for that, and payback was in his blood. If one day he decided to have his revenge, I would have to accept it. The Trasks could become my Gatlins, and even that threat had its comforts; it was something you could prepare for and stand guard against; it was forever, life everlasting, religion itself.

Celeste Carpenter remained in Bloughton after graduation. For a couple of years I read her name in newspaper recaps of local concerts, but over time those mentions stopped. By the fourth year I heard that she was living in another town, married and pregnant with her second kid and doing community theater. Every night for years I prayed for her forgiveness and to be worthy of it if it ever came. I did not know if she remained traumatized by what I had done to her or if she wore it as a badge, but regardless I knew she was the biggest star her new town had ever seen and that she surely captured the affections and envy of all who laid eyes on her. At night I continued to dream about touching her perfect skin, but even in dreams the sensation was weak. With three false fingers I could barely feel a thing, and no cheek that perfect should be scraped by weathered wood.

My grocery coworkers didn't really remember Foley, but they looked into it and assured me that he was gone. For a while I imagined him suffering a fate similar to Woody's, exiled to some strange town and left to suffer the repercussions of having known me. But then one of our butchers told me that Foley's family had relocated to Chicago. My heart soared. I saw again his fingers splayed in devil horns, saw him swishing his hair to the nihilistic noise of Vorvolakas and insisting that he wanted oblivion when in fact he wanted everything but. The city held its own dangers, but somehow I knew Foley would make it. He'd find a Boris. Probably a boyfriend, too. I missed him but knew he was better off on his own. Unlike my parents, Foley and I had made no formal pact that I had to avoid Chicago, but I told myself I would. It was Foley's now. He deserved it.

Ted, of course, is still Ted. When we get together over dinner he apologizes for our failure to see *Faust* at the Met but promises that he'll make it happen soon—it's an exciting prospect, as New York was never my territory. And when we run into each other at the store or on the street, he grumbles about the no-accounts filling up his band and how this will be the year that Ted's Army officially goes down in battle. Then he'll relent and his eyes will sparkle just a little. "There *is* this one girl," he'll say, or, "This punk walked in today, never picked up a sax, and started wailing like Impulse-era Coltrane." He has also begun telling me about a used trumpet sitting in the window of the local consignment shop. I can see his old refrain prickling the edge of his mustache, waiting to come out.

Aside from Ted, the one person I still see is Heidi Goehring. She remembered me from our few Fun and Games pairings, and to my shock that remembrance was fond. She had graduated at the top of her class, went to Northern Iowa, graduated at the top of that class, too, and had returned to Bloughton to intern at a doctor's office while saving money for med school. She comes into the store regularly and lately the items she brings me to scan seem pretty arbitrary—a wine bottle opener, a tube of Chap Stick. Sometimes she comes in late when we're slow and lingers at the counter and talks to me for fifteen or twenty minutes. Once she even showed up on my break and we had coffee in the diner down the block. She doesn't ask me about my father but she asks plenty about me. At first she wanted to know what TV shows I watched. I didn't really watch any, so that night I picked a few and started watching them so we could have something to talk about. The next time she came in she laughed at my choices—a sitcom about four black women trying to find love in the Big Apple, a reality show where people vied for the pleasure of dating twin blond bisexuals, and a late-night politics roundup hosted by someone Heidi called "an insane right-wing nut-sack"—but nonetheless she had plenty to say about all three. She knows everything about TV and enjoys schooling me on the backstory of every program, the careers of its stars, the number of Emmys won, and so forth. I'll never know as much as she does and wouldn't want to. That wouldn't be anywhere near as much fun.

It was after one of these visits from Heidi that I began to think again about Harnett. By any rational assessment my life had improved without him. My apartment was clean, I took daily showers, I kept healthy hours, I had a steady job, I ate well, and I almost had a friend or two. I was calmer and stronger and beginning to remember who I was: not the Resurrectionist, not Baby, not the Son—just Joey. Yet I missed my father. He had always seen a division in life, us and the dead on one side and the rest of the universe on the other, and he had died in search of a treasure he had thought I needed to survive. He had been wrong about that, but I couldn't fault him for it, and soon I began to regret having buried him in a random plot in North Carolina. Almost five years from the day he died I began making arrangements to move his body to Bloughton.

I didn't tell anyone, but somehow the story got out. At significant expense to me his coffin was disinterred and shipped to a holding office the next town over. I sent word to Knox and arranged for a local pastor to say a few words. I purchased the cheapest stone possible, a small square rock engraved with a simple H.

The night before his reburial I pushed my bed away from the wall and pried open a floorboard. From the hollow beneath I withdrew my only secret possession: the Rotters Book. The soaking it had taken five years ago had bloated it almost beyond recognition, and more recently mice and termites had found it delicious. It creaked when I pulled back the cover, and dust billowed as I ripped each page from its opposite. The stained and curled photos inside were still quite coherent.

I had intended to invent an excuse to spend a moment alone with my father's remains, pry open the lid, and tuck the book under his arm as evidence of the life the Diggers had lived. Then I heard my father's final word: *Wait*. It's all too easy to ascribe meaning to someone's last words, and I knew that; still, I took it as a sign. Looking at the book in my apartment, with the rock-and-roll sound track of another reality show clamoring from the TV and the microwave beeping to alert me that my burrito was done, I changed my mind. Maybe there was a God, maybe there wasn't, but on the off chance that He wasn't looking, I figured it was worth trying to ditch some evidence.

My first idea was to bury it, but I knew too well that anything buried could be unburied. Instead I burned it in the sink. It took all night. A small part of me screamed that I was making a mistake, that it belonged in a museum, that it was the only record of its kind, a photo album of the largest family in the world. But I burned it anyway. I felt satisfaction when the pictures of my mother incinerated; I felt even better when my own picture was consumed and lost. The others cremated that night were no longer rotters to me, they were people, and if I ever wanted to rest in peace, they would have to rest in peace first.

So Ken Harnett was buried in Bloughton as he had been buried in North Carolina: alone. The pastor finished his mediocre reading and blessed us. Behind him, a Jesus with all of His fingers blessed us better. An automated device lowered Harnett into the machine-cut ground. Six feet, flat surface, no rocks, no roots, an easy score—I blinked and looked away. Ted was patting me on the shoulder and saying he'd bring over some casserole later. Knox was taking my hand and saying he would swing by and say farewell after he grabbed a nap. Soon I stood there unaccompanied as men moved in with a backhoe.

I got out of their way, and that was when I noticed the faces. They were still there, all of them, watching from the other side of the cemetery fence. I specified as many of them as I could and wondered if Harnett's pessimism had been dead-on. Perhaps there would always be this division: they on one side of the fence and we on the other. Perhaps the desire to dig still ached in my bones. Perhaps the age wasn't over. It was just a few days earlier, after all, that I had been handed a shovel and told to clear an early snowfall from the sidewalk outside Sookie's, and as I'd labored, the tool had suddenly locked into perfect synchronicity with my body. A name for her had even popped into my head, the perfect name, the perfect grip, the perfect instrument. Such a shovel, it seemed a waste not to use it.

ACKNOWLEDGMENTS

Richard Abate, Joshua Ferris, Beverly Horowitz, Craig Ouellette, and Grant Rosenberg—none of you are rotters in my book.

About the Author

Daniel Kraus is a writer, editor, and filmmaker. He lives with his wife in Chicago. Visit him at danielkraus.com.